## Praise for Bill Ransom
## and *ViraVax*

# BILL RANSOM

ACE BOOKS, NEW YORK

This Ace Book contains the complete text of the original hardcover edition.

BURN

An Ace Book / published by arrangement with the author

PRINTING HISTORY
Ace hardcover edition / September 1995
Ace mass-market edition / September 1996

The Putnam Berkley World Wide Web site address is http://www.berkley.com

ISBN 0-441-00362-1

ACE©
Ace Books are published by The Berkley Publishing Group,
200 Madison Avenue, New York, NY 10016.
ACE and the ''A'' design are trademarks
belonging to Charter Communications, Inc.

PRINTED IN THE UNITED STATES OF AMERICA

10  9  8  7  6  5  4  3  2  1

# GOOD FRIDAY
## 2015

*Blessed are the meek: for they shall inherit the earth.*

—JESUS

*If we conclude that only the things which are in our power are good or bad, we have no reason for finding fault with God or taking a hostile attitude to man.*

—MARCUS AURELIUS

# 1

FATHER LUKE FREE encountered the line for confessions a block from Mary, Mother of Mercy Cathedral. He picked his way through the stalled traffic on the Avenue of the Martyrs and joined the line for confessions in the slim blade of shade beside the cathedral. He straightened his cassock, blotted his sweaty forehead with a sleeve, then walked slowly up the line, working his way against the flow of rosary vendors, holy-card vendors, Pope comic book vendors. He heard nothing but the blare of car horns, boomboxes and hawkers as he walked, his gaze fixed a few paces ahead. The crowds and vendors parted for him with silence, a nod, a sign of the cross.

He knew better than to look up. Some people got nervous if the priest saw them in line. More than once when he stepped out of the stifling confessional for air, Father Free noticed that the first few in line when he left had moved to the end when he came back. Or to another priest's line, on those rare occasions when there were two priests to spare in one region. Here, in La Libertad, there were the embassy priests, the seminary priests, the university priests and the hospital priests. Confessions would be heard in the

capital city in time for Easter Duty, but in the *campo*, where
he felt he belonged, there would be silence.

Father Free carried his Breviary in his left hand and a
packet of schedules for the archbishop's Broadcast Ministry. His turn in the hot seat began in a few minutes, and he
hoped that Father Umberto had not spent his two hours
eating raw onions again. Two Innocents charged batteries
on a tandem Lightening just inside the double doors, the
rasp of their chain and the squeak of their pedals a mantra
to the god of electricity.

He set his straw hat and Breviary on the table in the
vestibule. He placed most of the radio/TV schedules into
an empty slot in the pamphlets rack, then fanned a few and
laid them out for display. He heard with satisfaction the
quick hands that snatched them up behind his back as soon
as he entered the cathedral. The little broadcast station was
popular enough that it just might get him killed.

The clamor and glare outside gave way to the cool spa-
ciousness of the granite church. All of the statues huddled
in their Lenten shrouds as two young seminarians prepared
the altar. A *penitente* left one side of the confession-box,
another entered, and Father Umberto heaved himself out of
the center cubicle. He knelt for a moment, dripping sweat
in the nearest pew, then greeted Father Free inside the doorway.

"*Lo siento*," Father Umberto whispered, fanning his
face with his hat. "I have been an hour thinking about the
bathroom."

He winked, availed himself of the holy water, genu-
flected and then left Father Free with a sweaty pat on the
back and the unmistakable ripeness of raw onion in the air.

Father Free knelt for a moment, as Umberto had, gathering himself in the near pew for another bladder-busting
marathon of guilt and despair. He used his hat and fanned
the thick air out of the confessional before entering, and
heard a few giggles up and down the line. He latched the
door and sat on the bench, which switched on the light
outside, identifying his presence.

*How long will some Innocent have to pedal to keep my light on for two hours?*

Father Free's boot kicked against an empty bottle. In the dim light he saw the empties that Father Umberto left behind under the bench: EdenSprings Water. He himself never drank anything in the confessional; it was too risky on the bladder. And if he did, he wouldn't drink Eden-Springs because it was made by the competition, the Children of Eden. Competition who played dirty, very dirty.

He took a deep breath, let it out, touched his rosary and slid back the black wooden barrier.

"In the Name of the Father . . . "

Father Free recited his introductory in his most dispassionate voice, reserved for confessions and for the army roadblocks.

*Mezcal*, he thought. He also smelled tobacco, sweat, Mayan incense.

The young man's Spanish was bad. Father Free switched to Kakchiquel.

"Speak, Nephew. I am the ear of God."

"Well, Holy," he began, "I confessed two months last. I lied to my brother."

Father Free waited the accustomed time.

"You lied to your brother," he said. "What else?"

In the silence between them, Father Free felt the young man's perfect posture, heard the liquid *click* of his eyelids and the skitter of something across the ceiling.

"I did the man and the woman thing with my brother's wife, Holy."

Kakchiquel was an adequate language for theological discussion, but not Father Free's grasp of Kakchiquel. He did his best.

"Stay away from her," Father Free said.

"Well, Holy, it is good. But we share a room, and I have to sleep some time. And that is when she has me, when I am asleep and can fight no more. She straddles me under my blanket, then takes my member. . . . "

"Wait, Nephew," the priest interrupted. "You say you

were asleep. Is this a dream? Did you commit adultery with your brother's wife in a dream?''

''Well, Holy, it is true, when I wake she is not in my blanket. But it is so real! Every morning I must face my brother. Now he wonders what I, his closest of brothers, am keeping from him.''

''How often does this happen? Every night?''

''The once only, Holy.''

''You are confessing you had an affair with your brother's wife in a dream one time, and you lied to him about it. It's affecting your life with your brother.''

''Yes, Holy. And we work the coffee together.''

''So, this also affects your work, your pay.''

''Yes, Holy. It is a difficulty.''

''Well, Nephew,'' Father Free said, ''go home, and ask your brother and your sister-in-law to say a rosary with you. Tell them it is something I asked of you, that the three of you pray together that you might find a suitable bride.''

The miasma of tobacco and mezcal burst through the screen: ''Yes, Holy.''

Father Free imagined a blushing smile on the slight figure behind the curtain. He coached the young man through his act of contrition, and passed absolution as he slid the barrier closed. He hesitated only a moment before sliding open the barrier on his other side.

As the barrier *banged* open in its slot, a tremendous explosion popped Father Free's ears and set the confessional to rocking.

A woman across the screen shouted, ''Jesus, Mary, Mother of God! Oh, I'm sorry, Father!'' She hurried on, in a whisper, ''If they're going to kill us, please hear my confession now.''

He began, ''In the Name of the Father . . . ''

Many running inside the church. A knock on his closet door.

''Yes.''

''It is the embassy, Father. The U.S. Embassy. Many will be wounded and dying.''

"Thank you."

"Aren't you coming?"

"These people, too, are wounded and dying," he said.

Another knock, but Father Free ignored it. He turned instead to the mango and hot tortilla smell of the frightened woman sobbing her tiny sins into a handkerchief across the curtain.

*Fight to the death for Truth, and the
Lord God will fight on your side.*

—ECCLESIASTICUS

# 2

THE RETARDED TEENAGER struggled with his burden of
cameras and cases, trying to get out the hangar door to the
Mongoose, but a pair of pimply security guards wouldn't
let him through. The boy and the two Children of Eden
guards sweated heavily in the still humidity of the uncon-
ditioned Costa Bravan afternoon.

Isaac Green saw the struggle from the back of the hangar
and yelled, "Get that stuff on board, Paul, we're late and
there's another load to go."

Paul surged forward against the arms of the security
guards, then one of them got rough with him and Paul
started to cry in his peculiar bellow. It always put the hair
up on Isaac's neck when Paul did that. Mirian was sorting
the last of their equipment from the pile of incoming bags
and said, "You take care of it. I handled him last time."

Isaac Green left Mirian and the other Innocents to prepare the second load for their hop out to ViraVax. The
security guards were getting pushy, which made Paul bellow even louder. Isaac slapped the back of Paul's head.

"Shut up!"

Paul turned to hug Isaac, but Isaac pushed him away.

Paul shuffled to the back of the hangar and joined the other two Innocents, who tried to comfort him. Isaac turned to the dimwit security guards and indicated the Mongoose, idling on the lift pad outside.

"We've got to get this stuff aboard, we're already behind schedule. . . ."

"Your crew stays here," one of the guards said. He tapped his Sidekick for emphasis. "Orders."

"But *we're* the camera crew," Isaac said. "The Master invited us here himself to document the Easter Sabbath. You've made a mistake."

Isaac reached for the strap of one of the cameras, and the security guard tapped his wrist lightly with a rifle barrel. It sent a shock all the way up to Isaac's teeth.

"*You're* making the mistake," the blond kid said, his blue eyes as hard as his weapon. "Hump your stuff back there to your area, and wait."

"But the Master himself . . ."

" . . . Handed me this manifest," the guard said, brandishing a pokesheet on a clipboard, "and you're not on it. Neither is your partner, or your three pets. I don't know what's going on, but I do know you're not authorized on this lift."

"Let me speak to your commanding officer."

Both of the security guards smiled, and the Mongoose wound up in the background, screaming for vertical lift. Then it sucked in its landing gear and wallowed towards the Jaguar Mountains to the north.

"Shit!"

Isaac kicked at the canvas duffle at his feet.

"Yeah," the younger guard laughed. "Now, what was it you wanted? The CO? He'll see to the Sabbath shutdown out there, then he'll be back here for shift relief."

Isaac clenched his teeth and held his temper. Shouting would not get him what he wanted now. He spoke through a tight jaw, watching the heat ripple off the tarmac where the Mongoose had stood.

"And what time will that be?"

"They'll shut down at eighteen hundred hours," he said. "That's six P.M., your time. That's three hours, you might as well get comfortable." He pointed his weapon towards the back of the hangar.

Two cots sat next to their pile of bags and equipment, and Isaac had a bad feeling about how long they would be waiting in this oven of a hangar. Mirian had finished separating their gear from a supply shipment and was recording some background shots to test the cameras. She narrated as she shot.

"Good Friday afternoon, 27 March 2015, in the Confederation of Costa Brava, Central America. The Master goes on to the mystery facility without us and we're stored here like these cases of vaccines and bottled water. . . . "

Isaac pulled his headset out of the duffle, plugged it into his Sidekick and keyed in his access to the Godwire. As his hardware snaked its way through the electronic maze between La Libertad, Costa Brava and McAllen, Texas, he noted the blinking time display in the lower, left-hand corner of his vision.

The highlighted numbers blinked *1500:00 low batt*, and Isaac mumbled to himself, "Good Friday, and Jesus died at three." He felt he should honor the moment with a prayer, but worry drove prayer from his mind. Commander Noas had authorized them to accompany the Master for this story, but Isaac didn't have the proper security access code to speak with Noas personally. He left a brief message on the Godwire, describing their situation, and requested permission to complete their mission.

The two security guards, knowing that the news team was stuck, retreated to their office beside the hangar doors and began stuffing themselves with illicit tamales in anticipation of the coming bread-and-water fast of the Sabbath.

"Hey!" Isaac hollered. "We've got some low batteries. Can we plug in here?"

"Not on our grid," the youngest answered through a full mouth. He nodded to indicate a Lightening beside his office. "Put one of your pets on that ballbuster; you're welcome to it."

The Lightening would give all three Innocents a workout, but at least they'd be powered up if they ever had a story to chase.

"You should have argued with them," Mirian grumbled. It seemed to Isaac that she grumbled a lot, lately. "There's been a bombing at the U.S. Embassy. Things are happening down here."

"We weren't sent here to cover the politics."

"Well, we aren't going to cover diddly squat unless we get out of this hotbox."

"The whole country's a hotbox," Isaac said.

Mirian powered down her camera and marched past him to the pair of cots and patch of concrete that was their new home. The three Innocents fussed over their blankets and belongings on the floor, nervous about the change in plan. At twelve, thirteen and fifteen, they humped bags of gear with the best of them, but to get the best out of them required delicate handling, a lot of hugging, patting, kind words and fresh fruit. Isaac swallowed his frustration as he watched the three glum Innocents unpack their few things.

"Put your beds together later," Isaac said. "There'll be plenty of time for that. Let's get all of our batteries topped off, first. Who wants to be the Lightening Bug?"

Maggie, the twelve-year-old, stepped forward.

"I be the bug, Isaac!"

"No, me! Me!" Arthur insisted.

Paul sat on his blanket, arms folded, looking at the jungle hillsides past the open hangar door.

"Everybody will have a turn," Isaac said. "Let's let Maggie go first."

Isaac pulled the Lightening away from the wall, set four of their batteries into the appropriate slots, and diverted overflow power to the hangar's grid.

*If we're stuck here long, maybe we can deal on the power we produce.*

Isaac figured that the security guards took a turn each

shift on the Lightening, and they might look favorably on
the chance for relief. He set the overflow meter to zero to
record their contribution, adjusted the pedals for Maggie's
legs and said, ''Go for it, Mag.''

Maggie worked the flywheel up to speed, and Isaac ran
through the gears for her until she was comfortable. Then
he poked a straw into a chilled bottle of EdenSprings water
and fixed it into the clamp for her. She was the youngest,
but she had good legs and excellent wind, and she had
hardly begun to sweat.

Isaac patted her on the back, checked that the meter was
running, and said, ''Arthur will take his turn when you're
ready. We'll have something for you to eat by then.''

Maggie flashed him a smile and concentrated on pedaling
at a strong, regular rate. Many of the Down's syndrome
youngsters suffered from heart ailments, and Isaac believed
that daily time on the Lightening was their key to longer
life. He and Mirian also took shifts when necessary, though
Mirian remained unenthusiastic throughout their two-year
mission for the Children of Eden.

Isaac turned in time to bump into one of the ViraVax
flight crewmembers, who was preparing a cold pallet for
shipment. Metallic blankets called ''chill-coats,'' battery-
powered coolers, covered the cargo.

''Hey,'' Isaac said, ''any chance we can hitch a ride with
you guys? We missed our flight out to ViraVax.''

The loadmaster shook his head.

''Not going that way, bro. This here load's going to
Mexico City.''

The loadmaster guided Isaac aside as two forklift drivers
squealed tires in their enthusiasm for loading the plane.

''The charge in these blankets don't last forever,'' he
explained, ''and we'll be close getting off-loaded under the
wire for the Sabbath, so we've got to make some time.
Besides, this old 737 takes too much runway for the lift
pad at ViraVax. There you need the Mongoose, a chopper
or a parachute.''

Most of the bottled water was loaded already, along with

a dozen pallets covered with chill-coats. All that remained were these last two. The loadmaster tapped his Sidekick display that showed his shipping manifest.

"Isn't the Lord's work the greatest job?" he asked, and flashed a genuine smile. "Look what I get to send out into the world: the purest water, medicines, vaccines. I like a job where I get to be the good guy."

"What did you do before you joined the Church?"

The loadmaster ducked his head, scuffed a boot on the concrete.

"Point man for the Latin Death Boys in Tacoma."

This was the kind of story that Isaac wanted: "Vicious Gangbanger Redeemed." These real-life uplifting stories reaffirmed, for Isaac, a flagging faith. But the Godwire stringers got the human interest. Isaac and Mirian got the Master, and Isaac tried his best to accept the honor with grace. Mirian, however, grumbled the whole way that they were nothing more than cogs in a two-bit propaganda machine.

The loadmaster signaled the forklift operator, who tilted the forks back with a jerk and tumbled one of the luggage-sized stainless containers from under the blanket to the concrete. Condensation beaded the outside of the box immediately, and several smaller, thermos-like containers rolled out of the sprung lid.

Isaac saw that each bottle was marked with the characteristic "V/V" and a lot number. He also saw that Mirian was filming with the low-light unit.

"What's this?" he asked.

The loadmaster checked his manifest.

"Some kind of vaccine. Goes to World Health Organization in Mexico City for distribution. Those other pallets"—he indicated a row of cartons lining one wall—"those are the EdenSprings water shipments, for the Sabbath ritual up north and for the airlines."

"And those?" Isaac asked. He pointed to a palletload of larger cases covered with a chill-coat.

" 'Vaccine components' is all it says here," the loadmaster said. "Those go back to the U.S. of A."

He turned his back on Isaac, then, and directed the loading of the smudge-winged cargo jet. Already Mirian was
behind the stack of larger cases and under the chill-coat,
out of sight of security and the flight crew.

"What're you doing in there?" Isaac whispered.

"Snooping," she said. "Isn't that what real reporters
do?"

Before he could object, Isaac heard the *click* of a latch,
then a gasp.

"Omigod!" Mirian whispered. "Omigod!"

She burrowed farther under the heavy, cold blanket and
shifted her feet. Isaac almost allowed himself to think that
Mirian had a cute little butt.

She wriggled out from under the chill-coat wide-eyed,
her palm-cam still recording, her face whiter than he'd ever
seen it.

"What is it?"

Mirian pulled him by the sleeve and walked him to their
cots. She plugged a small preview screen into the palm-
cam and took a deep breath.

"This is weird," she said. "This is *way* weird."

She pressed "play," and the screen showed the lid of
the metal case lift a little bit, displaying what appeared to
be tidy packages of raw meat in some kind of solution.

*But we're all vegetarians*, he thought.

Then the palm-cam grabbed a close focus, and he saw a
dozen neatly packaged hearts, just the size of human hearts,
each awash in a very cold, clear liquid. A label on the
closest package read: "15 y.o. male." The lid dropped shut
and *clicked* into place. A stencil on the top read: "MH, 12
ea., 3/27/15." As the palm-cam pulled back, Isaac glimpsed
the markings on the adjacent case: "FL, 4 ea., 3/27/15."
Mirian's hand opened the latch, and he saw four livers
packaged in the same clear solution.

Isaac took a deep breath, let it out slowly, and tried to
drown out the voice in his brain that screamed, "Twelve

male hearts, four female livers. Sixteen lives in two suit-cases.''

"They're human, aren't they?" Mirian asked.

"Probably," Isaac agreed, and tried not to sound shaken. "They're obviously part of the transplant program. . . . ''

"But why call them 'vaccine components'? And where did they come from?''

"You mean *who*.''

"Whom," she corrected, and nodded towards the In-nocents. "We've taken in thousands of Innocents in hun-dreds of special homes for almost twenty years. The 'Down's-Up' program. Why don't any of them come out to work in the community?''

"They're all given jobs with the Church, like our assis-tants here.''

"Until when? Until some elder needs a pair of lungs? I *told* you it wasn't just a rumor. . . . ''

Isaac shushed her as the forklift driver returned for the pallet of organs.

"You don't know for sure. . . . ''

"And how are we *going* to know, stuck in this tin box on this two-bit airstrip. . . . ''

"Our job. . . . ''

"Our *job*," Mirian interrupted, with a finger to Isaac's chest, "is to parrot what the Church says and keep our eyes on the horizon. We're not reporters, we're secretaries, shills for the Children of Eden PR staff. Now, I came here to report, and I'm not going to stay locked up while the real news is happening out there. You can stay here if you want, but *I'm* getting a ride to town.''

That was when they heard the *clang* and grind of the hangar door coming down, and the *snap* of the latch as the dark-haired guard secured the lock. He unplugged his Side-kick from the locking unit, winked a brown eye at Mirian and sauntered into the office. The blond guard shoved a rattling kitchen cart towards Isaac and let it go, where it petered out a few meters short. The guard shrugged, his attitude easier and his rifle slung.

"Courtesy of the Master," he said. "Ice water and bread for the Sabbath. Basin and towels below."

"Thanks," Isaac said, trying to keep his voice casual. "We heard the embassy was bombed. Any scuttlebutt on that? Is the Master safe here?"

The attitude returned.

"We can take care of the Master," he said, "don't you worry about that. Now, who's going to take care of *you*, that's the problem. Willy and I got the nod. Okay? They shot a couple of Irish that bombed the embassy, but they're still looking for a yankee colonel, a Catholic. So, to take care of you we keep you here. The Mongoose picks you up at sunrise Monday. I am to remind you that you are not to perform work from sunset today until sunrise Monday. But you travel with the Master, you already knew that."

"Right," Isaac said.

He nodded towards Maggie wringing watts out of the battered Lightening.

"What about that? We need the batteries, you need power."

The guard shrugged, his blue eyes steady, intimidating.

"No souls, no sweat," he said. "The Innocents don't count."

"What do we do if whoever's bombing the embassy bombs the airport?"

"They won't. Everybody needs the airport, it's hands off."

*That's why they can afford two zitfaces on security,* Isaac thought.

"Where can we get a ride to town? We can get a room. . . ."

"You're to stay here until sunrise Monday and observe the Sabbath; those are my sole instructions."

"What if we just leave?"

"Then you'd be forcing me to work on the Sabbath, and I'd prefer not to think about that. And I'd prefer *you* don't think about it, either. Besides, you have zero chance to beat that lock. At least, while I'm alive." He patted his Sidekick and his rifle for emphasis, and he did not smile.

"I see."

"Good."

The guard jerked a thumb over his shoulder, towards the office door.

"The Master's speaking at eighteen hundred and we've got a peel if you want to come in and watch." His gaze flicked to Maggie, then back. He shrugged. "After all, it's your power."

"Right," Isaac said. "Thanks."

He turned the cart around so that the wobbly wheel was in the back, then spoke, trying to make it sound like a casual afterthought.

"Maybe you two could give me and Mirian an idea of what to expect down here."

The blond laughed a laugh much older than his years. He strutted towards the office, and called over his shoulder, "Expect anything. And *no working* on the Sabbath!"

Isaac pushed the cart to the rear of the hangar, where Mirian and the Innocents waited for the fresh spring ice water and the hot, fragrant mini-loaves of bread.

"What did he say? Are we locked in here?"

Isaac unpacked the ceremonial bowl and towels from the cabinet in the cart, poured them each a glass of ice water while there was still ice. They both downed a glass before filling one for each of the Innocents. The Innocents had no souls and the ritual meant nothing to them spiritually, but they liked being included, and this was the kind of thing that made them a team.

"*Well?*"

Isaac didn't answer. He filled the foot-washing bowl from one of the stainless-steel pitchers, then knelt at her feet and began the Sabbath ritual.

"I really hate being locked in," Isaac whispered, more to himself than to Mirian. "I got locked in the pantry as a kid. My parents said they couldn't afford a babysitter. Sit down."

Mirian said nothing and sat on the cot. Isaac removed

her tennis shoes and sweaty socks, placed a clean towel under her feet and began washing them slowly, carefully, as he would want her to wash his own. She would just take a quick swipe with the cloth over his shoes, this he knew, but he thought that with enough example she might become more patient and see the virtue in this small but intimate gesture.

*That's the nice thing about ritual, about instinct,* he thought. *It gives you time to think.*

Apparently they would have the whole weekend to think. And sweat. And remember what was in those cases from ViraVax.

A disagreeable smell soured Isaac's nostrils, and he swallowed a biting remark about Mirian's personal hygiene. The disagreeable smell turned putrid, a combination of burning hair and overdead meat.

"Whew!" Mirian said. "What . . . ?"

"Green!" Willy shouted from the office. "Green! Help me!"

Isaac and Mirian looked at each other for a blink, then Mirian snatched up the palm-cam while Isaac ran for the front of the hangar. What greeted him there stopped him cold, and he waved Mirian back. She stood fast in her bare feet and started filming anyway.

The blond's uniform lay crumpled across the communications console, and it leaked a foul organic goo from a mess of rubbery bones. Willy lay on his back under the desk, his brown eyes wide, unblinking, staring at Mirian.

"She's so pretty," he whispered.

Willy winked at Mirian and the eyelid stayed closed. His chest heaved one last shuddering sigh, and then his whole body sighed. His face and scalp slumped from his skull and his brown eyes liquefied in their darkening beds.

"God save us," Isaac whispered.

He covered his mouth and nose with his shirttail and couldn't take his focus off Willy's Sidekick, barely visible under the stinking viscosity that used to be the man who knew the access code. Isaac couldn't bring himself to cross the threshold of the office, much less reach for that Side-kick.

A pale blue flame licked across the blond guard's re-mains.

Isaac would have thought it a trick of holographic ani-mation if it weren't for the stench. He held his breath, reached a trembling hand to the half-empty water pitcher on the desk and tossed the ice water at the flames. There wasn't enough water to contain it all, and in a moment little tongues of flame flickered over Willy, too.

"Maggie!" Mirian screamed behind him. "Maggie! Oh, God, Isaac!"

Isaac didn't have to turn to know what was happening. He just stared, stupefied, as the spreading mess engulfed the office floor and burned up the Sidekick that controlled their hangar door, their prison, their sweltering, sheet-metal tomb.

*Branches were broken off that I might be grafted in.*

—PAUL, EPISTLE TO THE ROMANS

# 3

MAJOR EZRA HODGE of the Defense Intelligence Agency fielded the heat for the bombing of the U.S. Embassy in La Libertad because everybody was short-handed and fielding heat was part of his job. No one at the embassy or on the damage control team knew what happened, and Ezra the Invisible wasn't telling. Hodge, himself, had planted the bomb in Colonel Toledo's car. He had done it under orders, but these orders arose from a Higher Authority than the Defense Intelligence Agency. The New Prophet of the Apocalypse, the Angel of Eden himself, laid out the scenario and Ezra the Invisible pulled it off.

The children were all that mattered. Eden would be worthless without Adam and Eve, and it was wise of the Angel to gather them in while Revelations ran its course.

Dajaj Mishwe's part of the operation had been mightily screwed, but Hodge activated a contingency plan that might yet see him alive on the far side of the Apocalypse. His was a sweet dream of a plan that included an elegant sailboat and the perfect companion.

This companion was not yet a Gardener, but Hodge had faith that Rena Scholz would see the light when the flaming sword fell. She had been a nun, but abandoned Catholicism when she joined the Army. He'd done his research—she didn't drink, didn't date and read voraciously in theology. Hodge imagined that in her gratitude for saving her life, Major Scholz would love him, that they would let the Apocalypse run its course and then sail back with Adam and Eve to populate a fresh, new Eden based on the Angel's plan.

Hodge fanned his face with a fistful of papers. His tiny office was a sweat-trap across the street from the U.S. Embassy. The pea-green cubicles around him were jammed with tacticians, logisticians and propagandists of every stripe. The noise level was high, but not high enough to drown out the single word that followed the tone on his Sidekick.

"Revelation," his Sidekick said, and it repeated "Revelation" in its pseudobiologic voice until Major Hodge reluctantly replied, "Revelation. Acknowledge."

*The GenoVax delivery to Mexico City is secure,* he thought. *The last EdenSprings shipments went out today, as did the great sword that hangs over the Sanhedrin tonight. We will take off the heads of many serpents, the nearest one first.*

The Angel's Artificial Viral Agents floated in the ritual ice water of the Gardeners, in the bottled waters of nearly every market, vending machine cafeteria and airline. Similar AVAs slept in the communion wafers of the idolators. God would sort them out.

Hodge's job was to stir up the serpent, first, and get it to focus on the flute in front of it rather than the sword poised above. With the Master dead, confusion among the Children of Eden was already a strong ally. The Master's myocardial implant already had triggered its coded signal, verifying his heart's failure to Central Command. It was, perhaps, fortunate that it had to fail here in Costa Brava. Now that ViraVax was off-line, it fell to Hodge to verify the signal. Hodge took his time with this, thereby adding to the confusion.

He had no word from the Angel at ViraVax. Their backup communications ran four redundancies deep, and all were silent. Hodge could only imagine the madness of the final scene at ViraVax, with hundreds of bodies melting from their bones, and it was possible that someone or something had, indeed, killed Dajaj Mishwe. Flaming Sword was designed to unfold on its own even if he, Hodge, died, but Hodge preferred to live.

Major Ezra Hodge and Dajaj Mishwe had worked together before, in certain private experiments on the nature of death that the two of them ran while they were in EdenWood together. Hodge was fully prepared to carry on the mandate of Revelations and the Apocalypse without the Angel Mishwe.

Hodge would permit, even encourage, the Defense Intelligence Agency to investigate the ViraVax site immediately. They could find nothing that would save them, and any GenoVax residue that remained would eliminate the investigators soon enough. There was nothing to lose even if the Agency sealed the site in concrete, and Hodge might even gain a little more time.

Hodge did not care, now, whether ViraVax came to the attention of the outside world. In a few short weeks, the outside world—the *human* world—wouldn't even exist. The Angel of Eden had the right plan: "Destroy the believers and the unbelievers alike, let the Lord Our God sort them out."

Hodge himself intended to be sorted no sooner than absolutely necessary. The Angel had promised him immunity, and Ezra the Invisible held firm to the dream of the sailboat, to joining Adam and Eve in Eden with the beautiful, blonde Rena Scholz at his side.

Hodge prepared the first in a series of slapshots from a kit that Mishwe provided for him. He unfolded the text accompanying his first shot and read it aloud: "I have the keys of Death and of Hell," then he injected himself on schedule.

The series promised immunity from GenoVax and a doubling of his life span. He had a backup kit stored safely away to protect Major Scholz, the companion of his dreams.

Hodge performed a couple of data diversions on his console, then waited for acknowledgment from the Sanhedrin in Texas. The shutdown signal at ViraVax triggered an automatic computer feed into the Agency's file, which Hodge had already shunted. While it probably wouldn't matter much in the long run, Hodge didn't want to give too many heathens and idolators the chance to dig in. He might have to fight them later.

The major was only slightly disturbed that the feed stopped abruptly right after it started. The Angel had a backup plan, just in case, and Hodge was that plan. The world would be a lonelier place without the Angel, but Hodge was already far too busy to give it much thought.

In one sense, the breakoff of the feed was a relief to Hodge.

*It feeds into the Sanhedrin's Central Security and Communications, too,* he thought. *The Sanhedrin doesn't need to see their fellows melting down into sludge quite yet.*

Less information meant more time to spread the series of AVAs that the Angel called ''GenoVax.'' Hodge preferred ''Flaming Sword.''

Major Hodge knew, by the messages flowing into his own Sidekick, that phones were ringing in the homes of Children of Eden all over the world. They would be told that their Master was dead and a successor must be chosen. The Sabbath and their grief would keep them occupied just long enough for everything to be set into motion. They would meet, share bread and ice water, and they would die, successor or no.

Only Commander Noas and a few of his Operations staff in the Jesus Rangers knew the truth about ViraVax. They were too few and too far away to do anything about it. And they would never suspect that their own company had produced the catalytic agent of the Apocalypse, and used their own people to seed it into the rest of the world.

Lines also buzzed in the offices of the DIA and, by now, perhaps the White House itself. The White House had its own distraction—water wars in the countryside and turf wars in the cities. He had a few surprises in store for the administration, too. That had been easier for Hodge to arrange than the bomb in Toledo's car.

The purest, most contagious version of Flaming Sword was in a warehouse in Mexico City, this Hodge had confirmed, and it would be distributed as vaccine to the World Health Organization as planned. Special shipments were in place already—one each for China, India, the United States, Europe and the Middle East. Everyone else would burn in the fallout.

Even if Colonel Rico Toledo were found alive, he was already discredited and he wouldn't make it for long. If nothing else, Hodge would see to that himself. The two children that the Angel called Adam and Eve must be brought safely into his own custody eventually, but he had all the time in the world to locate them. Hodge didn't worry about the children; the Angel guaranteed him that they had been created immune.

Any virologist who survived at ViraVax would be no help to anyone. Flaming Sword was swift and deadly, too swift and too deadly for anyone to produce an effective defense. In the short time they had left, anything any virologist knew was moot. Besides, if there were survivors, Hodge would take care of them, too.

Hodge was proud of the stroke of genius that got his dummy corporation, a *Catholic* corporation, the contract for the Catholics' communion wafers. Easter Masses throughout the world would precipitate a great flambé over the next couple of weeks. The viral agents in the wafers were the slowest of the lot, taking up to twenty-four hours to hit critical mass.

The Gardeners, as the Children of Eden called themselves, would fall to the Sabbath water, swift and shocking, but painless. Or so he was told. The Gardener holocaust would provide the proper diversion while Flaming Sword did its work in clinics, churches, refugee centers, cafeterias and airlines throughout the world.

Hodge wondered about the inevitable mess, the billions of suppurating bodies, but he supposed the earth itself would clean that up, in time. The Angel had assured him that this would be no problem. He felt bad about all the animals that would starve in their pens, and worried about whether or not vermin would thrive in the aftermath. Ezra Hodge hated rodents of all kinds, but especially rats. He had asked the Angel Mishwe to eliminate them, too, but was told that, of all God's creatures, only this sinful pack of humans offended Him. Flaming Sword would spare the rats.

Hodge had to admit the possibility that he himself might not be there to see it, but his faith was so strong that this was something he did not regret. He had, in fact, no regrets and was eager to play such an important role in God's plan. Still, when he fingered his sidearm and imagined its cold steel in his mouth, his heart raced and his sweaty palms turned cold.

Major Hodge turned his attention to the closed-circuit view of the emergency communications center that he had provided at the embassy. He studied Nancy Bartlett as she spoke with her father, the United States Secretary of State, via satlink.

Nancy Bartlett, mother of the new Eve, stood behind the desk of the U.S. ambassador to the Confederation of Costa Brava while her aide finished the link to Washington, D.C. Nancy's blue eyes were red from crying and from the smoke. She kept her hands on the desktop in an obvious attempt to control their trembling. The clock on the console in front of her chimed once to announce the six o'clock hour. The office was a madhouse of people and makeshift electronics in the aftermath of the embassy bombing. In just a couple of hours, Hodge had converted the ambassador's personal quarters into the new embassy command center. He didn't care that they didn't thank him; it gave him the chance to install certain monitoring devices like the one he was viewing.

"Mrs. Bartlett," the aide said, "your call to the Secretary of State is ready. Go ahead."

Nancy's blonde hair was disheveled, and she tucked it behind her ears. Her blue power suit was streaked with plaster dust and water. Hodge presumed she hadn't cleaned up after the bombing because she wanted her father to see her this way. Nancy Bartlett was prepared to use every emotional tool at her disposal to get her daughter back. Hodge respected her for that, and thought maybe the woman would feel better knowing that her daughter had been chosen—no, *created*—to be Eve.

It didn't matter. Nancy Bartlett was a Catholic; she wouldn't live long after Easter Mass, anyway.

The peel-and-peek on the opposite wall lit up, and the Secretary of State appeared—ashen and exhausted.

" . . . Old," Nancy whispered, involuntarily, but not loud enough for her father to hear.

Hodge knew for a fact that Nancy had not spoken to her father since her husband had been killed over a month ago. He had studied the Bartlett family long enough to know that the secretary believed that Red Bartlett had stolen his daughter away to the ends of the earth. Staying on in Costa Brava after her husband's death had been the ultimate betrayal of her father and her native land. At least, that's how her father saw it.

Nancy Bartlett straightened her shoulders, cleared her throat and faced the video pickup to the right of the screen.

"Dad," she said, swallowing a sob in a tight throat, "my baby's missing, and so is Harry Toledo. A farmer saw Sonja's plane forced down by an unmarked Mongoose up in the Jaguar Mountains. He thinks the kids might be alive. . . ."

Here her voice betrayed her shock and grief by tightening up her throat too much to speak.

"I know, Nancy," he said. "I got a scramble from Colonel Toledo earlier, via an Agency field linkup. . . ."

"That *bastard*!" she snapped. "I *knew* he was behind this. He bombed the embassy and took the kids. . . ."

Secretary Mike Mandell raised a hand to calm her down.

"Nancy, listen," he said. "It's not like that at all. Let's take one thing at a time. You and Grace weren't hurt in that bombing, were you? The wires here say that six people died and a lot of us are worried about you."

"No, Dad, we're okay. Physically, anyway. And how very thoughtful of Rico to contact you instead of me, or his ex-wife. Look, I don't know what he told you, but you know you can't believe that slimy bastard. President García has troops all over the countryside looking for him. He's turned to the guerrillas and he's probably got Sonja and Harry in some hellhole in the mountains."

"Rico didn't take the kids."

Her father said it slowly, to make it clear.

"He didn't bomb the embassy," he said. "It was a diversion, to put the heat on Rico."

Hodge sat forward at this. He had not expected his efforts to be pinpointed so soon.

"But why?" Nancy asked. "Who's behind this?"

Her father's gaze faltered for a moment as he listened to someone off-camera.

"It appears that the Gardeners are behind both the bombing and the kidnapping."

"The Children of Eden? But why, Dad? What could two teenage kids mean to them?"

Mike Mandell sighed, and in that sigh Major Hodge heard the deep wheeze of death in the secretary's lungs.

*He won't have to worry about the smoking getting him,* Hodge thought with a smirk.

"It's ViraVax," Mandell said. "I can't give it all to you right now, but trust me, we're on it. We've diverted a SEAL team to help out, we believe that García is part of the problem, so we do *not* want his people to find either Rico or the kids before we do."

"ViraVax? But that doesn't make any sense."

"It does if you think of unauthorized experiments on human beings."

Nancy dropped heavily into a chair, her expression numb.

"Sonja tried to warn me about ViraVax," she said. "If I had listened, she wouldn't have gone out there on her own."

"Nancy?"

Nancy Bartlett's face betrayed a dizzying disorientation for a moment. She batted at something in front of her eyes, and Hodge knew what it was. The memory adjustment that he had arranged for her after the incident with her husband was coming unraveled. Right now he imagined that a flood of grotesque images, suppressed memories, crossed her vision—her husband, dead . . . a pistol in her hand . . . his body melting to sludge on the living-room carpet.

*It doesn't matter now,* he thought, and caught himself smiling. His part in Nancy Bartlett's memory adjustment had been a pleasant one. Creative.

Nancy shook her head and cleared the tremble out of her voice.

"Sonja was convinced that ViraVax had something to do with Red's death," she said. "She's been on a one-woman mission to prove it. But these kids are so high profile—American kids from embassy families. What would possess any sane person to take those particular kids to . . . to use as guinea pigs?"

"Nancy, there's a lot I can't say right now. But there are two unpleasant possibilities. They're using the kids as bait to get to Rico, who knows about a few of their experiments—including at least one on your husband."

"On *Red*? But he worked for them from the beginning, and it was a guerrilla who killed him. . . . "

"I *really* don't want to get into that right now," Mandell said. "That's the official embassy line, created by Rico under orders as a cover. . . . "

"But I was *there.* I *remember.* . . . "

Major Hodge smiled at this testimony to his handiwork.

"Nancy," the secretary said, "there's a lot that neither of us knows at this point, but believe me, Red was not killed by that man they executed. Now, the other possibility is that the kids have already been part of some study, and all this with Rico is to get him out of the way. If he's killed in a fight, then they can claim he was the only one who knew the whereabouts of the kids, and the search is hopeless."

Nancy felt sick to her stomach.

"Where is he now?" she whispered.

"He's gone in after them. And I'm trying to get him some support. The Children of Eden are making any operations in that country very difficult. García is fighting to save his presidency; he doesn't give a hoot about the kids. I really wish you'd come home. None of this would've happened if you'd been here."

Nancy pulled herself upright and looked her father's image in the eye. Her voice was steel.

"Dad, that was the kind of low blow I didn't expect from you. I don't need a guilt trip right now."

He sighed, and flicked at the tip of his bulbous nose, something Hodge noted that he always did when saving face.

"You're right, honey, I apologize. Sonja . . . she's your only child, but she's also my only grandchild. With the both of you down there and your mother gone, I'm . . . well, I'm alone. And I don't like it." He glanced off-screen again, and sighed. "Listen, Ambassador Simpson is being briefed now, and I want you to stick with her until this is over. What about Grace Toledo; how's she holding up?"

"She's here. Worried sick about Harry, of course. Hating Rico even more than ever, if that's possible. The best thing she ever did was divorce that sonofabitch."

Her father leaned off-screen to confer with someone, then came back looking even more harried.

"We've got our share of problems here, too. Someone managed to burn up two Gardener compounds, in Milwaukee and Tennessee. The President's sending the Vice-

President out for an appearance and assessment. Nobody's taking credit yet. Gardeners shut up tight for their Sabbath, so we hope they don't go off half-cocked when they find out.

"I would like for you and Grace to come up here to give some testimony when this is over. Then I'd like to talk you into staying. I'm not getting any younger, you know, and I'd like some time with you and my granddaughter."

Nancy started to interrupt, but the Secretary of State put up a hand to stop her.

"I'm sorry to cut this short," he said, "but I have to go. This line will be open for you until this is resolved, okay? We're mobilizing everything at our disposal to recover those kids."

Nancy grasped her hands together to keep the trembling from showing.

"Okay," she said, and sighed. "Thanks, Dad. I love you."

But the peel was already blank.

Loud shouts from the other side of the room startled her, and Hodge's screen showed a knot of aides crowded around a communications console. Nancy stood to see what was going on, but suddenly her legs were too wobbly to carry her the half-dozen meters across the room. The aides all talked at once into their headsets. The ambassador, looking hot and wilted, pulled her damp hair back with both hands, closed her eyes and walked away from the group.

"What is it?" Nancy asked. "What's happening now?"

Ambassador Simpson pinched the bridge of her nose and kept her eyes closed while she answered in a hollow voice.

"Somebody blew the Jaguar Valley Dam," she said. "ViraVax is gone."

Hodge leaned into the snoopscreen, his heart pounding. *The final coup,* he thought. *The Angel carried it off!*

"But the kids . . . Sonja and Harry. My dad . . . Secretary Mandell said that's where they're being held. What about them?"

The ambassador shook her head.

"We don't know," she said. "The Agency office received the ViraVax emergency shutdown signal just before the blast, so this may involve contamination, as well. García's forces say they shot down a Mongoose trying to get out. We don't know yet if there are survivors to tell us. . . ."

Nancy's legs gave out and for the second time she dropped, stunned, into the chair. This time Hodge was sure that her memories were flooding back; shock often overtook his most meticulous work. He watched as her wide, dilated eyes played back horrible images of Red Bartlett's shattered skull, along with the sensation of a hot pistol in her hand. Someone was screaming, then, and by the expression on her face Hodge saw Nancy realize that she was the screamer, but still she couldn't stop.

Major Hodge wanted his own team to get to that Mongoose first. If Toledo was on it, he should have an accident as quickly as possible.

"Excuse me, Major," his aide said. "Your scramble to McAllen is ready in booth A."

"Thanks, Sergeant. Any news on Colonel Toledo?"

"None, sir. The dam and ViraVax are gone. One plane crash-landed outside the compound, but we have no word on survivors."

"Get a team on the ground now!" he ordered. "Nobody leaves that crash alive until we're clear on contamination."

"Yes, Major."

Hodge dismissed her with a wave of his hand and proceeded to the ultrasecure transmission booth. Hodge had one last deception to carry off, the perfect theatrical finale that would decapitate the Gardener leadership and infect the United States in one fell swoop. The Angel had done his job; it was time for Ezra the Invisible to give Flaming Sword some breathing room.

*I am the Lord's trumpet, His plow and His sword. You who have the ears to hear, know this: The Children of Eden are sown, and it's a mighty arm guards the seed. Unbeliever, tread you not on the Garden of the Lord.*

—CALVIN CASEY, MASTER,
THE CHILDREN OF EDEN


# 4

MAJOR RENA SCHOLZ watched the clock on the warehouse wall turn 20:00 as she pressed Quik-Bond onto the last sheet of Plexiglas. She and her crew had removed several interview chambers from the nearby women's prison and converted them into makeshift quarantine Isolettes on less than three hours' notice. Each was three meters on a side, networked into a mainframe for communication and jiffy-plumbed by a drop team from the Corps of Engineers. The Isolettes were double-walled, sealed atop a fiberglass hold-ing tank salvaged from a freighter in the nearby harbor, and each contained a cot, sink and sea toilet from the same ship. The air was her biggest worry.

It seemed to be Sergeant Trethewey's worry, too.

"I can see how the air gets in, Major," he said, pointing to the compressor huffing away in the opposite corner. "But I'm more worried about the air that comes out."

The sergeant helped her lift the last piece of Plexiglas into place, then tightened the corner-clamps and stepped back. Like the major, Trethewey was drenched in sweat.

Major Scholz pointed to a firehose coupling Quik-Bonded to a hole in the glass.

"We'll run hoses from here to the cold-storage facility next door," she said. "We've got a dozen plastic water bladders in there from the airport fire crew, and more coming. The air fills them up, and the cold keeps the volume to a minimum. It's the best we can do right now, and with luck we won't need them for long. Frankly, I think it's just one big cover-your-ass."

"Who gets to seal them off and change the hoses when they're full?"

Scholz wiped the sweat from her forehead and smiled for the first time in hours.

"Some grunt," she said. "Presumably lower in grade than sergeant."

"Which reminds me, Major. How did you draw this lowly shit detail?"

"I've known those kids nearly all of their lives," she said. "If they're going to be held in security isolation, even for twenty-four hours, I want familiar faces around. That's why you're here, too."

"But I don't . . . "

"Yes you do, Sergeant," she said. "You've sneaked Sonja into every flight trainer and cockpit we've got out here. It saved their lives, Sergeant."

"It did?"

"Absolutely. Details forthcoming; you didn't hear it from me."

The teams setting up the other two Isolettes worked in a sweaty silence, the air in the warehouse almost too thick to breathe.

"They've been together all through this; why build separate chambers?"

"Orders," she said.

Scholz had asked the same question herself, and got the same answer. The guerrillas, the chopper crew, the ambulance team—they all waited out their fate in the adjacent warehouse without the luxury of these Isolettes. When she questioned this, the answer from her chief, Trenton Solaris, was, "We're doing the best with what we have."

The other question she had asked but received no answer to had to do with the Children of Eden hangar and warehouse directly across the airfield. They were locked up tight over there, presumably for their Sabbath. Still, she couldn't help wonder how they could sit quietly by when a couple of thousand of their personnel just disappeared under a few million tons of water. In spite of Major Hodge's hands-off attitude, Scholz put the place under surveillance, physical and electronic. If they tried to move anybody or anything out of there, she'd take action. Until then, it was easier for everybody if she let them sit tight.

Sergeant Trethewey dragged a couple of lengths of firehose to their work area and dropped them at the major's feet.

"Major, are you all right? I heard you were in the embassy when the bomb. . . . "

"I'm fine," she said. Then she shook her head and laughed. "A fluke. I hate to say it, but Hodge saved my skin. He called me out of the reception area back to snoop and sniff, clear on the other side of the building, just before it blew. By the time I got back through all the debris, Colonel Toledo was gone."

She shot some Quik-Bond into the threads and screwed them into the coupling in the Plexiglas.

"They say it was a suicide mission," Trethewey said. "That he did it to get his ex-wife."

"More complicated than that," Scholz said. "Believe me, he didn't do it. And he didn't blow the dam at ViraVax, either. The guerrillas verified that when they brought the kids in. Quik-Bond all these couplings until the bonding seeps out. We don't want any air leaks."

"The kids . . . they're still okay?" Trethewey asked.

Scholz patted her Sidekick.

"As okay as could be expected under the circumstances. They're in an ambulance out back—which we've been ordered to bury in concrete as soon as they're moved in here."

"Those goddamn guerrillas. . . . "

"It wasn't them," the major interrupted. "They discovered the charges when they went to help the Colonel get the kids. They're the ones who rescued the kids, and that woman virologist. She's the sole survivor out there, it looks like. García's people shot them down—*our* standing orders—and would have killed them all if they'd found them first."

"What happened with the team that Major Hodge sent out?"

"It was a faceoff," she said. "The guerrillas refused to hand the kids over. Things were tense until Harry used a Sidekick and Colonel Toledo's authorization code to get through to the Chief in Mexico City. Solaris called off Hodge and let the guerrillas bring in the kids."

"Shit."

"Yeah," Scholz said. "Shit. By the way, I understand you have a personal interest in the Bartlett *girl*, Sergeant. Isn't sixteen a little young for you?"

Trethewey shrugged.

"She's a genius who finished school at fourteen and flies planes at sixteen," he said. "I never think about her age and I've never . . . you know, done anything. Besides, when I'm forty she'll be thirty-four, and nobody sees anything wrong with that."

"Sounds like you have long-term motives."

The major held one coupling while Trethewey shot the glue to it and screwed it in. She hung it over a sawhorse so it wouldn't bond to the concrete floor. Trethewey dragged over a couple more.

"I might not be a genius, Major, but I'm not a jerk, either. Besides, she and the Toledo boy are inseparable. How's he doing?"

"Pretty shook up physically, but nothing broken. Recovering from a heavy trank that the Colonel slapped him with. But Harry had the presence of mind to grab a data drop that Red Bartlett made before he died. The sooner we get this stuff together, the sooner we find out what's on it."

"Can't you just run it through one of the machines at the office?"

"Not likely, Sergeant. The medicos don't want anybody touching it, and the spooks don't want it duplicated. Contamination risk, remember? I think we have enough hose on this one to reach."

She pulled another length of hose to the next Isolette, and Trethewey followed with three more.

"Harry's a very smart boy," she said. "He's pretty upset about leaving his dad behind just before the dam blew. . . . "

Here Major Scholz choked back her own feelings for Colonel Toledo—feelings which, until this nightmare hit, she'd hidden even from herself.

*He was a bastard,* she thought. *But under there somewhere was a good man once, trying to find his way out again.*

"Are you okay, Major?"

The voice behind her was that annoying and insistent nasal whine of Colonel Toledo's replacement in Costa Brava's DIA office, Major Ezra Hodge. Scholz had been in-country for years, but the Agency had put this greasy tenderfoot in charge of Operations. That did not sit well with Major Scholz, but she was accustomed to doing an excellent job for the occasional bastard, and this would be no exception. She put on the appropriate face.

"Just tired, Major," she said. "What's the latest?"

"We need another Isolette," he said, "on the double. And not with these three. I want it in the next building. Get a complete intensive-care setup from Merced Hospital and install it inside. Accommodations for two—a patient and caregiver. And communications. I want it ready within the hour."

Major Scholz felt the blaze of anger flash from her collar to her cheeks, and noted the theatrical rolling of the eyes from Sergeant Trethewey, who stood behind Hodge. Trethewey followed the eye-rolling with a quick jab of an uplifted middle finger, and, at a nod from Scholz, hurried out to start work next door.

"Who's our new guest, Major?" she asked.

"Toledo," he said, and the name spat from his tongue like a foul taste. "Our SEAL team picked him up. He's alive, barely. The corpsman who's treating him will have to stay with him, you understand. And post sentries. He'll be under arrest."

"Arrest?" Scholz was incredulous. "What for?"

Major Hodge was clearly agitated, rare for such a self-controlled little maggot.

"For the embassy bombing, of course. For kidnapping the kids. And for blowing the dam that killed who knows how many people. Including, it would seem, Calvin Casey, the Master of the Children of Eden. A little like dusting the Pope in the Vatican, wouldn't you say? Well, Major? Come on, let's hop to it!"

Major Scholz ignored Major Hodge's insulting tone and concentrated on getting her breathing under control.

*Rico's alive!* she thought.

Then she shook off her exhaustion and set to work with a vengeance to see that he stayed that way.

*Remember, I pray thee, who ever perished, being innocent? or where were the righteous cut off? Even as I have seen, they that plow iniquity, and sow wickedness, reap the same.*

—JOB

# 5

HARRY TOLEDO RAN a trembling hand through sweaty hair and studied his reflection in the glass of the Isolette. His dark hair hung into his eyes, and for the first time in his fifteen years Harry saw that he actually needed a shave. Except for a few nicks and cuts, and a major bruise on his right hip, he had survived two plane crashes remarkably well.

Sonja Bartlett and Marte Chang also survived that last one, and they were penned up in Isolettes flanking his own. His remarkable memory that had served him so well in his life got jarred a little in the last crash. Of course, the heavy dose of tranquilizer that his dad had shot him with didn't help.

"Dad!" he said to his reflection. "I hope you make it."

It felt good to say, after the bad years between them. Harry and Colonel Toledo could be twins if they weren't different ages—gray eyes, gallic nose with an *indio* flare of nostril, thick black hair, usually kept short for the heat. The new scatter of whiskers on Harry's cheeks added to their remarkable similarity.

*Physical similarity,* Harry reminded himself.

He was sure that he and his father were nothing alike inside. Harry couldn't stand the smell of alcohol, he was very shy around women, and he was sure that if he ever had a wife and children he wouldn't beat them. Still, in that few minutes that the two of them had worked together to escape from ViraVax, Harry understood that his father loved him in his tormented way.

Harry hated his father for so long that he got used to daydreaming him dead from a bullet, a bomb, an accident of the bush. He would review the memories of his father later and come to terms with that.

*When you wish somebody dead, and then they die, does that mean you killed them?* he wondered.

Father Umberto told him in confession that wanting to kill his father constituted a mortal sin in the eyes of the Church. What was there to keep him from actually doing it, then? Nothing but his own will, and his own fear. And did he really want his father dead? "No," he'd admitted, "I want him *back*."

Colonel Toledo had shot Harry with the trank gun to get him out of ViraVax alive. Harry had to admit now that his father had saved his life.

*Maybe in trade for his own!*

Harry hoped not, but it didn't look good. He thought back on all the times in his life that he had wished his father dead, and felt a hot blush wash his cheeks. He had gone so far as to figure out ways to kill his father without getting caught. He was glad, now, that he hadn't tried it.

"Good Friday," Harry told his reflection. "Dad always said that anything you do on Good Friday will die on you before sundown."

His father wasn't a by-the-book colonel or a by-the-book Catholic, but he believed in God and Country, in that order.

*That's it*, Harry realized. *If his family was anything to him, it was just another state in Country.*

Colonel Toledo had trained Harry in two different karate styles, Tong Soo Do and Tae Kwan Do, and lately he had considered the occasional beating to be part of his son's training. Karate, and a few other tricks that his father had taught him, helped Harry and Sonja in their escape. Harry wished mightily that his father had escaped with them.

Harry slapped the glass barrier of his Isolette.

*Escaped! What a joke!*

They crawled more than five stories of elevator shaft, stole a plane and got shot down in it, only to be sealed up again by their own government.

"For your own protection," Major Scholz told him. "No telling what you picked up out there."

That didn't worry Harry as much as being locked up and forgotten in some warehouse during a civil war. He had already figured out how to get out of this Isolette, but it involved mucking around in the septic tank, so he decided he could wait.

Sonja was another matter. He didn't think she could wait long, at all. Sonja's reaction when she first saw the Isolettes shook Harry almost as much as the ghastly scene at ViraVax and the plane crash. As the two of them and the virologist, Marte Chang, were escorted from the ambulance into the warehouse, Sonja collapsed.

"Oh, no!" was all she'd said, and she dropped, limp, to the concrete deck.

And then she cried. Harry had seen Sonja through a lot, and she never cried. Watching her sob on the concrete broke his heart. When he moved to help her up, one of their escorts pressed a rifle across his chest to stop him. Harry nearly tried the snatch-and-keep move that had saved them in ViraVax, but the neuropuff in his bloodstream wouldn't let him. It was a move his dad had taught him, and he hoped now that he would get the chance to thank him for it.

"At least we got Sonja's dad out," Harry muttered. "Even if he's just an image in a cube."

Red Bartlett had been dead for nearly two months. Sonja had convinced Harry that ViraVax had something to do with her dad's death, and she'd been right. He couldn't wait to get his hands on the information in that cube, and get it out to the world. Marte Chang would get to review it first, with the Agency's snoops on-line, as usual. Harry had taught Red Bartlett how to make the cube, and he was sure that neither Marte Chang nor the Agency could break it without him.

Harry could feel how much Sonja desperately wanted to see and hear her father in front of her one more time. Red had been largely an absentee father, working all week, and sometimes more, out at the ViraVax compound. Her relationship with her father was as loving as Harry's was antagonistic.

Some data was flowing into Harry's makeshift terminal already, spillover from Marte Chang's machine. That part had been easy. What he really wanted was to figure out how to get data flowing the other way. Every attempt he'd made to connect with the outside world had been terminated by an autoguard. And it really irked him that the autoguard operated out of his father's old DIA office, and that it was Harry who showed him how it worked.

*One of the few times Dad admitted that I actually knew something.*

Harry still didn't know what to feel about his dad, except he hoped that he wasn't dead. Scholz told him that the flood following the blown dam had scoured ViraVax and the entire Jaguar Valley. A SEAL team continued the search for Colonel Toledo, but from what Harry heard after he was lifted out of the valley, it sounded hopeless.

"How are you doing in there?"

The voice through the tinny speaker was Major Scholz's. He felt his cheeks flush as he realized he had been staring at his reflection in the glass, and Major Scholz looked back at him from the other side.

"Like any bug under glass," he said. "What about my mom?"

"She's still at the embassy," Scholz said. "We'll arrange for her to come out here in the morning."

"If we're alive in the morning, you mean."

"So far, so good," Scholz said with a shrug. "She and

Nancy Bartlett have been briefed on your situation. That console of yours includes a line to the embassy. You've already found that, I hear. She was probably relieved to hear from you."

"Yeah," Harry said, "she was. No thanks to you."

"They've got their hands full over there, as you might imagine. I know you're angry about this. . . . "

"You don't know the half of it, Major," Harry said.

Harry was mad because he escaped one trap to get into another, because he was exposed to God-knows-what Artificial Viral Agents, because the aftereffects of the tranquilizer left him trembling all over like a weak kitten and he hated feeling weak. It was too much like being at his father's mercy when he was on a rampage.

"Look at this!" Harry shouted, waving his arm at his tiny chamber. "You keep criminals better than this. Chill, you gave all of us Litespeeds. Crammed in here with a cot, a pump toilet with a see-through curtain and a camping sink in a goddamn warehouse. . . . "

"It's temporary, it's necessary and you know it," Scholz shot back. "Besides, you have your console with the usual network access. . . . "

"Don't give me that 'temporary' crap, Scholz," Harry said. "Ten minutes in here is eleven minutes too long. And I've already found the gates you put on that so-called 'network access.' Everything's triple-snooped, so that I'm shut down if I try to get out of the neighborhood. That Agency card you gave me is a major red flag."

"I thought they took that at ViraVax when they took your clothes."

"Yeah," Harry admitted, "they did. But I ran it through my Litespeed at home and got the coding sequences for verification and access."

"You mean, you *remembered* a sixty-four-digit code? *And* the random sequencing fuse?"

"I remember everything," Harry said, and shrugged. "But it didn't do me any good."

"This is a security matter," Major Scholz said. "You

can understand why we don't want . . . ' '

"Why you don't want the world to know what you've done," Harry finished. When Scholz's gaze went cold and distant, he added, "They couldn't have done it without you, you know. Or without my dad. Personally, I think we should tell everybody."

"What good would that do?"

"It would get a lot of good minds working on the problem," Harry said. "And warn people, in case it's contagious. *Is* it contagious?"

"Contagion-factor tests are being run now," Scholz said.

"This could be a multistage thing that doesn't flag the CF," Harry said.

Scholz's blonde eyebrows arched in surprise.

"Very good," she said. "That's what Ms. Chang thinks."

"I'd like to hear from Marte Chang what Marte Chang thinks," Harry said.

Scholz shrugged off his surliness.

"I think Ms. Chang wants you to help her research this problem within security parameters. I'll help wherever I can."

"Where are they taking our blood, by the way, if it's so dangerous? And what about the people who took our blood? And the suits we wore, the ambulance and chopper we rode in . . . ?"

Major Scholz put up a hand to stop him, and pointed with her thumb towards the back of the warehouse, farthest from the runway.

"Well," she said, "the ambulance and your hazard gear, the hazard gear and clothing of the two doctors, four nurses and six medics who helped you, the clothing and equipment of the guerrilla team who found you . . . those items are being buried in concrete behind this building as we speak."

"Chill," Harry said. "What about the people? And that chopper?"

"The people are quarantined, as you will be soon. The chopper's been sprayed with three kinds of death."

Harry flicked his right middle fingernail against the glass.

"What's the difference between 'quarantine' and this prison we're in now?" he asked.

"You're in 'isolation' " Scholz said. "Marte Chang says there is more than one variation on this AVA. You each may have none, all or several agents in your bodies. We don't want any of you acquiring more while you're in our care."

"And you don't want anyone acquiring them from us."

"No, we don't. And, frankly, I don't want to catch anything here myself, clear? We just found another pile of Meltdowns in the Gardener warehouse across the runway. There was a palm-cam in there with them, we're analyzing the record now. Ms. Chang suspects that it's their ritual water that carried the AVA package. There hasn't been time to see whether there's a stage two."

Harry shook his head.

"It might take weeks or months for a secondary to show up," Harry said. "And there's that brain virus with a twenty-year incubation period. Are you planning on keeping us nice and safe here for twenty years?"

"I keep telling you, this is only temporary. . . . "

"Frankly, Major," Harry snapped, "this setup you've got here is a kid's tree-house next to the accommodations at Level Five of The ViraVax Palace. I don't think you've isolated us from *mice*, let alone virions. It's a joke. Admit it, and let us out."

"We've done our best. . . . "

"Don't scare me more than I already am, Major," Harry interrupted. "You're monitoring anything that Sonja, Marte Chang or I might say to each other, right? Do you have a camera in that toilet, too, Major?"

Major Scholz's face drained to a marble-white under her blonde buzz-cut.

"Would you like to hit me, Harry? Would that make you feel better?"

"You bet your ass it would, Major."

"Then I promise you, Harry, that you can take your best

shot as soon as we can let you out of there.''

"That's another shuck, Major, and you know it. I might never get out of here. I want that shot *now*!''

Harry fisted the glass and found that, even in his weakened state, the panel flexed with a satisfying *whup*.

Major Scholz didn't flinch, and Harry was almost sure she didn't blink. In spite of his foul mood, he liked that about her. Then she *really* surprised him.

"All right," she said, and pressed herself hard against the glass. "Do it."

Her arms spread wide, and her thighs, pelvis, breasts and right cheek flattened under the pressure.

Harry curled his left fist and cocked it into his armpit for a quick, snapping punch. Then he flashed on all the times that his father hit his mother, who could only cover her head with her arms and take it.

"Do it, goddammit!" Scholz growled. "I can't stay here all night."

Harry took a deep breath, let it out slowly, and uncocked the fist. He reached out his hand and patted the place where her cheek met the glass.

"That's okay, Major," he said. "I don't need to do that."

She stepped back, a flush in her own cheeks creeping into her short, blonde hair.

"I'm on your side, Harry."

"I know, Scholz."

"And I do have *some* news. We've begun unraveling that data cube you lifted from ViraVax so that Marte Chang can tell us what they were up to. She's feeding it into her system right now, and you're on the same linkup. Have a look."

"Sonja's dad is the one who made that cube," Harry said. "Can she see it, too?"

"If she wants."

"Are you sure that's smart? I mean, no telling what's on there, and she's already been through a lot. . . . ''

"Harry Toledo, I don't believe what you're saying! You

just chewed my butt about limiting your access to the world, and now you want to limit Sonja's?''

Harry laughed for the first time in . . . a while. At least a couple of days. And it felt good.

"You're right," he said. "Thanks, Major. I don't want to become the enemy. We'll take everything we can get."

"I'm being selfish," she said. "Maybe there's a clue in there that'll let me let you out sooner. We just need to know what they made and what it'll do, first."

"And whether any of these little beasts survived?"

"Exactly."

Harry felt energized, suddenly, and the tremor was gone from his hands.

"Okay, Major. You got my full attention. I'll do everything I can." Harry turned his palms up. "But you have to let us out to do that."

"Soon, Harry." She patted the glass where his palm rested. "I'll see about getting your access cleared to the networks. Good luck."

The console included a sound system, and as the structures of the Artificial Viral Agents scrolled down the viewer, he keyed up the bridal procession from Rimsky-Korsakov's "Le Coq D'Or." It always helped him with memorization. For the moment he ignored the blinking symbols on his control panel that signaled messages from Marte Chang and Sonja. He wanted this brief time alone with his music and his mission.

"That gate of yours is a piece of cake," the console speaker squawked. "You taught me better than that."

*No such luck with the time alone*, Harry thought.

"Voice direct," he said, and his console made the switch. He was frustrated that they didn't have a video pickup. "Hello, Sonja. How's your head?"

"Throbbing," she said, and went on. "ViraVax, what a perfect name. All of the clues were there, out in the open. Look."

The word "ViraVax" appeared in front of him, then enlarged fifty percent.

" 'Vira' for 'virus,' " Sonja said. "They figured out how to make their own viruses. What did they use them for? Vaccines. That's the 'Vax.' But here's the good part."

She drew a circle around the "aVa."

"Artificial Viral Agents," she said. "That's what killed my dad, and all those people. That's what made the Down's syndrome kids."

Harry knew she was crying, and he was glad that the machine's primitive translator filtered it out. He didn't tell her that he was already into those files, starting pattern searches.

"So, you cracked your dad's files?"

"No," she said. "Marte Chang's working on that. I just saw an unscrambled memo that he made for me the day he died. They experimented on *us*, Harry. On you and me."

"Who?" he asked. "Your dad?"

"No," she said. "ViraVax. That dzee, Mishwe, he did something to us before we were born. My dad's message says the details are in one of the files; nobody knows *which* one. Marte's searching structures first because they need to know which of those AVAs is loose out there."

"I can help with that."

"I know," she said. "That's why I barged in."

"Well, if we synchronize our machines, we can do the rough search twenty-seven times faster than Ms. Chang can do it alone. This gives me the creeps, you know. The idea that Mishwe has been messing with us since before we were born. . . . "

"And he may not be done yet," she said. "Let's get Marte tied in and move on this."

"Yes, my Empress, my Queen."

"Don't be zed. You know what I mean. Now, Wonder Boy, tell me what we have to do to get out of *this* one."

> *Yes, the hour is coming for everyone who kills you to think that he is offering worship to God.*
>
> —JESUS

FATHER FREE HAD been awake now for over twenty-four hours, and he had a couple of hours to go before daybreak lifted the nightly curfew. He sat at a table with the beautiful Yolanda Rubia in the back of the restaurant El Ranchón Cuzcatlán. A single paddle fan stirred up the flies overhead and drained power from the lamp on the wall. With the checkered tablecloth, the softened light and their hunched postures, they might be mistaken for a couple. Every so often he caught a whiff of her perfume over the burned-diesel smell of his shirt and jeans.

"It was like nothing I have ever seen," Yolanda said, and rubbed her arms as though chilled. "And you, Father, know the kinds of things I have seen. You have seen as much yourself."

Not yet dawn, not yet the end of Holy Week, and Father Free sweated out the curfew with Yolanda, a half-dozen snoring guerrilla leaders and his third pot of coffee. Yolanda drank rum, sugared with lemon. He remembered it was Rico Toledo's drink, as it had once been his own. After the embassy, the Archbishop's office and its broadcast station had been bombed, and Father Free's room was behind the sound booth. The García government was a Gardener government, and they feared a Catholic retaliation.

*With good reason*, Father Free thought.

Both the Peace and Freedom guerrillas and the predominantly Catholic *campesinos* had looked for an excuse for an all-out uprising against the Gardeners. Father Free had fought the fire at the Archbishop's office for hours, while outside the poor people fought the Gardener army detachment with rocks and bottles. Twenty people died, including two seminarians.

Father Free had married Rico and Grace Toledo, baptized their son, and he did not believe for a moment that Toledo was guilty. But this news that Yolanda brought him now, of hundreds of people bursting into flame at ViraVax, had him scared. Few people knew of the ViraVax facility, and only a fistful of that few knew the kinds of things that went on out there. Father Free was one of those few.

"And none of your people got this melting sickness?"

"No." She sipped. "Not yet, thanks God."

*Five years ago she'd have made the sign of the cross when she said that*, he thought.

He remembered, too late, not to rub his eyes again.

"There's a good side," he offered. "Your team saved the kids and turned them over to U.S. custody. That's some negotiating clout that you've been needing lately, since Sonja's grandfather's the Secretary of State."

"And I intend to use it," Yolanda said. "This will be the time of times, Father. Truly, the final offensive. You should stay here at the *cooperativa* for a while. Many priests are shot in times like these."

"Easter is supposed to be a time of joy, and resurrection, and moving forward," he said, staring into his coffee. "I can't believe . . . "

A soft chirp sounded from his Sidekick, and Father Free pressed his earpiece to listen privately.

"Father Free? Chief Solaris."

Solaris and Toledo had both gone through his ethics course at the Academy. Father Free had always found Toledo a straight shooter and Solaris frightening, and twenty years ago he never would have believed that either of them would still be in his life. It was Rico who had given him the nickname ''Luke the Spook,'' and in an academy of intelligence officers, the name ''Spook'' stuck fast. It was Solaris the Sneak that he never trusted.

''Yes.''

''Give me your address. I'll have you picked up right away.''

''I'm comfortable where I am, thanks,'' Father Free said. ''It's been a long night.''

''It has, indeed,'' Solaris said. ''Toledo's here, badly injured. He'll want to speak with you when he wakes up. *If* he wakes up.''

''I'm at Restaurante Cuzcatlán,'' he said. ''Send some clothes, Rico's size; mine are ruined. And nobody comes inside, this is neutral turf.''

''There is no neutral turf anymore, Father,'' Solaris said. The word ''Father'' had a contemptuous edge to it. ''Those days are gone forever. Your escort will be outside in fifteen minutes. You'll have to excuse our limited selection of apparel.''

Father Free pressed the ''break'' button.

''Make sure your gear is screened,'' he told Yolanda. ''There'll be army outside in fifteen minutes and we don't want to tempt them to look in the back.''

''It's Rico, isn't it?'' she asked. ''He's alive?''

''So far,'' he said.

''Thanks God,'' Yolanda said.

This time she made the sign of the cross.

*It is not possible for civilization to flow
backwards while there is youth in the
world.*

—HELEN KELLER

# 7

FOR THE SECOND time in a half-hour, Sonja Bartlett
watched the image of her dead father run long, pale fingers
through his shock of thick, red hair. He always did that
when he was nervous, and so did she. Sonja knew now just
how scared he must have been when he recorded this cube.
She resisted the urge to run a hand through her own hair.
Her pulse throbbed against the stitches in her forehead, sou-
venirs of a Mongoose instrument panel.

Red Bartlett's flickering image queasied her stomach as
he explained to her how ViraVax had fooled him, fooled
the world.

All Sonja could think was, *Dad, for a genius, you were
way dumb.*

"I keep telling myself," the image was saying, "that if
you're seeing this, then we're all okay. We're probably
celebrating someplace nice while the good guys put the bad
guys away for life. But it doesn't look good. I'm using
some tricks Harry showed me to shunt data and keep it
feeding onto the web, in case anything happens to me. He
can find it if he looks; I can't say anything about it here.

"*If* something happens, your mom should get you, Harry

and Grace Toledo to Spook. He can be trusted, and he has connections outside the Agency. If I'm not with you when you get this, then there's only one thing you can do—hide. You and Harry, both. Get to Spook and have him get you someplace safe. Don't wait for anybody if you get this without me. Get yourself and this message to Spook.

"Dajaj Mishwe has gone way over the edge with his AVAs. He's found a way to get them into the DNA of our mitochondria, and to get them to work together. Each sub-assembly is smaller than a viroid, even. But when linked up and coordinated they form something completely different inside the cell, something bigger and slipperier than a virus."

The view behind her father showed little icons of gears and levers sliding through tubes inside a giant cell. "The gears and levers pick up other materials, meet in the DNA of an organ inside the cell and assemble themselves into a mechanical spider that bites off chunks of genetic material and spins an artificial replacement, which it tacks into place.

"Mishwe intends to infect the whole world with one of these. He called it 'GenoVax,' for 'Genome Vaccine,' to get the collateral work that he needed from uninformed people. A universal DNA repair kit, that's what he was selling. But what he was building and installing in humans was a bomb. It can be set to kill all blue-eyed females. All black-haired diabetics. All brown-eyed males. But Mishwe's not being that fussy. Anything with a basic human genome dies.

"The 'Geno-' is really for 'Genocide.' "

Behind Red Bartlett, banks of holographic batteries floated around the cell, linking up with golden wires. Other machines chewed up the cell to make littler machines that dissolved what was left, and they all gave off a gas that was sparked to flame by the chain of golden batteries.

*So* that's *how all those people melted down and burned up*, she thought.

"Maybe I'm already too late," her father was saying.

He clenched and unclenched his fists, knuckles blanching on long, freckled fingers. Fingers through the hair again.

"The worst of it is, ViraVax developed this technique by practicing on humans, including you and Harry. You're both . . . clones."

Here the image of Red Bartlett took a couple of deep, shaky breaths, rubbed his face, ran his fingers through his hair. When he spoke again, his voice was very strained, tight and high as an adolescent's.

"As a parent and a human," he said, "I'm disgusted by what they've done. But as a scientist, I know how excited I would be to study the first two successful human . . . clones. Mishwe's technique, infecting sperm with the proper AVAs, avoids the clumsiness of laboratory manipulation that ruins most attempts at cloning the higher animals. I hate the man, but I do admire the technique. So will others."

The cartoon behind him showed a robot rebuilding the inside of a sperm.

"That technique, by the way, used my genetic material as the Trojan horse for the Artificial Viral Agents that took charge of one of your mother's eggs and made you a perfect copy of your mother.

"They have done some horrible things down here at Level Five, many military projects for the U.S. and others, but this is where they stole my daughter from me. I'm not your father; you don't *have* a father. Just like Harry doesn't have a mother; he's a duplicate of Rico. Except you've been enhanced a bit, which explains why both of you blistered right through school and you did so well on your night flights.

"But you're always my daughter to me. I love you.

"Now, once it's triggered, this thing will move really fast. It will flash fast through crowds on water droplets but won't survive long outside the cell. Trouble is, these triggers are small and when the cell blows, thousands of them spill out.

"I hope none of us ever sees it. Tell Spook to smoke up some proverbs for me."

Sonja paused the cube and rubbed her aching forehead, trying not to disturb the Quik-Stitch that closed her jagged laceration. She didn't understand the reference to Father Free smoking up some proverbs.

"Harry," she said, her voice a croak, "can you hear me?"

"I'm here," her speaker said. "Going nowhere yet. What's up?"

"Have you looked at Dad's cube?"

"Just organizing the file index," he said. "I've been concentrating on how to get through these goddamn gates that the Agency's put up so that I can find that GenoVax stuff he talked about."

Sonja waved her hand at the Watchdog unit that recorded their every move, as though Harry could see her.

"Nice of you to announce that you're trying to defeat their system," she said. "That'll be a *big* help."

"They know," he said. "No big deal. If I get out, I get out. Besides, if I get the data, they get it, too. They're just worried that we'll tell the world about this before they can put a lid on it."

"We have to, you know."

"Yeah. I've been a bad boy. Computer-persistent. That doesn't seem to bother anybody. I want out of here, and I don't see why we have to be nice little kids."

"Yes," Sonja said, "that's right."

She picked up her chair and swung it with all of her strength against the air-intake glued into the glass. The incredible *bang* inside her Isolette popped her ears.

"Sonja!" Harry said. "What's going on over there?"

She swung again, another *bang* and this time the coupling loosened. Another *bang* and she could barely stand, her head wound pounding, as two guards and Major Scholz ran up to her cubicle.

Harry shouted over the intercom, "What's happening over there? Are you all right?"

Sonja rested on her knees, her pounding head in her hands.

"I bashed their hose-line out of the wall."

Harry laughed.

"Chill. You got their attention, wild woman. Now, what are you going to do with it?"

Two Marine guards in bio suits scrambled to hook the hose back up. Major Scholz approached the glass to speak to her. She wore the same sweat-soaked fatigues and looked dead on her feet. Sonja took a deep breath and blew it out the hole. Scholz jerked back as though Sonja spat fire.

"What's happening now?" Harry asked.

"I'm blowing through the hole to piss them off."

"Is it working?"

"Yeah. It sure is."

"Chill."

Sonja picked her chair up and popped it against the glass, to keep the two guards back. Scholz kept yelling at her, but Sonja couldn't understand what the major was saying. She popped the glass again and again, but finally couldn't lift the chair anymore, and she slumped to the floor. Her head hurt so bad that she had to crawl to her toilet and throw up.

"Satisfied, now?" Scholz said, over the speaker. "You know, Sonja, we can cut your power. There's a grunt busting his balls on a Lightening out back so you can breathe and play with your Litespeed. He'd love to take a break. Or we can send a chemical lobotomy in with your air. Is that what you want?"

"I . . . " Sonja cleared her sore throat and spat, "I want out."

"You two are like a bad recording," Scholz mumbled. She sighed. "Listen," she said, "we're having a bigshot meeting here that will include President García and Solaris from the Agency. They'll see what your dad had to say, they'll see the condition you're in, and you'll be out. Trust me."

"You keep saying that," Sonja said. "But my dad isn't

my dad, and I'll never trust anybody again.''

"Harry! Sonja!"

Marte Chang's excited voice came across her speaker much too loud for comfort.

"What now?"

"I've got the first clue. From your dad's cube. What we're dealing with is a trigger. The bomb is already in place. It's a catalyzing effect of AVAs, already in place, working together. Rapid onset, rapid contagion. We're going to need a lot of help, and fast.''

"Count on me," Harry said. "You divvy up the work and I'll do the snooping—that is, if we can get the Major to lift some of her network and satlink restrictions.''

Sonja stumbled back to her terminal, set up her chair and tuned out the others. She thought about Spook, about stealing a plane and flying out of this country, and sat down to hear the rest of what her father who wasn't her father had to say.

*The lure, the lore of the hidden. Every
side of refractory matter splitting
light. A deep blaze waiting to surface. . . .*

—MADELINE DEFREES

MARTE CHANG HEARD the *whoosh-swoosh* of incoming air
as the tray behind her opened and closed the positive-
pressure pump. She smelled fresh coffee and chicken soup.

*Feeding time,* she thought. She rubbed her eyes,
stretched, peeled off her headset and gloveware. *How long
has it been since I've had coffee?*

She felt for the cup in the tray behind her, and watched
the viroids she'd been studying fade from red to orange to
black behind her eyelids. She felt wide awake, but her eyes
were gritty and her shoulders knotted like fists. And her
right hip throbbed where the buckle of her seat belt had
caught her in the Mongoose crash.

Marte would not have slept, anyhow. Not after what
she'd seen, and heard, and smelled out at ViraVax. The
coffee was a luxury, one stage of freedom, a promise that
there was more to come. She had been locked up at
ViraVax for two months; a few more days in this Isolette
wouldn't bother her much.

*Except I'm so close,* she thought. *We could be moving
to production now if we were at a good lab.*

Marte heard some of the ruckus that Sonja and Harry

57

raised in their cubicles. They had saved her life, and she couldn't let them down now. Marte left ViraVax with nothing but her life—Harry had thought to grab for some data on his way out the door. They were young yet, those two, and righteous indignation was a privilege of youth.

She knew all too well how they felt. It was just how she'd felt when those automatic doors at ViraVax *whooshed* closed behind her that first time. And again, when she found the human experiments that Dajaj Mishwe had boxed up so neatly at Level Five. She had wanted to scream every night, but she had her own prison to maintain on behalf of the Defense Intelligence Agency. Marte trembled now, not with caffeine, but with the emotional blowup that bubbled inside her.

*I hope I can nip this fuse before I lose it.*

Marte desperately hunted the combination of proteins, amino acids and free radicals that would get all three of them out of the zoo. She couldn't do that if she went to pieces now.

She took a deep breath, then rotated her neck as she let the breath trickle slowly out her left nostril first, then her right. This was a trick of focus that her mother had taught her.

"Are you there, Major?" Marte asked, her eyes closed.

Her speaker hissed, and Major Ezra Hodge said, "Coffee, I see. They told me you were a Gardener, but of course Children of Eden don't drink coffee, and, obviously, you do."

Marte bumped her tray as she turned, and sloshed some bean soup onto the floor.

"But the chicken broth is made without chickens," Hodge added, "in case you're interested. A miracle of your own technology, I believe."

"I'm sorry," Marte said. This Ezra Hodge gave her a cold-belly feeling. "I thought you were Major Scholz."

"We met briefly last night," he reminded her, and manufactured a smile. "Major Hodge, Ezra Hodge. I'm sorry we can't shake hands."

Marte didn't like the way his eyes pinned her to her chair like some exotic bug. And he didn't *look* sorry at all. He looked greasy, and puffy, and even though she really wanted a man, she really didn't want this one.

"You're wasting my time," she said, and turned back to her console.

"You have to eat," Hodge said. "And there's your coffee, of course. We can chat while you . . ."

"I can *think* while I eat," she said. "I can't *chat* and eat. Not while you've got me in here. Get lost."

Marte touched a key on her console, and steel drum reggae drowned out his feeble squawking.

She ordered her computer, "Volume, up two," just in case.

Marte's soup was just cool enough to eat when Harry's signal, an orange comet, streaked across her vision.

"Voice," she said. Then, "Harry, did they give you mock chicken soup, too?"

"Yeah," her speaker said, "and EdenSprings water. I'm not touching anything made by the Gardeners. From now on, I'll stick to Coke for the rest of my life."

She laughed.

"That's the safest bet," she said. "I'm living dangerously and having a coffee."

"The chicken broth will get us, you'll see."

"Are we out of here yet?" she tossed back.

Her speaker was silent for a moment.

"Sorry," Harry said. "Incoming files on our GenoVax problem. They've been blown; I'll have to defrag and collate them before sending them to you."

" 'Blown'? You mean, somebody else has seen them?"

"No," Harry said. "Mr. Bartlett created the files, blew them into fragments, then mixed them up and stored them in various addresses. One fragment is an assembler. When activated, it brings the others together. It was the simplest trick that would give him the best results."

"Was that something else you taught him?"

Another pause. Marte drank off her coffee and sipped

her soup right out of the bowl.

"Yeah," her speaker said. "I taught Mr. Bartlett and my dad a lot of tricks on the web, which is one way my dad always found me so easily."

"You could have made that impossible, though, couldn't you?"

"Yes," he said. "Yes, I could. His stupid little messages . . . well, at least he kept trying to stay in touch."

"Sonja told me he used to stay in touch by beating you."

"Sonja had no business telling you about that," Harry said. "He wasn't always that way. I try to remember him before that. If he makes it . . . maybe things will be different."

"Things?"

"Well, I don't mean like my parents getting back together, or me living with him again, or anything like that," Harry said. "I mean, maybe he got it out of his system. I'd like to see him happy again, but I still wouldn't want to live with him. I'd like to get my own place now. Okay, here comes your feed. Good luck."

"Harry?"

"Yeah."

"Thanks for talking to me."

Static. Marte tipped her soup bowl up and chugged it.

"Thanks for listening," her speaker said. "I shouldn't waste your time."

"Never," she said. "Talk anytime."

Then he was gone; Marte could feel it. Or not feel it. What did she feel with the young Harry Toledo that was so noticeably absent without him?

*Happy.*

*Uh-oh,* Marte thought, *he's just a kid.*

He was just a kid, but he'd saved her life. She readjusted her headset, stretched her aching muscles again and sighed.

*The idle brain is the devil's playground.*

The GenoVax directory opened in front of her, and she moved to the customary abstracts to give herself an overview. Marte wondered how Harry had found the proper addresses for the blown files. She wanted to learn how to do that: search out anything or anyone on the nets and webs. If they got out of this, maybe he would teach her.

Marte twisted and untwisted her long black hair in her ungloved left hand while her right navigated through the ViraVax studies related to Artificial Viral Agents—specifically, "teams" of AVAs acting as smugglers, initiators and assemblers of microtubule expressways and biological engines within the cells.

*This thing is set up to work fast,* she thought. *A multi-system assault on the whole body.*

Any human being who had been vaccinated for anything over the past ten years was infected; ViraVax had seen to that. The cascade effect of the AVAs had to be stopped early in the process, so she concentrated on the supply lines, the microtubules, and the basic initiator-type structures.

*Once I identify these triggers,* she thought, *we still have to manufacture and distribute the blocking mechanism.*

Marte heard her mother's voice in the back of her head, urging her, "Don't let what you cannot do stop you from doing what you can."

So she didn't.

*No servant is greater than his master, nor is one who is sent greater than he who sent him.*

—JESUS

COMMANDER DAVID NOAS of the Jesus Rangers dreamed of fishes. The edge of his awakebrain registered this image as portentous while his dreambrain sucked him down a tunnel of warm water, aswarm with red, blue and turquoise lacefins. His dream self held his breath so the dreamer would not drown.

Silver, blue, yellow and green, stripes and calicos, these bright fishes drew David Noas relentlessly downward until their colors faded into shadowy reds and grays. Only luminescence flashed past him, now, and in the phantasmic glow he sensed the true hypnotic grotesqueries of the deep. The dreamself looked upward to where light and the surface were supposed to be, and the surface was gone. He knew, then, that he had been sucked into the maw of some leviathan, and if he could only outswim the current he might be spared.

A shrill, pulsing alarm startled him into letting go his one good breath and Commander Noas woke instantly, his Air Galil a chill in his fist.

"Speak!"

He relaxed his aim on the console and caught his breath.

"Sir! Special Ops Command meeting immediately at Sanhedrin Chambers, sir!"

Commander Noas flicked a finger and his bedside Watchdog displayed the image of a pale, distraught young woman at Central Security and Communications. Every light on her control board pulsed in a red fury. The woman's brown eyes stared, wide as a deer's, at the video pickup just to the left of his own display. The commander snorted his disgust.

*Another missionary.*

She wore the blue-and-white shoulder patch of a first-year missionary on a customary two-year rotation. That was his indictment of the missionary system of staffing—personnel were either coming or going, so continuity and long-term projects became very nearly hopeless. The commander made sure his own visual was off before he stepped out of bed.

"It's the Sabbath," he growled. "Who authorized a flipping meeting at cockcrow on the flipping Sabbath?"

*Probably her first flipping watch! Flipping amateurs!*

"Sergeant Tekel, sir."

Tekel. It was Tekel who'd been right about the Mormons and the Twin Falls Hot Bloods teaming up last fall. He was a pro, not likely to panic. The overzealous two-year wonders like the woman on his screen hallucinated Mormon infiltrators in the air-conditioning and Muslim frogmen in the hydroponics. This, thanks to the paranoia instilled in them by the weekend warriors who called themselves basic training instructors at Camp Calvary.

*Their parents probably never let them stay up after sunset.*

The actual enemy was much more subtle: a strategic marriage, a political appointment, a handshake over hot turf. This was the kind of danger that required experience to spot. Experience, and good intelligence.

Tekel was not one to cry wolf because he had breathed the wolf's foul breath himself, in the courtroom and in the street. And, like the commander, Tekel was Night-School trained in black ops, a service that the DIA and the U.S. government no longer provided independent contractors since consolidation of the intelligence services ten years back. Sergeant Tekel's office monitored the intelligence agencies of a dozen governments as well as the Godwire, and Noas trusted Tekel's judgment.

The commander pulled on his black pants and black sweater and finger-combed his blotches of blond hair before snugging them down with his black beret. The missionary was still on the line, and now she was crying. He slipped into his boots and squeezed the closures.

David Noas stood up to his full height of nearly two meters and activated the visual pickup on his bedside Watchdog. He knew that his rank, his size and the burn scars across his face cut an intimidating picture. That's why he kept the scars. That, and to remind him of what a government could do to a God-fearing people.

"If you know the situation, Corporal, by all means share it."

The commander heard a lot of shouting in the background, and Innocents weeping. The corporal started to speak, but what came out was a sob.

Exasperated, the commander snapped, "Are you under attack?"

She shook her head *no*, then tried again.

"It's . . . it's the Master." She pulled her shoulders back and took a deep breath. "He's dead, sir."

*His heart,* Noas thought. *He refused the replacement, after all.*

The commander felt the hot fingers of grief at his throat, but swallowed and shook them off. The Gardeners and their interests must be protected while they mourn, the Master's family notified. . . .

"Has anyone notified his son yet?"

Joshua Casey had been a geek of an older brother to the adopted David Noas, but he was a brilliant geek who lived to please his father. At times, his enthusiasm to please his father overstepped his theology. It was on this ground that

Joshua Casey and David Noas had formed a secret part-
nership to secure the Gardeners, their land and their installations worldwide. And to keep the Master alive by means
that the Master did not necessarily approve.

"He's dead, too," the missionary reported. "Somebody
blew up a dam in Costa Brava and he's dead. Every one
of them that went down there . . . they're all dead. . . . "

The rest trailed off into sobs.

The commander's belly went cold.

"ViraVax," he whispered.

A chill spread up his spine and out to his fingertips.

*ViraVax*, he thought, *means 'Artifical Viral Agents.'*

And AVAs meant an international incident and a big
cash-flow problem if he didn't get the cap on it right now.

"Pull it together, Corporal," he growled. "You have a
job to do. Your Master would not want you to let him
down."

"Yes, sir."

"Now, has anyone secured the area of the flood?" he
asked. "Anyone at all?"

The missionary dropped her headset into position, and
the commander watched a flicker of indistinct data blur the
air in front of her face. It reminded him of colorful fishes.

"Our source at the embassy reports a U.S. SEAL team
and a Costa Bravan merc unit on-site," she said. Angry
shouts of grief in the background distracted her for a moment. "No response on any facility channels."

The one piece of information David Noas wanted was
the one that was ultrasecure, one that he asked the corporal
for anyway.

"Is this a contamination situation?"

She showed no undue reaction to his question, and he
breathed a little easier for that. As far as she was concerned,
ViraVax produced vaccines, pesticides and certain agricultural enhancements in Puerto Rico. If the cover was still
good on the Costa Brava facility, they probably didn't have
to worry about a runaway biological catastrophe like the
one in Japan a few years back.

"No word on any kind of contamination, Commander. Should I ask . . . ?"

"No!" he barked. "No, I'll catch up at Sanhedrin. Monitor embassy output and route it to me in chambers."

Commander Noas cut the connection and rubbed the scars at his forehead.

*Who dares to smite the Master of the Children of Eden on my watch?*

*You are a little soul, bearing about a corpse.*

—EPICTETUS

# 10

MANUELITO KAX STRAINED the thin straps of his home-made harness and pulled his rickety cartful of treasures over the tree trunk half-buried in the muck. Though the light of dawn was just now making his way clear, Manuelito had been wrestling his cart through this thick red mud for several hours. He would beat everyone to the generous bounty of the flood. His sister, Lupita, and the two *deficientes* walked ahead, choosing the easiest route for him and his fat-tired cart.

"Yours will be the only cart up here," Lupita called back. "The others have the bicycle tires and they cannot challenge this mud."

Manuelito grunted. He was proud of his cart with the "Mitsubishi" chrome strip along the side. The automobile tires were heavier, truly, but they never went flat and they never got stuck. Well, except for that time in the river, but he was young then and knew nothing of the weight of fast water. He could not fault his cart for that.

Manuelito's cart had a bucket each for broken glass, bottles, plastic, aluminum, steel, iron. He had three buckets for brass, but he didn't fill these as often as he used to since

the army went to caseless ammunition. And he had his *caja*
with the German padlock nailed underneath his cart for his
very important finds and his money.

Up ahead, howler monkeys raised their morning ruckus
in an uprooted ceiba tree. The *deficientes* pointed out something in the mud to Lupita. She stepped up for a look, then
jumped back. Whatever Roberto had in his hand she
slapped out of it, and her wave to Manuelito was an urgent
one.

He slipped out of the traces of the cart, and for a moment
he felt like cottonwood floating on air. He trotted up to join
his brothers and sister, who gathered around several clumps
of hair twisted up with sticks and mud.

"Have you found the deads already?" he asked. "You
knew they would be here."

"No, skinny one, not the deads. Just the hair of the
deads. And look, Roberto picked these up because they
shine in the light."

Manuelito knelt close to Lupita's feet and flicked at the
pile of shiny scales with a stick. They were shiny, truly,
but they were not metal, not plastic, not scales of the fish.

"Fingernails," he whispered. He placed the end of his
stick under the nearest clump of hair and flipped it over.
"A scalp."

Other clumped scalps, fingernails, teeth and bits of bone
led up-valley, towards the great farm at the foot of the dam.

Manuelito and Lupita found bodies in the streets of La
Libertad almost daily, many with their hands cut off or their
tongues cut out or the ones he didn't like for her to see
with their penises jammed in their mouths, but never had
they found something like this.

"It must have been the weight of the water," Manuelito
said. "Truly, as I have learned, the moving water has a
great weight and a great force. We will find the rest of them
up there."

He pointed up-valley with his chin, his face displaying
a confidence for his sister that his belly did not feel.

Roberto pointed at something else shiny in the mud and snatched it up.

"Careful, quiet one," Manuelito said. "Remember what the mines look like. The *tigres*."

Even Manuelito was startled when the U.S. soldier leaped out of the bushes at them.

"Halt!" the figure ordered in Spanish. "You are not authorized to proceed. Go back the way you came. Your identity has been established and you will be arrested if you proceed."

The soldier repeated his message in English.

Roberto and Ricardo hid behind Manuelito and Lupita, who both laughed nervously behind their hands.

"It surprised me again," Lupita said.

"Me, too," Manuelito said.

His attention turned from the larger-than-life figure in front of them to the tree trunks nearby.

"There!" Lupita said, pointing at the base of a small ceiba tree. "I saw it first. It's mine!"

Manuelito smiled. It did not matter who found the Sentry; their whole family shared in all profits. Yet it was a point of pride. Manuelito himself had only captured six Sentries in six years, and they sold well at Saturday market. Lupita pried the sensor-transmitter unit from the tree while Manuelito dug the small staging plate from under the leaves on their trail. The Sentry delivered its message one more time before Manuelito could shut it off and lock it safely inside his *caja*.

"Such a toy might scare the *deficientes* or the mountain *indios*," Lupita said, her small chest puffed out, "but they don't scare me."

The Sentries didn't scare Manuelito, either. But the presence of a Sentry delivered another message, loud and clear: this had been no ordinary farm beneath the dam. Manuelito's heart beat a little wilder at the anticipation of something more valuable than farm implements to fill up his cart. And something more dangerous than a Sentry to protect it.

Manuelito had just stepped back into his harness when Roberto and Ricardo found the steel bottles.

"Ma'lito," Roberto called, lifting the shiny cup over his head. "¿Sí o no?"

Once again, the boy dropped his traces to inspect his brother's find.

"What is it?" Lupita asked.

"It looks like a little bottle to keep hot things hot," he said, turning it over in his hands. He rapped his begrimed knuckles against the top. "Stainless steel, I believe!"

"Look, Manuelito . . . a hundred of them!"

Indeed, many of the small metal containers poked out of the mud ahead of them. Ricardo and Roberto had already gathered an armful each. They dumped them onto the back of the cart and went looking for more. Lupita cleaned one of them with a stiff brush and tried to open it. After struggling with both ends, she handed it to Manuelito.

"Open it, skinny one. Maybe you have the hands."

Manuelito hefted the bottle and liked the feel of it in his hand. He shook it and heard only the barest rattle inside. Some writing was etched into one end, but he understood only one word: "ViraVax."

"This is the company that makes the vaccinations, the *medicinas*," he said. "Maybe this is the *medicina* that will make the *deficientes* normal."

Lupita laughed.

"Maybe it will turn clay into gold and pebbles into diamonds."

"You laugh," Manuelito said, and nodded towards Roberto and Ricardo. "I have heard it myself. They are working on such a thing."

"You can't open it, can you?" she said. "You're too skinny."

Manuelito snorted his disgust.

"You never see past your nose. If the package is stainless steel, what must the cargo be worth? If it is a *medicina*, perhaps it loses value when it is opened."

Lupita rolled her eyes and helped Roberto unload another armful.

"No one bids on an unknown cargo," she said. "One has to know what something is to know its value. One has to open the package to identify the cargo to know its value."

Lupita cleaned another cannister and handed it to Roberto.

"Open it," she said. "Twist the top, so."

She put his hands in the right place and showed him what she wanted. Roberto grunted, but nothing happened.

"No, amor," she said. "You have to twist *hard.*"

Roberto bit down on his tongue and put all his effort into it, and the top twisted off. Manuelito hurried over to see what was inside. He took the cannister from Roberto and pulled out a very cold rack of small blue bottles. Something was inside the center of the rack to keep it cold; already it was covered with a frost that appeared from the air like magic. The little glass vials contained a beautiful blue liquid, and Roberto reached out a finger to touch one.

"No, amor," Lupita said. "Don't break. You are very strong to open this bottle for us. What do you think, skinny one?"

"I think we should keep them closed. They are supposed to stay cold, so perhaps they lose their value if they warm up."

He replaced the rack of vials and snugged down the lid.

"And how will we know their value? And how will we sell them?"

"When we return to La Libertad, I will speak with the pharmacist, Juan-Carlos. I will bring one of the blue bottles. If they have no value, we can sell the containers for people to keep cold things cold."

"Ice cream cold," Ricardo said.

"Yes," Manuelito said, "ice cream cold. So, we fill the cart here with the bottles. Perhaps Mama can sell them while we come back . . . Roberto, no!"

Roberto had another cannister open, and he pulled out

the nesting-basket for the little bottles. He lifted them to the light and then cried out and dropped them. He shook his hand in pain and looked to Lupita for relief.

"*Caliente*," he said, around the fingers in his mouth. Then he offered them for her to see.

"Not hot," she said. "Cold. Very cold. Now, see. You have broken some of the *medicinas*. Some sick people won't get well now. Leave the rest alone, just bring them to the cart. We're not going to open them anymore."

Ricardo was squatted down beside the blue rivulet that ran into one of their wheel-ruts. He poked at it with a finger.

"No, Ricardo!" Manuelito said. "Leave it, it's broken. Let's fill up the cart and go home. Then I will get you an ice cream."

"Ice cream!" Ricardo said, and his face brightened. "Ice cream!"

Ricardo sucked the blue drop from his fingertip and turned back to the mud with his brother to look for more.

By the time the cart was full, Manuelito Kax was feeling lightheaded and queasy. He blamed it on his eagerness to get up so early and go to the flood. He'd only eaten two tortillas and a handful of beans, which usually got him through the day. But today he had worked harder than usual, wrestling his cart over debris and through the red muck that the valley floor had become. Mosquitoes and the botflies had swarmed him since daybreak. And his head hurt.

His cousin, Luis Ochoa, spotted him as they approached the village and came running to see what he'd found.

"Hey, skinny one, did you see many deads?"

"No," Manuelito shook his head, and lost his balance. He grabbed the traces of his harness to steady himself. "No, Luis, just parts of the deads. And don't call me 'skinny one.' You know my name."

Luis helped him pull the cart the rest of the way to his house.

"You have many fine steel jars back there, cousin. You

know, the soldiers turned everybody else back. Once again, you're the only one to come home with something.''

''I have another Sentry,'' Manuelito gasped. ''And a few bottles. Soldiers . . . they chased me back to the road.''

''Oh, yes, they're everywhere up there. They wear the space clothing and listen to no one. A Sentry, and these jars—truly a rich day for you, cousin.''

Luis stopped his chatter a moment and looked around.

''Where is Lupita?'' he asked. ''And the *deficientes*?''

Manuelito waved a hand to indicate the track he'd just followed.

''Back there,'' he said. ''The brothers have to look at everything, and she teaches them.''

''She should help you with the cart.''

''She cares for the brothers; it is much more work than this cart, my cousin. There, you see? They're coming now. I feel unwell. I want to unload the cart and lie down.''

''What was it like up there? Besides the soldiers. Did you see other gleaners?''

Manuelito shook his head as he unfastened his harness.

''No one,'' he said.

He stood still for a moment, drenched in sweat, feeling the relief of the weight. He took a deep breath to steady himself, and smelled the dozen charcoal fires of his neighbors cooking corn tortillas. From each house came the *pat-pat-pat* of tortillas being formed between a woman's palms. He heard the *clink* of steel as Luis examined the jars.

''Lupita!''

The shout was in his mother's voice, and Manuelito had barely the strength to turn and see that Lupita had fallen in the path, and the brothers were trying to help her up.

The next thing he knew, he was lying on his back, looking up at the shimmering leaves of the ceiba tree. His head buzzed, and people gathered around him, one face swimming into the other. Though they handled him, Manuelito felt nothing. But he saw, very clearly, a quetzal high in the tree. It cocked its head to see him better, ruffled its iridescent wings, and swung its long tail free of the branches. It preened a moment, then cocked its head at him again.

Manuelito heard snatches of his mother's voice crying: *Corre, Luis . . . una enfermera . . . la farmacia* and, finally, *la bruja.*

*I must be sick, indeed,* he thought. *Mama never calls for the witch woman.*

Then he felt like he was floating, upward, towards the quetzal, and all around him he was lit by a blue glow, the same rich blue that spilled from the silver bottles. And then he was not.

*No man can escape his destiny; and
he should next inquire how best he
may live the time he has.*

—PLATO

# 11

VICE-PRESIDENT CARL J. Carlson smelled Death as soon as
he boarded *Eagle Two*, and when he triggered his safety
harness he felt his leather recliner become a coffin. The
Vice-President smelled Death every time he flew, which,
even this early in the campaign, was almost every day.
Today it smelled sour, that moldy washrag sour of his
childhood. His nose had its fill of Death just an hour ago,
on the smoke-laden air that stuck to the remains of a Children of Eden compound in Tennessee. Death's thick perfume clung to fire trucks, the blackened clothing of
rescuers, to the breath of a glad-handing mayor.

He might be a politician, but he was no fool.

*The fire couldn't have been an accident,* he thought.
*These bodies . . . somebody set them on fire and let them
run.*

FBI investigators thought so, too, but the local medical
examiner claimed they had not had time enough to know
what they were looking at. The examiner was a big shot in
the Children of Eden, and it looked like all of the dead
were Gardeners, mostly Innocents.

*One hundred and twenty retarded kids, another eighty*

*adults. Maybe twenty-five staff.*

He shook his head to try to shake the memory of the pitiful remains of those children.

They called their compound "Revelation Ranch," and someone had engineered a flash fire to burn them out.

The question was, did that someone kill them all first, with something chemical or biological, and then torch them as a cover? And what's the immediate health threat to the neighborhood?

"Clever bit of engineering, eh?" asked Perkins, the obnoxious Toronto reporter. "Torching people without really doing too much damage to the structures?"

"Perkins," Carl Carlson said, "maybe up in Toronto you're accustomed to this sort of thing. Down here when somebody kills two hundred–plus people to *make a point* we take it seriously. They are not 'clever engineers,' they're bastards, pure and simple."

Perkins held up his Sidekick, its "send" light blinking.

"You're on record, Mr. Vice-President."

"Then strike 'bastards.' Make it 'dickheads.' "

The Vice-President had flown halfway across the continent twice in one morning, and now he was off again without even the chance to kiss his wife.

"Don't look so glum, Carl," Mark O'Connor said. "The best is yet to come."

Mark O'Connor was husband to President Claudia Kay O'Connor, and "The Best Is Yet To Come!" was the Knuckleheads tune that they sang for Carl that hot night at the convention when his name went up in lights. His name shimmered across the ceiling of the convention center, under the name "Claudia Kay O'Connor." The party had duped him into thinking he'd be their Number-One Guy, then trapped him into playing life insurance for the first woman President of the United States.

"It was an obscene song," he said. "We've been living it down ever since."

"That was three years ago," Mark said. "You've got those going-into-the-last-round campaign jitters, that's all."

He pulled an EdenSprings water from the refrigerator and offered one to Carl, who declined. Then he sat in his accustomed seat next to the Vice-President and triggered his harness just in time for the big push down the runway.

"Helps the ear-popping," Mark said, taking a swallow. "My ears are taking a beating from all this flying." He tipped back another swallow.

"You could talk your wife into taking her own team on the road for a while," Carl said. "Her exposure always spikes the polls."

"I hope that pun was unintentional," Mark said. "And we're keeping her under wraps as long as possible. That's a security thing, and it was my call and I'm sticking . . . "

Mark's left hand went to his ear, and he finished off his mineral water in three big gulps. His expression was one of intense concentration.

"You okay?" Carl asked.

Mark O'Connor pointed to his ear, made the "okay" sign, and continued to listen to whatever his Sidekick was telling him.

"You've been drinking so much of that goddamn water lately I thought . . . "

"Thank you, Jeff," O'Connor said, "I'll tell him."

"Jeff Wheeler?" Carl asked.

Mark nodded.

"Jesus! What kind of disaster does he have for us now?"

The plane leveled off, and O'Connor got himself another bottle of water. He leaned over Carl in that way he had that made the Secret Service nervous.

"You won't believe this," Mark said. "Another Gardener compound torched, this one in Arkansas. A hundred and twenty dead. Somebody's pissed at somebody."

"We better have something for the sharks," Carl said, nodding across the aisle.

Several Sidekicks sounded their tones among the journalists. The news was already on the wire, and O'Connor's people didn't have a statement for him yet. That was pretty goddamn sloppy interference they were playing. They'd better have something to say about it pretty damned quick.

As though reading his mind, Mark O'Connor handed him a slick, with big print, yet. The boys across the aisle started his way, but Carl waved them off while he read what it was the White House wanted him to say about this epidemic of fire.

The Vice-President never got the chance to read his opinion on the Gardener deaths, and no one had the chance to ask him about it, either.

As the traveling team closed in for their questions and a statement, Carl noticed that Mark O'Connor smelled like Death. Mark hovered, slack-jawed, over Carl's seat and the man's breath smelled like goddam *Death*. And this wasn't just the Vice-President's usual in-flight death fantasy. This smell was no sour washrag, and it was real.

Carl's first thought, even to himself, was a wisecrack: *Jeez, no wonder his old lady keeps us on the road!*

Mark shut his mouth, got a quizzical look on his face, then began scratching both his forearms.

"Mark?" Carl asked.

Agent Lampard, from Claudia's team, reached out to steady Mark O'Connor, who slumped against the bulkhead and slid onto the carpet. His body settled like hot jelly in its clothes.

Two sets of hands grabbed Carl by the shoulders and pulled him back as he saw O' Connor's face melt from his skull. Steam puffed out of his bulging shirt-front, and then little blue flames danced on the dark liquid that leaked from the splits in his skin. Agent Lampard grabbed a fire extinguisher.

Everything moved in underwater time for the Vice-President.

"Get him out of here!" Lampard yelled, and pushed Carl back with a shove to the chest. Then he triggered the distress call on his Sidekick.

By this time, Mark O'Connor was just a smear of greasy black smoke overlaying an intense blue flame that Lampard sprayed with a pitiful little fire extinguisher. The other two agents pulled the Vice-President through the hatch to the cockpit, and Carl's last glimpse into the passenger compartment showed Lampard and the Toronto reporter, Perkins, flailing at O'Connor's burning body with their coats. By the time the cockpit hatch was locked behind them, Carl and the others were gagging from the stench.

Alarms buzzed on the cockpit console, and Agent Carver gasped, "Fire in the passenger compartment."

"No shit, Sherlock," the copilot muttered.

"Activating fire suppression," the pilot said.

The pilot flipped a pair of toggles but the alarm persisted. The graphic on his screen showed the fire halfway up the aisle and already through the main deck. Fists pounded weakly at the locked cockpit door, and Agent Brown stopped Carl's hand on its way to the latch.

"National Control," the pilot said, "this is *Eagle Two* declaring an emergency. We have fire in the aft cabin."

The Vice-President's mind buzzed, and he realized he was hyperventilating. He cupped his hands around his mouth and concentrated on calming down.

*These guys are good,* he thought. *They'll get us down okay.*

"Roger that emergency, *Eagle Two*. We are waving off traffic and you are clear to come around and land on Three."

"Coming around," the pilot said, and began a hard, banking turn.

*I'm never going to be President,* Carl thought.

Then he felt himself flush with anger because first his party and then fate had cheated him of his lifelong goal.

*So close. So goddamn close!*

The anger that outwashed his fear felt good, made Carl feel like they might fight their way through this one, after all. Amid the flurried activity of the crowded cockpit, Carl couldn't help seeing O'Connor's face slumping from its bones.

"I'm losing hydraulics," the pilot said. "I've lost port flaps."

"He just burned up," Carl heard himself saying. "He just . . . burned up!"

Then the plane shuddered, dropped suddenly, shuddered again and more alarms buzzed across the control panel.

"No port side landing gear, no nose gear," the pilot said.

Carl wished he could bring up the kind of calm that he heard in the pilot's voice. The plane began to waggle and slew, and Brown pushed him down onto the deck and piled on top of him. He covered his head with his arms, felt Brown's assault Colt grind into his left shoulder blade and heard Carver on top of Brown whisper a prayer under his breath.

The plane almost straightened out, but by then the hot, stinking fire was at the cabin door, centimeters from his head. Then their wingtip caught the taxiway and the pilot hollered, "Shit!"

Through the tremendous tearing of metal and tumble of bodies around him, the last thing the Vice-President heard was Brown's desperate whisper at his ear: "God, please take care of my babies."

*And the angel which I saw stand upon the sea and upon the earth lifted up his hand to heaven, and swore by him that liveth for ever and ever . . . that there should be time no longer.*

—REVELATIONS

# 12

COMMANDER DAVID NOAS made record time through the morning streets of McAllen, Texas, pushing his new Thoroughbred past the red line on every straightaway. He arrived at Sanhedrin Chambers on the outskirts of town with a state cop on his tail. A wave of the commander's hand and a grim-faced, red-eyed sergeant at the guard shack took care of the frustrated cop, whose blasphemy was only outdone by his profanity.

*Probably a Catholic,* Noas thought.

The commander gritted his teeth. Even the gate sergeant had been crying. This show of emotion among his troops meant they were vulnerable, and Commander Noas did not like being vulnerable. Besides the Costa Brava disaster, two communities of the faithful had been wiped out during the night right here in the states.

*Vengeance is Mine,* he thought. *I am the instrument of the Lord.*

He activated the back entrance to Sanhedrin Chambers. With the Master and a couple of thousand dead, this would be no simple strategy meeting of Special Operations. The Master had made the process clear: "Within twenty-four hours of my death, the Sanhedrin will meet immediately and remain in session, under bread-and-water fast, until they unanimously choose a successor.''

Contacting the entire Sanhedrin during the most important Sabbath of the year had already wasted time that the Children of Eden could ill afford.

Commander Noas hoped that the selection would be inspired, and swift. If this was the first shot fired in a new war, he didn't want to be distracted by political posturing among the leadership.

Brothers of the Sanhedrin disembarked the shuttle terminal and shuffled towards Chambers. Shock, disbelief, anger, grief—these were the expressions on their faces. The scar tissue on his own face was a suitable mask.

Innocents outnumbered big shots two to one, and lumbered behind toting briefcases and luggage. The only women in attendance were Innocents, Down's syndrome workers, and these did not offend the Lord by their presence before the tabernacle because they were not truly human.

Commander Noas was thirty-three years old, and reflected that he was the same age as Jesus when he died, the same age as his own father. David Noas had seen his father and his father's people burned to death in the name of justice when he was eleven, not far from this very spot. He would have died with the rest, except his mother threw him out of a second-story window headfirst onto the sizzling turret of an advancing tank. The pain came later. What he remembered of that moment was the *hiss* of his face seared tight to hot metal, and the smell of burning meat. If he hadn't been a vegetarian before, he would have become one then.

Brother Calvin Casey, who broadcast *The Eden Hour*, took him in, trained and educated him, then organized the Jesus Rangers so that the security arm of his church would always be separate from the women and children. Never again would any enemy put Christian wives and children to the stake.

*Never again,* he thought, with self-contempt, *until now. During my own command.*

Brother Casey organized the Christian Economic Confederation—a delicate marriage of international businesses and ecologists that soon became the Children of Eden. Calvin Casey was the founder, Master and Prophet of the Children of Eden, the only family of David Noas. Protection of this family included Casey's "Jesus Is Lord Gas Station and Mini-Market" chain, the Godwire interactive network and the ViraVax research centers. In the end, the commander had failed the Master himself in his hour of need.

There was no love lost between the Children of Eden and the Catholic idolaters. Costa Brava was a lesson, indeed. A Gardener president did not mean a Gardener population.

*And now, the Master dead in a Catholic country!*

No matter what the Sanhedrin said, the commander vowed to have heads on platters for this. And he would serve them up to the Pope himself.

The commander saw Manus and Hubbard of Special Ops arrive by Flicker. He signaled them to wait for him in the Ready Room. They could sift intelligence while he debated policy with the rest of the Sanhedrin. No one approached him to chat. This was as he liked it.

The interior of Sanhedrin Chambers should have been left stark and soaring, suitably undistracting to councils of war. As it was, the Children of Eden had forgone the practical in favor of their passion for gardening. The structure rose to nearly thirty meters above the commander's head, but the proliferation of plants, trees and vines dropped the effective ceiling to under three meters. It was another security headache. As if for emphasis, David Noas had to duck his head several times to avoid one flowering thing or another while walking to his place at the table.

Commander Noas watched the surviving eleven of the Twelve and their entourage of pages, secretaries and advisors as they stumbled through the daze of their grief to their places in Chambers. Some of the Innocents, the ones the

young missionaries called "retreads," reflected the tension
and cried, too, as they set out the ritual bowls, towels, bread
and pitchers of water.

As Commander of the Jesus Rangers and overseer of the
northwest region, David Noas sat to the right of the Master
at the traditional crescent table. The Master's chair was
empty, draped in black cloth. These eleven remaining members of the Twelve represented the most powerful communities of North and South America. The Children of
Eden organized the Godwire Matrix, wealthy communities
operating in concert to control worldwide transportation,
petroleum, water, vaccinations and basic foodstuffs.

"He who controls the religion and the water supply controls all," the Master had said.

He didn't have to mention food, since ViraVax already
tailored Artificial Viral Agents to influence crop production
for better or worse—depending upon the farmer's religious
preference.

The commander's southwest region was a particularly
fruitful community, their precious water challenged mainly
by the Mormons from the west and the Muslims to the
north. Holding these rights required old-fashioned soldier-
ing, and warriors made Noas a lot more comfortable than
Artificial Viral Agents.

Pages, secretaries and the special advisors called Disciples sat at another table inside the crescent, facing the
Twelve. Each of these Disciples apprenticed to a particular
member of the Twelve. The commander's own apprentice,
Peter Bonyon, studied a desktop display of the ViraVax site
and entered a flurry of notes into his Sidekick. Freckles
stood out like buckshot on his ultrapale hands and face.

One apprentice would ascend to the Twelve before the
night was over, just as one of the Twelve would be named
Master. The commander knew, without doubt, that he
would not be the one. His value lay out of the limelight,
in the darker alleyways of God's plan and men's souls. In
the great movie of the world, the Master must always wear
a white hat. David Noas was the voice that is always at

the white hat's ear, the sword always at his side, hungry for Babylonian blood.

*Except this time,* he thought, *when it counted.*

He shook off the self-whipping. In all likelihood, had he gone down with the Master he would have died with him, like the rest. The commander had made valuable inroads in the fight against the infidels, the heathens, the idolators— and the Master recognized him for that, praising him publicly and often.

"Subcontract and Subvert" had been the Noas plan. He hired out units of his Jesus Rangers to any acceptable military force fighting a holy war.

"Choose the Christian side and fight the others," he'd told the Master. "Learn everything there is to learn about the Christians who hire you. You have said yourself that we will fight them later, during the Days of Fire. We must know their weakness. If they are in a spending mood, let them spend on us."

That was ten years ago. Now, even the United States government hired the Jesus Rangers for contract jobs and U.N. missions. In Latin America and Canada, they fought Catholics. They fought Muslims, Jews and assorted heathen in Africa and the Middle East; Catholics again in England, Ireland and Scotland; Sikhs in India and Canada; in China they got their butts burned by the breath of the godless dragon. That was an expensive and painful lesson in patience.

Then, at the commander's suggestion, the feds hired the Jesus Rangers as a Gang Turf Assault Force, specializing in taking the urban war into the homes of the enemy. The strategy was time-honored: identify a gang that they could work with, support that gang to destroy the rest until, in theory, it all boils down to the feds and one last gang per neighborhood. Commander Noas had finished negotiations with the Justice Department on that very lucrative contract just yesterday, and had been looking forward to presenting the good news to the Master.

"Bowl and water."

The thick-tongued voice snapped Noas back to the present. A female Innocent in a sky-blue service suit clunked the ritual vessels down on the table.

"Towel."

She was reciting to herself more than she was speaking to him. She folded the white hand towel neatly beside his bowl. Her cheeks and nose were blotchy and a little swollen.

*Could it be that even the Innocents grieve for the Master?*

"You've been crying," Noas asked her. "What's the matter?"

"Brother Lee, he mad. Brother Lee scare me when he mad."

The commander patted the girl's shoulder.

"Brother Lee's mad because the Master died and he couldn't stop it," he explained.

"I don't want nobody to die. I cry."

*They don't grieve for the Master, they grieve for us! And we harvest their organs like just another crop!*

"If you get your chores done, then that's one thing he won't have to worry about," he said. "What do you have next? Bread and water?"

She nodded and stroked his hand.

"Bread and water," she said.

"You go fetch them now," the commander said. "Everything will be all right."

He saw Sergeant Tekel enter the Acolyte's door. Beyond the Disciples sat the forty-eight Acolytes of the Diaspora. Many of these seats were empty, and one of these was also draped with black cloth. The indicator on his tabletop told Commander Noas that the missing man was Miguel Alonso, the representative from Costa Brava.

Noas nodded a greeting to Tekel, who pointed towards the Ready Room and shrugged. The commander nodded, and held up an index finger for "first thing."

Except for the persistent sounds of weeping, the customary ritual foot-washing proceeded in silence even as tabletop displays unreeled the Godwire news and the fragments of graphic footage from Milwaukee, Tennessee, and Costa Brava. Commander Noas took the bowl and cloth from Sebastian Ferguson, laid a perfunctory swipe over Ferguson's shoes before passing the items along.

Someone activated the peel-and-peek system throughout Chambers, and a dozen giant images of Major Ezra Hodge stared out at him from the flat screens around the walls. Hodge held no rank in the Jesus Rangers. He was a U.S. Army major in the Defense Intelligence Agency, stationed in the Confederation of Costa Brava, and one of the church's most valuable operatives.

*He can ferret out information, all right,* the commander thought, *but he has no idea what to do with it.*

Hodge was clearly uncomfortable, blotting his sweat and waiting on-screen for the seating and foot-washing to end. Some of the Acolytes still took the time to remove their shoes and perform the ritual properly. The commander redirected console output to his Sidekick for his personal analysis later.

Major Hodge's chubby face was pale except for his red-rimmed eyes and the red chafing around his nostrils. The major's eyes were sunken, haunted, and he hunched over his pickup like a crone. The   plant life in Chambers drowned out his tremulous voice beyond the first three rows, but pickups simultaneously translated and transmitted his speech to every console in the chamber.

"Brethren," Hodge began, "I am grieved to announce that here, in Costa Brava, the Master is dead and the Apocalypse is at hand."

"It was the Catholics!" a voice shouted from the back. "It's time we sent them all to Satan!"

An angry babble supported this judgment. Commander Noas noted that the original shout came from James Kane, a Disciple with well-known aspirations but little substance. A lift of his eyebrow towards Apprentice Bonyon, and a nod of recognition. The commander soon would know more of the recent movements and associations of Brother James Kane.

Hodge had enough stage presence to let them shout and pound their fists before raising his hand for silence.

"They will wed their filthy bridegroom soon enough," Hodge promised, his pudgy nose in high twitch, his double chin quivering over his tight, sweaty collar.

*Who put you on the high horse, Hodge?*

"Our entire ViraVax facility, which has fed the world's hunger and vanquished its diseases, was wiped out last night when the Catholics sabotaged our dam in Costa Brava. This very dam had been doomed to obsolescence by our recent patent for Sunspots, presented to this body not quite one month ago. One man, Colonel Rico Toledo, engineered this holocaust. He murdered the Master and hundreds more with full support of the papist conspiracy, here in Costa Brava and in the United States."

Here the huge screens rolled footage of the wall of mud that smothered ViraVax, filmed in the light of a dozen flares from an Agency Dragonfly. Ten kilometers of a lush tropical valley were scoured to stone. The valley floor was a sea of mud embedded with human debris—clothing, tools, farm machinery, twisted shards of metal buildings. But the one image that Noas had steeled himself against did not appear.

*No bodies!*

Commander Noas enhanced the image on his console and sat back in surprise.

*Where are the bodies?*

There had been no time to remove them, and the commander was one of the few who knew how many hundreds of souls lived on and under that site.

*Not counting the Innocents, of course.*

The Innocents, the Down's syndrome workers, were not human by a technicality. But they occupied bodies, very valuable bodies, and not one of those two thousand bodies on his roster was visible.

*They must have sealed off*, he thought. *They're buttoned*

*up in there, and either Hodge doesn't know it or he's throwing out a smoke screen.*

More than anything, this was what Commander Noas wanted to believe. If either possibility was true, then the Master may be alive. The commander had to admit another line of thought.

*What if something got loose with the Master there?* he wondered. *What if the dam was our own cover for a contamination incident?*

Contamination would mean, at minimum, a six-month shutdown for inspections, which might lead to further delays. But his real worry centered on the uncomfortable visibility of this vital facility when their camouflage had been working so well.

If the problem was only sabotage and the dam, then shutdown time would be cut from six months to the month that it might take to dig them out of there. Some value could be gleaned from exposing the Catholic terrorists. ViraVax out of commission for six months, however, meant that some very important Children of Eden would not get their prepaid replacement organs. It meant that the Catholics, the Mormons and the infidels squeezed in two growing seasons where they should have none—a delicate reversal that could offer hope to the hopeless.

*With hope comes resistance.*

And with resistance came the Jesus Rangers, and the inevitable casualties among his troops. David Noas would gladly sacrifice a dozen dams if it meant keeping ViraVax on-line.

Through his Sidekick Noas requested copies of any ViraVax transmissions from the weeks immediately prior to the incident, as well as aerial footage of the dam. The commander turned back to Hodge's soporific non-briefing.

"This is the time that we must act," Hodge said. "We must become the terrible swift sword of our own deliverance, and we must strike down the forces that murdered our Master and laid waste his holy work. Our flaming sword must smite the faithless vermin and these godless idolators from the face of the earth. The Garden of Eden is at hand, and the fruits thereof shall be plucked by the faithful. Are you faithful?''

The entire chamber shook with a resounding ''Yes!''

''Shall we take back the Garden from those who defiled it?''

''Yes!''

Commander Noas did not like this turn of events. Security was already on yellow alert, no other incidents had been reported and so far, no media. The deaths of the Vice-President and the President's husband occupied the secular press completely.

A sudden rush of Gardeners to arms in the wake of the Master's death would guarantee total confusion among their own people. If their blood-lust outraced their selection of a leader, then the life's work of thousands of people would be for nothing.

Coupled with a contamination situation in Costa Brava, the Children of Eden would be fragmented, paralyzed and hunted down as anathema all over the globe. This was not what David Noas had worked towards his whole life. This was not what the Master wanted. If Hodge knew contamination to be a fact, then he was way out of line by not disclosing it here.

Noas keyed the command channel on his Sidekick and whispered, ''Shut that idiot down!''

The first order of business was selection of a new Master, and it would be that Master who would give the orders. The danger, if any, was confined to Costa Brava, and it was the commander's job to see that it stayed there. Hodge usurped the Master's role and, with no explanation or by-your-leave, took command of the Sanhedrin under the pretext of delivering information. The Children of Eden had never suffered the death of a Master before, and Hodge, who did not even rate a seat in Chambers, was taking full advantage of the vulnerability of this tragic moment.

*As any rising young shark might.*

And why this sudden blood-lust from Hodge the Hedgehog? Sending the faithful willy-nilly into the streets was pouring gasoline on the fire. They needed to reaffirm their unity and, possibly, tap their reserves. Besides, orders to the faithful were not the place of someone like Hodge, who rated neither rank nor a seat in Chambers.

Hodge's image froze on the dozen wall-screens.

The Commander addressed Hodge in a calm, reasoned voice.

"This briefing is appropriate to Special Ops, Mr. Hodge. You will be transferred to the Ready Room where you can complete your report to Sergeant Tekel and Apprentice Bonyon. Our immediate duty is clear: we must select a Master who will consider your data and act accordingly."

The commander immediately switched his Sidekick back to command channel and whispered to Bonyon, "Was the dam a cover for a contamination? If so, what's our risk up here?"

The hubbub in Chambers indicated plenty of approval of Hodge's plan from both Disciples and Acoloytes.

"Very well, Commander," Hodge said.

His nose rose when he spoke, and the commander detected the slightest sniff of annoyance that would not be lost in transmission to the others.

"Our people must not let this heinous act go unpunished. . . ."

"Mr. Hodge!" The commander's voice boomed across the sound system and startled the Sanhedrin members. "You are out of line! I'll speak to you privately. Switch to command channel."

The commander stood to address the Sanhedrin and quieted the heated arguments in Chambers with a lift of his hand. He rubbed the throbbing burn scar on his forehead and sighed.

"We must see to some practical matters before getting on with our duty. First, upgrade to red alert to secure the gas station chain, refineries, power stations, reservoirs and communications systems. No merc units on these assignments! Go to communications on our satlinks, command channels only. Reserves, report to your units. All merc and gang teams, stand by for assault assignments. The new Master will decide whether we'll hibernate or not, and whether we have a fight on our hands. Hodge, scramble your transmission to the Ready Room *now*!''

Commander Noas snatched a loaf of ritual bread and a pitcher of water from the table, turned on his heel and left Chambers. When he opened the Ready Room door, the commander saw that Hodge continued his amateur theatrics on the peel. Hodge put on his martyr face for a couple of beats, then addressed the chamber.

''We, the faithful, await your selection of the new Master. Go with God.''

Hodge left them with a last glimpse of the destruction in Costa Brava before he blanked their screens—destruction that included a downed Mongoose *upstream* from the dam.

*What do you want, Hodge?* Noas wondered. *Where were you when that little dam blew?*

*Every kingdom divided against itself is brought to desolation, and house will fall upon house.*

—JESUS

# 13

PRESIDENT CLAUDIA KAY O'CONNOR thought that the long briefing-room table seemed gargantuan with only Secretary Mandell and Senator Myers to take up one end of it. One Secret Service agent stood beside the door, practicing her best blankface. President O'Connor initiated the third replay of the black box recording of the plane crash that killed her husband and the Vice-President. Myers and Mandell fidgeted with their ties, their cuffs and their paperwork as they sat, unspeaking, before the grisly record of the crash of *Eagle Two*.

The newshounds reported that a barrage of shoulder-fired missiles had destroyed *Eagle Two* on takeoff from National. For the moment, the President didn't dissuade them of that notion. The D.C. chapter of the Crack Head Slinks took the credit, though she could see for herself how the plane caught fire. She ordered an urban tactical team in to teach the Slinks a lesson in humility.

*If they want the credit, they can take the heat,* she thought.

The Slinks had done her one favor; they bought her some time. Precious time for the President and her advisors to figure out what did happen to her husband.

One New York daily insisted that her marriage was rocky and that this crash was not coincidence, but convenience. That paper was now suffering a massive audit by the IRS, Human Services, Immigration and the FCC.

The peel in front of President O'Connor displayed split-screen images of *Eagle Two*'s instruments, the pilot and copilot at their controls, and the plush office of the Vice-President in the aft compartment. Her husband, Mark, conferred with the Vice-President regarding some changes in the day's schedule. Three reporters, three Secret Service agents, a press liaison and The Football released their restraints and began the inevitable jockeying towards, and interference for, the Vice-President. Then, for the third time today, President Claudia Kay O'Connor watched her husband die.

The black box showed clearly what the FAA team, the FBI and the DIA had been unwilling to believe: Mark had collapsed, died and then *burst into flame* on the lamb's-wool carpet of *Eagle Two*.

Upon Mark O'Connor's sudden collapse, everyone rushed to his side and hunched over him. One Secret Service agent—Lampard, from her own team—doubled as the medical officer, and he stretched Mark out on the deck onto his back. The President couldn't see what happened next, with everyone in the way, but Lampard jumped back suddenly and shoved the Vice-President away. The other two agents immediately pulled the Vice-President into the cockpit and locked the cabin door behind them as Lampard fought a hopeless battle over Mark's bubbling, smoking body with only his coat and a small fire extinguisher.

The rest of the passengers fled to the forward cabin and hunched against the bulkhead, details of their babble indistinguishable on the unprocessed tape. One reporter had second thoughts, and returned to the agent's side to try to help control the hot, oily fire that had burst out from her husband's body.

The pilot and copilot hunched over their controls,

crowded tight with three extra bodies in that cockpit. The pilot practiced the same blankface that the Secret Service agents wore, only his eyes betraying the initial widenings of fear.

The pilot's voice was tight but clear.

"Activating fire suppression."

The President watched a fine foam splatter the aft cabin, but nothing more was visible through that thick, roiling smoke. A weak thumping of fists stopped completely.

President O'Connor kept looking for something that would explain what had happened to her husband. As a young girl she had read tabloid accounts of spontaneous human combustion, but even now, after watching her husband burn up from the inside, she could not bring herself to believe it.

*Somebody did this to him*, she thought. *They can run, but they can't hide.*

More alarms lit up the cockpit instrument panel.

"No gear, port side. No nose gear," the pilot recited, still as calm as ice.

The wings waggled up and down, then wallowed in a great seesaw as the pilot fought the throttles and reversers, trying to level off and straighten out for touchdown. The two Secret Service agents pushed the Vice-President to the deck and covered him with their bodies as the port wingtip caught the quack grass at the edge of the taxiway.

"Shit!" was the last word from the cockpit.

The onboard computer display lasted another instant. It showed the line drawing of an airplane touching down nearly sideways. The port wing acted as a great lever to flip the fuselage onto its top.

The rest of the tape was blank. The President's memory accommodated her when it rolled recent news footage of the crash. A full load of fuel spewed out of the mangled tanks; the fuselage flattened down to the baggage compartment and spun at nearly two hundred miles an hour across the taxiway and into two commuter planes on the terminal side of Runway One.

Secretary Mandell reached out and shut down the display when the President moved to replay the scene again.

"We've seen enough, Ms. President," he said. "Tormenting yourself serves no purpose."

She leaned her forehead on her folded hands for a moment, then sat up, slowly, not looking at either of the older men.

"You say a virus did this?"

"Yes. Or something like it. Probably in his bottled water."

"And the Gardeners are behind this?"

"Absolutely, Ms. President."

"How can that be?" she asked. "Those two communities that burned up, the ones Mark visited, they were Gardener communities. Who would do something like this to their own people?"

"Could be a takeover move," Myers said. "Their top preacher, Casey, died yesterday in a flood in Costa Brava."

"Mark was so healthy," she said. "He was a good Catholic, but he always bought Gardener products because . . . because they're supposed to be so *healthy*. . . ."

She stopped herself from crying with a sudden, deep breath that she let out slowly. She waved aside the offer of a handkerchief from Senator Myers.

"It was probably meant for you, Ms. President," Mandell said. "Or that you would be with him when it happened."

"Is it contagious?"

Senator Myers cleared his throat.

"We don't know that for sure, Ms. President. We're monitoring the surviving rescue personnel. . . . "

"What *do* you know for sure, Mr. Myers?"

The senator cleared his throat again, and massaged his neck as though that would make the telling easier.

"The secretary's son-in-law, a virologist, was killed in Costa Brava by an Artificial Viral Agent. The man went berserk first. He killed several people and attacked his own wife. She shot him, then he burned up. It was part of a

ViraVax project—he worked there. DIA speculates he stumbled onto something over his head, and they used him as a guinea pig.''

''And when was this, Senator?''

The President's brown eyes flashed with the fire she was famous for, and the senator cleared his throat again. Secretary Mandell interrupted and answered for him.

''Ash Wednesday,'' he said. ''Almost six weeks ago. This was an intelligence matter, and it was handled through channels. . . . ''

''It was *not handled*,'' the President snapped, and slapped the tabletop. ''It was *buried*, or I'd know about it.''

She pushed her chair back from the table in disgust.

''*Six weeks* we've lost here, gentlemen, because someone's asleep at the switch or pulling a fast one. This is one more example of how your precious little men's club has got this country's dick in a wringer. Now you tell me, gentlemen, and you tell me everything. Exactly how big is this wringer?''

''Very big, Ms. President,'' Secretary Mandell admitted. ''When my son-in-law died it was an isolated incident, confined to the ViraVax facility in Costa Brava. His hero was Jonas Salk, so when the official report said he'd experimented on himself, we believed it and concurred with the DIA's cover story. Officials in various agencies had conflicting orders on how this was to be handled. DIA had jurisdiction, and personnel overseeing that facility reassured us that this was an isolated, sterile incident.''

''Trenton Solaris is director for that region, correct?''

''That's correct, Ms. President.''

''Relieve him and get his ass up here, pronto. That officious little bastard!''

''ViraVax, the facility that produced this . . . thing, was wiped out by a flood last night. That's where the Master Gardener died. Solaris is overseeing the proper procedures now for sealing off . . . ''

''He didn't do such a hot job of overseeing procedures in the past,'' the President challenged. ''What makes you think he's doing the right thing now? Get somebody in there who can, or I'm sending you down there to handle things personally. Now, ViraVax is a subsidiary of the Children of Eden's holdings, correct?''

"That's right, Ms. President. And they've given us the best biologics for the best price, with nothing whatsoever to lead us to doubt either their judgment or their caution.''

"They're mercenaries; their loyalties are with their church or money. So, where do we stand now? And how do we get the bastards who killed my husband and the Vice-President and the hundred and ten innocent people at National Airport?''

Secretary of State Mandell unclipped several sheaves of paper from a stack in front of him and fanned them like a poker hand across the tabletop.

"Other people are dying,'' he said. "Specifically, other Gardener facilities. They've been going up in flames all night.''

Secretary Mandell told her the ViraVax story, as he had learned it from Toledo and the others, and related how his own granddaughter had been kidnapped in the plot.

"This looks like poisoning, not contagion,'' O'Connor said. "Talk to Atlanta and see if those kids can be quarantined someplace more comfortable. But I want these people kept together and under guard. Give them whatever they need to continue their work on this bug. They're closest to it; maybe they can get us some answers.''

"The virologist, Ms. Chang, says that she needs a quality lab. . . . ''

The President raised a hand to stop him.

"Nobody goes anywhere yet,'' she said. "Let's keep all exposures together, and out of this country. They can be isolated without being in solitary. We'll see what else this thing might do before we bring them up here. Seal off all of the incident sites, troops in full bio gear.''

"Surgeon General and the CDC director flew in from Atlanta, and they're reviewing the tissue samples now.''

"Tissue samples," the President said, and shook her head.

Nothing of her husband had been recovered. She would bury an empty box for the sake of the country. She would not weep over an empty box, and once again the press would call her "the Ice Queen" without knowing shit about her or her feelings.

Claudia O'Connor could see already how it would be. She would kneel on a blanket on the grass, within her shield of Secret Service agents, and place a rose bouquet atop her husband's empty coffin. The usual hundreds of shutters would click like mad insects and the reporters would trample the cemetery lawn into mud without a second thought.

The President loved her husband, in spite of what the press said. They were seldom together because he worked one side of the country while she worked another.

Mark O'Connor had been with the Defense Intelligence Agency for nearly twenty years. He had been aboard *Eagle Two* to assist the Vice-President on a couple of campaign hops and a disaster review. They knew about the embassy bombing in Costa Brava just before . . .

"Ms. President?"

The Secretary of State brought her back to the present.

"I'm sorry," she said. "I was already thinking about the funeral."

"You knew that your husband's initial field work was in Costa Brava," Myers said. "Before it was Costa Brava, of course. His roommate at the Academy, and his partner down there, was Colonel Rico Toledo."

"President García says that Toledo's the one-man show who pulled the plug on ViraVax," Mandell said. "García claims it's a smoke screen for a coup. He's asking me for troops and for Toledo's head."

"What do you think?"

"It's bullshit," Mandell said. "They kidnapped his son and my granddaughter, Lord only knows what for, and he went in to get them. It looks like a shipment of this stuff went to a warehouse in Mexico City. We've sent a contract team in to secure it.''

"You want me to believe Toledo's a good guy. Why?"

"President García's a Gardener," Mandell said. "ViraVax put him in the hot seat, and without them he'll cook for sure. He's running scared. Toledo risked his life to save my granddaughter, and a lot of other people," he added. "That's good enough for me."

*It always comes down to family*, the President thought.

And now she had none.

Claudia Kay had met Mark O'Connor at a shooting range outside Arlington, a mere five miles from where his head-stone would mark an empty grave. She was the most dec-orated police officer in Washington State history, which had helped her win a controversial bid to the House of Repre-sentatives. Mark had been reassigned stateside and was shooting in the lane next to her that night. He was angry at his reassignment, in spite of the promotion, and fired his Galil 10mm so fast and furious that it got too hot to hold. Claudia Kay O'Connor became the first U.S. President in modern history to carry her own sidearm.

President O'Connor had spent the toughest ten years of her youth behind a badge on the streets of Seattle. She knew firsthand the value of a good partner, good informa-tion and a good flak vest, and she knew the political im-portance of taking a stand when every cell in her body screamed, "Run!"

Mark had considered Toledo a good partner; they were tight for several years.

Claudia O'Connor wished now for some privacy. The only time the world gave her privacy was when she went to the bathroom. Even then, the Secret Service and The Football listened at the door.

A Mongoose set down on the White House lawn, its engines a shrill whine. The backblast had reporters on the lawn grabbing their coats and their equipment. Dwight Olafson, her Chief of Staff, entered the room with a stack of paperwork. Earl, her agent in charge, tapped her shoulder gently and indicated his Sidekick. He cupped his hand around her ear.

"Madam President, the Surgeon General recommends activation of Federal Emergency Management Agency protocols for isolating you, the Joint Chiefs and members of Congress. Three other airliners caught fire and burned in the last hour. The Vice-President is dead, and we're not taking any chances. We're taking you to The Mountain."

Outside, her agents cleared the reporters from the area, ignoring their shouted questions, clicking shutters and whirring cams. The President stood, brushed off her black skirt and let Earl take her elbow. She raised her voice enough so that he could hear over the engine racket.

"I told you before, Earl, I don't care what the books say. Don't call me 'Madam.' Isn't The Mountain a little premature?"

"We'll brief you aboard, Ms. President. Some of those mikes out there can filter anything."

"The Gardeners?" she asked.

He nodded, his expression grim.

"Shit."

"Yes, Ms. President. In the fan. They're selecting a new Master now. Meanwhile, that Noas guy's in charge. He's as paranoid as they get. The Children of Eden have secured all their facilities, placed their rangers on alert and called in contracts to every mercenary and gang unit they've ever dealt with. Intelligence suspects somebody inside their organization has eliminated the competition and is making a move."

"On us?"

"Exactly."

The President pursed her full lips, tapped her fingers on her thigh, then turned to her Chief of Staff.

"Change of plans," she said. "We're going to Camp David."

"Camp David? But . . . "

"A rabbit would go to The Mountain, and I'm no goddamn rabbit," she said. "Set up a meeting with David

Noas, or whoever's in charge of the Children of Eden. We've got some talking to do. If it comes down to shooting, we'll take care of that, too, when the time comes.''

"Yes, Ms. President," Dwight said. "Camp David."

Dwight Olafson's red-veined cheeks reddened all the way to the top of his bald, sweaty head.

"The Sanhedrin are meeting now to select their new Master," he said. "That hard-ass, David Noas, is a likely choice."

"We hired his people in the Gold Wars," Myers said. "He fought the Zulus in the bush while we worked the cities."

"History calls it the 'Independence March,' " the President said.

"No, it was done for gold, all right," Mandell said. "And diamonds. The Israelis got into it for the uranium. David Noas got into it for God."

"Does he hate blacks?" O'Connor asked. "I know there aren't many in their organization."

"He hates 'idolators,' " Myers said, "of any color or stripe. And, like most Gardeners, he doesn't think much of women in command. Oh, yes. He does hate the FBI."

"Why *them*?"

"Lots of Catholics in the FBI, in the old days," Myers said. "The FBI killed his whole family in a shoot-out when he was eleven. David Noas has always thought that Catholics are just Christian idolators, every bit as detestable and dangerous to him as Zulus. He considers the FBI the Pope's personal police force in America."

"Then let's show him some bite," the President said. "I want every Gardener warehouse, storage area, compound and weapon in this country secured by sundown. Now, get that prick Solaris on the line. And David Noas. I want him and the Surgeon General to meet me at Camp David. Clear?"

"Yes, Ms. President."

President O'Connor rubbed her eyes and stood from the table.

"Now, if you'll excuse me, I need to make some arrangements for . . . for my husband."

*Judge not by appearances, but give just judgment.*

—Jesus

# 14

Rico Toledo woke up inside a bubble of Plexiglas. He had IV lines in both arms, a tube down his nose, several machines beeping out of synch and a body that felt like it was skinned. He could only see out of his left eye, and that one was blurry. Rico tried to lift his head to get a look at his body, but he was restrained. If pain was any indicator, all of his parts were still attached.

"Relax, Colonel," a deep voice said. "We'll be here awhile."

A black man in fatigues loomed into view, the name "Clyde, J." stitched over his pocket. He wore SEAL and corpsman insignia on his fatigues.

"Where?"

"Joe Clyde Memorial Hospital," the medic said, with a chuckle. "We're in the back end of a warehouse in beautiful La Libertad, Colonel. Pearl of the Pacific."

"I'm not a colonel."

"You're reinstated, sir."

"Harry? What about Harry?"

"I'll ask the questions, Colonel, if you please."

The voice came from a speaker above his head, and was

not the deep voice of Joe Clyde. This was the effete voice of a career bureaucrat.

Rico turned his head slowly and saw his jowly, damp-handed replacement, Major Ezra Hodge, at a console outside the glass. He wore a telephone operator's headset and an expression of complete disgust.

"Okay, Colonel. Please tell us the last thing you remember doing today."

"You tell me about Harry, and I'll tell you whatever I damned well please whenever I damned well please. Clear?"

Something had taken the skin off the inside of Rico's throat, and talking felt like hot sandpaper in his larynx.

"Your son's okay," Clyde said. "The girl, too."

"Mr. Clyde," the bureaucrat snapped, "I'll speak to your superior about this. *I'm* conducting this interview. And I decide when, or whether, you get out of there."

"No you don't, Major," another voice said. "You're relieved. Do not leave the building. I'll speak to you when I'm through."

Rico tried to remember that voice. It was so familiar, and his mind was so unwilling. . . .

"It's Trenton Solaris, Colonel; do you remember me?"

Rico smiled in spite of his torn lips.

"Yes, sir. Vividly, sir."

"Fine. Then I'll brief you if you'll brief me."

"Fair."

"Harry, Sonja and the Chang woman are safe. Grace and Nancy Bartlett are still at the embassy for precautions, but they have talked with Harry and Sonja by phone. You are all in quarantine. We don't know what you may have picked up. How much do you remember?"

Images flashed through Rico's mind, like a stack of transparencies dropped into a whirlpool. He could pick out a melting face here, a burning building there, but nothing made sense. Solaris must have guessed his dilemma.

"Okay, Colonel, what's the last thing you remember clearly?"

"Cleaning out my desk," Rico croaked. "Turning in my keys."

"That was quite a while ago, Colonel. A lot has happened since then. You went on vacation. The embassy blew up, the Jaguar Mountain Dam blew up...."

"I remember the dam," Rico said. "The water ... I was smashed against the fence...."

"Do you remember which fence?"

"ViraVax," he said, and the memories started flooding back.

"ViraVax, south fence," he said. "I opened the access hatch covers to let the water in. That prick García shot down Harry and Sonja."

"Very good," Solaris said, and his voice sounded relieved.

"Now, what did you see there at ViraVax? Anything unusual?"

Rico started to laugh, but it hurt too much.

"Unusual?" He coughed as gently as he could. "*Unusual?* People melting off their bones and burning up by themselves, charges shutting down every available entry and exit. Guerrillas blowing up the dam...."

"It wasn't the Peace and Freedom people," Solaris interrupted. "The charges were planted and timers set before they got there. The squad leader says they tried to warn you, but you didn't receive the message."

Rico felt relieved. He remembered that moment of doubt before blackness, when he'd thought that El Indio and Yolanda had betrayed him.

"ViraVax, then," Rico said. "Whoever went into shutdown ..."

"Exactly. And the man who did it is the one who killed Red Bartlett. He also set up the incident at the embassy to turn our people against you. He kidnapped Harry and Sonja to lure you in. You were a loose end that needed tying up."

"How do you know this?"

"Harry rescued a data block that Red Bartlett set up. It was full of product that the Chang woman couldn't find.

You should be proud of Harry; he could have fled and we would never know what we're facing.''

Rico's flickering memory focused on Harry, bent over him at ViraVax, helping him to his feet.

"I am *very* proud of Harry," Rico said. "But I don't understand why I'm so important to ViraVax. I was out of their hair. Why go to all this trouble over me?"

Solaris was silent for a moment.

"I'd rather get into that later, Colonel. Right now, it's important that we find something that was shipped out of ViraVax to Mexico City, for distribution elsewhere. We need to know the locations of all Children of Eden clandestine operations in Mexico City. Do you have that information?"

Rico tried to remember, but nothing came up. He couldn't tell whether he simply didn't remember, or whether he had never known at all.

"I don't remember . . . I don't know," he said.

"How about your contacts?" Solaris pressed. "This is something big, something that could take out every human on the planet. We don't have the luxury of playing sides."

"Try Mariposa," Rico said. "She has several hundred people in Mexico City; it's their job to keep track of everything and everybody related to this country. She could do it."

"Who is 'Mariposa'?" Solaris asked. "How do we find her?"

"Get on the webworks and ask," Rico said. "She'll contact you."

"We don't have time for that. . . . "

"Then get me a priest," Rico said. "And get these restraints off me. It's bad enough I have to be locked up, I don't have to be tied up, too."

Solaris must have okayed the request; Clyde unsnapped the restraints right away.

"Why a priest?" Solaris asked.

"Because I still don't trust anybody," Rico said. "Make it somebody from the Archbishop's office, somebody I know. I'll tell him how to find Mariposa.''

With Clyde's help and a lot of pain, he scooted himself up to a sitting position. Rico's mind, the string of images that made his mind, felt shuffled and misdealt. He did not want to give away someone as precious as Yolanda or El Indio because of a basic miscaution. His superior should understand that better than anyone.

''What are you doing out at ViraVax?'' Rico asked. ''Are you going to dig it out, find out what happened?''

It was more of a probe than a question. Rico didn't want to take any chances on releasing whatever it was that holed itself up underground.

''Not a chance,'' Solaris replied. ''The Corps of Engineers has already diverted the stream. After what Ms. Chang revealed about their operations, we're going to cement over the whole thing and see to it that nothing and no one ever gets out.''

Rico weighed this for a moment.

''Do we have a phone in here?'' he asked Clyde.

''Phone, console, the works,'' Clyde said. ''Whatever you need, we've got.''

Rico addressed Solaris.

''If I get Mariposa for you, I want two things.''

''Name them, Colonel.''

''Amnesty for Mariposa. And I want to talk with my son.''

''Done. You know I've always been good for my word.''

''Yes,'' Rico said. ''I know. But before we do anything else, I want to talk with Harry.''

''There's a lot to tell you both, Colonel.''

''It can wait,'' Rico said. ''This can't. Put him on.''

The connection was made through a speakerphone, and Rico hated speakerphones. He preferred to hold something; it gave him a better sense of control. The screen cleared and Harry appeared, looking rested and unafraid.

*He looks like me.*

Rico had had this thought before, but this time the resemblance was more than striking, it was frightening.

"Hello, son," he croaked. "Good job."

"Thanks, Dad," Harry said. "Same to you. Are you going to be okay?"

"I think so," Rico said. "Feels like I've been skinned, but I think everything's here."

"Looks pretty rough," Harry said.

Silence.

"Harry, I'm sorry about the shot . . . I had to do it. I couldn't let you go back in there. . . . "

"I know, Dad," Harry said. "If I'd had the gun, I'd have done the same thing. Chill."

"Your mom's okay; Nancy's okay."

"Yeah, we just talked to them. They both say thanks, too."

"Colonel," Solaris interrupted, "we have some pressing business."

"Yes," Rico said, "we do. I'll talk with you soon, son."

"Okay," Harry said. "Take care."

The screen went blank as he added, "I love you, too."

Sitting was not the position for Colonel Toledo. His butt was crisscrossed with stitches and Quik-Stitch, so he lay on his stomach, waiting for the priest. He knew which one it would have to be.

Colonel Toledo and Father Free went back to the Academy days, when Father Free taught ethics and Rico and Solaris were just another pair of promising buzz-heads. Solaris was always in the administrative track. An albino couldn't do field work effectively unless it was above the Arctic Circle, and he sure as hell couldn't blend into a crowd. Father Free was a good Jesuit and a superb intelligence officer. Officially listed as a chaplain, he bore the rank of captain and taught many people who outranked him. At the Academy, they called him "Spook."

When Spook walked into the warehouse ten minutes after Solaris left, Toledo realized that Solaris had already called him in. That made him nervous. Colonel Toledo didn't like anyone anticipating his next move.

*Maybe he brought Spook in for last rites,* he thought. *I*

*look like somebody who should be dead.*

But he knew that wasn't it. Solaris must have guessed that Father Free had at least as many connections in the guerrilla community as Colonel Toledo, even though he had long ago quit the Agency to work among the poor in Central America.

Father Free looked pretty bad himself. As he approached the cubicle, Toledo noticed the dark-circled, sunken eyes, the filthy jeans and work shirt, and the ever-present kit for extreme unction.

"Spook," he croaked, "you look like shit."

"Thank you, Colonel," Father Free said. "You're looking your very best, too, I see."

The Colonel nodded towards the priest's kit.

"Expecting the worst?"

Father Free let his pale lips slip into a smile.

"Where you're concerned, Colonel, I always expect the worst. You don't seem to be dying, quite yet, and I haven't been a part of your social calendar for a few years. What's up?"

The Colonel turned to Sergeant Clyde.

"Sergeant, are you a Catholic?"

Clyde was reading a new hypernovel on his Litespeed. He chuckled.

"No, Colonel, I'm a Democrat."

"I'm going to make my confession to Father Free, here," Rico said. "You know what that means, legally?"

"Yes, sir," Clyde said, "I think so, sir. It means he's supposed to keep it secret and the court can't force him to tell."

"That's right," Rico said. "And it means I don't want any eavesdropping. The lives of some of my contacts are at stake. I assume we're fully wired, here."

"That's right, Colonel," Clyde said. "But look at this."

The big man squeezed out from behind his machine, pushed past Toledo's gurney and pointed out some of the cables and connectors that snaked through the triple-seal Plexiglas.

"The Father has his Sidekick, you have gloveware in here. Have him plug in the Sidekick; you plug in the gloveware on this end. You don't go through any circuits, nobody can pick you up on audio and visual doesn't count unless you use sign language."

"Set us up, Sergeant, if you would."

"Gladly, sir."

In less than a minute Colonel Toledo was typing, "Bless me, Father, for I have sinned. It has been years since my last confession. You know why I chose this route; I expect your absolute confidence."

"Guaranteed, Colonel," Father Free said. "God gets his sheep back to the fold in mysterious ways."

Colonel Toledo proceeded to arrange for Father Free to contact Yolanda Rubia and get her Mexico City teams to find and secure the Gardener warehouse that Solaris told him about.

"Tell her this is very dangerous stuff," he typed. "Tell her that one stray bullet in Mexico City today could kill us all by mid-week. They have to stop that shipment before it's broken up and distributed. They are guaranteed U.S. backup as soon as they've identified the structure. This is a straight contract job. Her team will be paid, like any other merc unit. That's it."

"I have nothing to absolve, here, Colonel," Father Free said. "Confession is for the remission of sins, not merely a confidential chat. Complete your confession; then I can give absolution and it becomes a true confession."

Rico hesitated, then remembered how good he felt when he was young, walking out of confession, thinking that he had a new life ahead of him.

*Okay,* he thought, *why the hell not?*

He didn't think for a moment that Father Free would betray him, anyway. But for the priest's sake, in case push came to shove, he had to give him some righteous protection.

"I've been drinking too much for fifteen years," he typed. "I've committed adultery more times than I can count. And I beat my wife and child.''

At the last, his fingers trembled inside the gloveware and sent lines of nonsense across the cable.

''Are you sorry for your sins?'' Father Free asked. ''Do you resolve to go and sin no more?''

''I am,'' Colonel Toledo typed, ''and I do.''

And he was relieved to realize that he meant it. He had a chance for a new life now; his old self had died at ViraVax. He vowed not to waste this second chance on a bastard like that.

''For your penance, you will apologize to your wife and son, and ask their forgiveness. It is not necessary that they forgive you, but you must ask. Since you will have a fresh start with this absolution, I suggest you get back on good terms with your God. Make a good Act of Contrition, and go, and sin no more.''

Colonel Toledo was surprised to find himself weeping as he typed out, as best he could remember, the Act of Contrition.

''Oh my God, I am heartily sorry for having offended Thee. . . .''

On the other side of the glass, Father Free murmured his absolution, delivered his blessing, and faithfully deleted everything that the Colonel had transferred to his machine. Colonel Toledo's tears burned the lacerations on his face, and he hid his face behind his hands as Father Free hurried to deliver to Yolanda the message that just might save them all.

*Men exist for the sake of one another. Teach them, then, or bear with them.*

—MARCUS AURELIUS

# 15

MARTE CHANG SCANNED her Litespeed's record of the ViraVax disaster, as though by review she could point to something on-screen and say to herself, "There, see, it was just your imagination." She froze and enlarged the image of a large sheet of gel riding the crest of a mud wall. In stop-action sequence the gel ripped apart and rolled into the rest of the debris sweeping along in the flood. She touched the gel's image, shimmering the air in front of her. The embassy's artificial intelligence filled her headset with a litany of organic models in a near-human voice.

"Biostat. Virometallic. Trade Name: Sunspots...."

"I know," she interrupted. "I made them."

"I know. Marte Chang, virologist, creator of these 'Sunspots,' returned to this image thirty-five times since oh-eight-forty."

"They were my children, and now they're dead."

"Not children," the voice corrected. "Ideas made real, but not children."

*As though a machine could know,* Marte thought, and shuddered.

How could a machine know about ten years of research,

ten years of her life? Like the musical prodigy or the math whiz, she had no childhood, a bizarre puberty and a crippled adulthood. No social skills whatsoever. What could a program know of that?

Everything is all this moment to a machine.

"Show: Sabbath Suicides."

Marte Chang's headset responded: "Searching: Sabbath Suicides."

"Correction. Sabbath Suicides, yesterday and today only."

"Sabbath Suicides, the previous forty-eight hours. Up."

Marte's view inside her headset was of the last moments of the ViraVax compound. Red lights flashed and klaxons blared their warnings that shutdown was in progress. Speakers around the ViraVax compound announced:

"Condition Red. Suit up and seal off."

Her viewpoint came from the monitor atop the water tower beside the landing pad. This was one of several security stations that Red Bartlett had jacked into and diverted to memory before he died. The program that he'd set up continued to monitor ViraVax from just before his death on Ash Wednesday until the dam blew at sunset on Good Friday, scouring the facility with thick, red mud.

Marte watched the security monitor sweep the compound below where small, blue fires bobbled about on the grounds or stopped in a *whump* of flame to simmer out in a smoky red glow.

Marte made a fist of her right-hand glove. The viewer zoomed in and enhanced. Each blue flame was a human being. Each red glow was just a simmer of tissue.

Some, apparently, felt no pain while others suffered acutely. The difference could be extremes of acceptance and fear, but the pain was the same for those who had it. Crews on the flight line shot one another as flames burst their flight suits. Loyal company men to the last, they kept each other away from the planes. Had they not, she and the others would have died there, too.

Marte Chang lifted her headset, removed her gloveware

and rubbed her exhausted eyes. Another cup in an endless supply of hot coffee appeared at her elbow.

"He's smarter than smart, Scholz," Marte said, without turning.

"Was," Colonel Scholz replied, her voice as soft as her tread. "He's dead. Old news."

"But his bugs are very much alive," Marte said.

"Cheer up, Chang," Scholz said. "So are we."

"So far," she said. "But I don't think I can keep us that way locked up here."

In the strained silence that followed, their gazes never met.

"Every journey starts with a single step," Major Scholz said. "We've opened up these Isolettes so that we can all work better. Next step is out of this warehouse. It's in the works, Marte, and works take time."

Marte brushed her black hair out of her eyes and reached for her headset, but Major Scholz stopped her with a hand on her arm. The major pulled another chair to the workstation and sat beside Marte. She slopped a little coffee onto the knee of her uniform, frowned and blotted it with a tissue she had wadded in her fist.

"How long since you slept?" they both asked.

Then they both almost laughed for a second.

"A couple of hours Friday night in isolation," Marte said. "A couple of hours today. You?"

Scholz shook her head, and Marte couldn't tell by that whether she hadn't slept at all, whether she didn't know when she'd slept or whether it didn't really matter. Marte guessed the latter.

"Rico's not doing so well," Scholz announced.

Marte didn't feel like small talk. Every second meant another person infected out there, and pretty soon it wouldn't be just "out there." She sighed, and resolved to give Major Scholz two minutes.

"He was pretty banged up in the flood," Marte said. "I thought they had him stabilized."

Rena Scholz shrugged, and her worry appeared to be

more personal than professional.

"They stabilized his injuries," Scholz said, "but ViraVax did more to him than just scratch his butt with barbed wire."

"And it's going to do more than that to all of us if you don't get me to a decent lab!" Marte snapped. "I don't have the luxury of worrying about one person."

"You're killing the messenger, here, Ms. Chang," Scholz said. "Besides, he risked his life to get your butt out of there and bury that place. You owe him."

"Don't guilt-trip me, Scholz. He put that place there in the first place. You kept it running. My sympathies are with those innocent people burning up in the streets. And with myself."

Scholz seemed a little stunned by that, and Marte was surprised, herself. It was the truth, but delivered in a voice that Marte had never heard from her own mouth before.

"We shouldn't be keeping this a secret," Marte added. "That's been the problem here all along. If I broadcast our problem to every qualified virologist out there . . ."

" . . . It would never leave the building," Scholz said. "Everything out of here is monitored; that's why you don't communicate with anybody in real time."

"But don't you see? I could transmit these structures to a half-dozen good people, and we could have a hundred variant antibodies in our hands in forty-eight hours. Besides, people should be warned so they can isolate themselves."

"We can't risk anyone else knowing how to make these things. Ever."

"Other people already know how," Marte said. "They just have the good sense to leave it alone."

Marte slumped in her seat and twisted her hair tight into her fingers; then she pulled on it to help her concentrate.

"You're never letting me out there again, are you?" she asked. "I'm going to disappear someplace with those kids, right?"

"Sorry," Scholz said. "It's not my call."

"You can't risk giving me my life back, not with what I know."

"That's not my call either, Marte. But I promise you, like I promised Harry and Sonja, I will not let them do that to you. I owe you that."

Marte stared at her hands for a moment. They were chapped from so much work inside the gloveware, but she didn't feel any pain.

"Does that mean you'll kill me, Scholz?"

Marte couldn't face her, and heard Scholz suck in a deep breath and let it out slow.

"If, at any point, things are as bleak as you say, and that's still what you want, *then* we can talk about it," Scholz said. "But I think we have plenty of options to run through before we come to that."

"And if they order you to kill me?"

Scholz reached out, put a finger to Marte's cheek and turned her so that they could look one another in the eye.

"I will disobey that order. Subject closed, okay?"

Marte nodded. But she had to find a way to get this information out. If she couldn't get it out, maybe Harry could. He was persistent, and confident. She sighed, and smiled for Scholz.

"All right, Major," she said. "Let's talk about Colonel Toledo. ViraVax installed several Artificial Viral Agents into him over time; we know that from Red Bartlett's log. But to isolate which AVAs, where they hide, how they interact and how to defuse them, I need a lot of samples and a good facility. Don't you understand how frustrating this is?"

Colonel Scholz's gaze never wavered.

"Well, we're stuck here until the Agency says different," Scholz said, "and the Colonel's wasting away in the next building. If you're so set on saving the world, why don't you start with him?"

Marte rubbed her eyes again, then took a long pull at her coffee. Before she set the cup down, she knew what they must've done to Toledo.

"They altered his metabolism when they made him a

drinker,'' Marte said. "When he drinks, he activates the AVAs that bring on his rage and . . . attraction to women. He's not drinking now, so everything should be pretty quiet; am I right?''

Scholz scooted her chair closer, until their knees touched.

"You wouldn't recognize him, Marte. He's a shadow. All of his resources go to keeping him away from alcohol. It's done wonders for his attitude. But his body can't hold out much longer at this rate. I'm scared, Marte. Things looked so good there, for a minute.''

"Well, I'm scared, too,'' Marte said. "The whole god-damn world is coming apart out there, and all I can do is sit here and theorize . . . Shit, to isolate the things that ViraVax turned loose I need . . . ''

"I know,'' Scholz interrupted, counting on her fingers. "A lab with the proper medium, assistants who can splice genes using AVAs, and time. Solaris is talking with the President about that today.''

"Everybody's *talking*,'' Marte said, and thumped the desktop. "Nobody's *doing* anything.''

"Calm down, Marte,'' Rena said. "We're all doing what we can. Besides, I understand from the web that your Sun-spots may make you rich *and* famous.''

"It's too late to start a garden when you're starving to death. I'm going to disappear, remember? So it's likely that riches and fame won't mean a damn thing. Remember, once we get the medium we still have to *grow* these things. Odds are that none of us will cash our next paycheck.''

"My, we're in a mood, aren't we?''

Marte sipped her tepid coffee and didn't answer. She didn't want to discuss her moods, her Sunspots or their sorry predicament. She wanted the key to Mishwe's Arti-ficial Viral Agents, his personal pets, because without that key, humanity and everything associated with it was moot. Images of the rows and stacks of cages of helpless lab an-imals that would die without humans haunted her as much as the deaths of the humans themselves. Marte had the drawings for a dozen AVA keys on her desktop, but no way to make them into real keys for real locks.

Marte twisted and untwisted her hair again.

"Since they wanted Colonel Toledo to drink and womanize himself out of their lives," Marte said, "maybe those AVAs need some alcohol input to trigger his metabolism."

Colonel Scholz raised a blonde eyebrow.

"You're saying that he *has* to drink to live?"

"Maybe." Marte shrugged. "Mishwe targeted the mitochondrial DNA, not the cellular DNA, for his most vicious pets. Interrupt the mitochondria, and the body can't metabolize glucose, doesn't get energy, then . . . "

"Then he starves to death, right?"

"That's what I'm thinking."

"Can you substitute any other substance for alcohol?" Scholz asked. "You know, something similar that might trigger the same response."

"Excellent suggestion, Major," Marte said, and smiled. "You've also been doing your homework the last couple of days. As a matter of fact, antifreeze binds to the same receptors. Trust me, he'd be better off with the alcohol."

"I see," Scholz said. "Now, what if he got it in an IV drip, very slow and very dilute? That way he wouldn't have to drink it and, frankly, he wouldn't have to know."

"It sounds good to me," Marte said. "But I'm no doctor. I do know one thing, though. You like Colonel Toledo. If you try to trick him or lie to him, you'll both lose the chance to see whether something might work between you." She emptied her cup. "Just my opinion, of course."

"So noted," Scholz said. "And you're right; I'll talk to him about it. Now, there's one other thing."

"Always," Marte sighed. "Now what?"

"They're moving you out to Casa Canadá. For safety. An attack on the embassy is imminent, in my opinion, and a move out of here will put you one step closer to that lab you're demanding. The Agency has put Harry on the payroll officially as your research assistant."

Marte glimpsed her sleepless, disheveled self reflected in the blank peel-and-peek on the wall. Her tangled black hair and bloodshot Asian eyes contrasted in spades with the clean-cropped, well-scrubbed, blonde and blue-eyed Rena Scholz. The thought of Harry working beside her was Marte Chang's first burst of excitement in days.

*Excited over a teenage boy,* she clucked to herself. *What have you come to, Chang?*

Marte's self-criticism wasn't completely fair; she knew that. Harry navigated the networks, the electronic web, the satlinks and hardware—all elements of her work that Marte hated to face. She preferred the lab, pure and simple. But she needed someone to sleuth the networks, and Harry was perfect. He single-handedly retrieved all of Red Bartlett's data that survived from ViraVax, and he was patiently seeking out more that the company had secreted away in the electronic web. Harry was fast, and tireless, and speed was important right now. The academic phase was over. Now she wanted somebody who could get a warning out to the world, and Harry would be perfect.

Rena Scholz flipped through a stack of transparencies, all variations on one viral base code that ViraVax had used for several vaccines.

"Have you found something here?" she asked. "They all look pretty much the same to me."

Marte set a half-dozen of the transparencies onto the light box and pointed to a tiny triangle on the shell of each virus.

"Those are all the same five-protein structure, except for one isomer in the protein of the coat. Each, therefore, is the key to a different lock, or a link in a different chain of messages or commands. If I can find and destroy one link in the chain, then this 'Deathbug' can't carry out its program within the cells."

"So how do you narrow it down to one of these instead of billions?"

Marte felt herself puff up a little with pride. Not for herself, but for Harry.

"Without a lab, you mean?" Marte couldn't suppress a smile. "Harry figured it out. I was explaining how viral sequencing was like computer programs except you had to grow the viral agents, and each agent grows best in a slightly different medium.

" 'Chill,' he said. 'If you had a recipe for the medium, could you tell what someone grew in it?' I realized that I might, and with his help I've narrowed it down to these six agents, with six more possibles.''

Scholz tapped her fingernail against each of the offending diagrams.

"Hard to believe that one of these can do so much damage in the body."

"The kind of damage we've seen requires the coordination of several of these things," Marte said. "One can carry the instructions to let the others inside, to build yet several others. They even use the antibodies that are produced against them as raw materials."

"And there's more than one of these loose?"

Marte shut off the light box and accepted another coffee from a passing tech. Thick, raw cream roiled on top, and the local crude sugar made it even sweeter. Marte had not had any coffee since infiltrating ViraVax six weeks ago. It was one of the simple pleasures that, after her recent brush with death, Marte vowed to never do without again.

"Six that I've found," Marte said. "We can hope the other five are buried under the concrete they poured over ViraVax. That major from the Agency was going to redouble a search downstream from the labs, just to be sure."

"Hodge?"

"Yes, him."

Colonel Scholz laughed.

"He couldn't find his butt if it didn't follow him around. He didn't think the ViraVax warehouse across the airstrip was worth breaking into. When I took a team over there, we found another heap of Meltdowns, and this."

Scholz held out the tiny palm-cam, scorched but intact. Marte had heard that the camera recorded the entire sequence of events inside that warehouse. It was this record that confirmed the worst about ViraVax: they harvested human organs for sale, and the Meltdown AVA was hidden in the EdenSprings water shipments as well as their standard vaccines.

"Well," Marte said, "if Hodge stumbles across one of these beauties, we'll all know about it soon enough. Meanwhile, we have to find one torpedo that will take out all six AVAs."

"You'll do it," Scholz said, "or nobody can. The team should be here to move you and your gear in about an hour. Maybe you should grab a nap."

"I thought the Agency was worried about contamination. . . . ''

"The country's coming apart. It's too risky for us here, too hard to defend, and you're our top priority. Security wants everybody closer to home, and Casa Canadá is more comfortable and more defensible right now. Besides, thanks to Harry it's already fully cabled and shielded for Litespeeds."

"It's as bad as that?"

Colonel Scholz nodded.

"Badder. Three Catholic churches blew up in the past couple of hours. Two of those homes that the Children of Eden had for retarded kids burned yesterday—looks like they were set by the Gardeners to make it look like the Catholics did it."

"The children . . . ?"

"Dead, of course," Scholz said. "But *not* from a virus. It was the old-fashioned way, a bullet to the head." She gulped a swallow of hot coffee and set the cup aside. "Records burned, too, naturally. I do believe we're about to have us an all-out war, Ms. Chang. Our Deathbug is loose down here, and I just got briefed on Mexico City. It seems things there have taken a turn."

Marte set her coffee down so that the chill that shot up her back wouldn't set her hands trembling. She cleared her throat, suddenly dry in spite of the coffee.

"I thought the mercenaries you sent secured that shipment of virus from the Gardeners," Marte said. "I thought everything there was under control."

The room began to fill with techs as they prepared to pack up the consoles, projectors, gloveware and endless snarls of cable.

"It's under control, all right," Scholz whispered, "but not under *our* control. The guerrillas we hired seized the shipment from the Children of Eden, yeah. Now it appears that one or more of those guerrillas got an idea."

Marte leaned her elbows on her desk and put her face in her hands.

"Do they know what it is, what it can do?"

"I don't think so," Scholz said. "They just know that we wanted it bad enough to hire them to take it."

"So they want money?"

Scholz laughed, and Marte envied her ability to laugh at a predicament that could destroy her along with every other human being.

"Always," Scholz said. "Always it's money and a plane ticket somewhere else."

"One stray bullet," Marte groaned.

Scholz stood to go.

"That's for me to worry about," Scholz said, patting Marte's shoulder. "Your worry is defusing the thing. With luck, it won't get the kind of start here that it would get in Mexico City. They have about twenty million people more than we do in the same area. Cheer up. You and your navigator should be elbow-to-elbow in another hour. That might take some of the load off. Harry's got quite the crush on you, you know."

*It's mutual*, Marte thought, and embarrassed herself at the admission.

She wanted something from him that might dampen their relationship. She hoped it wouldn't warp him for life. Marte Chang wanted a sperm sample from Harry Toledo, and she needed to get it immediately to a facility that could do a full-genome scan, including mitochondria. He might be carrying the secret torpedo, and she wanted a peek.

*Maybe this move will work out after all.*

"He's very helpful," Marte said, hoping the blush she

elt rising past her collar didn't betray her.

"Well, you've been a big help to him, too," Scholz said.
"He's buried himself in your work and doesn't even know
one day from the next. Sonja, on the other hand, doesn't
speak to anyone. I'm worried about that one."

Marte understood. They all needed the luxury of going
a little crazy in their own way, so that they wouldn't go
*really* crazy later, if there was a later.

If she had the leisure, Marte knew what *she'd* be doing:
drinking fruity rum drinks beside some pool and toasting
herself under this tropical sun that she'd not been allowed
to see. She would *not* be talking shop of any kind.

After ViraVax everything seemed so trivial. Marte had
to force herself to participate in the occasional small talk.
Only those who had witnessed the last gasp of ViraVax
understood what the others were going through. She felt for
Sonja, but had no time herself for sleep or food, much less
sympathy. Marte replaced her headset and gloveware, then
powered up her Litespeed. She could get in nearly an hour
here before they unplugged her, and she wasn't about to
lose it.

Scholz took the hint and stood to go.

"Sonja'll get over it," Marte said, as Scholz walked
away. "Or she won't."

> "But what about when I'm dead?"
> "Then you're dead."
> "But I can't stand to be dead."
> "Then don't let it happen till it happens. . . ."
>
> —ERNEST HEMINGWAY,
> THE GARDEN OF EDEN

# 16

TRENTON SOLARIS, THE albino Chief of Operations, prepared to board his private flight to Mexico City when the connection came through from the Secretary of State. He was well covered with his usual long sleeves, white gloves and floppy hat, so he turned his back on the Lancer jump jet and took the call in the sun.

Solaris found the secretary a personally repulsive and uncivilized man who thought of nothing but his edge on power. The situation was made more uncomfortable because nearly anything Solaris had to tell him would be negative, and disappointing the secretary always meant personal trouble for Solaris and money trouble for the DIA.

"It's his granddaughter, after all," Major Hodge whispered as he offered Solaris the Sidekick.

As if Solaris needed Hodge to tell him *that*.

The secretary didn't waste any time.

"Who authorized you to start a goddamn revolution?"

"Revolutions just start," Solaris said.

"Bullshit," the secretary said. "This project was your baby, and your ass is on the line. Not only have you been fucking with *me*, you've been fucking with my *family*, and you've been fucking with the *American people*. Now, I want some goddamn answers and I want them *now*!''

Solaris hesitated, and was very uncomfortable to be receiving this dressing-down in the presence of Major Ezra Hodge, the geek of the DIA. He watched heat waves wash the tarmac and wished himself into the lush foothills of the Jaguar Mountains beyond.

"What are your questions, Mr. Secretary?"

"Don't be cute with me, son," Mandell growled. "When I was a senator, I voted against your pet project down there and you know it. Now, you tell me straight. Did they give her some new virus down there? Is my granddaughter going to die?"

In an uncharacteristic moment of hysteria, Solaris wanted to shout, *Mr. Secretary, everybody dies*. But he knew what the secretary wanted, and he knew what he meant, so he answered the best he could.

"Absolutely not, Mr. Secretary. She's in the best of health and in good hands. So is the boy who was with her."

"What about Costa Brava?"

"There's some activity, yes. But that's not unusual, as you well know, and things are moving in our favor."

"But you're holding my granddaughter in isolation. Why is that?"

Solaris knew that the secretary was setting him up for a fall over this mess. He just hoped he could stave it off long enough to redeem himself. He moved into the shade of the Lancer's wing so that he wouldn't have to worry about the sun.

"A precaution," Solaris said. "They were kidnapped by a madman at ViraVax, a man acting completely on his own, and we took the prescribed precautions. You, yourself on the Intelligence Committee . . . "

"I know what we said about that," Mandell said. "Don't snow me with legalese. You say there's nothing to worry about, so they're clean. The President says let them out, but keep them together for observation."

Hodge made a dramatic gesture of supplication to the sun.

"Right," Solaris said. Then he delivered the proper political lie: "I gave the order just minutes ago. . . ."

"Fine. Now. Mexico City?"

"It's under control."

"It's *not* under control," the secretary snapped. "You're getting your butt kicked there, my friend. I don't have time here to dick with you. Now, how hot is this cargo?"

"Very hot, sir."

"Would you like the area cleared without a lot of folderol?"

Solaris felt some relief. The Secretary of State was not an admirable man, but neither was he stupid.

"Yes, sir, I would like that very much."

"Fine. Earthquake Watch got a three-point-oh prediction for that area; we'll upgrade it to an eight-point-oh with warning and get as many people out of there as we can."

"Thank you, sir. That will be most helpful."

"And, Solaris?"

"Yes, sir?"

"There's a biplane for sale in Punta Gorda. Buy it with some of that contingency fund of yours that I voted against in the Senate and give it to my granddaughter."

"I don't think there's any way we can . . ."

"That Mongoose that forced her down and wrecked her plane, it was on lease out of your command, was it not? In flagrant violation of several international policies and at least one U.S. law?"

"I'll locate the plane right away, sir."

"No need, son. It's already loaded on a Fat Boy and headed your way. It'll land at La Libertad in about fifteen minutes. You take care of the funds transfer, and arrange an appropriate place to keep these people together. Your presence is required at Camp David. Instructions to follow. End."

Solaris's hand trembled when he gave the Sidekick back to a smug-looking Major Hodge. The albino had to admit that the earthquake warning was a good idea. The guerrilla team was supposed to be crack at entries, but something had gone wrong; there was much more of a fight than they'd anticipated. He prayed that none of the deadly concoction was hit in the battle.

Solaris felt safer here in Costa Brava, in spite of the infighting, but he needed firsthand information on the siege in Mexico City. Plus, he needed to placate Mexican officials, several of whom were Gardeners, as well. He sighed, and presented Hodge with the updated plan.

"Release them," he said. "Remand Colonel Toledo to Merced Hospital, the Catholic hospital. Get the Chang woman and the kids out to Casa Canadá. Give Chang whatever she needs but keep her there. Set up a security and communications post at Casa Canadá. Once those kids are out there, lock up their plane and don't let them leave."

"Yes, sir."

Small-arms fire crackled in the distance. Solaris lowered his sunglasses for a moment and noted the smoke of several large fires from the city.

"If this gets bad, relocate your people to their farm," he said. "It's got an airstrip and a defensible perimeter. As soon as this plane shows up, I'll hand it over to the girl and head back to Mexico City. I'll return tomorrow to put the lid on ViraVax. You've ordered the concrete and equipment?"

"Yes, sir," Hodge said. "It'll take every cement truck in the five provinces, and more than double-time to get them to work on Easter. . . . "

"Fine. Just so it's done."

The albino squinted up at the whine of engines overhead and saw the wide-bodied Fat Boy transport lining up on its approach.

"Good," he mumbled. "We can get this done and get out of here." He turned to see Hodge watching the transport, too.

"Major Hodge," he said. "Don't you have duties to carry out?"

"Yes, sir," Hodge said, and snapped a salute. "Right away, sir."

Hodge turned on his heel and hurried to the unmarked warehouse beside the taxiway, where the Isolettes had been installed.

*Maggot*, Solaris thought, and wiped his sweaty brow with a handkerchief. His hand trembled and he jammed it back into his pocket. He rapped the fuselage of the Lancer to get the pilot's attention. "Stand down," he said. "We'll be here awhile."

*It is ridiculous for a man not to fly
from his own wickedness, which is
indeed possible, but to fly from other
men's wickedness, which is impossible.*

—MARCUS AURELIUS

# 17

COLONEL RICO TOLEDO admitted to himself that he looked
like shit warmed over, and it wasn't a trick of the hospital
lighting. He barely had the strength to hold himself upright
at the sink, so he could not spare a hand to shave himself,
and shaving around dozens of stitches would be tricky anyway. It had been decades since all he had to do was stare
himself down in the mirror, and what he saw there now
was his grandfather on his deathbed.

Rico was only an hour out of isolation, and his day at
Merced Hospital looked to be a long one. He had expected
to feel better just for getting out of that cage at the airport,
but now he hurt too bad to enjoy it. What he really wanted
was a couple of uninterrupted hours in the Costa Bravan
sun. What he really wanted was a drink.

"Tough shit," he told his image.

His image told him that it *was* tough shit, but he knew
from experience that all tough shit would pass. He just had
to hold on. For now, it was all he could do to hold on to
the sink.

For the first time in a very long time, Rico Toledo was
afraid. It showed in the way his arms and legs trembled,

barely holding him up. It showed in his gaunt, unshaven cheeks crisscrossed with stitches and in the lusterless hollows of his eyes. He hadn't even had the strength to tie the hospital gown, and it hung on him like a shroud.

His face had taken only sixty stitches after the flood, but he'd wound up with over a hundred in his butt. The medic, Joe Clyde, had lost count of the rest after three hundred. All of the field stitches put in by the SEAL team corpsman had infected, but those had closed the bad holes that opened up his belly and his back. Without some Quik-Stitch in the field, he wouldn't have lived long enough to get infected. Still . . .

*Something got in there*, he thought. *Something's not right.*

It was fear. He could see it in his eyes and smell it on his clothes, and he couldn't do a damned thing about it. He threw his kill face at the mirror, and it tossed back a death mask.

"Cute butt, Colonel. Looks a lot like a road map of southern California, with that fault, and all."

Colonel Toledo couldn't let go of the sink without falling, so he shuffled himself behind his gown as best he could. He positioned himself so that he could see Rena Scholz in the mirror.

"You wouldn't say that if you were still a major, Scholz," he rasped.

"Yeah, but I'd still jot it in my diary. The promotion's still a rumor, by the way. Nobody's handed me any silver for my collar. Can I give you a hand?"

Rena Scholz pulled Colonel Toledo's gown closed for him and tied it at the back. When she took his elbow to guide him back to the exam table, he pulled away.

"Thank you, Scholz. I got myself into this, I'll get myself out of it."

"You've used up most of your strength just hanging onto the sink," she said, then shrugged. "But suit yourself."

Twice he started to step to the table, and both times he knew he was too weak to make it.

*What's happening to me?* he thought. *I'm supposed to be getting better, not worse.*

He breathed deep a couple of times; then he was grateful for the promotion rumor. The official word was to come out today or tomorrow, probably when they cemented in all the holes that led to ViraVax. It gave him something to stall with.

"So . . ." His voice came out a squeak, so he tried again.

"So, Scholz, it's *Colonel* Scholz now. Congratulations. Solaris said last night that you were long overdue. How's that maggot Hodge taking the news?"

Scholz flushed, and flashed him a paralyzing smile.

"He's stayed completely out of my way since the whisper started around last night," she said. "The most intelligent thing I've seen him do so far. Now, quit bullshitting me. Can you make it over here or not?"

Rico grunted. For virtually all of his fifty years he had honed his body to a fighting edge and had been accustomed to having it perform flawlessly on cue. These injuries he could tolerate; he'd lived through others. Weakness, however, had never been in his personal vocabulary.

Scholz kicked the brakes off the exam table and wheeled it behind his knees.

"It's an old nurse trick," she said. "Going my way?"

"Scholz, goddammit, it was the principle of the thing."

In spite of himself, he was grateful to let go and sit down, even with the stitches. But his body kept going, and if Scholz hadn't caught him in time he'd have dropped flat on his back on the table. His reflex to save himself turned the rest of the stitches on his body into a hundred fishhooks of fire.

"Shit!"

"Sorry. Slow, deep breaths."

Rico hurt too bad to argue, and after a few deep breaths the hundred little fires started dying out.

"You made a smart move, Scholz," he gasped.

"Which one was that, Colonel?"

"Getting out of nursing and into intelligence."

"Why, thank you, Colonel. Coming from you, that's downright complimentary."

Somehow, pillows appeared under his knees and shoulders, and Scholz had managed to make him relatively comfortable. His body was one throbbing web of pain. Rico's mouth and throat were raw and dry from sucking a ton or two of mud, but he tried talking as a distraction from the rest.

"What about Harry?"

"Well," she said, "Solaris came up with a new plane for Sonja—don't ask me how—and she flew Harry out to Casa Canadá. Of course, Hodge immediately seized the plane and hired a squad of Pan-American Security to keep them in the house. Solaris wants the place as a pull-back in case the shooting gets serious in the city. The *campesinos* have thrown the kids quite a party. They're staying out there, under guard, of course, until this gets squared away. Harry's spent every waking minute working for Chang on the webs. Your ex is working with Philip Rubia to set up the interim government. Most of the fighting is church-to-church, by the way, and nobody seems to care who's president. Nancy Bartlett has taken a bad turn."

"She remembers what happened to Red?"

"Afraid so," Scholz said. "The bombing and the kidnapping were shock enough, but seeing Bartlett's last message and security tapes of those Meltdowns . . . "

"Yeah," he said. "I never believed in that memory adjustment shit, anyway. Especially with Hodge at the helm."

"Well, then, why did you . . . ?"

"Don't start, Scholz. Okay? I've hammered myself enough over that; I don't need any help from you."

Rena said nothing, and the silence between them lay too heavy for Rico's comfort.

"The Chang woman?" he asked.

"Really, Colonel," Scholz said, with a shake of her head. "Her name is Marte. And your son has quite a crush on her, by the way."

"Well?"

"Well, she's got a makeshift setup that Hodge threw together for her at the embassy compound. For security. No lab, though, just a Litespeed and access to the web. But between Bartlett's files and what she'd already observed, she's almost got an immunization worked out. Doesn't do much good without a lab to produce it."

Rico snorted in disbelief.

" 'For security,' " he mocked. "You mean that the same guys who let that bomb into the embassy are now keeping the only virologist who might stop this thing locked up instead of flying her to a decent lab?"

"Our virologist might not be necessary," Scholz said. "Spook . . . I mean, Father Free, put Solaris together with the Peace and Freedom people, like you recommended. Solaris contracted their assault team that happened to be on R&R in Mexico City. They captured the warehouse and secured the shipment of AVAs a half-hour ago. Yolanda herself made the deal; she thought it would add some clout if she blew her own cover to him."

"She's pretty sure that García is through here," Rico said. "And I think she's right."

"Well, she's meeting Solaris in Mexico City after the cement job on ViraVax tomorrow to see that the shipment is all accounted for. They'll pour concrete around the shipment while the suits worry about where to put it."

Yolanda Rubia had saved Rico's skin, what he had left of it. Then she had rallied her people to help save Harry and Sonja. It wasn't out of generosity. She wanted the Gardener government out of Costa Brava, and ViraVax controlled the Gardener government. Her motives may have been different from his own, but the result was the same— an alliance that got the kids, and Marte Chang, out of ViraVax alive. He had to admit a certain weakness for Yolanda's perfume and her dark brown eyes.

Scholz looked uneasy on the subject of Yolanda; her flush showed through the roots of her blonde crewcut.

"You have a question, Scholz?"

"I'm not sure whether it's professional or personal."

"Shoot, Scholz. We're not going to live forever."

"Why Yolanda?" she asked. "Why go to the Peace and Freedom party instead of an independent contractor?"

"I didn't go to her," Rico said. "She came to me. The bombing, remember? She drug me out of there. Things got so wild after that. . . . But I knew she had people in position already, and the move had to be a fast one, before the end of the Sabbath."

Scholz shook her head.

"Okay, before that," she said. "When Red Bartlett melted down, you just *buried* it, and he was your best friend. I just don't understand. . . . "

Rico began to shift position, then thought better of it.

"Okay, Scholz, I'll ask you the same thing. You were there, you saw Bartlett melt down in person and got it on tape. You maintained security and came to me instead of going public. Why?"

Rena pursed her lips, but didn't let her gaze slide from his. Rico suspected that if she did, she would cry, and Rena Scholz never let anyone see her cry.

"The only other person I could have gone to was Spook," she said. "Some in the Agency consider him a traitor. He'd want me to resign before working with him. Even if he didn't, the Agency would force my resignation, or worse, if they found out I'd gone to him. I'm surprised Solaris let him see you."

"Well, there you have it," Rico said. "I was too close to retirement pay to write that off. But I didn't want Spook to see me . . . you know, as I was. As something less than he remembers me."

"As a drunk, you mean?"

"Shit, Scholz. You sure have a way with words."

"Takes one to know one, Colonel. That's why I'm the only one around you who knows what you're going through right now. I'm the only friend you've got who can really appreciate the fact that you haven't asked for a drink since you woke up. In fact, Colonel, I'd have to say I'm pretty goddamned proud of you. And I'll be there for you anytime you want to talk about it.''

Rico coughed nervously, then croaked, "Too water-logged to think about drinking.''

"Don't sell yourself short, Colonel, and nobody else will, either—not me, not your son and not even Spook.''

The worst of the pain had subsided, and Rico felt his mind clearing. Besides, the personal chatter was getting too close to the bone for his tastes.

"Scholz, as a former nurse you're probably familiar with medical charts and such.''

"If you're going to ask me what I think you're going to ask me, you'd better start calling me Rena,'' she said. "Scholz is for the boys, and I'm no boy.''

"No,'' Rico said, exaggerating an appraising glance, "that you're obviously not.'' And he managed to snap his hand in that way that the Costa Bravans used to say, "Hot, very hot!''

"Well, I see there's nothing wrong with your testoster-one production.''

"You saw the ViraVax files; they messed with that, too. So, my records are in that rack in the hallway beside the door,'' he said. "Would you tell me what they know about what's going on with me?''

"How long before the doc gets here?''

"They're bringing in a guy from the Catholic clinic up in Santa Ana. I didn't trust anybody here. The Flicker left to pick him up a half hour ago.''

"Plenty of time,'' she said. "I'll speak to your nurse and see that we're not disturbed.''

"Don't get my hopes up, Scholz. I'm a sick man.''

"Dream on, Colonel.''

Scholz stepped out, and Rico tried a few more deep breaths before reaching for his canes. He popped a sweat getting his fingers on one, and with it he hooked the other. He wanted them beside him on the bed, as though they were his legs that seemed to be giving out. He had refused the walker, even though he felt more secure with it.

Crutches were out of the question because of the lacerations under his armpits.

His left armpit, upper arm and shoulder were covered with a matrix of shark cartilage and his own skin cells. Rico had refused the Second Skin that the Children of Eden developed, as he had refused their doctors, equipment and medications. The Gardeners and their medical meddling had got him into this mess with their secret potions inside their legitimate treatments; he wasn't about to let them get their hands on him again.

Scholz came back in, and the quick smile that she arranged for his benefit wasn't quick enough to fool him.

"More bad news?" he asked.

Scholz hefted the reader that contained his chart, as though more data increased its weight.

"Fifty thousand words already," she said. "Your chart is already longer than the average movie."

"More interesting, too, I'll bet."

He patted the covers beside him and she sat, gently, reviewing the files.

"Very interesting," she agreed. "We know from ViraVax records that they infected you with at least three AVAs—that hitchhiker in your sperm that made Harry your clone instead of your son, the little tracker assembly that you found in your neck and some kind of aggression package like the one that killed Red Bartlett. None respond to the contagion-factor test, so you're not catching. We can assume other changes in your biology that these facilities can't find. Other than your obvious injuries, your clotting factor is much higher than normal, which saved you at the scene. It was probably a function of that aggression package. And your glucose metabolism rises and falls for no apparent reason, which is why you're so shaky right now."

"Yeah," he said, "it comes and goes. But it's more come than go right now. I just want to get out there and see them cap that zoo tomorrow."

"You looked God in the face just yesterday, Colonel," Scholz said. "However, if you're a good boy, I might help you out to the ViraVax pour. If they let you out of here by tomorrow, that is. I want to see the place covered in concrete myself. But save your plans until the doc checks you out."

"Now, what exactly is this clotting factor?"

"It's a chain of events in the body that leads to clotting. Some people don't clot at all, and a small cut can kill them. Some people form clots spontaneously, without an injury, and these can lead to stroke, heart attack, kidney failure. . . . "

Rico waved a hand to stop her.

"What are they doing about it?"

"The clotting? After all your lacerations, you should have bled out in minutes. But your body mounted an exceptional clotting reaction and stopped it. Some of that pain in your legs is from clots that lodged in your major veins. They've given you a couple of drugs that stop the clotting, but with all your lacerations they don't want to give you any of the thrombolytics that dissolve clots already formed. You refused their Artificial Viral Agent designed for that purpose; no surprise there."

"Now, what about the glucose?" he asked.

"Nothing, yet," she said. "You got plenty in your original IV, but your body doesn't always metabolize it. They tried insulin, but for some reason it didn't work and, besides, there's nothing wrong with your insulin production so they don't want to suppress that by giving you more."

"So," he mused, "if I don't have a stroke I'm going to starve to death?"

Scholz couldn't hide the shadow of concern behind her professional mask.

"Marte Chang will have a handle on things by then. She and Harry are making excellent progress. . . . "

A heavy-handed knock at the door interrupted Scholz. The door *swooshed* open and a large, red-faced man with long, dark hair snatched the reader out of her hand.

"McCarron's the name," he said, "*Doctor* McCarron. I see you've found the chart that the nurses' station lost."

He leaned past Scholz and shook Rico's hand.

"Not much of a grip for a colonel, Colonel. Excuse me, ma'am." He tugged at Scholz's sleeve and, when she stood, he sat heavily on her spot at the side of the bed. "Now, tell me what happened."

Doctor McCarron focused an intense, blue-eyed gaze completely on Rico. Rico shrugged and glanced at the door. Scholz took the hint, winked at him and left the two men alone.

"It's a very long story," Rico croaked.

"Well, then you'd better begin. You've already given me an excuse to miss a medical staff meeting, but I'll be damned if you'll cheat me out of an afternoon of fishing."

"The story involves some national security matters. . . ."

"So? I keep my mouth shut. I always do, and I'm sure your investigators can verify that. Tell me just what pertains to your own body and mind. I have all the drama in my personal life that I require, thank you. I do not go looking for more."

Rico liked this brusque, no-nonsense manner and, after a couple of deep breaths, he began to pick his most delicate path through the immense story of ViraVax.

*The Way of the warrior is resolute
acceptance of death.*

—MIYAMOTO MUSASHI

# 18

THE MEDIC BERT Frank tightened the side-panel straps of
his flak vest, lowered his entry visor to the tip of his long
nose and took up his position directly behind the Powell.
The three-story building in front of them was painted "Gardener Green," and the techs reported no movement inside.
Bert Frank was nervous. Deploying in the nation's capital
was serious shit.

"Rapid Entry Tactical Display A-211" flashed in red
against his visor. Sergeant Frank turned the brightness
down so he had to squint at the ghost of a map that hovered
before his eyes. He'd rather squint than sacrifice what little
night vision he could muster out of broad daylight. The
techs would cut the building's power on entry, so no telling
what visibility would be like.

*It'll be bright enough when that Powell cuts loose,* he
thought.

This raid made Bert Frank very nervous. This complex
in northwest D.C. was home to more than a hundred
Down's syndrome people, children and young adults, and
he feared more for them than for himself. If the Gardeners

started shooting, Frank would have his hands full, and it wouldn't be pretty.

*Not "if,"* he corrected himself. *When. These are some mighty trigger-happy Christians.*

The army contracted a unit of Jesus Rangers to work with Frank's unit in South Africa. Their enthusiasm for killing the heathen included the knifing of a Catholic lieutenant, a woman, in his own unit. They were arguing over the translation of a biblical phrase, Frank never found out what.

He rocked up on the balls of his feet a few times to warm up his calves. This entry reminded him of a situation just last year, with a hundred soft targets jammed into a tight space. Everyone had come out of that one alive, even the five Dancing Devils who called the party.

*But those were college students,* Frank reminded himself. *They learned fast and took direction well once we got inside. But these are . . . ?*

Sergeant Frank sought for some word other than "retards." The Captain called them "retards," but Sergeant Frank preferred the Gardener term, "Innocents," even if he didn't think much of the Gardeners. Especially after today's briefing. Even now, afterimages of a man melting from his bones played at the edges of his vision.

Ramiskey's sign, a parachute, blinked him to open a channel. Frank glanced at the parachute and it turned green. He glanced at the number "3" on his visor's pad, and the channel opened.

"Ramiskey?"

"Don't worry, Doc. I'm on your clumsy butt like a diaper."

"Just don't shoot me, Ramiskey, that's all I ask."

A sudden hand slapped Sergeant Frank's shoulder, startling him more than he cared to admit.

"Ramiskey, goddammit!"

"Dummy-up, Doc. They give you that expensive gear, you could at least switch it on."

Frank activated the flank-and-rear scanners that he hated

so much. Typical military overkill. More information, but more distraction, too. Besides, the close-fitting, constantly moving images made him seasick.

"Makes me sick," he mumbled.

"Sick?" Ramiskey barked a laugh. "You can *live* with sick. Now, *dead*? Naw, man. Can't live with that."

"Cut the chatter, two-three. Two, dig into your pack and solve your problem."

Samuels the Snake, squad leader for a day.

*What a prick!*

"My pack's for my men, Snake."

"That's right, Doc. Now you keep quiet, keep your men alive and don't puke in your visor. Three, that goes for you, too. Ready up."

Sergeant Bert Frank breathed deep and tried to orient himself inside the wide-angle holo of his helmet. He hadn't felt well since this morning, when the CO had made them watch the helmet record of some nurse major in Costa Brava. The constant scanning and rolling of the 360-degree pickups unseated his scrambled eggs, but what they recorded would have unseated a vulture's breakfast; he knew that.

A few years ago Bert Frank would have been shocked at today's general briefing. This one made him numb. They were going in, supposedly to liberate a hundred Down's syndrome kids from a handful of missionary mercenaries that called themselves "Jesus Rangers." Bert had that bad feeling. They were going in to die, and to die on-camera, and to stay alive as long as possible before they died.

Sergeant Frank closed his eyes against the dance of his visor's displays. His traitor cortex immediately flipped him inside a rerun of last night's briefing.

The nurse, a Major Scholz, had lived through her encounter. Her patient and her entry team lived. The record from that Watchdog unit, and Major Scholz's helmet records, verified that this dead guy's body melted from its bones and burned to a few fragments under a light blue flame.

Bert Frank's brain replayed that scene for him again: Major Scholz, who had removed her biohazard suit to treat her patient, hurries into it now. Her heavy breathing punctuates her verbal report, and camera tracking intensifies Frank's seasickness.

*The colonel says it's some kind of artificial virus.*

ViraVax made the virus. And tested it on their own Innocents. And something got away from them. And now medic Sergeant Bert Frank was headed into the middle of them, his bio suit conspicuously absent. That meant that he, Ramiskey and the rest of them were guinea pigs and he'd bet a year's pay that they were all going to wind up in quarantine by nightfall. Someplace fireproof, like this building they were about to enter.

This church, the Children of Eden, bred retarded people for their organs and their labor. That was the next big news at the briefing. These Gardeners had some Artificial Viral Agent that kept organs from being rejected. Their "Innocents" were universal donors, and the Gardeners claimed that it was okay because these Down's syndrome people weren't human and didn't have souls.

Bert Frank didn't care. They bled when cut and screamed when shot and they would rely on him to keep them alive. He was saddened by the briefing, but not surprised. He'd been a medic now for twelve years, and nothing surprised him anymore. And, anymore, he didn't *want* to be surprised.

A red strobe at the lower left-hand edge of his visor alerted the sergeant to the one-minute warning. He checked his watch out of reflex, even though he could read the digital display at the top of his visor. The Powell hummed, its electrics at full power, and it surged against its tread, prickling the air with ozone. Everything was still, no challenge or sign of life from the target. Broad daylight, and Bert Frank had a bad feeling. He rubbed the Powell's rubberized armor for luck.

A quick wave from Gray at point beside the wall, a few deep, slow breaths and his visor flashed green for "go."

The Powell dug in; then the wall in front of it snapped, twisted and shrieked as the narrow little vehicle nosed right through to an interior courtyard of cement and rock.

There, and in other simultaneous raids of Gardener buildings throughout the world, all similarity to known forcible entries ended.

Sergeant Frank found himself slipping on a foul, thick muck that churned up hair, teeth, charred bits of bone and clothing with every step.

A glimpse of something blue in and out of a doorway across the courtyard.

He heard bitter curses and the sounds of vomiting around him, but Sergeant Frank focused on that quick, blue movement.

No shots fired yet. He was medic, not point.

Ramiskey had seen it, too, because he duck-walked in his fast crouch along the wall and came up tight against the doorframe. Frank tuned channel three and worked his way to the doorway without looking down at his soggy boots. He heard Ramiskey take deep, gulping breaths to calm himself, but Frank sucked as little of the fetid air as possible. It lay like a sour blanket across his tongue.

"Ramiskey, Frank, do you have contact?"

Snake's voice sounded raw, and Frank guessed that he'd been the first to toss his breakfast.

"We have movement," Ramiskey said.

He hand-signaled for Frank to cover the left as they entered.

Sergeant Frank didn't like to put himself in a shooting position. As a seasoned medic, he'd carried his weight in many a firefight when the action came down to himself and his patients. He liked doing the impossible—putting together blown-up bodies. Shooting people was entirely too possible for his tastes. He acknowledged Ramiskey's signal, checked his load and took the deep breath that he'd been avoiding.

And he heard someone crying on the other side of the doorway.

Ramiskey jumped inside and swept right, and Frank was a half-step behind him to the left. Several shapes huddled in the far left-hand corner of the bare room; small, frightened shapes without weapons. Frank flooded the corner with his spotlight and paralyzed a half-dozen very young, very filthy children. He remained still while Ramiskey checked another doorway to the right.

"Clear," he said, and closed the door.

"Check," Frank answered. "Now let's see what we can do with these little guys."

Frank sensed movement behind him and spun on his heel, Snake squarely in his sights as he stepped through the doorway.

"Too late, Frank, you're dead," Snake said. "What have we here?"

"Kids," Frank said.

"Scared and hungry kids," Ramiskey added. "We'll have to . . ."

"Halt right there, Ramiskey," Snake ordered. "Don't touch them."

"They're just kids, Snake," Ramiskey said, "and they're hungry, for Chrissake."

"Orders," Snake said. "We're to isolate and quarantine any survivors for study. . . . "

"Well, they won't survive long without food and water," Sergeant Frank interrupted. "Look how sunken their eyes are, and their cracked lips. They're dehydrated. They need attention, and they need it now. If Operations wants these kids alive, then you'd better let me take a look."

"Yeah, Snake," Ramiskey chimed in, "whatever it was that we waded through back there will kill us long before these kids do. They lived through it, maybe the bright boys can find out how *we* can live through it. Because even an ignorant shithead like yourself must know that we are all dead men here."

"My orders say . . . "

"What do they say, Snake?" Ramiskey demanded, his visor clacking against Snake's. "Do they say you'll shoot me if I feed these kids? You know you're not fast enough, and you know how much I'd love for you to try . . . ''

"Can it, gentlemen," the captain interrupted. "Ramiskey's right, we need these kids alive and well. Frank . . . ?"

Sergeant Frank was already in the corner, tilting his canteen for the first of six very thirsty, very frightened children. Sergeant Frank tried hard to control the tremble in his hand, and there was no way that he could control the hair that stood up on his arms and the back of his neck. These six kids weren't Innocents, after all. At least, they displayed none of the physical characteristics of Innocents. Brownskinned, with wide brown eyes, they looked like the Muslim kids in his old neighborhood back home. He was a little nervous that they didn't speak or even whimper; they just looked at him with those huge, brown eyes. What *really* scared him was that they were identical.

*All six of them identical*, he thought. *And they lived through whatever happened out there.*

Sergeant Frank dictated what he saw and his conclusions as quickly as he could. He was afraid that he wouldn't live to report in person, and he was sure that these children harbored the key to surviving the virus or viruses that killed everyone else in the building. He only lived long enough to know he was right on the first count.

*Alas! Alas! that great city Babylon,
that mighty city! for in one hour is thy
judgment come.*

—REVELATIONS

# 19

DAVID NOAS WANTED to discuss his suspicions and his plans with his most intimate advisor, but that was impossible. The Master, the father who made him a son, was truly dead. It took the commander a couple of deep breaths to swallow this wave of grief. Everyone in the Ready Room stood at his entrance, so he waved them to their seats. Headsets, holos and peels were aglow throughout the room, and the background chatter of a dozen phone conversations picked up where they had left off.

Commander Noas opened the scramble channel and lit right into Ezra Hodge.

"What do you think you're doing, Hodge? Inciting panic and sending our people willy-nilly into the streets furthers no one. And how many of our faithful do you think would survive the kind of blood bath you're instigating?"

The expression, and the answer, were smug.

"At least a hundred and forty-four thousand, Commander, and that's all that prophecy requires."

"Mr. Hodge, does the word 'Custer' mean anything to you? We are sorely outnumbered in this world—*thousands* to one. Do you want to go down in history as the man who single-handedly destroyed the only true church on God's green earth?"

The commander's voice had risen to a shout that silenced the Ready Room.

Before Hodge could answer, the commander's Sidekick interrupted with an incident warning tone.

"Speak!" he ordered.

"Sir! Ranger unit in Mexico City reports that they've taken heavy fire by unknown bandits. Casualties. Requests backup strike force, emphasis countersniper, and medevac for twelve."

*"Twelve . . . !"*

The Jesus Rangers' field units were twelve-member teams.

"Have Senator Plata protest the Joint Chiefs *now*," he ordered. "And request intervention—U.S. nationals, U.N., OAS—whoever. Our nearest Ranger backup is in Veracruz; order them a jump immediately and get me a link to the Mexico City unit."

"Yes, Commander."

The commander took a long pull at his ice water.

"It was the Peace and Freedom people and your old pal Colonel Toledo that did the job on ViraVax," Tekel announced, over the commander's shoulder. His expression was grim, and his tight voice close to a hiss. Tekel tapped a cube and set it on the commander's Litespeed. "ViraVax shutdown dumped the data to our system. It's all in here. He's been a mighty busy boy."

*Toledo!*

David Noas had hoped that he would never cross swords with his old sparring partner. Now, on top of the loss of the Master, the commander felt that special loss reserved for betrayals. After a few moments this special loss became anger, and the anger an uncharacteristic but infinitely satisfying rage.

"I will harvest his organs myself," the commander whispered to no one. "That is a promise."

"First vote in," Tekel announced, pressing on his earpiece. "And it's unanimous."

"Who?" the commander asked, and at the same time offered a quick prayer of thanks for the speed of the vote and another prayer of support for the man who had been handed this tremendous cross.

Tekel didn't move, and he sported a wide grin.

"What's so amusing, Mr. Tekel?"

"Well, sir . . . they voted for you. You're the new Master of the Children of Eden."

The Ready Room broke out in an enthusiastic applause. Sergeant Tekel accompanied a stunned David Noas back into Sanhedrin Chambers, where the applause was thunderous. David Noas offered a quick prayer of supplication, then accepted a bowl from one of the Innocents and began to wash the feet of the Sanhedrin. So it was that he began his day as prophet and Master of the Children of Eden.

An hour later, the Master David Noas stood alone in the courtyard of the Sanhedrin and pretended to meditate in the privacy of a stand of bamboo. His dark hands worried at one another, two twitchy little animals at the cuffs of his new white robe. Those scars that seemed so vivid when he wore black seemed to blend in better when framed in white.

David had never believed that he would be chosen Master of the Children of Eden. He realized now, for the first time, that this had been his greatest fear. As a child he'd watched his father, first, and then Calvin Casey go to strangers' doors, pamphlets in hand, to introduce them to Jesus. David always hung back, on musty porches, hot sidewalks, in blustery rain, and he admired these holy men who faced grim-lipped strangers with a smile and a handshake. After the deaths of his parents and the others, as he moved into the white heat of adolescence, David Noas trusted no one but the Master.

The Master had honed him into a fine tool of vengeance, though vengeance was not what he preached in the streets nor on the airwaves. Always a thoughtful, obedient boy, David set out to repay the Master's kindness by routing the unbelievers and infidels and those loudmouth murderers of

Jesus Christ. When gangs of Jewish boys vandalized Jesus Is Lord mini-marts, David and his followers sought them out, one by one, and pacified them in most unpacifistic ways.

"An attack on the faithful is an attack on the faith," he reasoned. "And an attack on the faith is an attack on the Lord Himself."

When the doubters challenged, "The Lord can take care of Himself," the young David Noas shot back, "Yeah, that's why he made *me*."

In those days, as a Bible-mad hotblood, he raged against the spinelessness of the Lord's disciples and vowed to defend the true word of God with his life, as his father and mother had.

"The Holy Spirit threw you out that window to save you for a higher purpose than death in some squalid little village," the Master had told him. "It's up to you to find that purpose. Pray on it, son, and you will know the truth in your heart."

Up until now, he thought that his purpose had been revenge. Now, after twenty-two years of it, the cup tasted bitter and he wanted to put it away for good.

*But how?*

Now he was the Master, and his followers expected revenge, and he wanted none of it. David Noas was, for the first time, afraid. Not afraid of the infighting that might devil them all, but of his unworthiness and of the great emptiness that sat where he was supposed to have vision. A walk in the afternoon sun had not helped lift this blackness and this doubt from his soul.

In spite of the fear, and his surprise at the vote, he had come to understand that this was the path that his life, and Calvin Casey, had been leading him towards all along. He realized now that Calvin Casey had not been any more at ease. The Master had merely worn his discomfort in grace, and persevered. David Noas vowed to do the same.

"Commander," Hubbard broke into his reverie, "Master, I mean. The White House calling. You can use my Sidekick.''

David waved it away.

''I don't want to talk to some bureaucratic termite,'' he said. ''I want the queen.''

Hubbard smiled, and it must have been painful through his chapped lips. He offered the instrument again.

''Her highness herself,'' he said.

President O'Connor wasted no time on pleasantries.

''Mr. Noas, have you followed the incident in Mexico City?''

''As best I can. Your administration has seen to it that information is at a premium.''

''I can say the same thing about your organization, Mr. Noas. We're not getting the full background here, and the rumors are very ugly. This does neither of us any good. I'd like to remedy that.''

''What do you propose?''

''I propose that you and I meet at Camp David immediately to discuss it.''

Hubbard's eyebrows quivered a little, as they often did when he was excited. David decided that the President could use a little humility.

''O'Connor,'' David said. ''That's an Irish name, isn't it? Are you Catholic?''

Hubbard smiled again and made a twisting-the-knife motion in the air.

''I am President of the United States, Mr. Noas, within which you and your organization reside. Don't play games with me.''

''As you must know, Mrs. O'Connor, our organization is experiencing a difficult time. . . . ''

''You have my sympathies, Mr. Noas. I, too, have a grief to handle. As commander of your military arm, you are in a unique position to enlighten us.''

''And I am obligated . . . ''

'' . . . to do what is right for your people. I know. I will send a flight for you. . . . ''

"I am obligated neither to you nor to my people," David said. "My obligation is to the Lord, His Word and His Work. . . . ''

"If we don't talk *now*, there may very well be no one left to hear the Word or perform the Work, including yourself. Now, I suggest . . . ''

"No, Mrs. O'Connor, *I* suggest something. Read Ezekiel 9, and then if you want to talk with me you can come here.''

The Master broke the connection, handed the device to Hubbard, and spat into the bamboo.

"Bet she can't even boil water,'' he muttered. "Get Hodge on the line. It's time he told us exactly what's going on in Mexico City.''

"Why do you suppose she's so hot about that Mexico City thing?'' Hubbard asked. "A couple of dozen people in a firefight over a warehouse doesn't warrant a summit meeting. Not with the President of the United States.''

He keyed in the proper codes for Hodge's scrambler and handed over the Sidekick.

"That's exactly what I'd like to talk to Hodge about,'' Noas said, and slipped his earpiece into place.

*I hope it doesn't have anything to do with ViraVax*, he thought, but that falling-elevator feeling in the pit of his stomach warned him otherwise.

"I'll check the networks on Mexico City,'' Hubbard said. "Hodge will want an update, too. I'll connect, if you'd like to do that now.''

The Master David Noas nodded, took a deep breath and prepared for the inevitable frustration of dealing with Ezra Hodge. Noas reminded himself that he was now the Master, and Hodge was a tool, to be used or tossed. He could afford to be more patient with the man. He decided to appoint Hodge Commander. This would disappoint Hubbard, who would expect the promotion himself, but it would bring Hodge into the fold, make him easier to watch. And his little on-screen drama had proven surprisingly popular with the Sanhedrin.

*I can always change my mind after I'm sure we know everything that he knows.*

Hodge knew plenty, of this David Noas was certain. The man had been assisting ViraVax programs for years, for the Children of Eden as well as the Agency. With this new confidence that Hodge displayed, Noas was sure that he was hip-deep in this ViraVax mess.

*Hodge doesn't seem surprised,* Noas thought, *like all of this is old news.*

Yes, he would get Hodge closer to hand, even though it might mean losing a good mole with the Agency in that region. There were others more to his liking in the Agency; Hodge could be replaced there without much trouble.

Hubbard put the connection through, and in a brief and fairly painless conversation the Master informed Hodge of his new position.

Then he put Hodge on hold for a moment while he and Hubbard turned to see what all the sudden screaming was about in Chambers. Noas split-screened Hubbard's Side-kick and keyed in the security cameras, but all he could see in the tiny viewer was pandemonium.

*And what is that ungodly smell?*

He hurried to close with Hodge.

"You have my priority code," he told Hodge, "and I'm transmitting Hubbard's now. Something's wrong in Chambers; I have to go."

The Master's whole body prickled, suddenly, and began to tremble. One second he felt unbearably hot, and the next he felt himself rising, like smoke or steam. This was peculiar, since he could see that he had fallen, unfeeling as stone, backwards into the bamboo. His mind groped for a prayer, but there was nothing there.

*And the fourth angel poured out his vial upon the sun; and power was given unto him to scorch men with fire.*

—REVELATIONS

MAJOR EZRA HODGE rubbed his eyes and checked his watch.

*I've been up almost thirty-six hours!*

He was once again surprised and thankful for the energy that was his gift from the Lord. It had enabled him to make his own investigations of the ViraVax site and to ascertain that destruction of lower levels had been complete—thanks to Toledo. After Toledo was picked up, Hodge had mucked about in the godforsaken jungle most of the night, then developed and delivered his own strategies to the albino at the Defense Intelligence Agency before daybreak.

This morning Chief Solaris ordered the entire compound buried in concrete immediately. Hodge concurred, because argument would be fruitless, and might expose him as a sympathizer. He would get out there once more in the daylight for another recon, just in case there was trouble lying about, some unknown factor that might put a hitch in Flaming Sword.

"Trouble lying about" reminded him of Toledo, and the humiliation he'd just suffered at the hands of the albino.

*The albino's treating Toledo like some kind of hero,* he

thought. *Relieving me of the interrogation in front of the enlisted men undermines my authority here.*

Major Hodge reminded himself to relax, that it didn't matter, that in a matter of weeks there would be no Chief Solaris, no enlisted men.

All was going as planned.

More a hasty collage than a plan, Hodge tried to make the best of the sabotage wrought by Colonel Toledo and the children. Toledo was a mosquito awaiting a swat, but the children required a delicacy and resources that Hodge feared he did not have. He turned his fears to prayer, and one by one the obstacles fell from his path as the scales had fallen from his eyes.

Colonel Toledo had convinced Solaris to mercenize a Mexico City guerrilla team to liberate the warehouse. He was sure they'd be no match for the Jesus Rangers there. What could a straggle of ragtag idolators do against the Mighty Men of the right hand of God?

*They could delay distribution of those World Health shipments until there aren't any more planes to fly,* he thought.

That would be a serious setback. Timing was the key. He and the Angel had counted on the vaccine shipments going out on Monday, following the doctored EdenSprings waters in service with the airlines, among many others. These AVAs would still encompass the globe, but not with the swiftness generated by a few hundred thousand personal injections in the name of medicine.

Hodge looked out his office window onto the sullen, battered compound of the U.S. Embassy across the street. Two extra security detachments betrayed the frantic activity that he knew roiled in the bunker-like interior. Every piece of the bristling rooftop electronics should be aglow with overuse, such was the level of panic inside. Even now his own equipment monitored every word, every signal for his perusal later. None of it had much value.

Major Hodge smiled at his shadowy reflection in the one-way duraglass and smoothed his rumpled shirt over his pot belly. He knew the picture that he presented: short, pudgy, pasty-skinned, nearly bald at thirty. In other words: bookish, invisible, threatless. The thought brought a sparkle to his blue eyes. This morning his cheeks and nose were blotched with mosquito bites, but he had to admit he'd enjoyed his slog into the boonies.

Today Ezra Hodge enjoyed everything, because the Eden he had prayed for all his life was finally at hand. He had Adam and Eve in his care, just as the Angel's contingency predicted.

*And those drones at the embassy don't have a clue*, he thought.

If he were loyal to the Agency, he would have let Mishwe come down to the wire with his plan, then nabbed him and the invaluable AVAs. But that would not suit his plan at all.

*And for what?* he thought. *A commendation? Recommendation for promotion?*

That was nothing compared to nearly two hundred years in Eden. More, if he took care of himself. Where the Agency was concerned, Ezra Hodge had bigger fish to fry.

The tone on his Sidekick brought a wry smile to his full lips. That would be the Sanhedrin, perhaps Noas himself. By now perhaps they had reviewed the supplemental materials he'd parceled out from the ViraVax records. They would see that the Advent of Eden was at hand, and that Ezra Hodge held the key.

He strolled to his console and double-checked the Litespeed, reassuring himself that the satlink to Godwire was secure and any listening devices in the office were useless. He straightened his tie, tugged the wrinkles out of his shirt and commanded the machine, "Scramble one. Open."

The flat-screen image of David Noas did the man no justice. Captured in front of the giant bamboo, the Goliath was truly a David, and Ezra Hodge did not have to suffer neck cramps looking up at him in person. The commander's scarred and swarthy face tried for a neutral expression, but Hodge's experienced eye read fatigue, shock and an un-

dercurrent of anger that came out in dark-circled, wide eyes
and a twitch of muscles around the jaw. The major breathed
evenly, smoothly, confident that his expression did not betray his triphammer heart.

"Good morning, Commander Hodge," Noas began,
"and congratulations."

"Thank you, Master," Hodge managed, with a suitable
nod of respect.

He did not want Noas to see that the promotion had
caught him off guard.

"Congratulations, yourself," he said, "and thank you for
your confidence in me."

"You knew?"

Hodge enjoyed the flicker of uncertainty that passed over
the dark-circled eyes of David Noas. He did not know for
sure, but the laws of probability were behind his bluff, and
the bluff paid off. Even if Noas were to survive Flaming
Sword, he never would be sure just how much Ezra Hodge
knew about anything.

"It could be deduced from your introduction," Hodge
allowed. "If you were no longer Commander, then it fol-
lows that the Sanhedrin must have selected you Master. I
could not imagine them voting you out in this hour of
need."

Noas seemed unimpressed by the logic or the flattery.

"We have both been chosen for our military and intelligence skills," he said. "The Sanhedrin fears the coordination of a worldwide coalition against us, and we are
expected to stop it. My only question for you is this: will
you give up your position with the DIA to serve us?"

"Do you think that's wise?" Hodge asked. "I'm in a
unique position here, and it has cost me thirteen years of
torment and humiliation among the Babylonians. With a
strong first officer, I believe I can hold this position and
serve the Lord as well."

Noas nodded absently, and Hodge realized that he was
receiving another conversation via his earpiece.

*We need focus at a time like this, not distraction!*

"All right, Commander," Noas said, finally. "You may remain in position for the time being. We will assess our threat, and you will continue your work with the Mishwe materials from ViraVax. Your assistant on the Twelve will be Tekel. He's reliable, and up to speed on our current situations. I recommend Hubbard as your first officer, but that choice is yours."

"Thank you, Master," Hodge said. This time the title did not stick quite so hard in his throat. "I expect to have an update to you in the next few hours."

"We are assessing a situation in Mexico City where our people are under attack for unknown reasons. Hubbard will brief you within the hour."

*More of Toledo's meddling,* he thought. *He and the albino wasted no time.*

Hodge considered informing Noas of the situation, then thought better of it. The Jesus Rangers could hold their own, and Noas didn't need to know how Toledo had slicked him on this one. Nor did he need to know quite yet what the fighting was about.

"Thank you, Master. I'll investigate from this end."

"Could this be linked to the ViraVax disaster?"

Hodge hesitated. Noas was no fool, and had been instrumental in cloaking certain military applications of the AVA technology. Hodge concluded that it didn't matter now whether the Mexico City shipment was exposed. All the others were in the pipeline.

"It's possible, Master," Hodge said. "Several coded shipments left here for Mexico City just prior to the sabotage. Transplant units and vaccines for World Health. I should know more in a couple of hours."

"If the situation sours in Mexico City, a couple of hours may be eternity."

"The fight in Mexico City is over nothing," Hodge said with a smirk. "Don't get drawn into it. I'll have all the data to you within twenty-four hours. You will gain much and lose nothing by cooperating with the Babylonians on this one, trust me."

"All right," Noas said, and it came out a sigh. "I have a couple of speeches to write and a lobbyful of interviewers. And the Termite Queen wants to meet in person. She's got a wild hair about this Mexico thing. Maybe they've winded the organ harvest and want some evidence. . . . "

Noas was distracted by something off-screen, and Major Hodge heard shouts and screams in the background.

Suddenly, David Noas looked very agitated.

"You have my priority code," he said, "and I'm transmitting Hubbard's now. Something's wrong in Chambers; I have to go."

The Children of Eden logo filled the screen, and Hodge switched it off.

Hodge had been cut off for most of his adult life from open practice of his religion, a religion that he felt with a passion that surpassed any corporal desire. Now his hour had come around at last, and his heart made a joyous cry to the Lord. Soon, he would be able to shout his love of God from the rooftops.

" 'Trouble in Chambers,' " Hodge repeated to himself, with a laugh. "I'll get back to you, trust me," he whispered, and patted the hot scrambler.

He would wait until GenoVax threw the children into his hands, and he would urge Rena Scholz to help him protect them.

*She'll be safest with the children,* he thought. *I can offer her the antidote at the last possible moment.*

He took out the compact metal kit and prepared to administer another shot. He had not yet concocted a good story for his possession of the antidote, but for one who had been writing disinformation for the news media for years, this should present no challenge.

*And if she, too, is swept up by the pale horse of pestilence?*

He did not intend to live out his days in the Garden of Eden without a companion. Ezra the Invisible would improvise, as he'd been doing successfully all his life.

*Whatever you do, you must drive the enemy together, as if tying a line of fishes, and when they are seen to be piled up, cut them down strongly without giving them room to move.*

—MIYAMOTO MUSASHI

# 21

PRESIDENT CLAUDIA KAY O'CONNOR pulled at the side panels of her body armor, smoothing the wrinkle that chafed under her shoulder holster. She put her hands flat on the dining room tabletop, leaned across a chocolate White House and looked Agent Robideaux in the eye.

"I'm going to church," she said. "People expect it of me—for Easter, and for Mark."

"Give them a new Vice-President," Robideaux said. "Make your announcement today, but from the Camp. They will forgive you a Mass."

"It isn't a matter of forgiveness," she said. "They need confidence in authority right now. The public needs to see their President fulfilling the office while managing her grief as a spouse. They need reassurance, and not by word, but by action."

"The Gardeners have been dying in clumps," he argued. "Somebody used their own ritual against them. We don't want to take any chances in case they decide to take on Catholics next. . . ."

"John Kennedy went to this very church whenever . . . "

"My point exactly, Ms. President," Agent Robideaux

interrupted. "Look what happened to him. Father Delahunty's already up at the Camp, you can use the chapel there. You're a widow, Ms. President; you want some privacy."

Claudia agreed with Robideaux at the last. She approved "Worm in the Apple" status for troops abroad, collaring her defenses and snubbing them up a short leash. This would be an unmistakable sign that she anticipated trouble from within and intended to deal with it boldly. In reality, it would get most, if not all, of her armed forces back home before all of the airplanes in the world fell out of the sky.

The *Nixon* was serving its eleven hundred hands an Easter mess in an unusually calm Bering Sea when Chief Petty Officer Dean Welch burst into flame. He had waved off the ham, being a vegetarian, and took another swig of water while waiting for the yams. The EdenSprings label had shown up clearly in the security recording transmitted through a DIA relay to Naval Operations.

"We should organize collection centers," Dwight Olafson said. "Get the Guard out at fire stations, city hall, with big bins. . . ."

"Not a chance," General Gibson interrupted. "First, if you treat it like it's dangerous and then stockpile it, sabotage is inevitable. You create the need for troops that you don't want to spare."

"But we have to get control of that stuff," Dwight blustered, "and it's everywhere. It's in every refrigerator in the goddamned White House, for God's sake."

"What do you suggest, General?"

"Tampering warning and product recall," he said. "Warning symptoms are high fever and sudden death. Offer immediate on-site, full-price rebate for every Eden-Springs container. We'll want to follow up on those empty ones, so they have to complete a questionnaire to get paid. Entered right there at the check-out counter, flagged for us. We get some quick baseline demographics cheap."

An hour later FDA issued a tampering warning and recall against all EdenSprings bottled waters. None of the leadership of the Children of Eden remained alive to protest this action against their second most profitable export worldwide. The President joined Father Delahunty and a small press cadre for a photo-op mass in the Camp David chapel. That was where she heard of the death of Speaker of the House Dell X.

"Burned to death at a barbeque on the Carolina coast," Advisor said through her earpiece. "State is being briefed now, and will remain under cover at Langley."

"Mike Mandell," she said.

"Yes, Ma'am," Advisor said. "Next in line."

Claudia O'Connor rapped her knuckles on the table.

"Swear Mike Mandell in as Vice," she said. "Announce new State at check-in one hour from now. I'm asking Cady, then Root. Get Mandell for me; I'll be in Communications."

*Pestilence will walk the earth
and many will denounce
the great gods,
form packs of unbelievers
causing illness to descend
with even greater fury
on the heads
of the afflicted Maya.*

—Chilam Balam
    (translated by
    Christopher Sawyer-Laucanno)

# 22

RICARDO KAX LED the only survivors of his village out of the dark jungle to the road that would take them to the city. Their clothes smelled of burnt meat and hair, and everyone except Ricardo was crying. Most of their group had never been to the road before, and the fast traffic so close by and the imminent darkness terrified them almost as much as the horror of their families, and their entire village, burning up before their eyes.

Ricardo looked carefully up and down the road. Maria wailed and ran in a circle, holding her burned arms away from her body. She had held onto her father even as he melted, and only let go when his smoldering body slumped into a stinking hot sludge. Her hair, like Roberto's, was melted to her head in a clump. Ricardo had walked to town many times with his brother, Manuelito, but never alone. The doctor was in town. People who help were in town.

"This way," he said, taking Roberto's hand. "We go this way."

The others followed in a line, stumbling along the roadside and crying. Maria fell down and Daniel, the dark one, tried to help her up. She screamed all the more, and thrashed at him, bloodying his nose.

Ricardo wanted to help her, but it was getting dark and Manuelito told him that the wild pigs came out at dark and the wild pigs would tear them up with their teeth and their sharp little feet.

Many cars passed but none stopped. They were all going the wrong way, anyway. A few honked at them and shook their fists, frightening the younger ones even more. Ricardo saw a flatbed truck coming out of a muddy drive across the highway. He remembered the time he and Roberto and Manuelito rode to the market in the back of such a truck. He stepped out into the middle of the road and waved his blackened arms.

The empty truck's back tires smoked and bounced along the road as it came to a stop in front of him.

"*Mierde, peloto!*" the driver shouted. "You want to die so bad?"

Then he looked closer.

"Mother of Jesus! What happened?"

"Doctor," Ricardo said. "Doctor, *por favor.*"

The driver and his passenger got out to look at them. For one moment, everyone stopped crying.

"Where are you from?" the driver asked.

Ricardo pointed back towards their village, towards the column of smoke flattening above the trees.

"They burn up," he said. "Mama, papa, Manuelito . . . they burn up."

"Was it the army?" the passenger asked, his eyes narrowed. "We don't want no trouble with the army."

"They get sick, burn up," Ricardo said. He pointed towards town. "Doctor, doctor, doctor . . ."

"All right, all right!" the driver said, his hands in the air. "We'll get you all to a doctor. But what happened? People don't just burn up."

Roberto, who never spoke, stepped up and said, "They fall down. The fire come all over them. They burn up."

Ricardo didn't want to waste time talking. Maria and some of the others looked very bad, smelled very bad.

"Doctor, doctor, doctor . . . "

"Okay, okay," the driver said. "Get in and hold on back there; it's a rough ride."

The men helped the worst of the injured into the back of the truck. It took both of them to carry Maria, who no longer screamed but whose skin slid like soap off her wrists and ankles where they picked her up.

The men were both afraid, Ricardo could see that in their wide eyes and their fast talk. The passenger man threw up after lifting Maria into the truck. Ricardo did not want them to be afraid. He wanted them to look at the burns and say, "Hey, foolish one, this is nothing. We will do this and this and this and you can all go home."

But there was no home, and he hadn't been able to keep his uncle's pigs out of what was left of Manuelito.

Through the cab window he saw the men gesturing at each other. They would glance back at him and the others, shake their heads and drive even faster.

Ricardo rocked back and forth and focused on the road unraveling behind them. The back of the truck smelled like the big dead horse that he and Roberto had found one time. It was dark now, and everyone shivered with the wind. Maria shivered so hard that her feet knocked into his back, and she breathed very, very fast and when he turned around she looked at him with only the whites of her eyes.

Ricardo was the first one off the truck when they got to the hospital. He helped his brother, Roberto, whose hands were burned from trying to help Lupita. The passenger man helped, too, while the driver ran inside for the doctor. They left Maria in the truck. She lay limp and quiet, eyes half open, her skinless arms covered with dirt. Already the flies had found them all.

The doctor people came running out of the hospital, some of them pushing the skinny beds on wheels. They led Ricardo and the others inside. Four of them lifted Maria out of the truck and covered her with a sheet.

Everyone was shouting, asking questions, crying or screaming so that Ricardo couldn't understand anything. He stood back and watched them cutting off shirts, poking needles into arms, washing them all down with cold water.

It seemed like everyone was shouting questions at Ricardo.

"Was there a fire?"

"No, no fire."

"A bomb?"

"No, nothing."

"*Gasolina? Un químico*, a chemical?"

"No, no! They get sick, they fall down, they burn up!"

A man in a suit interrupted.

"They're all *deficientes*. You won't get anything from them. Get the army to send somebody out to their village and see what's going on there."

Ricardo held his hands to his ears to stop the noise and he closed his eyes against all the faces shouting in his face.

Suddenly, all of the shouting, crying and screaming stopped. Ricardo opened his eyes and saw the truck driver stagger through the doorway, holding his belly.

"*Por favor*," he said, to no one in particular. "I believe I am sick. I feel . . . "

The truck driver grasped at one of the green curtains between the skinny beds but he couldn't hold on. He sat on the floor with a *thump* and knocked over a tray full of things. All of the air went out of him as he toppled over onto his side, and the air that came out of him smelled like Maria. The hollow-eyed survivors stepped back as the rescue team moved to help him.

"Get him onto this bed!"

"Jesus! He has a great fever. . . . "

"His shirt's on fire!" someone shouted. "Get it off. . . . "

"*Mierde!* It's not his shirt, it's his body. . . . "

"Get some water down here. . . . "

" . . . fire extinguisher . . . "

Then Ricardo looked outside and saw the passenger man slump against the door of his truck. He slapped at himself as he collapsed, steam rising out of his misshapen face. Ricardo bulled his way through the gathering crowd, out the back door and ran to a park across the street where he could finally get some air.

*It is not the healthy who need a physician, but they who are sick.*

—JESUS

FATHER FREE ACCOMPANIED Yolanda Rubia through the darkened Restaurante Cuzcatlán, the purifying smell of bleach wafting around them like cheap incense. The restaurant belonged to the *Todos Santos Cooperativa* that Father Free had started when he finished his tenure at the academy. In the success of the *cooperativa* he celebrated the modicum of earthly pride that he permitted himself. A handful of hard-working people had turned several abandoned waterfront buildings into livelihood for more than a hundred. Besides Restaurante Cuzcatlán and its private bar, their holdings included a small vegetable and chicken farm on the outskirts of the city, a fishing boat, two tour boats, a carpentry shop, a mechanic's shop and a guesthouse. The idea and organization were Father Free's. The silent startup money was Yolanda Rubia's.

Father Free called the superprivate bar the ''National Security Alumni Club,'' but the ex-agents who frequented the place called it ''Spook's Bar and Grill.''

''We have heard nothing for hours, Father,'' Yolanda was saying. ''I am thinking perhaps it is the equipment.''

They left the restaurant by a secret door in the back and

hurried behind the freshly painted building to a drab three-story structure of metal and wood next door. The low-tide smell of the harbor mixed iodine and seaweed with the inevitable smell of the death that high tide leaves behind. Sometimes, when the world was too much for him, Father Free slept in the office behind the bar where he could be lulled to sleep by the *slap-slap* of waves and the *clink-clink* of rigging against masts. Tonight, if he slept at all, would be such a night.

Yolanda pressed a key on her Sidekick, and a lock *snicked* open. Father Free pushed the door aside and Yolanda secured it after them.

"It's not the equipment," Father Free said. "It's El Oso. He has his own agenda. It was a mistake to trust him with an Agency mission."

"You have never liked him, Father. His team is our best, and they were a half-kilometer from the target when we needed them. Could it be that even judgment such as yours can be colored?"

"Perhaps," he admitted. "Even priests are human."

He could not tell her how strongly he was reminded of this truth as he followed her lithe form up the stairs to the bar. Father Free was fifty years old, and he had never experienced sex with a woman. Or with a man, for that matter, but it was the occasional woman who had him burning under his collar in his youth. Now, when he thought of it at all, he studied the matter more out of a scientific curiosity than anything else. There was never lack of opportunity; many women in his life had made that clear. But he had not fallen, would not fall, which made sex one less threat that he had to face in a dangerous country in a dangerous time.

And the danger was real. President García's government was of the type that disapproved of the poor getting a hand up. García and his kind were more inclined to step on their fingers. From the center of the city, near the U.S. Embassy, came the *pop-pop-pop* of small-arms fire to punctuate this point.

The darkened bar, too, smelled of bleach. He could make out the legs of chairs sticking up like dead animals atop the tables. He drew a cold, dark beer from the tap for each of them. They clinked their glasses and stood, looking into each other's eyes, as they sipped off the top. Yolanda was one of the few women who would meet and hold a priest's gaze. There were women who would flirt with a priest, tempt him out of his cassock more as a trophy than a man. Yolanda was not one of these.

"A good batch," he remarked, savoring the astringent aftertaste of the *cooperativa's* fine hops. "Perhaps we should attempt to improve the sacramental wine. Every priest in Central America would be profoundly grateful."

Yolanda laughed.

"Father, you're always thinking. You should have been in business."

"I am in business," he said. "My Father's business. But I see no reason for the people to suffer while they prepare themselves for Glory."

A pair of shadows moved behind the bar's huge mirror, and a sudden shaft of light filled a rectangle of wall.

"There you are," a woman's voice said. "We were worried."

"A busy time," Father Free said with a sigh, and set down his glass. "Now, let's have a look at that machine."

*I am quite sure you all see the lesson learned here. It is very simple. It is that all of you must have strong hearts.*

—HYEMEYOHSTS STORM,
SEVEN ARROWS

# 24

HARRY TOLEDO SLIPPED out of the trap door at the top of his closet and into an attic stairwell. The Defense Intelligence Agency's security had done an electronic sweep of the Casa Canadá compound, but they had not found this escape route that old Mr. Marcoe had built into the house and outbuildings.

Before Costa Brava, before Quebec, the old Frenchman who built the place had grown up in French Indochina, which became Vietnam. His family had been trapped and slaughtered in their own house on the outskirts of Dien Bien Phu. Mr. Marcoe attended a small Catholic school in Saigon, and a sympathetic Vietnamese nun got him onto a plane to Canada. The old-timer built escape routes into every building he owned, and named his small coffee farm after the country that took him in.

*Now the DIA and their goons won't even let him on the place.*

They'd moved the Marcoes and the *campesino* families to a tent encampment on the perimeter of the farm.

Harry worked his way up the steep, narrow stair in a darkness so black that his excellent night vision was no help at all. Two latches at the top released a slab of roof. Harry slid it back and was greeted with a gust of cold air and a dazzle of stars. He pulled himself up and over the edge, onto the rooftop. His silhouette was swallowed by a false gable to his mother's bedroom.

After nearly twenty-four hours at the terminals Harry didn't feel the least bit sleepy, but he did feel a whole lot trapped.

*At least I'm trapped at home; that's an improvement,* he thought. *Marte Chang's right. If you can't sprint to freedom, take what steps you can.*

He squatted low and still in the shadow, and listened for night-calls in the coffee trees. Nothing. So many patrols secured the plantation that even the birds and small animals were lying low. Harry wondered how he could get to see Marte Chang again.

Harry really liked Marte Chang. She listened to him when he simply needed to jabber, and she made sense of the jabber. He liked the sound her long, black hair made when it moved across itself. Harry reminded himself that a lot more fish got collared in this net than just himself and Marte Chang.

*Mom, Dad, Sonja and Nancy Bartlett, Colonel Scholz and Sergeant Trethewey. . . .*

His mother was Liaison Officer between the U.S. and Costa Bravan diplomatic corps. With a bombed-out embassy, a two-day civil war and the resignation of a president in the works, Grace Toledo had her hands full. He saw her for a few moments when they were released at the airport, and she looked okay. She took the clone news pretty hard, but then, so did he.

*She isn't the specimen under the microscope, either.*

Harry stepped out to the edge of the roof, careful not to lean across the plane of the Watchdog's alarm. Holobursts and traditional fireworks bleached out the stars over La Libertad as the confederation celebrated the announcement of President García's flight from the country. Harry suspected that a few of the blazes against the sky were not celebration, but evidence of the growing religious war between Catholics and Gardeners.

The U.S. Embassy sent up a traditional Stars-and-Stripes volley that lit up the sky from ten klicks away, then a follow-up holo of the Costa Bravan flag flickered against the thick, black smoke. Harry caught a whiff of burning rubber and diesel on the gunpowder wind.

"Hello, kid."

Harry started at the voice in his ear, then froze when he felt the zapper at his neck.

A chuckle at his other ear. A second voice said, "Well, he's a cool one, I'll give him that."

"It's okay, kid," the first one said, with a pat on his back. "We know who you are."

The zapper was gone. Another pat on the back.

"This here's The Druid, kid. Don't matter if it's dark, you can't see him anyhow. He a Stealthman. C'mon, let's watch the show."

Harry recognized that voice—it was Joe Clyde, the SEAL medic who'd dug his dad out of the mud below ViraVax and kept him alive.

Two dark shapes made holes in the fireworks as they walked with him to three lounge chairs set up along the edge of the roof. A cacophony of music and cheer rode the cooksmoke up from the *campesino* encampment at the perimeter.

"I do love to see people happy," Clyde said. "Here, kid, have this one."

Clyde sat in one chair and tapped the arm of the next one. Harry smelled fresh coffee—good coffee, not that boiled slop that they brought over from the embassy cafeteria. It was ironic that he lived on a coffee plantation and had to drink instant from town. The Marcoes had sold every ounce of this year's crop before Nancy and Sonja Bartlett bought the place.

Clyde turned to Harry.

"So what about you?" he asked. "You're sixteen years old, got locked up naked with a girl who's a ten-point-five and you ain't smiling. I don't get it.''

Harry jerked a thumb towards the *fiesta* fireworks in the distance.

"I'm sixteen years old, and this is the third time I've seen those fireworks. You're down here on a gig. I *live* here. Every time they say it's for freedom, and every time things just get worse.''

The Druid handed Harry a cup of coffee.

"For them, maybe," Clyde said, "but not for you. Even with the trouble with your dad, your life . . . ''

"My life is over," Harry said. "Sonja's, too. We're bugs in a jar, Joe, for the rest of our lives. At best, we'll be studied in the same facility so we'll at least see each other. And maybe Ms. Chang will do the studying. With luck, they won't peel us apart muscle by muscle. And you're the lid on the jar, right? Joe?''

"That's being a little hard, kid. . . . ''

"Then why don't you just stroll me out the front gate and down the road to the bus depot?''

Clyde shook his head.

"You a real party-pooper, kid.''

Harry took in the fireworks, car horns, bonfires across the slopes of the volcano Izalco.

"You ain't seen nothing yet, Joe," he said.

He set his unsipped coffee down and walked back to the rooftop hatch.

"Whatever you're planning," Joe hollered after him, "don't pull it on my watch!''

Harry returned to his room on the first floor the same way he went up.

*No use waking up the whole house,* he thought. *As though anybody could sleep.*

He slipped out his bedroom window, found the ladder that the two SEALs used to get to the rooftop, and quietly laid it on its side before climbing back into his room. They couldn't unlatch the hatch from the outside to get in through the attic, but they'd think of something. That was what they were trained for. Harry couldn't escape Joe and

The Druid yet, but if they weren't going to help he could make himself a pain in the ass.

Harry decided to get back to the terminals and see what's cooking with Marte Chang. All of the equipment that the Agency could muster was set up in the living room and front parlor. Both Nancy Bartlett and Grace Toledo had brought Litespeeds and access boxes from the embassy. Harry had his own, now cabled through to theirs. It hadn't made much difference; they blocked every move he made to send data out to the web.

The primitive air-conditioning only serviced these two rooms and the kitchen, and it couldn't keep up. Yellow pine walls beaded sweat to match the worried, scurrying humans whose vacant eyes betrayed an almost universal hopelessness. Security outnumbered residents by three to one, but at least a few of them knew the hardware and made themselves useful. Harry hoped that one of the cables they were laying would be a mistake that would get him a line out.

Two hand-lettered signs taped beside the open doorway indicated that someone retained a bit of humor in the face of the inevitable: "Mitochondria Manor" and "Deathbug Suite." This place was definitely not a home anymore, and he wondered whether it would ever be a home again. Harry couldn't bring himself to jump back into the breach just yet.

Sonja Bartlett's room was down the hall at the opposite end of the house from Harry's. It was late, but time didn't mean what it used to to any of them, and he was sure she was awake down there. She'd been locking herself in, not talking and not eating.

He soft-stepped down the hallway and saw Sonja's door ajar. Inside he glimpsed the ever-present console and the unlit peel-and-peek staring down at him from the wall. In the past, she always had the Knuckleheads on the peel playing "Skyborne" full blast. Harry knocked, and when she didn't answer he let himself in.

Sonja was as he'd left her, sitting cross-legged on the floor, staring at a larger-than-life holo display of herself

beside her mother, Nancy. Except for Sonja's cuts and
bruises, they looked identical—twins at different ages—not
just the same shade of blonde hair and blue eyes, but the
precise positioning of eyes and nose, the exact line of jaw,
full lips, tilt of nose. The reason for that, and for his own
twinship to his father, churned his belly with a fast nausea.
He breathed deep and choked it back.

"I can't believe it," Sonja said, without looking at him.

"What?" he asked. "That you two look so much alike?
We knew that even before we had the gory details."

The images vanished at a flick of Sonja's gloveware, but
she continued to stare at the afterglow.

"Not that," she said. "I *know* the biological conse-
quences of . . . cloning. What I don't know is . . . *what am
I?*"

Harry sat next to her, not touching, aware that she was
very spooky. So was Harry. Now, in their own house, their
every word and gesture was monitored, security patrolled
the rooftop and the coffee trees. It was claustrophobic, but
it was bigger than a cell. They were moving in the right
direction.

*So far.*

He had to get some of Sonja's fight back.

"That doesn't seem very productive," he said.

Sonja turned on him in a flash.

"Oh, yes," she hissed, "you're Mr. Productive. You and
Ms. Chang seem to be making great progress on your little
terminals. There's nothing I can do here and this time we
can't run."

"Wanna bet?"

"We're *surrounded*," she said. "And we blabbed to
them about how we got out last time. Damn! Damn! I *hated*
them when we landed here. They gave me a hand down
from the cockpit, then wheeled the plane into that hangar
and locked it up. We were *so stupid*!"

"No," Harry said, "we're not stupid. We're tired, frustrated and scared. Even without this AVA thing, you know,
we've had a pretty hard day. Nobody else in the world

knows what it's like to get the news we got today. Clones! Jesus! And they think everything'll be chill if we just talk to the embassy shrink.''

Sonja leaned against him and he leaned back.

"I can't make sense out of relationships, now," she said. "Think about it. You're a clone of your father, right? Doesn't that make him your twin, but with a head start? Your father is your brother—the rest of the world calls that sort of thing incest."

"I might be my father biologically, but I'm my own person in here." Harry tapped his temple for emphasis. "Except for the augmentations, of course."

"Oh, yes, the augmentations." Sonja hissed the last word out long and hard. "We learn fast, we forget nothing. What else did they pump into us? An 'off' switch? An abort mechanism? Attack mode?"

"That's what all the testing is about. . . . "

"All this testing is about keeping us locked up," she said. "They had their nice little ceremony to thank us for what we did, they gave me a pretty new plane to replace *Mariposa*, and when we landed here they took the prop off the plane, sealed this place off and we haven't seen the light of day since."

Harry knew that Sonja was glum about losing *Mariposa*, her little yellow biplane. Crashing twice in one day would stomp the ego of any pilot. Surviving two crashes in one day should merit *some* strokes. Harry wanted Sonja thinking less about airplanes and clones and more about getting *out*.

*Out to where?* was one of the questions she would ask that he didn't have an answer to, yet.

"I've seen the light of night," Harry said. "I was just sightseeing on the roof."

"If I were up there right now, I'd probably jump off."

"Glad I didn't bring you along."

Harry reached into her wastebasket and pulled out a sheet of paper. He leaned close to her ear and crumpled the paper near their faces as he whispered: "On your airstrip in back—two choppers and a Mongoose."

Sonja looked at him for a moment, her lips pressed into a tight, white line. Then, for the first time in two days, her expression softened. She reached for her own piece of paper, and crumpled it as she whispered back, "You get us there and I'll get us out. Where can we go?"

Harry shrugged.

*One thing at a time.*

"Let's hit the kitchen," he said. "I could use a snack."

*Besides,* he thought, *it's noisy down there. Maybe we can get some planning done.*

*When Phidias saw the claw, would he
ever have known it for a lion's if he had
never seen a lion?*

—LUCIAN

# 25

COLONEL RICO TOLEDO propped himself against the wall
of the embassy's makeshift communications center. Two
canes took the weight off his lacerated feet, but nothing
eased the pain in his butt.

The ambassador's inner office was the last place Rico
would've set up communications, but that was Hodge's
problem, not his. Hodge was flinging orders willy-nilly the
last couple of days, and it looked to Rico that, as usual,
Hodge was more a problem than a solution. He'd hoped to
find Hodge at this hearing so he could rattle his cage. It
wouldn't be the same without a few drinks, but it would
still be fun.

Rico watched Marte Chang, with her back to him, face
a closed-circuit interrogation. It was her turn to testify on
a scramble to the Senate Intelligence Committee. They'd
accepted a taped statement by Rico that he'd made for
Scholz at the hospital, but they wanted Marte Chang choppered in from Casa Canadá to face them in person.

Rico chuckled.

*They know that if they hook up a broadcast unit out
there, Harry will find a way to piggyback on it.*

Rico was working on that very problem himself. He was sure, now, that Spook was their only hope. Everything else had either been royally screwed or stonewalled, and he was getting a bad feeling about the silence in Mexico City.

Rico itched all over from the sweat in his stitches. Condensation dripped from walls of the tight-packed room as the early-morning sun went to work on the plastic windows. The air-conditioner was overwhelmed by the Costa Bravan humidity and the press of Agency officials, witnesses, experts and a one-to-one security cadre. They weren't afraid of anyone getting in. They just didn't want anyone to get out, particularly Marte Chang and the Colonel.

Getting out wouldn't be easy, but it was exactly what the Colonel intended to do. He just couldn't move fast, or far. Even with the canes, he could barely put one foot in front of the other. Moving around helped, but he didn't move much. And when he did move, he exaggerated grimaces of pain.

*—That'll make 'em careless,* he thought.

It was an optimistic thought, his first in a while.

He thought of Harry, and smiled.

*I taught him that elevator shaft escape trick in this very building.*

At least one thing they'd done together turned out all right. He hoped that they'd have to bring Harry into town to testify at the last minute, but he'd heard they, too, would be taped instead. He intended to snatch Harry out of here at the first opportunity, but first he had a couple of favors to call in from Spook and the Peace and Freedom guerrillas.

Major Scholz entered the doorway, caught his gaze and worked her way through the crowd and cables to join him. As she crossed the room, Rico saw everyone perk up at her presence, and greet her as she passed. She left smiles on their faces, and on his own. Why hadn't he noticed that before?

*I didn't dare.*

"Is this the line for butt transplants, Colonel?"

"Scholz, you're merciless. Please, don't ride my ass. Is Harry coming in?"

"No," she said. "It's confirmed. They'll interview him out there at the farm, with Sonja."

"I'd sure like to figure a way to see him."

"Well, Grace forbids us to let you set foot out there, I'm afraid. Something about some punched-out cupboards and a raging asshole."

"That was before all this," he said, waving a hand at the wreckage of the embassy and the frenetic workings of the hollow-eyed staff. "I was drunk then. I was stupid then."

"And now you're smart?"

"Smarter, Scholz. It's a start."

Rico resisted the urge to scratch the gel seal that covered the left side of his face and pretended to focus on the painful sluggishness of the inquiry at hand.

"When *can* I see him?" he whispered.

"When we pour the concrete over ViraVax, at the latest," Scholz said. "This afternoon."

She fingered the top brass button on her jacket.

*Wearing a bug,* he realized. *And she wants me to know.*

"I'll be glad to see *that* show, Major, for three reasons."

The peel-and-peek wall holo showed the jowly, red-nosed face of the Intelligence Committee Chair, the Honorable Frank Myers. His sensitive mike transmitted the rustle of off-screen paperwork from Washington, D.C. to La Libertad, Costa Brava.

"Three reasons?" Scholz asked. "What are they?"

Marte Chang took off her own headset and shrugged a question toward the floor director. She accepted the liaison's headset and nodded her okay.

"Harry, of course," Rico said. "I don't know what I'll say to him, but maybe he's got something to say to me."

"I know for a fact that he does," Scholz said. "What are the other two?"

"ViraVax," the Colonel sighed. "Not that it's anything but symbolic, but I still want to see that place buried."

The Senate Intelligence Committee began its interview of Marte Chang.

"Ms. Chang," Senator Myers said, "you were a virologist for the company known as ViraVax, is that correct?"

Marte Chang, her smooth features wan and her eyes dark-circled, sighed.

"Yes."

Rico was unimpressed by the Intelligence Committee's intelligence except for one thing—they were intelligent enough to interview all survivors by satellite. His tape had rolled first, and Marte Chang's statement would cap things off. It had been a very long night.

Major Scholz whispered so close to his ear that Rico felt the barest flutter of lips.

"What's reason number three?" she asked.

Rico placed his hand over Scholz's top jacket button, the one right between the swell of her breasts.

"You," he whispered back. "I'll get to see you."

Scholz patted his hand, then removed it from her chest. She gave it a squeeze before she let go.

"I'll be in touch," she said.

Rico didn't answer. He watched her walk past his hired security and return the man's salute. The guy was a rent-a-gun who didn't have to salute, but he probably thought she'd be impressed by the move. Scholz turned to the guard on just the right beat.

"Sergeant," she told the guard, "Colonel Toledo will give you the slip. Page my on-call line when he does."

"Yes, Major," the young man said. He blustered on, "I'll see to it that he doesn't give me the slip, Major."

Scholz was already walking away. When the sergeant turned around, Colonel Toledo was gone.

Colonel Toledo intercepted Marte Chang at the side door. Sweat-soaked security guards waited impatiently to take her back to quarters.

"They're going to study the kids," he said. "Whisper says they're shipping them to the States in a day or two."

Marte shook her head.

"That's the least of my worries. And theirs . . . "

"Your work," he interrupted. "It's all theoretical, isn't it? I mean, it's computer work, not tissue work, right?"

Marte hesitated, glanced at their guards, then stepped back inside.

"You're up to something, Colonel," she whispered. "What is it?"

"Insurance," he whispered back. "For all of us. And a way you can continue your work in private."

She raised an eyebrow.

"Trust me," he said. "Have yourself and all your data ready to jump immediately."

"But, *look* at you. How can you travel . . . ?"

"Motivation," he whispered. "Someone *will* turn loose that virus, and you know it."

"Yes," she agreed. "Someone will. But what can I accomplish on the run?"

"Warn the world, help people protect themselves. Until somebody comes up with an antidote, it's the best we can do."

One of their escorts interrupted.

"Colonel . . . ?"

"Shut up, soldier," Colonel Toledo ordered. "Step outside and give us some privacy. I'll let you know when I'm going to escape."

The young sergeant backed away, his face a pale blur.

"The recipe is one thing," Marte reminded him. "Manufacture and distribution on a worldwide scale is another. How . . . ?"

"You can't do it here, either," he said. "We take one problem at a time. Like the flight attendant says, 'In case of loss of cabin pressure, place your own oxygen mask first.' We're no good to the rest of the world if we're dead."

"Good point."

"Unassailable. Try to get a little sleep. Be ready."

With that Marte Chang hurried out the door, her escort just a pace behind her. Colonel Toledo took less than a minute to give his greenhorn guard his second slip in ten minutes. He left a scrambled message with Rena Scholz via Sidekick, then caught a cab to the harbor in La Libertad. They would find him soon enough, this he knew, but by then arrangements would be made with Spook and there would be nothing they could do to stop him.

*And the smoke of their torment*
*ascends up for ever and ever; and*
*they have no rest day nor night.*

—REVELATIONS

# 26

MAJOR EZRA HODGE carried a duffle of supplies to Pier 9 in La Libertad's filthy harbor and dropped it at the feet of a heavily armed Costa Bravan security detachment. This was regular army, not those Pan-Pacific mercenaries that he'd been forced to hire to cover Casa Canadá. None of the five uniformed faces looked older than twenty, and none smiled.

A corporal reached out his hand and demanded, *"Papeles!"*

Hodge handed over his diplomatic passport, military ID and visa without comment. Martial law had everybody jumpy, and in Hodge's experience it paid to be calm, quiet and to have the right stamps in the right squares. The corporal spat, handed back his papers and waved him through without a salute. Just days ago Hodge might have had this kid busted so low that sewage treatment would look like good duty, but today he just smiled and nodded as he passed.

*They'll be dead in a day or two,* he thought. *What does it matter?*

Hodge activated the security gate with his Agency card.

184

A lot of other people had the same idea—the crowded harbor was the site of frantic activity as several hundred people pressed against the fence and gates, coveting the forbidden boats inside. The chosen few who had the right rank or the right papers busied themselves making their boats ready for open water. These vessels ranged from rowboats to forty-meter yachts. Hodge himself stopped at the *Kamui*, a fifteen-meter schooner that the DEA used for sting operations and the DIA used for entertaining dignitaries. He unlocked the cabin and tossed his duffle inside.

The boat was spacious and comfortable, much nicer than his bachelor apartment in Zone Four. It had a double bed and toilet fore and aft, as well as fold-down bunk space for six more people. The cabin smelled of stale beer and mold. He cracked a pair of portholes and mopped his sweaty brow on his sleeve.

Before doing anything else, Hodge opened his antidote kit, removed the vacuum-sealed injector and unwrapped its rice-paper cover. The message inside read:

*All nations shall come and worship before thee; for thy judgments are made manifest.*

He unfastened his pants and slipped them down to get at his hefty thigh.

*One shot to go.*

Hodge swallowed the cherry-flavored paper and positioned the injector over the thickest part of his thigh. It hair-triggered, and startled him so that half of the antidote sprayed onto the deck.

*More than half!*

The Angel assured him that even one drop in his body was plenty. Still, this GenoVax hit the victims' bodies like a dirty nuke—what if this antidote didn't have a chance to diffuse? Would chunks of him—whole limbs and organs—rot in place in a matter of seconds? He had a sudden vision of himself as a modern leper, forever slinking from doorway to doorway in the cover of darkness.

*As though there would be anyone alive to see.*

Rena Scholz would be alive, and she would see. Hodge

eyed the spare kit, the one he saved for Rena Scholz. He
could make up the difference by splitting a shot with her.
She was playing the whore to Toledo now. The part was
unlike her, but she played it superbly.

*She keeps him talking,* he reassured himself. *It's busi-*
*ness.*

That's what the spook business had in common with
whores and journalists. Hodge smeared the evaporating antidote into the teak with his boot and forced his gaze from
the spare kit.

*I'll get Solaris to loosen up the quarantine,* he thought.
*Then at least she won't be paired with Toledo all the time.*

Hodge had seen familiarity breed before, in the liaisons
between his coworkers. Some of those fornicators and adul-
terers were Gardeners, and he would be happy to watch
these hypocrites burn in the flash of the sword.

Meanwhile, Scholz, Solaris and the rest of them pursued
their useless gesture of cementing a cap onto every access
to ViraVax. It saddened him, in a way, because now he had
to admit that the Angel was truly gone, and the handle of
Flaming Sword snugged firmly in his own grip. And he
would ride out the storm, comfortable and secure offshore
aboard *Kamui*. A few thousand million rotting bodies was
going to make terra firma pretty unattractive for a while.

"Compost for the Garden of Eden," Mishwe had told
him, nonplussed.

Hodge's drive through the city to the harbor had revealed
the glittering edge of Flaming Sword. Dozens of fires raged
unfought, including two hospitals and the Jesuit university
on the hill overlooking the embassy. This last sight gave
him great pleasure. The Jesuits were the Marine Corps of
the papists, and their deaths would be occasion for much
despair among his enemies.

He would have to rescue Rena Scholz soon; already the
streets were clogged with roadblocks, patrols, abandoned
cars and buses. Command was breaking down; he had seen
one soldier leave his station to hijack a car at gunpoint,

while an entire patrol carried armloads of electronics out of a broken storefront.

*I'd better have her back here before those communion wafers kick in from Easter Mass.*

Hodge thought about moving *Kamui* upcoast, in case the mob at the fence broke through, but then realized he would have no way to get to Rena Scholz. He had been out on the boat twice before, with a hired crew, and he knew nothing about sailing. But he knew navigation, and he was confident that he could handle the boat well under power. The fuel gauge showed both tanks of diesel full, and he had plenty of propane.

Hodge started the propane freezer and stocked it from his duffle. The cabinets and stowage already held enough sealed goods to keep four people fed for months. Fishing gear was in place and in good condition.

He hurried topside and topped off his freshwater tanks, then locked up and rehearsed his approach to Scholz as he negotiated the difficult trip back through the tormented city to Casa Canadá.

*Whose sins you shall forgive, they are forgiven them; and whose sins you shall retain, they are retained.*

—JESUS

# 27

GRACE TOLEDO KNELT beside a trembling Nancy Bartlett in the open-air church of Santa Ana. Grace tried to recapture some of the spiritual calm that she remembered from her Catholic girlhood. This was a difficult enough chore with the horrors of the past few days eating at her. She had not made her Easter duty in years, but since her life was crumbling around her she was willing to try anything for hope. Spiritual focus was hard when she shared the kneeler with Nancy Bartlett, who was a bundle of tics and tremblings. Nancy's condition gave Grace Toledo one more reason to hate her ex-husband, and she did so knowing full well that hatred had no place in the house of God.

Father Free, on loan from the Archbishop's office, presided over this unusually solemn Easter Mass. Father Free had been a friend of her ex-husband's for over twenty years, and the ill feelings she held towards Rico spilled over to include Father Free. Besides, she was divorced, and this church no longer welcomed her to its bosom.

Grace was as proud of her friend Nancy as she was hateful of her ex-husband. Nancy's suppressed memories had burst through in a rush, triggered by the kidnappings and the security camera replays of all those burning bodies out at ViraVax. After being sedated into a night's sleep, a very shaky Nancy Bartlett had ridden the embassy limo with Grace to greet their children as they were released from their Isolettes. Grace's pallor and waves of trembling did not stop her from a loving reunion with Sonja, whom she had borne and raised as a daughter but knew now as her double, her clone, her beautiful unauthorized self.

Grace agreed with Nancy that the children did not need to know the truth about Red Bartlett's death; they were burdened with enough emotional garbage already. But Grace was sorely burdened, and hateful, and completely unforgiving. She avoided glancing up at the wafer as the Sanctus bells rang in the Great Mystery.

Grace's reverie was broken once again by the scream of sirens outside on Camino Esperanza.

*Something big must be up,* she thought. *They've been doing that all morning.*

The revelations about ViraVax had triggered a civil war between the Catholics and the Children of Eden, a two-day bloodbath that she hoped would resolve now that García had resigned. The embassy expected trouble, since the interim government hadn't had time to secure itself and there was some question about the loyalty of the military. Fires burned throughout La Libertad, but they burned the heaviest in the outlying districts, the Gardener districts. All the whispers said that the Catholic underground was getting even for twenty years of genetic manipulation at the hands of the Children of Eden. Grace looked around at the fearful crowd packing the board-and-batten church, and hoped that it wasn't so.

*If not us, then who?*

Ambassador Simpson told her that the Gardeners were burning the Reichstag, setting fire to their own to whip the survivors into a rage against the Catholics. Much as she hated the Gardeners, she refused to believe that anyone would burn their own families in their beds as a political ploy.

Tapes of the ViraVax Meltdowns had been bled off the web and played for nearly twelve hours on every screen in the country, and across the world. Another whisper claimed that the Innocents had been a ViraVax engineering project, and that one made sense. No Gardeners birthed Down's syndrome children, yet they were eager to take them all in.

In Costa Brava, most Catholic couples had recently come up sterile. Nobody doubted, now, the perpetrator of that curse. Dozens of Gardener homes for the *deficientes* went up in flames overnight, and Grace Toledo prayed for the poor, frightened Innocents who died there. Some said it was a well-coordinated firebombing, but no one had stepped forward to take the credit. Firefighting response had been suspiciously slow, in many cases nonexistent. Most of the firefighters were Catholic.

Grace bowed her head at the Sanctus bell that startled Nancy Bartlett. Grace had been a political Catholic, a check mark on the census to challenge the rising tide of the Gardeners. Today, she wished for more, and regretted that she could not receive communion with the rest of the faithful even though the priest dispensed a general absolution to his congregation. Though faithful in her way, she was divorced, and the sacrament of penance did not cover divorce. That most intimate bond with the church was closed to her now.

The time came for communion, and Nancy Bartlett whispered, "Come up with me. God knows what's in your heart."

Grace smiled and whispered back, "God knows what's in my heart, so I don't have to go."

"No," she insisted, "you come, too."

Nancy took Grace's hand and led her through the benches to the makeshift communion rail. A new calm seemed to wash over Nancy as she knelt before the picnic-table altar. The people of Santa Ana had no way of knowing that Grace was divorced, excommunicated, but Father Free would know. How could she bear the shame when he passed her by or turned her away?

Before she knew it, he stood over her with the wafer. He smiled warmly, nodded, and offered her the host. She opened her mouth for an old-fashioned communion, and he placed the wafer on her tongue with a blessing and a "Body of Christ, Amen," in English. While she didn't necessarily feel holier, she felt better about Father Free, and resolved to have a long talk with him as soon as this mess blew over.

She followed Nancy Bartlett back to their seats and knelt beside Nancy for a moment in silent reflection. Nancy Bartlett's nerve-wracked body was still for the first time all day. Presently she sighed, crossed herself and patted Grace's arm.

"Let's go bury those bastards," she whispered.

Grace choked back a laugh, and followed Nancy Bartlett out to the beat-up Lada taxicab that they shared for city driving. She would have to hurry if they were going to catch a flight out to ViraVax; the concrete pour was already started. The badly rusted car looked hopeless, but it fired up every day at the turn of an old-fashioned key.

*Kind of like me,* she mused, *except it's been a while since I had anybody's key in my lock.*

The old cab slewed in the gravel as Grace gunned it east, towards the Jaguar Mountains. The day was plenty hot, and she was glad the sun was behind them. She vowed to buy a real car with air-conditioning first thing, but she had to admit she enjoyed the anonymity of the cab.

"It's like a tomb out here," Nancy remarked. "I've never seen it so quiet."

Sirens continued in the distance, in the heart of the city, but it was true; there was little traffic out here on Camino Ezperanza. Columns of black smoke formed an ominous cap over the city, and at Avenida Alcaine Grace saw fire-fighters hosing down a burning ambulance that had crashed through the front of a shoe store.

"No shooting and no roadblocks," she said.

"Thank God for small favors."

Nancy Bartlett clutched the dashboard with both hands,

her eyes wide and fixed straight ahead.

"Did you see them?" Nancy asked.

"See who?"

"The two bodies beside that ambulance," Nancy said.
"They were . . . they were *melting*."

"No," Grace said, and patted her friend's arm. "No, I
didn't see them."

And she hoped to God that Nancy Bartlett didn't see
them, either. She hoped against hope that it was stress, hal-
lucination, lack of sleep. They drove the rutted back roads
in silence towards Casa Canadá, neither of them speaking.

They missed the last chopper out to ViraVax, and Grace
was relieved. She had wanted to see the place sealed under
a concrete slab, but she did not want to face her ex-husband
out there. What she really wanted, in spite of the heat and
humidity, was a long, hot bath. And time to think about
what it meant to bear a child that wasn't her child, but a
clone of her ex-husband.

*What will happen to Harry?* she wondered, in anguish.
*Will I have to hate him, too?*

The Pan-Pacific guards wouldn't let her enter Casa Canadá, so she let Nancy Bartlett off at the gate and watched
her shuffle and jitter her way up to the house. One tire
rubbed a fender as Grace turned the car around and headed
towards the city, and the luxury of a long, hot bath.

*A fast, busy spirit is undesirable . . . when your opponent is hurrying recklessly, you must act contrarily and keep calm.*

—MIYAMOTO MUSASHI

# 28

HARRY TOLEDO HELPED pull a tarp tight over the last pour of fresh concrete.

"Tack that stake in and we've got it," Sergeant Trethewey said. "I'll wet it down good so the mud won't crack."

Harry hammered the tent stake through the grommet in the tarp and stepped back to let another water tanker through. His part of the day's work had been intended to be more ritual than real, but Harry had worked himself hard. He had to know what his body could do, because he wanted out and he wanted out *now*.

A very nervous, very deferential Solaris offered him the first chopper ride to the site, and Harry took it. He was glad to work outside for a change, even under Costa Brava's tyrant sun. Besides, Scholz told him there was an outside chance that his dad would be there, and Marte Chang. He had some things to say to his dad that he'd prefer to say in private, and there was no privacy at Casa Canadá.

The squad from the Corps of Engineers was a young one, the oldest being twenty-two, and they all showed the dry, flush faces of heat exhaustion. Harry might be a few years

younger, but he had lived all of his fifteen and a half years
in Costa Brava's heat and humidity. Besides, he had
something personal at stake, and he would do whatever it
took to see the horrors of ViraVax entombed forever. He
brushed his sweaty brown hair out of his eyes and watched
the last of the cement trucks pour its load into the access
shaft up at the dam.

*In two days they punched in a road, commandeered
every cement truck in northern Costa Brava and buried the
Double-Vee,* he thought. *Why can't the government work
this way every day?*

"Boys will be boys. Always playing in the mud."

Sonja's voice behind him was huskier than usual, and
Harry guessed that she'd been crying again. When he
turned around, she was squinting at him in that way that
said, "Who is this person, really?"

Both of them had plenty of reason to wonder. Next to
the Meltdown virus, their mystery genetics was the hottest
topic of conversation among the embassy crowd. He did
not feel the magnetism that he used to feel when their gazes
met. He felt a little leap of fear, instead, and saw that she
felt it, too.

*Are we biological time bombs?* he wondered. *Like those
Innocents?*

Hundreds of Innocents and dozens of missionaries had
died on this spot, melting into sludge before his eyes. Besides Sonja, only three other people knew how that felt—
his father, Rena Scholz and Marte Chang. The leap in his
heart at the thought of Marte Chang used to be reserved
for thoughts of Sonja. Harry saw a smile on Sonja's lips,
but fear widened her stark blue eyes.

"How is this going to change us?" he asked.

"Subtlety is not your strong suit," Sonja said.

Her gaze held his, searched him. . . .

*For what?*

"No one else could understand what happened here," he
said. "I get really nervous when you're gone. I . . . you're
*part* of me."

"Yes," she said, "we've changed for the closer. At the last, when you were still in school, you frightened me." She hesitated, a blush coming to her cheeks. "What was happening to you at home frightened me, so I stayed away. So did my mother and father. We would have grown further apart. I can't imagine that now."

Harry would have cried if she hadn't hugged him in time. *We're almost like a different species*, Harry thought.

"We're almost extinct already, and we just got started," he whispered. "We have to stick together."

"Let's play whatever we have to play to get out of here," Sonja whispered, and took his hand. She nodded towards the nearest chopper, beside the mess tent, and they started walking slowly, affecting a casualness that Harry didn't feel.

Major Scholz spoke privately with his father nearby, and helped Rico discreetly as he caned his way into the mess tent from the other side. Harry liked the influence that the major had on his father. He wished that his parents could live happily ever after together, but that was impossible now. He wished them well in their separate lives. ViraVax had removed him from both of his parents in a kind of death, and now, if he escaped with Sonja, he might never see them again.

"Can you get that thing off the ground in less than a minute?" he whispered.

"Probably not," she said. "You'd better think of a distraction; I'll have my hands full."

Harry and Sonja were a half-dozen steps from making their second break in three days when a guard stepped from around the back of the chopper and leaped aboard for some shade.

"Shit!" Sonja hissed.

"It's okay," Harry whispered, and squeezed her hand. "We'll get our chance. Think hideouts, and supplies, and don't leave without me."

Harry let go of Sonja and moved to catch up with his father, but Trenton Solaris stopped him. Solaris had always looked ghost-like to Harry, but now his eyes were dark-circled, sunken, wild as a whipped dog's.

"Harry!" the albino called. "One moment, please."

The albino walked out of the tentside shade, removed his right glove, then reached out into the sunlight to shake Harry's hand.

"Congratulations again, Harry," he said. "Your performance was first-class. Your country is very proud of you."

"Thanks," Harry said. "My father taught me a lot more than I realized. We have our differences, but I'm glad he's alive. I'm glad it worked."

Solaris's gaze shifted away from Harry's, then back. He didn't seem to know what to do, so he shook Harry's hand again. The albino congratulated Sonja, too.

"Give some thought to what you want with your lives," he said. "You both have skills that your country—and your adopted country here—can use. I urge you to consider making a career out of what you do best—learning, and helping others."

"If you mean working for the Agency, I'm not sure I'd care to be in my father's command," Harry said. "I mean, I've learned a lot, and one thing I've learned is to not press my luck."

Solaris laughed.

"I think you would make a better statesman than an agent, Harry," he said. "But I, personally, and the Agency will support you in anything you choose. And we have many, many resources."

Solaris waved a pale hand to indicate the mass of concrete in the middle of a high jungle river valley.

Sonja cleared her throat and said, "I'd like to be part of the Mars colony shot, but with all the trouble in the U.S. it looks like it'll never get off the ground."

"I promise you all of the flight time you want in anything you want," Solaris said, his smile-wrinkles fully deployed. "That's the first step. The rest is up to the politicians. Good politicians."

Solaris winked at Sonja and nodded at Harry.

"You need somebody like him to get their attention. If you do that, the sky's the limit."

Harry's stomach flipped at the thought of Sonja going anywhere without him, but *Mars* . . . ?

She must have read his mind, or at least his expression. Sonja laughed, and took his hand.

"Hey, baby," she said, "wanna be Mayor of Mars?"

"Chill," he said, and laughed. "With you? Anytime."

But Harry knew it was all a sham, a joke, a way to lighten a heavy afternoon. The Agency wasn't going to let them out of its grip, not until they teased out every secret tangled in their genes and their mitochondria.

He loved Sonja, that was true, but it was no longer the blush-cheeked, stammer-tongued infatuation he'd felt for her before. Theirs was the love that bonds two people who have firewalked the holocaust together and survived.

This new drymouth feeling he had for Marte Chang was something else again. They would have to find a way to save Marte, too. For now he would play the Agency's game, but he and Sonja were ready to run, and he hoped they'd get a chance soon.

*We escaped one hellhole*, he reminded himself. *We can get ourselves out of this one.*

Sonja gave his hand a squeeze, cupped her free hand to his ear and whispered, "It'll be okay, Mayor. Have I let you down, yet?"

He swallowed back a wisecrack about her flying.

"Never," he said.

Solaris and his entourage entered the mess tent, which was really just a large tarp stretched over a dozen poles. The conversation among his father, Rena Scholz and Yolanda Rubia was fast and furious until Solaris walked in. Harry eyed the chopper again and the lone, sweltering guard.

"Not yet," Sonja said, reading his intent. "Besides, choppers aren't my strong suit. These other good old boys would just tag along until we put it down, anyway."

"Then let's take a little stroll by the mess tent," Harry said. "The Agency always says that 'Information is Power.' We could use a little of both, right now."

They put on their strolling-lovers act and skirted the outside of the tent. The sides were rolled up to admit a hint of breeze. Sonja's arm around his waist gripped Harry a lot stronger than their act required, and he hoped that didn't mean she was really in love with him. He couldn't take that, right now, and he couldn't take hurting her, either.

"Yolanda's Peace and Freedom team has secured the warehouse," Solaris was saying. His hollow voice had a raw rasp to it. "Another squad of Jesus Rangers jumped into the area, but they don't seem to be a match for the guerrillas."

"Is the shipment intact?" Rico asked.

"You'd know if it wasn't," Solaris said. "Any fighting or accident in the vicinity of that GenoVax threatens us all. That's why it's important to evacuate the downtown area immediately."

Scholz barked a nervous laugh in response.

"Evacuate downtown Mexico City?" she asked. "Without anyone knowing why? Impossible."

"Not so," Solaris said, a trembling index finger striking the air like a lecturer's pointer. "Earthquake Watch issued a warning yesterday for a three-point-five quake near the Zócalo. They say three P.M. tomorrow."

"That's not going to faze anybody in Mexico City," Rico said. His voice sounded raw and painful. "They eat that kind of quake for breakfast."

"Not if it's upgraded to eight-point-five," Solaris said. "And not if Earthquake Watch predicts that it will hit one day after the three-five that they've already predicted."

"What if the three-five is a no-show?" Scholz asked. "And how do you evacuate twenty million people in twenty-four hours?"

"Good questions, Major . . . ah, that reminds me."

Solaris fished around in his pocket and handed something to Rena Scholz.

"My apologies for the lack of ceremony, Lieutenant Colonel Rena Scholz," he said. "Your promotion cleared this morning, and I'm proud to present you with these silver leaves, on behalf of Military Assistance Command Central America and your Commander in Chief. It is too small a token of our appreciation of your excellent service to your country."

The small gathering applauded as Colonel Scholz contemplated the two shiny objects in the palm of her hand. Rico struggled to his feet and leaned heavily on Colonel Scholz as he removed the brass leaves from her collar and replaced them with the silver. Harry found his father's gesture moving.

"Now, *Colonel* Scholz," Solaris said, "to answer your questions. The three-point-five quake is a certainty. Earthquake watch hasn't missed a prediction by over an hour in two years. Second, we focus on evacuating the damage zone around the epicenter—which just happens to lie between my office and the U.S. Embassy, and includes Coyote Warehouse. . . . "

A shrill tone from Solaris's Sidekick shattered the moment. As he listened through the earpiece to the unscrambling message, the albino's complexion remained unreadable until a last-second flush betrayed his anger.

"Trouble?" Rico asked.

Solaris nodded, and the hand that removed his earpiece trembled conspicuously.

"Trouble," he admitted. "Here and Mexico City. Much more than we bargained for. You will reconvene at Casa Canadá, which will be your temporary headquarters, in fifteen minutes."

Solaris turned and tipped his hat to Yolanda.

"Ms. Rubia," he said, "please secure your troops in Mexico City. They refuse to release the shipment to anyone but you. This chopper will lift you to the airport immediately. The sergeant will escort you aboard. We have already initiated the earthquake scenario so that Mexican authorities will clear the immediate area of the warehouse as a precaution."

Yolanda hesitated, but when the armed sergeant stood at her side she threw a quizzical glance at Rico before leaving the tent for the chopper.

When Solaris turned to speak privately with Rico and Colonel Scholz, Harry saw a blankness in the man's eyes, a shutdown of emotion so complete that it could only come from fighting back unbridled fear. And Harry knew for a fact that Solaris did not frighten easily. He did not come to any emotion easily. Harry pressed Sonja closer to hear what more Solaris might have to say.

The Agency veteran spoke in a low voice, and he spoke very quickly.

"I've been recalled to Washington," he said. "I'm delaying that as long as possible. I'm sure you can appreciate why I want to have this matter fully under control before reporting to the President. I'm returning to Mexico City immediately to oversee operations there. The Gardeners' houses here haven't been firebombed. The fires came from the bodies. It seems our friend here at ViraVax managed to taint their ritual water nationwide before he died."

Harry didn't care who knew he was eavesdropping now. He interrupted Solaris's briefing.

"The dead ones we saw at ViraVax, they didn't give it to any of us," he pointed out. "As long as we don't drink that water . . . "

Solaris ignored him.

"We will seal off Casa Canadá for you now," he said. "Expect to be airlifted from there to an emergency shelter within twenty-four hours. Save your questions; we don't have that kind of time."

Harry started to ask about his mother, and all the others working at the embassy compound, but Solaris was already boarding his chopper for liftoff. Two rent-a-guards grabbed Harry and Sonja at the elbows, and guided them silently but firmly towards the chopper that they had hoped would fly them to freedom.

*Outward show is a wonderful per-
verter of reason. And when you are
most sure that the things you are
busy about are worth your pains, it is
then that it cheats you most.*

—MARCUS AURELIUS

# 29

EL OSO AND El Tigre waited at the International gate while
the traitor Yolanda Rubia cleared Mexican customs. El Oso
remained calm; the prospect of killing always rendered him
calm. His hulking, bear-like form moved with deliberation,
and once set into motion it could not be stopped easily. El
Tigre jittered beside him and lit yet another cigarette, the
backs of his hands revealing the stripe-like scars that gave
him his name.

Yolanda Rubia, Comandante of Costa Brava's Peace and
Freedom Brigade, presented herself to the customs officer
in her disarming elegance—gold watch and chain, rings
encrusted with diamonds, a teal jumpsuit of wrinkle-free
silk.

*How many mortars could we buy with that?* El Oso wondered. *How many rifles? How many rounds?*

Yolanda Rubia flashed a bright smile at the officer; he
flashed one back, and with that she was through the line.

"The bitch," El Tigre whispered. "Let's do her now and
teach the rest of those arrogant bastards a lesson."

"She has something to tell us."

"We have the shipment in Coyote Warehouse. We know

it's a new weapon that frightens even the northamericans enough to empty the pink zone with an earthquake alert. Our people are in place. What more do we need?''

''You were a fool once, Tigre,'' El Oso growled, nodding at the scars. ''Don't be a fool again. This weapon could kill us all; that's why we're here and the northamericans aren't. She is here to tell us what it is and how to use it.''

''Then can I do her?''

''Then you can do her. And the rest of them. They're all in bed with the northamericans. They're all whores.''

As Yolanda Rubia stepped through the gate, El Oso manufactured his biggest smile and El Tigre reached for her bag.

''With much pleasure,'' El Oso said, adding a slight bow. ''You have been away too long.''

''It's been a tough time,'' she said. ''But now that García is out of the way, our prospects for the presidency are excellent. For the first time, Costa Brava will be in the hands of the people who love her.''

El Tigre broke out in a coughing fit.

''The car is this way,'' El Oso said, taking her elbow.

He turned to El Tigre. ''Really,'' he said, ''you should quit smoking for good.''

''After this operation,'' El Tigre said. ''I'll take better care of myself after we've disposed of the weapon.''

''It's not exactly a weapon,'' Yolanda said. ''What is the situation now?''

El Oso opened the passenger door to the gray Bushido van and steadied Yolanda with his hand as she stepped in. He and El Tigre scanned the parking lot visually and electronically. El Oso double-checked their Watchdog system to make sure the van hadn't been tampered with while they waited at the terminal. He activated the scrambler on the Watchdog. Any conversation now would be secure. Any call for help would not be heard.

''We took their position this morning, as you know,'' he said. ''The missionaries moved in their pathetic Jesus

Rangers, but they were no match for us. Alfonso says he saw another team drop on the rooftops across the way, but they have made no move. We barricaded ourselves inside, and whoever they are we know they are no match for our snipers, particularly El Tigre. The missionaries are dead, all Rangers dead. El Tigre slipped inside last night before the battle. Their security was terrible and they paid the price. Even the Jesus Rangers were lightly armed. Except, of course, for whatever is in those boxes. They seemed to be waiting for something.''

"Yes," Yolanda said. "Their own Sabbath killed them. They were waiting for orders and reinforcements. Their entire facility in Costa Brava is gone, along with that television preacher, Casey. He was the pope of their church, and it will take them time to reorganize. The northamericans wanted to keep it out of the news, even after we secured this shipment.''

"Shipment of *what*?"

El Tigre had been impatient for the entire twenty years that El Oso had known him. Still, he voiced the question that had nettled El Oso himself for two days.

"Shipment of death," Yolanda whispered. "The man who invented it wanted to kill every human being on the planet.''

El Oso whistled his surprise.

"And this could do it?"

Yolanda nodded.

"Just the slightest fraction could do it," she said. "It is a virus that melts people from their very bones. Our sources tell us that even one virus cannot be permitted to escape, or every human being is lost, no matter what their religion or their politics.''

"And your sources?" El Oso asked. "How do they intend to dispose of this plague?"

"They intend to pour concrete around it, place it in a hole in the center of the desert, encased with a neutron bomb.''

Again, Oso's whistle of surprise. This was deadly stuff indeed.

"But they don't want to be here for the capture."

"No."

El Tigre leaned forward, his lips nearly touching Yolanda's ear.

"Why don't they just burn it where it lies?" he asked. "Are you sure they're not using us merely to capture it for use against us later?"

"They don't burn it because fire makes steam, and some of the virus might escape on the steam before it's burned," she said. "This way, it is killed twice—by the radiation and the explosion."

"Why don't the northamericans just drop their bomb on Coyote Warehouse?" El Oso asked. "Surely Mexico City is expendable."

"That's exactly what they plan to do if we don't succeed," she said.

El Oso drove in silence for a moment, wrestling with this troubling news.

*Bomb Mexico City! Truly, the northamericans were scared shitless!*

He negotiated the roadblocks that kept unauthorized vehicles and looters out of the abandoned downtown corridor. The earthquake alert broadcast by the northamericans was working, to a degree, but it would not work for too much longer.

The diplomatic code broadcast from their Watchdog cleared them all the way to what was left of the National Palace, a short distance from Coyote Warehouse.

"If someone started shooting," El Oso said, "and by accident hit one of these boxes, what happens?"

"Everyone in the room is dead within twenty-four hours. Everyone in the world, within thirty days."

"And the antidote? Where is that?"

"There is none."

El Oso sucked air through his teeth in a wet hiss.

"What kind of fool builds a weapon without a defense?"

"An American fool," Yolanda said, her grim lips cracking a smile. "A Gardener fool. He is now a dead fool."

El Tigre's jitters cranked up to a new level.

"Shit," he hissed. "And I was in there with it. And there was much shooting."

"As there may be again," El Oso said. He was no longer smiling. He turned to Yolanda. "Do you have anything else for us?"

"No," she said, shaking her head. "The northamerican Agency doesn't want a panic, so no one is to know. The strategy is up to you."

"Who will replace García as President of Costa Brava?" El Oso asked. "You?"

"No," Yolanda said, and sighed. "It is as it has been all along. It will be Philip Rubia. I will be Minister of the Interior."

"I see," El Oso said. "You and your rich ex-husband."

He pulled into a rubble-strewn alley off Avenida El Salvador. He edged past three children sleeping in a cardboard carton, stopped the van, shut off the engine, took a deep breath and let it out slowly.

"What are we doing here?" Yolanda asked.

"Giving El Tigre a moment to refresh himself," El Oso said.

He nodded to El Tigre in the mirror, and swifter than it could be said El Tigre pulled Yolanda's head back, slipped a sharpened piece of stiff wire into the outside corner of her right eye and shut off her brain.

El Oso busied himself looting the body of its gold and mopping up the inevitable mess on the seat, regretting only that they had too little time to retrieve certain fillings that later might be worth safe passage to Singapore. El Tigre scattered a fistful of pamphlets over the body, religious pamphlets from the pack of a dead Jesus Ranger lying inside the back door of Coyote Warehouse.

*The more deaths over a thing, the more valuable that thing becomes*, El Tigre thought.

He would have to tell that one to El Oso.

Had El Oso taken the time, he might have noticed the peculiar electronics within one of Yolanda Rubia's teeth. Its battery was her body itself, and because it lay on its face it continued to broadcast her whereabouts for another six hours.

By the time the Agency contracted for a SEAL team, El Oso and El Tigre were barricaded safely inside Coyote Warehouse, refining their new plan to hold the whole world hostage. By the time the SEAL team located its target in Avenida El Salvador, El Tigre had shot the last of the wounded resisters.

El Oso backed in the truckload of earthquake relief that they'd liberated from a Red Cross encampment at the *hipódromo*. They set up watches, sentries and fortifications, including a thick jacketing of cement bags around the pallet of cold cases full of the Devilbug. Then they waited to make the deal of a lifetime, to buy their country back from the traitors who took it from the traitors who took it from their great-grandparents eighty-three years before.

*I will make mine arrows drunk with blood, and my sword shall devour flesh....*

— DEUTERONOMY

# 30

THE ALBINO WAS aboard his Lancer and on approach to Mexico City before he took the call he'd been avoiding from Senator Myers. The senator didn't waste any breath on pleasantries.

"Mr. Solaris, it appears that everything you touch turns to shit."

Solaris sat stiffly in his harness with the video pickup off and didn't respond.

"Are you receiving me, Mr. Solaris?"

"I hear you."

"The committee and the President have agreed that your contract be suspended immediately. You will return here voluntarily for a debriefing tomorrow at oh-eight hundred at Camp David, or I will have you brought here in hand-cuffs. And you will bring with you all records pertinent to ViraVax. Is that clear?"

"Yes, Senator. Perfectly."

"Do you have a problem with that?"

"No, Senator."

The connection ended as the Lancer's wheels scorched the concrete. Solaris didn't ask who would replace him, because that was none of his concern now. Now he would be disgraced, his thirty years of service to his country held up to ridicule, and as scapegoat he would spend the rest of his days in a forgotten corner of some federal prison.

*Shame!* he thought. *They visit shame upon me now, after I kept their hands clean and saved the country a dozen times over!*

He knew it was coming. The nature of bureaucracy is to peck its own to death at the first sign of blood. He had not got so far from the chicken pens of his childhood, after all.

As he choppered to his office from the airport, he passed over the mess at Coyote Warehouse. The entire block was cordoned off by U.S. and Mexican troops, and he saw bodies in the street and on the rooftops. He spoke to no one as he made his way to his office, and he relied on his com alone for a briefing. He could not bear to speak to another human quite yet.

The com showed him the chilling images of the rebel standoff at Coyote Warehouse. Five of the fifty-eight bodies that bloated in the street were rebel comandantes who had tried to reason with their dissident troops. The rest were Jesus Rangers who dropped in a tight formation that accommodated the guerrilla snipers nicely.

Trenton Solaris hoped that this turncoat sniper was not a subcontractor on his own payroll. As though that would make a difference. As though there would be a *later* to worry about.

*Those fools will kill us all!*

The Peace and Freedom faction that held the warehouse now called themselves the Death Brigade. They didn't care who they killed—they knew they would die soon no matter what the outcome. Trenton Solaris had a personal backup plan that would guarantee it, but he prayed to all the gods that he wouldn't have to carry it out. Everything rode on Yolanda Rubia's ability to reason with her people, and her people had proved to be beyond reason. She faced death in the street to do what must be done. Solaris would do the same.

The rebel leaders must have known from the start, as he did, that their elimination was nonnegotiable. Their immediate goal would be to put off that inevitability as long as possible.

From his position in the Agency, Solaris commanded more than two hundred agents, and a tone from his Sidekick mobilized entire divisions. Usually he felt much taller than his one hundred and sixty centimeters, but today he felt small, and weak, and old.

*I wish the Colonel were here.*

Colonel Rico Toledo's recovery in La Libertad was fraught with setbacks. He'd barely had the strength to tape his testimony for the Senate Intelligence Committee.

*ViraVax could have done anything to him when he went in after those kids,* he thought. *They did plenty to him before.*

He had been shocked at the level of betrayal perpetrated upon him by Casey, and Mishwe, and ViraVax. They had worked many projects together over the years: military, health and agricultural projects that had made Solaris the darling of the Department of Defense—and a rich man. He had invested heavily in ViraVax, though he was no Gardener.

Solaris was disgraced already, that was clear. His life was over. The bugs were loose in La Libertad, but a shutdown of the country's airports, ports and highways should contain it there. But this one in Mexico City was the worst. Mexico City was the largest city on the globe, and the center of worldwide travel and commerce. If that virus got loose here, Washington itself would die only three days to a week later. Or so his analysts told him, and his analysts were never wrong.

The lights on his com and on his Sidekick winked insistently, but the albino ignored them.

*In a few days, whatever they want won't matter.*

For a moment he regretted not having children, then in the same breath he was thankful that he wouldn't have to watch them die. The Agency had been his parent and his

child; ViraVax had been his child. The albino had a very
bad feeling about this one.

Trenton Solaris swiveled his chair to face the mural behind him. It was a plasticized carbonite reproduction of the
Maya calendar superimposed upon the Aztec Temple of the
Sun. Hidden behind the swarthy mural, a double-filtered,
triple-glazed window framed the famous Zócalo of Mexico
City. Trenton Solaris thumbed a switch that lifted the mural
with a series of clacks and hums. The Agency's engineers
built the finest filters into this glass for the albino's comfort—still, Solaris squinted under the sinking, unforgiving
eye of the enemy sun.

He blinked his vision clear and surveyed the abandoned
Zócalo—the well-picked rubble of the cathedral, one pre-
carious wall of the National Palace, the restored and un-
shaken temple of Tenochtitlán. Crude barricades protected
the surviving half of a Diego Rivera mural from souvenir-
seekers, and a nun in her habit whirred past on her electric
scooter, skirting debris, her traffic-flag barely mustering a
flap behind her. Earthquake warnings didn't frighten off the
street kids, or the few, like this nun, who tended them.
Solaris donned his shades and sipped his ice water. As always, the Zócalo belonged to the poor, the pigeons and the
tourists. There had been no tourists since Earthquake Watch
issued their doctored warning. Possibly, very soon, there
would be no poor, either.

"The pigeons shall inherit the earth," he muttered.

The great earthquake of '13 had flattened a third of Mexico City and inspired his own mural—a practical piece of
art that shielded his office from the enemy sun, enemy electronics and from the shrapnel that his previous window had
become at the eye of an earthquake. Though the Aztec em-
pire had eclipsed the Maya, Trenton Solaris commissioned
his mural with the Maya calendar foremost—an oblique
testament to his own ancestry. It was an ancestry that he
had spent a lifetime denying, down to his pseudo-Blackpool
accent and his anglicized name.

In a rare gesture, Trenton Solaris drank to the past, because the last-ditch plan that he'd formed in case the virus got loose here ensured that, for himself and a few hundred thousand collaterals, there would be no future. If his personal plan failed, there would be no future for any humans on the face of the planet. He drank to the memory of humans, of humanity, of intellect and poverty and greed. He drank to the inspiring lecture that Marte Chang had given him on cell-mediated immunity. Sometimes, the cell had to die to protect the body.

Solaris debated dying now and avoiding the horror to come, but he could not raise the pistol to his head. He drained the last of his water, instead, and thumbed the mural closed. He reviewed the three most likely scenarios:

In the first, the deadline that he'd imposed on the rebels approaches, the rebels fight to the last man and the virus is released as a side-effect of the fighting.

The second scenario finds the rebels beating his deadline by releasing the virus themselves out of frustration and spite.

His personal option responds to either number one or number two: detonate a neutron device presently siderailed near Coyote Warehouse, atomizing all of the rebels and their vials of virus as well.

It was Solaris who had recommended to the Joint Chiefs that stockpiled devices be planted in the rail yards, freighters and hangars of every major city in the world. Paying freight and storage was much cheaper than building missiles, and much quieter. Solaris had used up every favor he had to get the detonation codes to the devices in his own back yard.

*Better with a bang than a whimper.*

The albino made this decision because none of his analysts' options included the surrender of the Death Brigade with their cache of virus intact. He shuddered at the memory of what had happened at ViraVax.

*And that version of the virus wasn't even communicable,* he thought. *Thank God we put that place in the middle of the jungle.*

He wondered how many other versions were buried under the mud in Costa Brava. And how long they would stay buried. The way things were devolving in Mexico City, it probably wouldn't matter.

The ViraVax satellite clinics in the United States had been fooling around with the water supply for some time, that was now apparent. These new AVAs were puzzle pieces, undetectable until they assembled themselves inside the cell. And then it was too late. Just a few little twists of protein that made the uninoculated very ill, that did not show up on contagion-factor tests because, at first, they weren't contagious.

It was obvious to him, now, how the Children of Eden had taken over towns, cities, whole regions by altering the water supply with one AVA and adapting their people to it with another. Nothing showed up in standard tests. When entire neighborhoods got sick, property became worthless. The Children of Eden bought up whole towns and villages for pennies on the dollar, blaming the "unhealthy lifestyles" of their non-Gardener neighbors as the culprit.

Solaris recalled a stanza from a poem he'd memorized in grammar school:

> "And when it comes to slaughter
> you'll do your work on water
> and you'll lick the bloomin' boots
> of 'im that's got it."

Kipling, another child of colonial days with one foot in two cultures.

He sighed, and continued to ignore the pleading electronics around him.

*And to think I was proud of the project when they came up with that marijuana AVA for the DEA to turn loose!*

He and the Director of the Drug Enforcement Administration had laughed when they saw film of the results: one toke on a joint, and the subjects vomited themselves into exhaustion. At first he was disappointed that it wasn't applicable to opiates or cocaine. Then the scales fell from his eyes and he saw the truth: it *was* applicable to opiates and cocaine. The big payoffs were in the big drugs. Nobody was willing to tamper with the big stuff. Marijuana was, as Colonel Toledo had put it without apologies, "a smoke screen."

Solaris comforted himself with the thought that his motives had always been pure. Everything he did in his career, including ViraVax, had been for the benefit of his country. He had never taken a penny for throwing his weight around; his investments had been legitimate. He saw now that his colleagues in the intelligence community and in Congress saw him not as an altruist or a hero, but as a fool.

Trenton Solaris poured himself another ice water, and this time he added a slice of fresh lime. The citrus mist at the top of the glass refreshed him.

Yes, the whispers coming in from Costa Brava were bad. It was not a major nexus, as Mexico City. The Deathbug worked quickly, and movement in Costa Brava was slowed to a stop right now. But Mexico City was the hub of the world, and the concentrations in that warehouse tremendous. Solaris knew that his life was finished. If this solution required drastic measures, he would have to be the one to take them.

*This bug must not leave this city, or human beings are through!*

Sacrifice for the good of the people was in his blood. Trenton Solaris was now the captain of the great Mayan ball game, and it was the winning captain who got sacrificed to renew the crops. He would have to be strong, now, and merciless. Nothing must stop him from redeeming himself in the eyes of his country.

He stared through his shades at the enemy sun and tried to muster an affection for the heat and for that unfamiliar gift of radiance that he might have to pass on.

> *When your thinking rises above con-*
> *cern for your own welfare, wisdom*
> *which is independent of thought*
> *appears.*
>
> —YAMAMOTO TSUNENORI

# 31

HARRY TOLEDO TRIED to sleep, but after what he'd heard out at ViraVax his mind still wouldn't let him rest. He'd thought the real threat was over, that the Deathbug, what-ever it was, had been buried forever. The embassy shrink had been sympathetic, but sympathy didn't stop the night-mares. And Harry didn't want to take any drugs that might slow him down.

*They rotted, dissolved, burned themselves up.*

All of those things. Now it wasn't just ViraVax, but peo-ple in downtown La Libertad. There was no doubt in his mind that the U.S. would be off limits for any flights from Costa Brava. When the international word got out, there wouldn't be an airport in the world that would let them in.

*And now this thing's behind us!*

Behind, and possibly surrounding. Harry sat up and rubbed his eyes in frustration. Only four people had made it out of ViraVax alive, and Harry was one of them, tossed like a bag of coffee onto the deck of the plane.

*And we're still alive*, he thought.

Marte explained to him that even the most devastating

214

viral pandemics left about twenty percent of the infected population alive.

*But those are natural viruses.*

"This one might be too fast for its own good," Marte had told him. "I hate to say it, but infected people may not have the time to travel far enough to spread it. And the mitochondria is a tougher little critter than Mishwe gave it credit for."

Small comfort to those people who were now a black smudge on the breeze.

This afternoon as they prepared to lift from ViraVax, Harry's father had taken him aside for the one moment they'd been permitted together.

"You see my situation," Rico said, tapping his canes onto the fresh concrete. "Scholz and I are working every angle we can think of, but I might not be able to move fast enough. You get yourself and Sonja out, any way you can. Understood?"

"But what about you, and Mom, and Marte Chang?"

"Help them if you can," he said, "but don't look back if you can't. You're no good to anybody if you stick around and get dead. Scholz and I, we're working on an angle of our own with Spook. We'll try to get everybody out together. But if an early bus comes along, you get on it, understood?"

"But I . . ."

"No heroics here," Rico said. "The important thing is isolation. If you risk yourself, you risk everybody else, too. I saw you make your move on that chopper, and I was rooting for you, believe me."

*At least Mom and Nancy Bartlett made it back from church,* Harry thought. *The whole country's getting pretty wild.*

Harry had lived through several insurrections in Costa Brava, but this one was different. This time the real enemy didn't wear a mask and carry a gun.

Harry lay back down and tried to relax. The recurring movie behind his eyelids always started the same: Marte

Chang's black hair whips the breeze as she runs towards him like she did that day at ViraVax, except this time she melts down and burns like all the rest, her scream and her beautiful brown eyes the last to go.

This he saw nightly in the reverie before sleep, in that gray dusk when his guard was down, just before the twitch. Harry had taken up daydreaming about Ms. Chang, and this new hitch in his nightmare made him think about her even more.

*Marte.*

She'd made him stop calling her "Ms. Chang." The two of them worked night and day to wring out codes from a data cube; then he'd worked day and night unraveling the files that those codes unlocked from hidey-holes throughout the electronic universe. Two days' time seemed like years, and in that time, they met in person once at a debriefing that the Defense Intelligence Agency held at El Canadá for all survivors.

"Witnesses," Marte had said at the meeting.

The briefing officer raised his eyebrows.

"Ms. Chang?"

"A survivor is a victim," she'd said. "I'd prefer to be called a witness. I've *seen* the victims."

Harry and Marte couldn't keep their gazes apart and, while Harry had memorized her face long ago, what attracted him the most about her when she testified was her hands. When she talked, her slender fingers moved to the rhythm of her voice and played out some secret tune on the tabletop in front of her.

So when he thought of her at night he pictured her sensitive hands dancing their subtle semaphore, as though they worked her gloveware or played a small keyboard. And if that got him through the next image of her burning alive, then he'd won the privilege of sleep, and the plane-crash dream.

Harry's real memory of his second plane crash in two days blurred behind the heavy dose of trank that his father had shot into his thigh. He had been conscious, but helpless, when the Mongoose pancaked into a jungle hillside. That awful helplessness scared Harry the most.

Helplessness was not new to Harry Toledo. His father beat him, but not anymore. His mother stuck a pair of scissors into his father's neck one night to stop him, and now the whole *country* knew what happened. Harry needed to be in control, even if it meant doing the wrong thing. That's why he hated flying, something he couldn't explain to Sonja.

*She lives to fly.*

Sonja hadn't been out of her room except for the quick trip to ViraVax since the Agency grounded them and locked up her new plane upon return to Casa Canadá. "For your own protection" was getting to be a stale old lie. Harry thought it was pretty chickenshit himself, but he had to admit it's what he would have done if *he* were in charge. The deathbug had everybody ultra-paranoid, and their own bodies could be secret weapons now, for all they knew.

He and Sonja were the world's only *in utero* clones, and everybody would want a peek and a poke, so he tried to be thankful for the temporary privacy. Harry was sure that, unless they escaped, the two of them would never see privacy again.

The Agency shrink explained that the nightmares always picked up on his fear of helplessness.

"You're vulnerable when you sleep," Dr. Olsen told him. "And in sleep your body goes numb, like it was on the lift pad that day at ViraVax. Like it was when your father beat you."

Each time the dream began the same way. A horde of Innocents, the *deficientes* that ViraVax manufactured for themselves, surrounds the Mongoose. Harry is strapped inside, but through the magic of dream he can see Innocents all around the plane. They all want out of ViraVax. They're reaching towards Harry and crying as the engines wind up, but Harry's paralyzed. Harry can see the back of a bald head at the controls. Not Sonja. It's the dzee that kidnapped them, that virologist who "made" them, Dajaj Mishwe!

Harry tries to shout, to get Mishwe to shut down the engines, but Mishwe laughs and revs them higher, until the Mongoose trembles and its landing gear tapdances in place. Gravel ricochets off the fuselage as the Innocents melt from their bones amid screams and that rotten, burnt-hair smell. Harry's dream paralyzes him as they writhe beneath the wings, slopping their dead sludge over the concrete. As always, they flicker with the clean blue flame of death as the Mongoose lifts off.

Harry didn't feel like going through the whole program tonight. He kicked off his sweaty sheet and gave up trying to sleep.

*Maybe tomorrow I'll take Dr. Olsen up on that sleeping pill,* he thought. *If we're still here tomorrow. If there's a Doctor Olsen tomorrow.*

His experience at ViraVax had soured him on any kind of medication, particularly the kind that made him helpless. And it was nearly impossible for him to think about the future.

He slipped out of bed quietly, though the household had been designated a communications center and the noise level was uncharacteristically high. Still, he would leave the few sleepers nearby to whatever rest they could find. Each of them: Harry, Sonja, Sonja's mom, Harry's mom— and the other survivors in La Libertad—had lived through hell, and it wasn't over yet. The faint electrical switching of muffled security tracks patrolling the farm roads was reminder enough. But Marte Chang had discovered some disturbing possibilities in her search for what ViraVax had done to Harry, his father and Sonja Bartlett. The Agency suspected something, too, because they all were under some kind of house arrest, though even Colonel Scholz denied it.

*Marte was right; we're witnesses, not survivors. The survival part isn't over yet.*

Harry strapped on his Mosquitex, pulled on a shirt and shorts, then slipped into the shadows of a banana tree outside his bedroom.

Three meteors carved their silent streaks through the

warm Costa Bravan night. He wished that Marte Chang were here to see them with him. A couple of times he'd caught himself daydreaming about Ms. Chang, but he always stopped himself because all dreams these days ended the same: the ground racing to meet him, or her beautiful face melting from its bones. The Agency had sequestered her in La Libertad, so he'd been working with her by satlink, and even *that* was exciting. But he wanted to hear the *hiss* of her clean black hair shifting across itself and he wanted to . . .

"Pilot to navigator," a voice whispered. "Where the hell are we?"

Harry spun around.

"Mom!" he said, his heart racing. "You scared the hell out of me!"

Grace Toledo stepped out of the hedge of bougainvillea that skirted his room and gave Harry a hug. She wore shorts and a T-shirt, too, and in spite of the warm night her skin felt cool. A slight dampness slicked her cheeks. She had been shorter than Harry for a couple of years, now, but tonight she felt small, frail.

"I like it when you call me 'Mom,' " she said.

"You *are* my mom."

Grace let go the hug and patted his arm. Harry's night vision was one of his augmentations, one more proof of his tampered genetics, and he saw the sad shake of her head.

"ViraVax even took *that* away from me," she said. "Their Artificial Viral Agents destroyed your father, our marriage, and now . . . "

"You carried me for nine months, Mom," he said. "You've taken good care of me for fifteen years. And you saved my life when Dad . . . you know. What does a little hitch in genetics mean after all that?"

She sniffed, fumbled for a tissue and blotted her nose.

"It means that the part of you that's supposed to be *me* isn't," she said. "I know that's small of me, and I know I love you no matter what genetic stew they gave you. But I still feel *robbed*, you know?"

"Burgled," Harry corrected. "Robbed means they did it face to face."

"What*ever*!"

They stood, side by side, listening to the night sounds swell to fill their silence. Harry heard the electric tracks of the patrols as they crisscrossed the gravel roadways of the coffee farm around them. The coffee workers' housing had been taken over by security, and he heard the *slap* of playing cards down there, and the occasional laughter.

Patrols had tripled since the Archbishop's office in La Libertad leaked a few of the terrible facts about ViraVax, then tripled again when the Deathbug hit the Gardeners in some kind of suicide pact. Only this suicide was designed to take everybody else with them. They had engineered the sterility of millions throughout the world, focusing on Catholics, Mormons and Muslims. They had manipulated tens of thousands into giving birth to Down's syndrome babies, then supplied "homes" for the children through their "Down's-Up" program. These "homes" provided ViraVax with a malleable labor force, human stock for experimentation and plenty of organs for transplant. And now, a vector for horror and death.

"What are you doing with that Chang woman?"

Harry had known that his mother would ask this.

"Helping her on the web," he said. "She found evidence that ViraVax developed several versions of the Meltdown virus. It could be dormant in any one of us that they tinkered with—including you. I want to know what I'm made of before . . . "

Grace interrupted, "What do you mean, including me? I've never even been to that facility."

Harry could tell by the strain in her voice that she was scared—a lot more scared than she'd ever been at the hands of his father. He told her what he knew, what he'd learned from Marte Chang.

"They could alter you the same way they got me," he said. "Through Dad. They tagged his sperm with a couple of AVAs so that they'd get a new, improved clone of Dad instead of a normal child. You could have anything ticking inside you. Marte wants to find out what went where so that we can shut it off.''

''I see. So it's 'Marte' now?''

''Yeah.''

''Do you like her?''

''I like her a lot, Mom. She's *really* smart. . . . ''

''And nearly twice your age. What does Sonja think about all this?''

''She's only ten years older,'' Harry corrected, ''and I don't know what Sonja thinks. She seemed cheerful enough at the pour, but since the Agency grounded us she stays in her room.''

''I thought you two were a number.''

''We were *bred* to be a number, Mom,'' Harry said. ''How would that make *you* feel? To find that you'd been . . . engineered . . . to be the ideal breeding pair? It doesn't feel very good to me.''

''But you two have been inseparable, long before you knew. You make a great team; look what you did to ViraVax. Before you knew what they did to you. . . . ''

''That's it, Mom,'' Harry interrupted. ''Everything in life now is divided into Before and After. Before we knew, and After we found out. Like it or not, everything's changed. Most people won't associate with us, you know. Even security's scared we'll breathe something terrible on them.''

Grace Toledo heaved a great sigh for such a small woman and patted his arm again.

''I really wish I had a cigarette,'' she said.

''You don't smoke.''

''Maybe it's time to start. They're moving some embassy personnel and equipment out here by morning. Your friend, Ms. Chang, will be coming with them. Maybe even your father and Colonel Scholz.''

''I thought they were worried about contamination. They . . . ''

Grace exhaled in disgust. She wasn't listening. Harry's father was not a welcome topic in Grace Toledo's house,

even when she brought it up. This time she skipped the
usual blistering diatribe that she kept warm for Rico Toledo.

"You've been engrossed in your research," she said,
"so you haven't been on the newswire. Churches are burning up all over this country—Catholic and Gardener. The
Agency releases say it's a bombing war, but . . . "

*She doesn't know,* he realized. *Or she's in big-time denial.*

Denial was something that Dr. Olsen covered with him
in their videophone conversation earlier today.

She shrugged, and audibly choked back a sob. Harry finished for her.

"It's really the Meltdown virus."

"The Agency already thinks anyone associated with
ViraVax—and that now includes you and Sonja—is more
important than ever, and more in danger than ever," Grace
said. "Even from our own people."

" 'Our own people,' " Harry muttered.

"What do you mean by that?" Grace snapped.

"Sonja and I, we're not like anybody else alive," he
said. "It just gives a different meaning to something like
'our own people.' "

"Then that leaves me out, doesn't it?"

"Is that how you want to feel?" Harry challenged. "You
and I have gotten through all of this so far because we stuck
together. Do you think it's all hopeless now? Is that why
you're down?"

Grace dried her eyes on the sleeves of her T-shirt, a
child-like gesture that showed Harry just how vulnerable
his mother was, and how much he wanted to protect her.

"I'm down because I wanted us to have a nice life here,
and now it's all ruined. Forever."

His mother put her arm around Harry's waist and they
walked to the smoldering remnants of the bonfire that off-
duty security had built at the edge of the compound. Harry
kicked the charred pieces together and, as the fire caught,
they watched a spiral of sparks ride the thermals into the

night. Harry saw movement among the coffee trees.

"More security," he whispered, nodding towards them. "It's going to be like this for the rest of of our lives, isn't it? One kind of prison or another."

"One kind of prison or another might just save you from this virus," Grace said. "Don't be so harsh with these people right now. They're doing their best for you."

Harry didn't feel the fear that he knew he should feel over this obvious setback to their freedom or to the update on the virus. He knew now how stressed he'd been waiting for the other boot to drop, and now it had.

"At least you'll be closer to Marte," his mother added.

Her voice was softer, fishing for response, but Harry didn't reply.

*Chill*, he thought. *Now maybe we can get something done.*

The something on his mind was noble, but the stirrings in his body were slightly less than that. At least his *body* believed there'd be a future, even if his mind had serious doubts.

*"There aren't any sides anymore,"*
*David said.*
*"No," Marita said. "And we didn't*
*try to make sides. It just happened."*

—ERNEST HEMINGWAY,
THE GARDEN OF EDEN

# 32

SONJA BARTLETT UNDID the long French braid and brushed her blonde hair straight down over her breasts. Sometimes the brush flicked the top of a breast and sometimes a nipple, and by the time she was done the tops of her pale breasts glowed an angry red. She brought out the scissors while the bathtub filled with her lavender bubbles.

Sonja eased herself into the steaming bath and reached down the hand mirror from the back of the toilet. She soaped her hair, rinsed it and shut off the faucets. She propped the mirror across the faucets and lay back into the hot luxury. No matter how hot and humid this country got, Sonja still found a hot bath the only way she could unwind.

Her dead father's comb lay in the soap dish, and when she cut off her hair she used his coarse comb to keep her work more or less even. He'd had springy, red hair and hers was straight blonde, nearly white, identical with her mother's. After his death, she had picked a solitary red hair out of his comb and put it into an envelope. The envelope waited in the bottom of her underwear drawer for her to buy the proper locket she'd promised herself.

*This* is *my mother's hair*, she thought.

Sonja piled her long, blonde hair neatly on the floor next to her tub and tried to ignore the fact that the Agency recorded her every move. She tried to ignore their prying eyes but, in fact, she was drunk for the first time in her sixteen years and she had discovered already an age-old truth: drinking to forget never works.

And for sixteen, she had so much she wanted to forget. Two planes had crashed while she sat at the controls, one while she fled a nightmare epidemic of a thousand bodies melting from their bones. The lavender of her bath helped cut the stink of her memory, but it didn't cut the memory itself. She knew, now, what all combat vets learned, that death is the only complete perfume.

Two *lagartos* chattered from the wall above the toilet, then skittered together for a quick mating. The female accommodatingly moved her tail aside and when the male finished he performed a half-dozen triumphant push-ups. The female raced after a spider in the corner, and the male continued his push-ups.

Sonja piled a hatful of fragrant bubbles onto her head, then submerged herself to rinse them off.

"Sonja?"

Yes, her mother would be worried. Sonja was having trouble facing the woman who was and who was not her mother ever since she found out what she'd begun to call "The Clone's Truth." She had the same trouble facing Harry Toledo. In fact, she couldn't seem to face anyone. She sipped another mezcal.

"Sonja? Are you all right?"

Sonja started to giggle uncontrollably.

"Sonja!"

"Yes, Mother, my twin?"

There was a pause, and Sonja could envision her mother's sigh.

"I was afraid you'd drowned in there. Sergeant Trethewey is here to see you."

Sonja placed two handfuls of bubbles onto her breasts and admired them in her mirror. Her first inclination was

to tell her mother that she didn't want to see Sergeant Trethewey, or anybody else, ever again. But then she thought
of how much she'd wanted to talk with Harry—*really* talk,
not just plan—the last couple of days even though his presence reminded her of the ViraVax horrors. Besides, now he
was always working for Marte Chang, and he got disgust-
ingly dewy-eyed when he talked about their work. Harry
had been ignoring Sonja, too, so he hadn't noticed how she
had been avoiding him. And everyone else. She'd gone to
the pour to see ViraVax buried in concrete and to steal a
chopper, not to socialize.

"Sergeant Trethewey?"

Her mother must be desperate. She would never let Sonja
talk with men, particularly enlisted men, unless she thought
it was a last-ditch effort. Or maybe she saw that Trethewey
was a nice guy who had helped Sonja get a lot of free flight-
trainer time. Never once had he made a pass.

"Sonja?"

"Yes, okay," Sonja said, raising her voice. "I'll be out
in a few minutes."

"That's great, honey. We'll be in the kitchen."

Sonja let herself slip under the surface of the hot bath,
then sat up and rinsed her close-cropped hair with the
sprayer. The haircut made her look older, tougher. When
she narrowed her eyes at the mirror, she imagined that she
looked like Colonel Scholz.

*Okay, Sergeant,* she thought. *Let's see what you're really
made of.*

Sonja drained the tub and toweled herself vigorously.
The muggy Costa Bravan night overwhelmed the bathroom
fan, and sweat replaced bathwater on her livid skin. Only
a few rooms of Casa Canadá were air-conditioned, and the
bathroom was not one of those.

Sonja wrapped herself in a fresh towel, left her hair in
blonde clumps on the floor and steadied herself on the door
handle before facing her mother. She took three deep
breaths, as her mother had taught, and listened to the clatter
that filled her house.

*I'll sleep in the hangar from now on,* she thought. *Whether they like it or not.*

Casa Canadá had become a homeless shelter for Agency Operations, and she bitterly resented this most recent violation of her life. Sonja Bartlett was an unhappy girl determined to spread this unhappiness like a deadly virus among these invaders that dogged her every move. She tucked her towel wrap tight, lifted her chin and threw open the bathroom door with a crash.

Nancy Bartlett stood in the hallway, massaging her temples with long, slender fingers. Her blue eyes were rimmed in red from crying and from exhaustion. She wore her long blonde hair gathered back in a loose braid, tied with a blue ribbon. As Nancy's eyes widened in shock, Sonja ran her fingers through her hair stubble and giggled.

"Oh, baby, what have you done to yourself?" her mother asked.

"It's the new, streamlined me," Sonja said. "Like the women in that Seattle band you like so much, Genital Puppets."

"You know I hate that band," Nancy said. "Why are you doing this now? We've been through so much. . . . " She stopped and rubbed her forehead again. "I feel so rotten, and they want me to go back to the States in the morning. . . . "

Nancy sniffed, stepped up to Sonja and sniffed again.

"You've been drinking, haven't you?" she asked. "Where did you get it?"

Sonja shrugged.

*Might as well admit it.*

"Down at the hangar," she said. "Mr. Marcoe always keeps a couple of bottles hidden down there."

"Sonja, we still have a lot to do. . . . "

"*You* have a lot to do," Sonja said. She put out a hand to steady herself against the wall. "I have nothing to do but wait for them to take more blood, more tissue and samples of everything that goes in and comes out. *That's* my life, Mother, and I can't stand it. . . . "

Just then, Nancy Bartlett gasped, clutching at her chest and throat. Her eyes rolled back into her head, and before Sonja could react her mother dropped to the floor in a heap. Sonja knelt down to help her mother, and felt the telltale heat radiating through her clothes.

"Oh, no!" she whispered.

Sonja didn't dare call anyone because she didn't want others exposed. Without hesitation she grabbed her mother under the armpits and dragged her into the bathroom.

It took two tries for Sonja to get her mother into the tub, and by that time tissue had already sloughed from Nancy's arms and her face sagged in a way that betrayed more than exhaustion. Sonja opened the cold water faucet all the way and held her mother's head as the tub filled.

Sonja began to cry when she saw it was hopeless: her mother leaked away from her bones, out of her clothing and formed a gray scum on the surface of the tub. At the worst, bubbles roiled through the water and Nancy's scalp and right ear came off in Sonja's hands as she tried to keep her mother's head above water. Finally, she had to let her go.

Sonja sat on the floor with her back to the tub when Sergeant Trethewey appeared in the doorway.

"Sonja, my *God*!" was all he could say.

The tub water flowed over and spilled the stinking debris of Nancy Bartlett across the bathroom floor, mixing with the huge clumps of blonde hair that Sonja had left behind. Sergeant Trethewey became the bravest man Sonja knew when he stepped into the mess, reached past her and shut off the water.

*Both in fighting and in everyday life you should be determined though calm . . . even when your spirit is calm do not let your body relax, and when your body is relaxed do not let your spirit slacken.*

—MIYAMOTO MUSASHI

# 33

HARRY TOLEDO RUBBED Marte Chang's shoulders and watched her fall asleep in the reflection of her dead screen. He lightened his touch, but continued working his fingers between her shoulder blades. His left hand cradled her forehead while his right kneaded the strain out of the back of her neck. Neither of them had slept for two days, and Harry tried to pass some energy through his fingers to the exhausted body of the virologist.

"I love it when you touch me," she said.

"You're supposed to relax. Ten minutes, remember?"

Harry had never really touched a woman before. Not like this. Marte stayed quiet, and he worried that he'd offended her. At twenty-six, she was ten years older than Harry. He'd grown up in Costa Brava and loved the flirty eyes of the latina women. Marte Chang flirted, too, and something more.

*She's a goddamn scientific genius.*

All his life, everybody thought it would be Harry and Sonja. Even Harry thought so, especially when they were locked naked in that decontamination chamber at ViraVax. But since their escape and the revelation that they weren't . . .

*normal*, the two of them had avoided each other for the first time in their lives.

Marte Chang was easy to talk to, she actually *listened*, and with Harry's teamwork on the satlinks and the webs she had cracked the code of the Deathbug.

*Codes,* he reminded himself.

There were several, all marvels of molecular manipulation. It was a puzzle-code, fragments that worked together in a cascade effect to fool the immune system. They tricked the cell into betraying its own mitochondria. Now Marte had to find someone to manufacture an antidote, and the working conditions put on them by the Agency made that impossible. But Harry had a plan.

*If the whole world knew about it, there wouldn't be any need for secrecy,* he thought. *Then every virology lab in the world could get going on this.*

Tonight, when the Agency vans showed up with more techs and the equipment, Harry noticed that the usual security gates for the computer linkups had been left behind. Casa Canadá was a madhouse of confusion, and he was sure that he could get the word out. But it had to be the right word, to the right place.

Harry worked his fingers back down Marte's neck, across her shoulders, and he kissed the top of her head as he finished. Her hair was oily after three days without a shower and smelled of sweat. But it was *her* sweat, and sweet as plumeria to Harry.

"It's time," he said.

"You know, you'd better be careful doing that," she said, her eyes still closed. "I could wind up in a lot of trouble with your parents."

"Chill," he said. "It might be a relief to them if I go in trouble for something normal."

"Don't tempt me, young man," she said.

She spun her chair around, stood to stretch, and Harry kissed her. Much to Harry's surprise, she kissed him back.

"Well," she said.

"Yes, well."

They kissed again, and this time she pressed herself tight against him and caused quite a jam-up in his jockey shorts. The techs would be back any minute, but Harry and his body didn't care.

Casa Canadá was a large French Colonial home in the heart of several hundred acres of coffee. Marte's Litespeed and peripherals were installed in a sitting-room just outside Harry's bedroom. He had fantasized for two days about how to get Marte Chang into that bedroom. She had gone from ten kilometers to three meters away in a matter of hours, and now that she was this close Harry didn't know how to ask.

Fortunately, he didn't have to ask.

"Harry," she whispered into his neck, "we don't have much time."

"No," he sighed. "We're lucky to have this."

She kissed him again, running her hands down his back, his hips and up his thighs. She grasped his belt buckle and tugged.

"Which way to your room?" she asked.

"Right there."

"Does it lock?"

"Yes."

Marte pulled Harry by the belt buckle into his room and closed the door. Harry flipped the latch, and Marte already had his belt undone and his zipper unzipped. Harry thought he'd explode when she kissed his belly just above his pubic hair. He didn't know what to do with his hands, so he pulled her blouse out of her pants and over her head without unbuttoning it. Her small breasts jiggled in her bra as the blouse came free.

Marte kissed him again, then skinned his T-shirt off and pressed herself against him. Somehow she had already slipped out of her bra, and her firm, brown nipples drew little circles on his chest.

Harry fumbled with the catch on her pants, so she unhooked it herself and they stood there, holding tight, naked except for their shoes, socks and shorts bunched around their ankles. Harry glanced at his bed and saw that, as usual, it was covered with books, papers, disks and cubes. He grabbed a corner of his bedspread and dumped everything onto the floor. It didn't matter; they never made it to the bed.

Marte sank down onto the lamb's-wool rug and pulled him with her. She kicked off her shoes and got one leg out of her shorts as Harry struggled to kiss her and get out of his things at the same time.

"Okay?" she asked.

"Yes, okay," he whispered. She was so small, and he felt self-conscious about pressing his full weight on top of her. "Am I smashing you?"

"Smash me," she said. "I'm not as fragile as you think."

He kissed her and her little tongue flicked around his lips, tapped the end of his own tongue. He kissed her hard brown nipples and nuzzled her belly before Marte pulled him up to her and slipped him inside.

They lay still for a moment, tapping their tongues and catching their breath. Harry was afraid to move because he knew he was right at the verge of bursting through. Marte had almost triggered him off when her fingers explored him lightly, and he didn't want to ruin things for her. Her body gripped him in a tight, fierce heat that he felt pulsing hard around him.

"It's all right," she said, as though reading his mind. "It's all right."

He moved slowly, then, once, twice and heard the small sucking sounds of her passion as she trembled against him, her legs locked against his hips. Then what little control he had was gone, and Harry poured out of himself in tremendous bursts while Marte moved on him in a near-fury until she fell back with a little cry, racked with spasms that clutched him even tighter inside her.

In the dim light he saw her, eyes still closed, as she smiled broadly and started to giggle. He had been supporting his weight on his arms but she pulled him down to her,

still giggling, and rocked him on top of her tight in the grip
of her thighs.

"You feel so good," he whispered.

"Yes," she giggled, "I do."

He kissed her, but she started giggling again and nestled
her face against his chest.

"I'm sorry," she said. "I'm just so *happy* to feel *good*
for a change, you know?"

"Yes," he whispered, and kissed the top of her head.
"Yes, I know. Thank you, Marte."

" 'Thank you'? My, aren't we polite?" Marte tilted her
head back and looked him in the eye. "Well, Harry, thank
*you*."

"You probably guessed that it's my first time."

"I guessed . . . *hoped* that it was," she said. "It's my
first time being somebody else's first time, and I wanted it
to be nice for you."

They kissed, long and soft. Marte's body shuddered in
another spasm, and in spite of himself he slipped out of
her.

"Oh, no," she whispered. "I didn't mean to throw you
out."

Then someone pounded on the door.

"Harry! Harry! Are you in there?"

It was Joe Clyde, the SEAL team medic.

"I'm here," Harry said, holding Marte tighter. "What's
up?"

"There's been an incident here in the house. Are you
alone?"

They rolled apart and Harry grabbed for his shorts.

Marte, too, struggled with her clothes.

"I'm here, Joe," she said. "Marte Chang. It's just the
two of us."

"Jesus! Listen, stay put for now. We're just trying to get
a fix on everyone and some new orders. I'll be back in a
few minutes."

"Who was it?" Harry asked, but Joe Clyde was already
gone.

*When you walk toward the light, the
shadows fall behind.*

—PIERRE TEILHARD DE CHARDIN, S.J.

# 34

RICO TOLEDO STRUGGLED up the dark stairway to Spook's
bar, his arms trembling to the point of cave-in after a long,
hot day on crutches and canes. A crystal doorknob outfitted
the ornate, antique door, and Rico was sure that the doorknob provided Father Free's *cooperativa* with a palm-and-
thumb scan of everyone who entered. Father ''Luke the
Spook'' Free was nowhere in sight, which meant he was
probably behind the two-way mirror, repairing the damage
to the Archbishop's transmitter. Martial law locked up the
phone system, so Rico had a strong personal interest in
several of Father Free's toys, including his transmitter.

Rico ordered a tonic water with a slice of lime from Al,
an ex-cryptographer. He hoped that Father Free wasn't below on the pier working on his fishing boat. For Rico, a
boat was an isolated environment, and this evening he made
a serious study of isolation. But he was not the least interested in hauling his two hundred lacerations back down
those stairs and working his way out to the end of a floating
pier.

*Tonight will have to be the night,* he thought.

''Things are heating up out there,'' Rico said, toasting

Al and taking a long pull at the tonic.

"That's the world," Al said. "We don't do the world any more."

"What do you call that?" Rico asked, and nodded towards the video screen.

Al shrugged.

"Forewarned is forearmed."

Two Ministry of Intelligence types sat in one corner, making notes on the programming. The screen at Spook's offered an unwashed version of U.S. and international affairs, straight off the satellites. This version was as rare as it was illegal, and Spook didn't care about legal. He knew how to siphon anything off the airwaves, how to get anything on the air, how to move anything or anyone anywhere, and he was always a step ahead of the Agency. The Ministry of the Interior left Spook alone because he let their intelligence people drink in his bar and make notes on things they couldn't find out for themselves. It was almost a symbiosis.

Four suits that had to be Pan-Pacific Security goons tried to look invisible, two at a table in the far corner, two beside the exit. Rico toasted them in the mirror but none responded. They were contractors, probably drawing double for the holiday, so whatever they were up to was nothing personal.

"Tightasses," Rico muttered. "No sense of humor."

He hoped he wouldn't have to wait long for Spook; the liquor bottles were calling him with a strong, insistent voice. He chewed the pulp out of the center of his lime, and saw the flick of a shadow behind the bar mirror. Rico smiled a broad smile and toasted the shadow.

Father Free had been Rico's ethics instructor at the Academy, and his advice on matters of philosophy was sound. But it was Spook's improvisational acting course that had saved Rico's life more times than he could count. Spook was a weaponless wonder, and he would have made a helluvan agent in any intelligence service. But he was also a priest, and when his tenure was up at the Academy, he went

where his superiors sent him—Costa Brava, before it was
Costa Brava. Rico asked for and received Central America
duty the following year.

Spook bankrolled his initiative and a handful of wide-
eyed young rebels into the *cooperativa*. Colonel Toledo
bankrolled ViraVax for the Agency. It was little wonder
that Father Free didn't have much to say to Colonel Toledo,
these days.

Father Free helped Costa Brava upgrade its telecommu-
nications, and in exchange the country granted the Archbishop the only non-government broadcast license. Officials
also looked the other way when Father Free started the
*cooperativa*, mainly because they expected it to fail. They
didn't know that the private bar was the international office
of the "National Security Alumni Club." Father Free
wanted everyone to have the chance to right the wrongs
they'd done through his Agency, or any other. His bar was
home to countless ex-operatives from dozens of countries.
There was never any trouble at Spook's.

Some bars sold drugs or weapons under the table, but
Spook sold possibilities. For the right cause, he even gave
them away. He wouldn't wage war, but Father Free often
waged rescues. Other than the brief confession, it had been
five years since he'd even spoken to Rico Toledo.

Rico sipped his drinkless drink and checked the suits in
the mirror. They could have been mannequins. The Interior
Ministry boys continued entering incriminating notes into
their Sidekicks, though they must have known that no authority in Costa Brava was about to slap the hands of the
man who had brought them into the twenty-first century.
They wouldn't even have those Sidekicks if it hadn't been
for Father Free.

The unwashed Washington, D.C., news did not impress
Rico, no more than that slow-motion obstructionist committee had. Congressional attention was on the water wars
that had the western half of the U.S. in flames, and the
ghetto wars that charred their own doorsteps in the east.
They were not about to listen to a beat-up bush colonel

warning them of a rogue virus two thousand miles away.

Rico glimpsed himself in the mirror, and he could see why. Crisscrossed with scars and stitches, his dark face looked singularly deniable. He also saw Lieutenant Colonel Rena Scholz standing behind him.

"Scare yourself?" she asked.

"Every day," he said. "I'm just too damned handsome for words. Have a seat. Buy you a drink?"

Rena Scholz hesitated, her expression questioning.

"Tonic and lime," he explained. "Don't worry, the bogeyman's still in the bottle and I hammered the cork in tight."

Toledo patted the seat beside him to hide his shakiness, and she sat. Father Free himself appeared with his effervescent grin and flourished a napkin onto the bar. Rico assumed he'd been watching from his special office. Father Free couldn't resist Rena Scholz. Before the Army, she'd almost become a nun.

"You look like shit, Toledo," Father Free said. "But that's not unusual. What'll you have, young lady?"

"A double shot of that flattery, Father. And a Virgin Mary while you dish it out."

Rico studied Rena Scholz's reflection beside his own. She was beautiful. It had taken him ten years to realize that, mainly because the aura from Rena Scholz had been barbed wire—all business, no question. The hatchwork of fresh scars on his face flushed a deeper pink when she caught his gaze.

Rena Scholz was a blue-eyed blonde who wore the effects of the Costa Brava sun like a beauty queen. Tan had gone out of fashion with the ozone layer, but Rena Scholz always turned heads with her tan, her buzzed-down crop of blonde fuzz and her ice-blue eyes.

"This place should be called 'The Oasis,'" Scholz said. "Costa Brava's heating up, big-time. It's still quiet in here."

"Heat's what you're after, isn't it, Scholz?" Rico asked. "Don't you just love adrenaline?"

Scholz had been raised by some nuns in Idaho who made the news when they'd actually done battle with the Aryan Nations back in the 90's. "Pistol-Packing Nuns Flush Huns" had been the headline, and Solaris had recruited her fresh out of nursing school as a result. Scholz fought her own demons, on her own time. She sucked on a chili from a bowl on the bar.

"Adrenaline's the only drug that's still free," she said.

"The kids?" he asked her.

"Still at the farm. Still ready to jump. Chang's out there now, too. Mostly hired guns, like your shadows, here."

Scholz nodded towards the Pan-Pacific Security drones.

"Chang have a vaccine yet?"

"Microtubules," Scholz said. "She might not need a vaccine."

Rico turned on his stool for a better look at Rena Scholz.

"What the hell are microtubules?"

"Chang says they're little subways that one AVA builds to smuggle the rest of them into and throughout the cells. She's found a way to prevent the microtubules from forming."

"Great!" Rico said. "Then she beat this thing!"

"Not exactly. We still can't get authorization to get any labs involved."

"Why the hell not?"

Rico knew why not—he'd built these frustrations into the system himself, to give the DIA time to cover their asses if anything ever went wrong.

Scholz shrugged, and helped herself to a swallow of his tonic. "Intelligence Committee's still arguing about who should be trusted with the technique. Marte says it won't matter anyhow."

"What do you mean?"

"She thinks it's self-limiting. Mishwe made a key mistake. It's *so* fast-acting, *so* contagious that it'll burn itself out, like those fires up there on the peel. We just have to stay out of its range until then."

Rico barked a hoarse laugh. He nodded at the peel-and-peek beside the mirror. Raw network footage depressed him as much as whitewashed network footage. The sound was off, but split-screen showed four different airports fighting burning planes and terminals.

"Look at them. Squabbling over who gets to shower this week. The Water Wars and gang alliances are small potatoes. Maybe this bug will thin things out enough that turf wars will be obsolete."

"We've had turf wars ever since the first human swung the first club," Scholz said. "And there are a lot of ways to define 'turf.' "

Father Free reappeared with Scholz's drink.

"The Pope's dead," he announced. "A fire in the Vatican, about an hour ago."

The priest set a large goblet in front of Rena Scholz. Stalks of celery and pickled string beans stood in a thick tomato froth. Father Free pushed the bowl of chilis closer to Scholz, then turned to leave.

"A fire?" Rico asked after him. "What kind of fire?"

But Father Free was already gone. The man Rico knew as Spook always came and went silently, with a practiced invisibility.

"First Casey, of the Gardeners, and now the Pope, of the Catholics," Scholz mused. "You don't suppose that's coincidence, do you?"

She sipped her drink and affected a nonchalance that he found . . . stimulating. This was the first time since he'd known Scholz that Rico sat with her in a bar. Outside, the faint wail of sirens backed up the *whump* of mortars working the neighboring zone.

Scholz swirled a celery stalk through her drink and sucked it dry, then began to crunch it systematically from the bottom up. Her gaze was distracted, focused somewhere on the other side of the mirror.

Father Free appeared at Rico's left elbow.

"I heard you were smart, and dry, to boot," he said. "Congratulations. But don't you get it yet? The light's always red."

"Which light, Spook?"

"The traffic light on The Hill," the priest said. "White House, Congress, doesn't matter. All that comes out of there is excuses. You want something done, you've got to do it yourself."

Rico smiled. He had the perfect challenge for Spook, the perfect hook.

"What we need done can't be done without Congress."

"Like a surgical strike?" Father Free laughed. "You been in the bush too long, amigo."

"Well, you've been out of it too long, Spook. You retire, confess your sins, start a bar for remorseful ex-agents and let the world go to hell. You were good, Spook. You could talk a nun out of her bra and panties. . . ."

" . . . and *did* . . ."

Scholz shook her head in disgust.

"Shit, Father . . ."

"Sorry, Scholz," Father Free said. "It wasn't . . . you know, a sex thing. It was a bet, that's all. Look, I wish I could help you two, but you're still inside. So are the four gentlemen who have waited for you all afternoon without buying so much as a coffee. You don't deal with the outside, and I don't deal with the inside."

Rico checked the mirror, then looked Spook in the eye. Spook didn't waver. Rico smiled, and winked.

*If we've got tails in here, we've got wires,* he thought. *But if I know Spook, they're probably not working.*

Father Free hadn't lost his healthy paranoia.

"You couldn't get an item out on the newswire, could you?"

"Of course not," Father Free said, his grin lopsided, his gaze steady. "An idea like that gets around, even a priest could get in trouble. I specialize in fishing charters. If you're interested in fishing, we can talk business. Let me get you two more. The ice is on the house."

Then Spook turned on his fluid invisibility, and was gone.

Rico used the mirror to scan the bar. He recognized three

patrons as ex-informants from his own district, now working for CostaTel, thanks to Father Free. The four squeaky-
clean types moved, two covering the door and two flanking
him and Scholz. As he'd suspected, they wore the gold
lapel pins of Pan-Pacific. Spook's was the kind of bar anyone could love, but few could find from the outside. There
was no sign, no official name, no logo on the napkins or
matches. Rico would bet his retirement that no one had ever
wandered in off the street and that these guys weren't regulars.

"I've been thinking," Major Scholz said.

"Sounds like trouble."

"What doesn't? Look, I think you should party without
me."

Rico sucked an ice cube, watched two squeaky-cleans
whispering near the door.

"What's your plan, Scholz?"

"You party with the kids and Chang, invite Spook to be
neighborly. I'll meet you afterward for ice cream."

"Eat all the cake ourselves, and while the ice cream
melts you sit in the dark? I don't think so."

*The ears on the wires will have a time with this.*

"There's a poker game back at the office," she said. "I
feel good about my strategy and could use a little bonus.
Finish your formalities, and we'll meet up."

*Everybody has a goddamn plan,* he thought, *but nobody's coordinating.*

Rico sucked an ice cube, resisted the urge to scratch his
stitches and shifted his weight from the more sore buttock
to the less.

"I don't like it."

"Why not?"

"I'm sure this will shock you, Scholz," he said, turning
to face her, "but I'm getting selfish in my old age. There
are some tough hombres in that game, and I don't want to
lose you, that's why not."

Rico's attention switched from Rena Scholz to the peel-
and-peek beside the mirror, and what he saw there raised

the few fine hairs on his arms. The pain and itching from
his wounds washed away.

Clumsy camera work panned Mexico City through the
window of a commercial airliner. Dust, black smoke and
steam boiled up from acres of rubble. The thick plume flattened out as it hit the colder air atop the city. One finger
of smoke reached out towards the camera, and the international airport.

*And there was a great earthquake,
such as was not since men were upon
the earth, so mighty an earthquake,
and so great.*

—REVELATIONS

# 35

EL OSO SHAVED the part of his new beard that irritated his neck, his boot knife gliding nicely over the cold, hand-soap lather. In this brief standoff he had lost nearly ten kilos, and the image that regarded El Oso from his mirror was hard, lean, noble.

"Take your time, Oso," El Tigre called from the sniper's roost. "We are in charge here. The albino *pendejo*'s message is *mierde*, nothing more."

El Oso rinsed his face and neck, then toweled himself dry. He put on Hernan's clean shirt, since Hernan would no longer have need of shirts, and called back.

"Pay attention. We lost four men who did not pay attention. We have to think of food, soon, or we will be too weak to shoot the gringos when they come."

"We can eat Hernan," El Tigre said. "He was hit yesterday, but he didn't die until this afternoon."

El Oso shook his head, chuckling at the joke, but when he looked up and saw the fear in the others' eyes, he stopped.

"No more talk of eating Hernan," El Oso ordered. "No more talk of eating, period."

"They say they come tonight," Guillermo said. "Then what? If we kill them all, they'll send more tomorrow night. We will run out of ammunition. They pick us off one by one. . . ."

"What would you have us do?" El Oso interrupted. "Surrender, and be shot against this wall like pigs? No, when the phony earthquake never comes—one day, two days more—the city will fill up again and we will all leave here rich men."

"But how . . . ?"

"El Oso has a plan," El Tigre cackled in his unnerving way. "And shadows collect on the roof across the street. It is time, Oso."

El Oso heard the hard *blat-blat* of Tigre's compressor.

"One less shadow, Oso," El Tigre said. "Tell them the plan."

"Osvaldo, bring me that tape!" Oso ordered. "Umberto, Miguel, unpack two of those cartons. With care, you two! Don't do to us what the gringos cannot."

Osvaldo handed Oso three rolls of duct tape that he'd found in a tool box. Oso pulled off a dozen meter-long strips and placed them on a workbench beside the pallet of cartons. Twice more El Tigre's compressor coughed.

"These are very careless men, Oso."

"Continue to instruct them in their carelessness, Tigre," El Oso said. "Osvaldo, Umberto, over here."

El Oso unpacked one of the shiny cylinders from its protective carton and carefully twisted off the top. He lifted out the rack of cold, blue vials and set it gently atop the carton. Wisps of vapor slipped from the vials as Oso removed them one by one and stuck them onto the tape. Then he wrapped the tape around their chests and foreheads.

"Everybody see this?"

"Sí, Oso."

"Sí."

"Sí."

"Then come down here one at a time and prepare yourselves this way. We will transmit a portrait of each of you

> *This is a truth: when you sacrifice your life, you must make fullest use of your weaponry. It is false not to do so, and to die with a weapon undrawn.*
>
> —MIYAMOTO MUSASHI

TRENTON SOLARIS PICKED himself up from the floor of his office, tested his arms and legs and found nothing broken. He had ridden out more earthquakes than he could count, in Mexico City and in the old Guatemala, but this one was the Big One. Everything from his walls—books, disks, cubes, his personal collection of Mayan artifacts—lay in a tumble of shards and paper on his office floor. The walls still held most of the ceiling aloft, but the lining of acoustical tile hung in great white shreds.

This thick silence, after the terrible grinding shrieks and the groans, made him test his hearing as well.

"Yes?" he asked himself aloud.

Yes, he was alive. Yes, the gods had punished him for his presumptuousness.

*Declare an earthquake, human,* they said. *We will give you a shake to remember.*

His mother would have expected as much.

The albino checked the instrumentation on his console. As expected, the local hard-wire was out but the battery-powered satlinks persisted. Had he planned on surviving the afternoon, Solaris would have sent a congratulatory

memo to the Corps of Engineers. As it was, he had some
ugly business to be about.

Solaris tried his window shield, and it would not open.
The building's emergency generators must be out, as well.
That meant his communications abilities lay within the
range of his battery packs—four or five hours. He did not
feel like communicating. He knew that he should see about
the condition of his staff, other people in the building, survivors among the poor on the street. But that which was
required of him now made all of that moot. None would
survive his final duty, and nothing would stay his trembling
hand from that duty.

The confirmation was solid. The lot numbers on the
cannisters inside Coyote Warehouse matched the numbers
in the logs that Harry Toledo extracted from ViraVax.
The Deathbug was, indeed, alive and well in Mexico
City. Perhaps the stainless steel cannisters could have survived the earthquake intact. But Solaris had watched the
transmission from the observation post across the street
from the rebels. The greedy fools had removed at least
fifty vials from their nests, and there was no denying
what that meant. Even now, survivors of the earthquake
inhaled the great death.

*Our air processing is gone with the generators,* he
thought. *Right now I could be breathing that virus myself.*

Solaris admired, for the last time, his Maya mural. Born
to a poor village in the Petén region of Guatemala, he had
learned Spanish from a medic who came through with polio
inoculations. Being the only villager who spoke Spanish,
Solaris found himself indispensable by the time he was
twelve. At fourteen, he spoke English and German. At sixteen he changed his name to a form suitable to one who
desired more fluidity in the greater world. His father was
already dead at forty-four, an elder by village standards,
burned alive by the Guatemalan army as a lesson to their
village. The point of the lesson was never clear, except that
they *would* do these things simply because they *could* do
them.

The albino recalled how his father taught him that the end was near—not the end of the world, which would survive, but the end of time.

"That is why the Old Ones quit building the cities of stone," he'd said. "The stars told them that time itself would end when the planets aligned in their two-thousand-year cycle."

"When will that be, father?" he'd asked.

"By the *ladino* calendar, about 2020. You will have more years by then than I do," he said. "It saddens me that you will endure such a thing, but surely it will be glorious to behold, this end of time."

"How can time end without the world ending?" he'd asked.

His father had merely shaken his head and pursed his lips in his way that meant, *I don't know. Discussion ended.*

But Solaris thought that he knew, now, how time would end. Time would die with the last timekeeper, the last human being.

"Five more years to go, by the Mayan calendar," he muttered. "Maybe I can put it off that long, at least."

To do what needed doing, he had to get to the rail yards, and to a nondescript freight car that awaited the ultrasecure coding sequence that was stored in his Sidekick.

Solaris cleared rubble from the doorway and found the little clay dog-shaped whistle that he had uncovered with his own hands at Chacben Kax. A front foot was broken, but the whistle remained intact. The whistle always made him smile because the ancient potter was quite the jokester. One had to blow into the dog's butt to make it work. He slipped it into his jacket pocket and wrestled open the door to his outer offices.

Terrelle and Workman were dead, crushed under a failed concrete truss and ceiling debris. Hot water sprayed across the room, and a tangle of wires and cables blocked the only exit. Solaris picked up a twisted metal bookend and threw it into the wires. Nothing. He wrapped his Sidekick in a shred of plastic film, covered his head with his arms and bulled his way through the tangle to the far door.

In his struggle down the dark stairwells to the ground floor he met not one living human. He grew ever more apprehensive of the thickening dust, smoke and steam billowing around him.

*What if it kills me before I make the rail yards?*

Then nothing would matter, and time would stop on time.

He slipped and scrabbled his way through the rubble that used to be the Hotel Majestic. Fires raged in the remnants of downtown Mexico City, lighting the dusty scene with blood. All around him he heard the *hiss* and *pop* of explosions. More and more screams pierced the night. The screams didn't usually last long before shifting to hopeless moans or hopeful shrieks for help.

*They should have left as they were told,* he thought. *We warned them to get out.*

What did it matter now that the warning was a fraud, a cover for the struggle over the supply of virus? As the stars would have it, the lie could have saved them anyway. Rescue from the rubble would mean only the horrible melting death awaiting them from the virus, so Solaris struggled on with his mission and ignored the pleas for help rising from the devastation around him.

Dust and smoke watered his eyes, and already he was wracked with the long, deep cough that comes with the inhalation of pulverized stone. For the first time in his adult life, Solaris wished for the full onslaught of the sun. No moonlight pierced the pall over the center of the city, and he struggled towards the little sun that he himself was about to create.

The Agency had prepared his building well. As he glanced back through the firelit haze, he saw that only his operations center remained standing. The National Palace, gone. Diego Rivera's murals, gone. The national cathedral, gone. Gone, too, was his sense of direction. He took his bearings from his office, and estimated that he was entirely too close to the mess that used to be Coyote Warehouse. He checked the subway, hoping the tunnels could lead him past the enemy bug, but huge blocks of beautiful old stone blocked everything—streets, subways, alleys. Gouts of water burst from the buckled pavement.

Though Solaris was small, and unused to physical exertion, he persisted in this mission with a fever born of absolute fear and desperation.

*I got us into this,* he thought. *It's up to me to get us out.*

The "us," of course, would not include himself, nor the few survivors back at Operations who were, even now, helping dig the dead and injured from tons of collapsed ceilings and walls. Nor would it include any of the international rescuers and firefighters who faced crushed propane tanks, live electrical lines and shifting wreckage as they shouted and poked their way into what used to be the Zócalo.

He had forgotten how hot exertion could be. In his adult gentility he had forsaken the hard physical work of his childhood.

As a child in Guatemala, a Maya of an American father, Solaris had always been special. His mother's father told the village that this albino child represented the advent of the coming of the end of time, which their calendar had predicted a thousand years ago. Now, by playing both ends against the middle with ViraVax, he had become the agent of that end. Things would continue, but time itself would unravel and existence as we know it would cease. It was, he admitted, a marvel that his people saw this conclusion so clearly from so very far away.

He looked over his shoulder and saw the humped shapes of the dozen armored vehicles that had surrounded Coyote Warehouse. He heard no cries from within, and the three vehicles that were not buried in brick appeared abandoned.

*They knew what they were fighting,* he thought. *But they can't outrun the bug, or my penance, here.*

He mounted the closest track, popped the hatch and instead of the cool dark guts of the machine he was greeted by fresh blood cloying the air. He resisted the reflex to run, and as his eyes adjusted to the dark he saw the three crewmen, dead at their posts. Two had been shot in the back of the head. Their faces and brains clotted the gauges. The third sat propped against the rear plate, a Colt 10mm beside his hand and a huge halo of blood behind his back.

Solaris swallowed, swallowed again, frozen just inside the hatch. His trachea spasmed and he breathed in a tight wheeze, his body unwilling to accept the fouled air.

*Yes,* he thought, *they outran the Deathbug.*

The albino forced himself down the few rungs of ladder. The cabin of the Powell was crowded with its crew of three, made more crowded by their splatterings about the cabin. Solaris didn't take the time to send any of them out the hatch. He didn't want to waste the time, and he wasn't sure that he had the necessary strength of body or mind. He peeled the two faceless ones away from the controls and let them fall back against their executioner.

The Powell was the newest of the Rapid Entry Armored Vehicles, designed for urban use against the gang armies. Extremely narrow, it could punch through walls without bringing the building down on top of it. Electric motors drove the rubberized track in near silence. In extremely hot situations, it could be directed by remote and deployed as a drone. In low-visibility situations, the crew could lock into a satlink and follow a screen-generated simulation to its target.

Solaris located the console's input cable and plugged in his Sidekick.

"Initiate starting sequence," he commanded.

The machine hummed to life, a far cry from its loud-mouth diesel brothers. The rubberized armor would protect him from live power lines, and his passing would not spark any leaking gas to flame. He called up a district map, penned in the shortest path to the railroad yard, and forced himself to breathe.

"Run," he commanded, and the machine set out in its

indomitable twenty-kilometer-per-hour crawl toward its goal.

The ride was a rough one. At times the Powell achieved near-vertical as it clamored over rubble, and when it crawled down the other side Solaris had to push off the three bodies that crushed him against the console. He finally managed to wrestle the smaller man, the executioner, up the ladder and out the hatch. The effort and the close quarters had Solaris drenched in sweat, the muscles in his arms and legs trembled, and he concentrated on slowing his rapid breathing. He regretted that he had to breathe at all, in part from the stench of the dead, in part from fear of the Death-bug. He did not want it to get him before his mission was complete.

For the few moments that the hatch was opened he heard the terrible cacophony of death and grief, and realized that he had sorely underestimated the effectiveness of their evacuation. He had wanted to believe that twenty-plus-million people could pull out of the city in twenty-four hours, and he had wanted to believe that at least fifteen million *had* pulled out, but of course the math made a mockery of this. Roads had been blocked within hours of the alarm, vehicles abandoned, and millions of people tried to walk their way to safety. The rest simply stocked up and dug in. Now the living tried desperately to dig out.

The enormity of what he was about to do struck him with the screams and the pleadings of the survivors. Already the Powell carried a dozen or more humans clinging in hope to its rubberized shell. Solaris had imagined that a few thousand might die, but his mind had been incapable of picturing death in the millions, in the ten millions. Death at his own hand. If he saved history, he would go down in its pages beside Hitler.

Yet to stay his hand at this point would mean the deaths of nearly ten billion.

The railroad yard looked, through the monitors, like the aftermath of a child's tantrum. His floodlights revealed box-

cars tossed askew as far as he could see, and ruptured tank-
ers poured their chemistries into the soil and the air. Even
if he knew which siding held the container he sought, Solaris knew he could never find it by sight.

He entered the signal-locator code, his personal authorization code, and held his breath for the few moments that
it took for the satellites to chat. Numbers had been his
blessing and his curse all his life. Solaris never forgot a
number—com number, address, Social Security number, license number. When traveling, he had to force his gaze
away from license numbers, house numbers, numbers on
boats, planes and railroad cars.

This railroad car, like others throughout the world, held
a special cargo. So, too, did shabby freighters in myriad
ports. Ballistic missiles still targeted the nuclear nations and
their installations, but through Solaris the Agency had
found a cheaper way to cover the bets in the rest of the
world.

It took the President and The Football to launch a ballistic strike, and "Red Alert" only applied to a situation
directly threatening the United States or its holdings. A
dozen people in the world had access to the RCC—Re-
gional Contingency Codes—and Trenton Solaris, as the
DIA's Latin America Chief, was one of those dozen.

His Sidekick inquired, in its flat voice, "Do you wish to
declare Red Alert?"

"Negative," he answered. "Run search."

Somewhere in the Department of Defense complex in
D.C. a red light was blinking away valuable time. Suddenly
the Powell lurched ahead, spun on its left track and wove
its way through a propane fire to a rusted, nondescript container lying on its side. The end doors were accessible, and
Solaris magnified the view fifty percent. The numbers were
correct, and he saw with relief that the locking mechanism
and plug were undamaged.

Solaris scrambled out of the track and into hell. The
Powell had protected him from the searing heat of the propane fire and from the caustic vapors from nearby tank cars.

In this industrial area even more screams rent the air, these from the thousands of families who lived in and among the empty cars.

A blackened husk of a man pleaded with him.

"*Por favor*," he begged, pointing through the wall of flame just meters behind them. "My wife, my babies . . . "

Solaris already had his Sidekick plugged into the lock. He nodded towards the Powell.

"Take it," he told the man. "It will take you through."

"*Gracias*," the man said, wiping the tears from his eyes with the black smears of his hands. "*Muchísimas gracias, señor. Vaya con Dios.*"

"Yes," Solaris answered without looking, "go with God."

The lock buzzed free and one of the double doors dropped down, nearly crushing Solaris, who jumped aside barely in time. Inside the container, bolted to the floor, lay the device that he sought. It did not look in the least bit deadly.

The neutron device was over thirty years old. Except that it was stainless steel, it looked much like an old steamer trunk. Solaris found the arming plug on the side facing away from him. As the Powell backed away from him and into the inferno, Solaris plugged his Sidekick into the receptacle and uploaded the arming sequence.

He knew, from Marte Chang's report and lot number confirmations, that some virus already swirled aloft with the smoke and debris. Fire created its own wind, and the wind from a thousand fires even now spread the Deathbug throughout the city. He knew that the effective range of this device was not great, but by destroying as much virus as possible as quickly as possible, he hoped that the delay would give Chang the precious time she needed to protect the rest of the world from any of this horror that slipped through. A horror that, though indirectly, was his sorry contribution to human biology.

*And maybe I'll get them all,* he thought. *There's absolutely nothing to lose.*

He keyed the final code verification sequence into his Sidekick, took the clay whistle from his jacket pocket and looked upon the pitiful struggles of his fellow humans one last time. He put the dog's butt to his lips, blew a shrill, clear tone as loud and as long as he could. Then, as his breath ran out, he pressed the command key: "Run."

Time, for Trenton Solaris and millions of others, ended right there.

*Waiting is bad.* —Miyamoto Musashi

# 37

PRESIDENT CLAUDIA KAY O'Connor had two minutes to herself in the relative silence of the Communications booth bathroom. Two com-line headsets hung above the toilet paper beside her, and a row of status lights blinked their green, yellow and red semaphore at her from above the urinals against the opposite wall. Two flat screens flanked the status slate, and a peel shimmered on the back of the door. All were blanked, at her command, and speakers muted.

President O'Connor sat on the toilet seat lid and shook out her fingers, trying to relax. Her black wool pants itched like mad because she'd been sitting and sweating most of the day. In less than a minute she would explain to Juan-Carlos Herrera, President of Mexico, and Raphael Klein, Prime Minister of Canada, what she knew about Eden-Springs water. The media called it the "Sabbath Suicides," and it was especially virulent among Gardener outposts throughout Mexico.

The President opened the door to Communications, and Dwight shoved her formal statement to Herrera into her hand.

"They need to hear that help is on the way," Dwight reminded her. "This is for their media people."

A piercing *whoop* blared from a speaker overhead just as static replaced Mexico City on the status screen.

"We have a nuclear situation, Ms. President," General Gibson told her. He ran a hand through his thinning gray hair. "A detonation. Mexico City."

"Shit," President O'Connor said.

No one was trying to outshout anyone else. She watched the light on the Defcon panel go to Red Alert.

"Authorize?" the panel asked her.

With the flick of her thumb she would mobilize the world's largest nuclear arsenal to counterstrike anything construed as an attack. She pressed her thumb to a plate on her desk, and it recorded her print.

Babble was picking up.

"Who?" O'Connor asked the general. "Who hit Mexico City?"

She leaned her elbows on a hexagonal tabletop that housed six control stations. She sat at one of six captain's chairs that rolled freely atop the shiny oak floor. The oak covered twelve feet of reinforced concrete which, itself, was lined with steel, lead and reinforced with concrete beyond that. "Nuclear" had been spoken in this room before.

General Gibson was uncharacteristically pale, and slow to answer.

"It's a Trojan Horse, Ms. President," he said.

"One of ours, then," she said.

He nodded just slightly, and his gaze of steel held steady.

"I'm afraid so, Ms. President."

"Media's calling it an aftershock," Dwight said. "Let's keep it that way, for now. . . ."

President O'Connor tuned Dwight out. She was now the second American President responsible for a nuclear massacre. And she still had a country to protect.

*What would I do if I were Mexico?* she asked herself.

"I'd attack," she answered. "As soon as I knew they'd betrayed me."

"You're reading my mind," General Gibson said.

Suddenly, something behind the general frightened her more than the bomb. As General Gibson explained how he would deploy southwest units to discourage a Mexican invasion, President O'Connor watched a plumber working under a sink across the room. The man slid out from under the sink with a white canister in his hand. He tossed it into a bucket on his utility cart, unwrapped another cannister and began crawling back under the sink.

"Hey!" President O'Connor shouted. "What are you doing there?"

The plumber crawled back into the room.

"Me?" he asked. "Replacing water filters."

"It looked new from here."

"It *is* new," the tech said. "But we're getting complaints on the taste."

She had noticed a mineral undertaste to the water, but it wasn't unpleasant.

"It doesn't taste bad," she said.

"It's not supposed to taste at all," he said.

By the time she asked the next question, the noise level had dropped again as everybody listened in.

"Who made the filters?"

The tech pulled the last one out of the garbage.

"Eden Well Supply," he said.

"Gardeners," the general said.

"We're fucked," the President answered. "You better warn the others."

She saw for herself that it was already too late for General Gibson.

*A wise man fears and departs from evil: but the fool rages and is confident.*

—PROVERBS

# 38

RICO TAPPED SCHOLZ on the shoulder to get her attention as the rest of the patrons got to their feet behind them. Their focus, like his own, was the smoking rubble of Mexico City that a shaky camera operator broadcast to the bar screen.

"Are you sure your game's still on?" he asked her.

Rico called up the volume, and a hysterical reporter off-screen tried to deliver the story of her career.

" . . . worst predictions came true. The controversial evacuation that followed Earthquake Watch's timely warning has undoubtedly saved millions of human lives. Once again, I'm Michelle Spencer, live from our airliner over Mexico City. We are witnessing live an earthquake that has just flattened the center of the most populous city in the world. Earthquake Watch was right, and as a result millions of people are alive tonight, though homeless.

"Fewer than half of the citizens of Mexico City evacuated reluctantly after geologists confirmed an eight-point-oh buildup in progress and the U.N. moved armored units in to clear the Zócalo. Critics of the evacuation warned that billions of production dollars would be lost and looting would be a 'feeding frenzy.' Both points are now moot.

"Many of the city's poor stayed in defiance of the evacuation order, and rescue teams worldwide will have the task of digging them out. Fortunately, hundreds of volunteer rescue workers are on hand, but considering that millions of lives are in question, that number may prove insignificant. Property loss, from our vantage point, is immeasurable. It's horrible, the worst I've ever seen. But, again, thanks to the Earthquake Watch early warning system, millions of lives have been spared. . . . ''

The news clicked off, and the two suits behind Rico and Scholz pressed closer.

"White House requests your immediate return to the States, Colonel."

Rico didn't move, not even his lips.

"Isn't babysitting cripples kind of light duty for war whores like yourselves?"

"You're in no condition to piss me off, Colonel."

"What about my boy? And Sonja?"

Scholz shifted her weight slightly, and Rico knew she was ready to play.

"Don't do it, lady," the other suit said. "You're booked on the same flight."

"I'm no lady," Scholz said. She held her drink in the "throw-and-go" posture.

"My boy and Sonja," Rico insisted.

"I don't know anything about that, Colonel. My orders are to move you two immediately to the airport. This comes directly from The Man. Let's go."

Rico felt the unmistakable press of an airgun muzzle against his ribs and decided against pointing out to the contractor that, since the President was a woman, orders no longer came from The Man. He glanced down and saw an eight-shot disposable Hornet convincing him that the contractor could say whatever he liked. One suit by the door jacked a high-pressure hose into the side of his briefcase, and jacked the other end into the hardware under his coat. All of the patrons showed their hands on tabletops without further encouragement.

*Eight shots apiece for these two,* Rico thought. *But that guy at the door could take the walls out of this place.*

Rico didn't hear the dart that dropped Mr. Briefcase, but he glimpsed the white blur as it streaked across the mirror. In the same instant, three more white-feathered darts pricked the necks of the other three suits. Each of them swatted out of reflex at the bug that bit them, and each crumpled to the floor without a twitch. The rest of the patrons studied their drinks very carefully.

"What the hell . . . ?" Scholz asked.

Spook, Al and two strangers smiled, tapping small blowguns in their palms. Rico picked up one suit's Hornet, and Scholz grabbed another. Father Free slid his blowgun into his back pocket.

"Handy, aren't they?" he said, then laughed. "Of course, it's just an artifact. For display purposes only."

"Thanks, Spook," Rico said. "Listen, the lid's off. We need your help and we need it right away."

"Does this have to do with that warehouse standoff in Mexico City?" Spook asked. "And the sudden arson problem we're having here in La Libertad?"

Rico and Scholz raised eyebrows at the same time.

"What do you know about that?" Rico asked.

Father Free smiled, his perfect teeth brilliant. He pulled a faded white collar out of another pocket, and slipped it into place in his shirt.

"I know that the Agency has been sweating blood over a Peace and Freedom subcontractor that took a warehouse away from the Children of Eden," he said. "I know that you managed to pull off an earthquake alert and evacuation, and that you lost Yolanda and a dozen other high-level contacts." His gaze took in Rico's bruises and stitches. "I know about ViraVax."

"Lost Yolanda?" Rico asked. "What . . . ?"

"Sorry," Father Free said, "I thought you knew. One of her own people, apparently, in an alley in Mexico City. I just heard, myself."

In the few seconds of stunned silence, Rico heard the

*whup-whup-whup* of ceiling fans and rifle fire from down the street.

"The kids wouldn't be here now without her," Rico whispered. "Neither would I."

" 'She should have died hereafter,' " Spook quoted, " 'there would have been a time for such a word.' I don't know why you didn't square with me in the first place."

Father Free turned to the mirror and hand-signaled someone behind it. Two women came out of the back to help Al and the others quietly drag the suits through a doorway behind the mirror. Rico glimpsed another half-dozen people back there, intent on the holo projections shimmering in front of them. They took absolutely no notice of the unconscious men dragged through the room and into a closet behind them.

"I don't know what was in that warehouse," Spook said. "But it cost the Agency plenty—people, contacts, money. And favors. *All* favors, even from me. Even, it appears, from you." His gaze flicked over Rico's stitches, scabs and scars. "And now, Yolanda."

One of Spook's men tossed him the briefcase and the automatic. He tossed it to Rico.

"Here," he said. "You might need it."

"Thanks," Rico said, "but this enemy can't be shot. We've got ourselves a Jonestown Special."

Father Free's blue eyes glittered a hard acknowledgment. The Agency considered a Jonestown to be the destruction of an isolated population from within. A Jonestown Special was destruction of unlimited population, also from within a single group. A nation- or worldwide poison or plague.

"Special?"

Father Free looked to Scholz for confirmation, and got it.

"Absolutely," she said. She nodded to indicate the toll of earthquake destruction being run on the peel. "This could be every human being on the face of the earth."

"We need a broadcast team with satlink capability,"

Rico said. "We need security, transportation and quarantine facilities for a virologist and two kids."

"All we were going to do was snatch the kids and this virologist and hide them out in a safe house up in the Jaguars," Scholz said, "Now it looks like a nuclear sub would be about right."

Father Free smiled.

"I can still help you," he said. "I don't believe that *St. Elias* is booked up this afternoon. She's not nuclear, but she's reliable. Now, this 'Special.' There's no antidote?"

"The virologist says she can neutralize it," Scholz said. "But there's production. Then distribution. She also says this thing spreads *very* fast, and that we can't beat it. With luck, we can outrun it."

"How fast?"

"Two days max, from exposure to Meltdown."

"Meltdown? What do you mean, '*Meltdown*'?"

"Spontaneous human combustion," Scholz said. "You get a fever and you melt off your bones and you burn up. Something to do with virions and the mitochondria, Chang says."

"That's the source of the fires around town?"

"Probably," Rico said. "ViraVax tainted their ritual water supply, so they'd all start going up on Easter."

"Why didn't we hear about this before?"

Rico swallowed hard, but didn't let Spook's accusing gaze stop him.

"Because I buried it," Rico said.

His face, a painful mask behind the stitches and the gels, betrayed no expression.

"It killed Red," he added. "Then I followed orders and buried it."

"Will you let your guilt bury *you*, Colonel?" Father Free asked. "And the rest of us along with you?"

"Lay off, Father," Scholz snapped. "Yeah, we had orders."

She put her nose to Rico's nose.

"But we didn't want every tinhorn politician with a thick

wallet to invest in the idea, either. Remember?''

"Yeah," Rico nodded, "I remember. And that goddamn committee's doing the same thing. . . . "

Father Free cleared his throat.

"My sympathies," he said, his voice flat. "The facility shouldn't have been built in the first place."

"You cashed our check when we consulted you on the communications job," Rico said. "Let's get back to the bug. The virologist says it's designed for contagion. Besides the ritual water, it's in vials of childhood inoculations, millions of doses, that's what's in the warehouse. . . . "

"So, what's the problem?" Father Free asked. "If you can't snatch your cargo, destroy it. That earthquake did us all a favor. It's destroyed."

"Not this cargo," Rico said. "Open one of those vials, and anyone within ten meters is dead in two days. You'd have to nuke it to stop it, and nobody wanted to nuke Mexico City."

"And this earthquake just turned it loose?"

"Exactly."

The busy room had grown quiet, hotter, thick.

"What's the survivability?"

"Zero," Rico said. "Chang computes the maximum exposure-to-Meltdown time at forty-eight hours. Infants and old people can go in two or three."

Father Free blinked a couple of times, as though to clear his vision.

"Two *hours*?"

"Two hours. In two hours your baby gets sick. In ten minutes it melts down and burns before your very eyes. . . . "

" . . . And who wouldn't pick up a sick baby?" Scholz said.

"How much of that time are they . . . can they spread this thing?"

"Don't know," Rico said. "But if you're exposed, you're contagious within moments and dead within two days."

"*Could* you nuke it?"

Father Free's voice was soft, smooth. Rico was sure that Spook thought what he thought—if someone *could* nuke it, they probably *would*.

"Too late," Rico said. "That air's contaminated already. According to Chang, it will ride on steam, smoke, dust. It will run off in rain and collect where the poor collect water for their beans. If one vial's broken, it's too late for Mexico City."

"So, it's loose here, too," Father Free said. "If we can't fight, we run. But where?"

"Underwater," Rico said. "Underground. The space station or a biosphere. The only solution is to get ahead of it and seal off."

"Exactly," Scholz said. "Seal yourself off completely from the outside world. Then you have to stay inside for at least two months—air, water, septic, food ... the works."

Father Free's Sidekick interrupted with three bell-like tones.

"Yes?" he answered, and triggered the "unscramble" toggle.

"Targets on the move," the machine reported. "Pan-Pacific Lancer out of hangar and fueling. Flight crew arriving."

"Check," Spook said. "Position Team Two for intercept. We'll want that plane, too."

"Roger that. Secure targets and aircraft."

Two scratches of a microphone signaled, "Out."

*He's pretty casual about who listens in,* Rico thought. *Or he's that well shielded.*

"What's up?" Colonel Toledo asked.

Father Free smiled and tried to look humble.

"Thanks to a few whispers, I anticipated certain of your needs," he said.

His voice hardened.

"I did not anticipate such extreme needs. Not even with Yolanda on the inside."

It was Rico's turn to blink.

"Yolanda worked for you?"

Father Free shrugged.

"Not exactly," he said. "We . . . well, we go way back. She worked for you, of course. And for the Peace and Freedom people. We do . . . did . . . some private work from time to time, just the two of us. . . . "

Father Free's jaw muscles twitched as he clenched his teeth. He motioned the Colonel and Scholz into the office behind the mirror.

The Colonel had made it his business to survey Father Free's office, as well as his two stories of "storage" and "living quarters," years ago. Spook had upgraded his personal electronics considerably since then.

*Same four walls,* Rico thought. *A lot more sophistication.*

He realized, now, where the Peace and Freedom party got its electronics. It wasn't through El Indio, after all.

*Shit*, he thought, *El Indio's probably another "private partner."*

Rico realized, now, why Yolanda rescued him after the embassy bombing. It was a favor from his old ethics professor, Spook.

*Yolanda and Spook!*

No wonder the Peace and Freedom people were gaining popular ground. Yolanda had kissed Rico as he prepared to break his son out of ViraVax. He tried to recall the press of her body against his, but he'd worn coveralls and a tool belt, so there had been no body-pressing. All he remembered clearly was her perfume, "Poison," and the cooling of her kiss on his lips.

He could imagine how bad Spook wanted the men who killed her. That wouldn't be possible now. Nor necessary.

"Which of our needs did you anticipate?" Rico asked.

"Your kids, of course," Father Free said. "And escape. Whisper told me that somebody was taking them someplace for study. I didn't like the sound of it. I presume that whisper came from you."

"It did."

"You could have ordered their study yourself, Colonel," the priest said. His steely eyes glittered in his dark face. "Remember, Colonel, I've known Harry since birth. Sonja, nearly as long. Frankly, Colonel, you've been in the bottle for the last ten years, and I didn't trust your judgment. Instead of studying the possibility, I made some arrangements."

Rico froze. That was the sting of things as he'd come to see them in the past few weeks, but the verbal slap nearly drew blood coming from Spook.

"He doesn't deserve that from you, Father," Scholz hissed.

"You don't know the first thing about it, Scholz," Father Free said. "Those kids deserve having me to watch out for them; that's who deserves what."

"Where were you on Good Friday, when they needed you?"

"At the dam, with Yolanda," he said. "One step behind our hero, here. Check this out."

Colonel Toledo shifted his position as a wall peel came alight across from Spook's desk. Rico's body turned to fire when he moved, as the abrasions and stitches cracked their crusts and tore the pink new flesh underneath. He tried to slow down, relax. . . .

And saw Major Ezra Hodge on the peel, leaving the embassy with a well-stuffed dufflebag over his shoulder.

"What's this?" Rico asked.

Hodge tossed the duffle into his jeep and drove through the gates in a big hurry.

"That's what I was wondering, until I heard your story," Father Free said. "As you know, I have a significant interest in the harbor."

"He went to the harbor?" Scholz asked.

"Right. Pier Nine."

"Isn't that where the DEA keeps that sailboat?" Rico asked.

"Right again," Father Free said. "It's been in my interest to know what goes down on that boat. . . . "

He signaled one of the techs, and the image on the peel switched to the interior of the *Kamui*. Hodge filled the screen as he followed his duffle through the hatch, then took out a small package.

"Motion- and voice-activated," Father Free explained. "Utilizing their own alarm system. I thought maybe he was diabetic, or something—too old-fashioned to accept the pancreas repair."

Hodge unwrapped the paper around a slapshot, read it, ate it, then hit himself in the thigh. Rico noted the panic on the man's face when he blew the shot.

"He's planning a trip," Rico said. "That's clear. And I've seen his records; Hodge doesn't have diabetes, or anything else."

"Junkie?" Spook asked.

"Intramuscular injection," Scholz explained. "He didn't need a vein. It's like the old setups for nerve gas, remember?"

"And what was on that paper he ate?" Rico asked.

The three of them stared at each other for a moment.

"He has an antidote, doesn't he?" Scholz asked.

"That would be my guess," Spook said.

By then Hodge had left the frame of the camera. They heard him locking up topside, and then the camera switched off.

Rico pushed himself to his feet.

"We've got to get Hodge *now*," he said. "And if that's an antidote . . ."

"Father!" one of the techs hollered, pointing to a blank screen in front of her. The woman was so shaken she couldn't speak right away; she just continued pointing a shaking finger at a blank screen.

"What is it, Susanna?"

"Mexico City," she said. "I . . . it's gone!"

"Earthquake," Rico explained. "We saw it on the bar screen."

"No," Susanna said, standing, still unable to turn from the blank screen. "Not the earthquake. This was a flash and fireball. The pulse wiped out our feed. My God, Father, twenty million people!"

*For even now the axe is laid at the root
of the trees.*

—JESUS

# 39

HARRY TOLEDO WATCHED the panic roar like a forest fire
through the tiny compound at Casa Canadá. Joe Clyde and
the other SEALs had flown to Mexico City, leaving the
house and outbuildings to the contract security forces. Now
Mexico City, and any semblance of chain of command, was
gone.

Fear pasted the faces of the hired guns. Their tight-
lipped, wide-eyed scramble for authority left one man dead
and the kitchen shot up beyond repair. Once the shooting
started, it didn't stop until every Litespeed and console was
converted to hot splinters.

Six of the dimwits herded Harry, Sonja and Marte Chang
like lepers into the front parlor and locked the doors. That
prick, Major Hodge, called the shots, but he called them
from a dozen kilometers away.

"Shoot me!" Harry challenged the burly, bald-headed
security guard with the TransNational patch.

"Don't be that way, kid," the man said. His eyes were
wide and his brow sweaty. "Just move into the parlor."

"You're gonna have to drag me in there or shoot me,"
Harry said, and spat at the man's feet.

Everybody moved back a couple of steps at that, and Harry grinned.

"Booga booga," he said, wiggling his fingers at them. "You can't shoot me, I'm a goddamn national treasure."

The TransNational response was to pull back from the entryway and seal it off. The entryway, parlor and screened front porch became home for the three refugees from ViraVax. Sonja pressed her blotchy face against Marte's shoulder, and Marte quietly stroked the shaggy blonde head. That's what showed up most clearly in the dark—Sonja's cropped blonde hair.

Marte, being small and dark, was nearly invisible except where her dark hand stroked Sonja's hair. Marte had said little since Nancy Bartlett's death. When the crazy guard shot up her Litespeed, Marte let out one long shriek of frustration and despair. Her face looked haggard, beyond exhaustion, and she'd shown no reaction to the news about Mexico City.

Harry heard Sergeant Trethewey arguing with one of the guards.

"What about me?" the sergeant yelled. "I've been exposed; shouldn't I stay with them?"

The door opened just a crack, and the sergeant slipped through. Since Trethewey had handled Nancy Bartlett there at the end, nobody in the security cadre wanted to be near him anyway. Sonja greeted him with a hug. She wasn't crying now, and Harry saw the flash of fight coming back to those sky-blue eyes.

Harry stepped to Marte's side and took her hand. It was warm, but otherwise as limp and unresponsive as her expression. He put an arm around her shoulder and hugged her, and still she only stared past the screen at the tongues of flame rising from the darkness along the road.

The rest of the techs and staff remained locked up in the back of the house. Several had tried to get away after Nancy Bartlett died, but the TransNational boys brought them back. Harry had the feeling that a couple of the security guards had slipped away, themselves. Harry hadn't seen his

mother for hours, and didn't know where she was, or
whether she was still alive. None of the security guards
thought this a priority question, so it went unanswered.

"Well," Harry asked Sonja, "can we get four people off
the ground in that biplane of yours?"

Trethewey cleared his throat.

"Not likely," he said. "Hodge took the prop and wheels
as a precaution."

Faint screams came to them on the wind, from out by
the highway, where the coffee workers had been moved.
Everyone listened in a strained silence, and Harry double-
checked their guard. Three of them stood watch in front of
the porch, weapons at the ready, their nervous fingers flick-
ing safeties off and on.

Trethewey saw where Harry was looking.

"I really wish they wouldn't do that," he whispered.
"Somebody could get hurt."

Sonja giggled nervously.

Marte came alive with a deep breath and slipped her arm
around Harry's waist. They said nothing as little blossoms
of fire opened up in the surrounding hills. Harry was cal-
culating speed, and odds, and firepower.

"I have something for you," Marte whispered, and she
slipped a data cube into his palm.

"What's this?"

"Everything," she said. "The original data that you recovered from ViraVax, plus everything we've accomplished so far. I yanked it when that asshole started
shooting."

"Why give it to me?" Harry asked. "You'll need it
when . . ."

"When what?" she interrupted. "When we get out of
here? You have a better chance than I do, Harry."

"Don't talk like that," he said. "We'll all get out of
here. It's dark, we'll shake these rent-a-guns, get to the
airport and Sonja will fly us out. Right, Sonja?"

Sonja's voice was muffled because her face was pressed
into Trethewey's chest.

"We'll do *something*," she said. "You're goddamn right about that."

Cries of shock and pain and the sounds of furniture falling came from inside the house. Harry tried the door, but it was still locked. The thumping and thrashing settled down, and now Harry could smell the unmistakable stench that they'd come to know all too well.

"Shit!"

Just when they were all about to take their chances on a breakout through the screens, three pairs of headlights wound down the drive from the highway. Harry was suspicious from the start when the three black cars pulled up in front of the porch. Three Pan-Pacific suits, a black, an Asian and a caucasian, dismissed the TransNational trio with a simple flash of ID. The TransNationals glanced at the house, then turned as one and jogged to their track down by the hangar.

The black guy, Mills, did all the talking.

"You," he said to Trethewey, "step back. Harry, Sonja, Ms. Chang, you'll come with us, please."

"We're not going anyplace with you," Harry said.

"Why, we're taking you home, son."

His exuberance indicated that he thought Harry was a ten-year-old who would jump at the chance to fly in a real airplane.

"I'm not your son," Harry said. "Check your ID if you don't believe me. But I *am* home. I thought we were staying here, that everything was being taken care of from here."

"You've been misinformed," Mills said. "Whoever told you that had no authorization. Everything will be fine; we'll be flying with you."

Harry didn't move or speak, and Mills looked perplexed.

"Well, I mean, you get to go back to the States," Mills said. He turned to Sonja and bowed slightly. "And your grandfather is the new Vice-President of the United States. You can't disappoint the White House."

"Oh, but I can," Sonja said, also standing firm.

Mills's expression slid from perplexed to pissed.

"Plane's waiting at the airport," Mills said. "We couldn't bring it into this rinky-dink strip. After you."

Mills gestured toward the car.

Harry still didn't move.

"What about my parents?" he asked.

"They're not on my dance card," Mills said.

"Don't I get to pack?"

"I'll buy you a toothbrush," Mills said. "I'm a big fan. I didn't get to tell you yet how proud I am to meet you."

Mills extended his hand, and Harry shook it out of reflex. Mills did not let go, but put his other arm around Harry's shoulders and started to guide him out the door. Harry went limp for a blink, and when Mills was off-balance, he swept the man's foot and dropped him to the pavement. Instantly, Mills had a pistol out and pointed at Trethewey.

"Let me put it this way, son. You come quietly, or the sergeant here is history. I can't shoot you, but I sure as hell can shoot everybody else."

Sonja and Marte had remained silent throughout the exchange. Each of their guards also held pistols on Trethewey.

"Never felt so popular in my life," Trethewey said, and forced a casual-looking grin. "You kids go on without me. I'll catch up."

Sonja groaned, threw her arms around his neck and kissed him.

"Get on the networks as soon as you can," she said. "We'll find you. Trust me."

"Always," he said, and kissed her back.

Harry blushed, and felt himself squirm just a little. He still cared for Sonja more than he wanted to admit, particularly in front of Marte Chang. He turned to Mills.

"What about my dad? He knows more about this than we do."

"He'll be following in a couple of days," Mills said. "He's still in no condition to travel."

Casa Canadá was uncharacteristically deserted, and the humidity made the air nearly too thick to breathe.

Sonja, with the Asian guard holding onto her arm, glanced up at Harry. Her face paled and her lips thinned to grim. She shook her head "no" at him, and he knew that she was ready and waiting his move. No matter what, they would not get into that plane that Mills had waiting.

This was a scenario that Harry had practiced a hundred times with his father in the gym: the kidnapping. He and Sonja had both attended dozens of classes over the years aimed at getting them out of just this situation. Children of embassy personnel in Costa Brava were well versed in the psychology and tactics of kidnapping and hostage-taking.

"Let's go," Mills said, propelling Harry forward with a shove between the shoulders. "We have a plane to catch."

The expression on Mills's face was neutral, but the look in his eyes was that combination of anger and fear that Harry remembered so well from the bad days with his dad. And from what the Agency referred to as "the ViraVax incident."

*Why should he be worried about taking us to the airport?* he wondered. *He doesn't care whether we're lab rats for life.*

Harry glimpsed Sonja's pale face looking back at him from the car ahead, and her expression was one he had not seen from her yet: absolute fear, and panic. She could not survive a lockup; that was clear. Harry doubted that he would, either.

Harry's stomach churned. The drills that he practiced with his father emphasized never getting into the car in the first place.

"Make them do whatever they're going to do in public," his father had said. "Don't let them get you into a vehicle. If you get inside, you're dead."

But this vehicle was taking them to the airport, and Harry thought it worth the risk to get the free ride. The cars jolted down the chuckhole driveway and rattled Harry's teeth. When he looked out the back window at Casa Canadá, he saw Sergeant Trethewey fall facedown into the dirt. He couldn't tell from that distance whether he'd been shot, or

whether the Deathbug got him. He caught the driver's gaze
in the rearview mirror, saw the unmistakable flicker of fear.

"You've seen what it does, haven't you?" Harry asked.

Mills and the driver stared straight ahead. The driver
swerved around two charred lumps to get out onto the highway and then swerved again to avoid a group of *deficientes*
shuffling towards town, many of them crying. The little
band of retarded kids had stepped in front of the car from
a trail in the bush, and there was no caretaker with them.
One of them tried to wave down the car, and Harry's mind
tricked him into seeing them all aflame, like those poor
bastards at ViraVax.

They passed dozens of burned vehicles along the roadside, and other blackened lumps of humanity, some of them
still steaming. No one stood by any of the bodies. Wild-
eyed drivers careened hundreds of vehicles along the highway, most of them headed away from the city.

At the frontage road to the airport, Harry decided it was
time to make his move. There would be more security at
the airport, and even though they'd have their hands full
with panicked mobs desperate to get out, Harry thought the
odds were best right here.

"You guys fucked it up, didn't you?" Harry said. "You
dropped the ball and let that virus loose in Mexico City,
didn't you? They nuked a whole city because you guys
*fucked up!*"

"You've got quite a mouth on you, kid," Mills said.
"Why don't you just shut it up?"

"Why don't you just try to make me, Mills?" Harry
challenged, and spat at the back of the man's head.

*Make them come to you*, his dad had taught him. *The
madder the hornet, the worse his vision.*

"I'm not taking that shit from you, kid; you need to get
that straight right now."

Mills reached back to give Harry a slap, and Harry
grabbed his hand, turned it around, folded it back against
the wrist and drove his fist into the man's elbow. He felt
the wrist snap and heard the satisfying *pop* of the elbow

separating. Mills screamed in pain and curled up on the seat, too stunned to grab for his gun.

Harry popped the driver's ears with both hands, then fisted both carotids just above the man's shoulders.

Their car swerved across the road and nosed into the ditch. While Mills lay vomiting from the pain, Harry reached over the seat back, grabbed his Colt and his Sidekick, then rolled out the back door, waiting.

Taillights blazed in the car ahead, and it backed up with tires smoking. The Asian who jumped out spoke into his Sidekick and the third car, with Marte Chang, accelerated down the road. Harry watched the Asian approach the car and pull Mills's door open.

Mills hollered, "The kid, goddammit! The fucking kid's got my gun!"

"Right here," Harry said, and leveled it at the very surprised guard. "Take your pistol out with your fingers and put it on the ground, and put your Sidekick beside it. If you've been briefed at the right level, you know I'll blow your brains out before you can say, 'Adios, motherfucker.' "

The guard did as he was told, and Mills alternated spitting and cursing in the front seat.

"Now kick them over here, and walk around to the driver's side."

Harry glanced up to see that Sonja was struggling with her driver. She was in the seat behind him with a crude stranglehold around his neck. The security guard kicked the gun and the Sidekick over to Harry and walked around to the driver's side. Harry picked up the Sidekick and the gun, then shot out both tires on his side before he rescued the other Pan-Pacific from Sonja's death-grip.

"Out!" he ordered, and the gasping driver crumpled to the pavement.

Harry took his weapon and Sidekick, too, then started to get in on the driver's side. Sonja scrambled over the seat back and grabbed the wheel.

"I'll drive," she said, "you shoot."

"We've got to get Marte," he said. "Step on it; maybe we can catch them before the airport."

When Sonja slid through the airport's side gate off the frontage road, Harry saw that nobody was going anywhere from this airport. Two planes blazed in the center of the runway, and various security forces fought a mob that tried to get to the small private planes tied down on the parkway. Sonja slammed on the brakes and they screeched to a stop about a dozen meters behind the car that held Marte Chang. The car was on fire. Both front doors were open and the Pan-Pacific men were sprinting for a Lancer on the taxiway. Harry saw, with horror, that the fire came from a small, disintegrating figure in the back seat, her black hair swirling with the greasy smoke and her hand held out as though she'd just blown him a kiss.

*You get angry about a lot of things
and you, yourself, dying uselessly is
one of them.*

— ERNEST HEMINGWAY,
"NIGHT BEFORE BATTLE"

# 40

RICO WATCHED IN brittle silence as the images of Mexico City's destruction flashed across Spook's high-class displays. Action in the street below had escalated into full-scale combat, and Spook's people frantically scrambled to get disks, cubes and other portables into dufflebags. They worked in near-silence, well organized, as though they'd abandoned their quarters before. None, including Father Free, carried a weapon.

Rico's real fears lay with Harry, Sonja and Marte Chang. He had to find a way to get to them and get them out. Slipping his two-bit security guard a couple of times had been a joke. But taking on a whole contingent, even a merc contingent, was a grossly different matter. In Rico's condition, his next best bet was to find somebody who could get through security for him. Somebody like Father Free. Rico allowed himself a grunt of approval when Father Free lifted the colorful rug and showed him the escape shaft. The lights failed as Spook's team pulled batteries out of their slots and slid them into backpacks.

"Used to be a laundry chute," Father Free said. "We just took some liberties."

Rico looked through the open hatchway and knew that he could not force his battered body down that three-story ladder. Even if he could stand the pain, he didn't have the dexterity to make it, and he would only slow up the others. There was shooting now at the front of the building. Rico didn't say anything, but helped Scholz drag a full duffle to the edge of the shaft. That alone took most of his strength.

"Can you make it?" Scholz whispered.

Rico didn't answer, but remained bent over his cane as he tried to calm the thousand little fires burning his skin.

"Move your butts, boys and girls," Father Free mumbled to no one.

Through the two-way mirror, Rico saw one of the patrons collapse out in the bar. He tapped Scholz's shoulder, and by the time she swung around for a look, the rest of the patrons were already scrambling for the doors. That familiar smell of hot gangrene wafted through the doorway.

"Hand me that extinguisher, Scholz," he said. "We don't need this place burning up around us."

She pulled it out of the case on the wall and handed it to him. He didn't have the strength to hold onto it, and the heavy cylinder crashed to the floor. Everyone looked up from their work, startled, and Rico waved his hand toward the smoke already filling the bar.

"I'll take care of this one," he said. "Just get moving."

Rico pulled the fat fire extinguisher behind him like a child's wagon. This man was someone that Rico used to know, but he couldn't remember his name. Most of the fire was concentrated around the man's trunk. He lay, face down, the bones of his hands frozen in supplication. Rico pulled the pin and slathered the astringent foam over the bubbling body. The floor was scorched, but the fire was out. He tottered into Spook's office in time to see the top of Susanna's head disappear down the shaft. Scholz waited for him, a backpack of batteries slung over each shoulder.

Scholz's Sidekick interrupted with its urgent tone.

Scholz took the message in her earpiece, and her tan seemed suddenly sickly pale.

"What now?" Rico asked, gasping.

"The kids," she said. "State Department sent some Pan-Pacifics to pick them up and get them to the airport."

"Back to the U.S.?"

She shook her head.

"Doesn't matter," she said. "The kids beat them up, took their weapons and their cars, and made it to the airport on their own."

"He's his daddy's boy," Father Free mumbled.

He lowered the last duffle by rope down the shaft. The three of them were the only ones left, so Father Free unlocked the closet door that held the Pan-Pacific security team. They were still unconscious.

Rico felt hopeful for the first time in days.

"Did the kids get a plane out?"

"No." Scholz shook her head. "Airport's a mess—fires and debris on the runway. Mobs trying to steal planes that they can't fly, and our people have orders to shoot them down anyway."

Rico was grateful that she didn't stress the fact that the standing orders to shoot them down were cut by one Colonel Rico Toledo.

"How can we get to them now?"

It was hopeless. The kids were lost, the whole goddamn human race was probably lost.

"Hodge is out there now," she said.

"Hodge? What the hell . . . ?"

"He's the one who called in from the airport. He didn't trust the Pan-Pacific goons, so he drove out there and saw the whole thing. . . ."

"And you believe it was coincidence?" Father Free interrupted. "I think he's been after them all along. Look at the preparations he made on the *Kamui*. Three supply trips in one day. He's got plans for leaving, and he's not leaving alone."

Rico nodded.

"He's had control of the kids all along," Rico said. "He ordered the isolation, then the quarantine at Casa Canadá."

"And the one time they're out of his command, he happens to run into them at the airport in time to save their skins," Father Free added.

"Hodge is an idiot," Scholz said. "He's a self-centered little maggot who . . . "

"Who got command of this station," Rico reminded her, "even though you were next in line. Even though you got promoted over him." Rico took a deep breath, squeezed his aching temples. "And in that data that Harry recovered from ViraVax, there was something that bothered me, but I couldn't place it."

"And?"

"It wasn't something, it was the lack of something," Rico said. "There were detailed files on all of us. You, me, Grace and the kids. Even Spook, here."

Scholz's blue eyes widened as she saw where he was headed.

"But nothing on Hodge."

"Not a word," Rico said.

"Well, well," Father Free said. "Solaris's little garden had a mole, after all."

Scholz's Sidekick toned again. This time she didn't bother with the earpiece, and Rico heard Hodge's whine loud and clear.

"The embassy and the airport's lost," he said. "We'll have to evacuate from the harbor. Meet at C-dock. Would you confirm that, and confirm Colonel Toledo's presence with you?"

Scholz's eyebrows lifted with curiosity.

"Roger that, Major," Scholz said. "The Colonel is here, and we can meet you at C-dock."

Rico pulled her sleeve.

"The kids?" he rasped.

"What about Harry and Sonja?" she asked. "And Marte?"

"The kids are fine," Hodge said. "Harry's holding a pistol on me right now. Marte Chang burned up here at the airport. Harry wants to talk to his father."

Scratching sounds came across the airways as Hodge handed over his Sidekick.

"Dad?"

"Here," Rico croaked. "Do what he says. Get to the harbor."

"What about you?"

"We're already there," Rico said. "A boat is the safest place to be right now. Get here with or without Hodge."

That was when he saw one of the Pan-Pacifics in the closet start to slump off his bones.

"Looks like we're in some kind of second stage of this bug," he said. "Get your butt down here and let's get gone. Keep that gun on Hodge; I'll explain later."

"Good luck, Dad."

"Good luck, son."

One more glance towards the closet, and Rico knew he'd make it down that ladder or die trying. If he was going to die, it would be with his own people, not with some pissant, tinhorn, rent-a-gun security team.

Father Free was already over the edge and halfway down the ladder.

"Let's *go* up there!" he hollered, sounding more like the old Spook and less like a parish priest.

"Go ahead, Scholz," Rico said. "I'll try not to fall on you."

Boot heels clattered up the stairwell out in the bar, and Rico checked the loads on his airgun.

"Go!" he shouted at Scholz, and gave her a shove.

The army squad burst through the doorway, and the first one through snapped off a quick burst from his Bullpup that stitched the peel-and-peek behind Rico. Rico's stitches didn't slow his reflexes any. He felt, more than heard, the satisfying *putt-putt-putt* of the briefcase compressor as it coughed out a withering stream of pellets. The two men in the doorway went down immediately. The other four looked at the Meltdown in the bar, at their buddies twitching on the floor, and scrambled back downstairs without a fight.

Rico abandoned the heavy compressor, stepped down the first few rungs of the ladder and slid the trapdoor back into place overhead. He was sweating so hard his eyes stung, and he couldn't catch his breath. Scholz hung onto the ladder about five meters below him.

"Rico, can I help you?"

He summoned all of his breath and growled, "Get your sweet ass out of my way, Scholz. I might be coming down hard."

He heard her climbing towards him.

"Scholz, goddammit, you can't *carry* me down, for Chrissake!"

She was already working her shoulder into his belly. She grabbed his knees and said, "You've got to trust me; now let go."

By that time, Rico didn't have a choice. He collapsed across Scholz's shoulder, and was barely aware that his head and feet scraped the walls of the shaft as she worked her way down the ladder.

"This is how I like my men, Colonel."

"Helpless?"

"No." She paused, shifted his weight. "Trusting."

"I . . . didn't know . . . you liked men . . . Scholz."

"Only one so far, Colonel."

They were more than halfway down, and Rico tried to help her balance by holding onto her waist. His face hung only a hand's-breadth from her solid rear, and for the first time he realized how incredibly strong she was.

"Nice butt, Scholz."

"About time you noticed."

And then they were down, gasping like dead fish on a heavy plank floor that smelled of creosote and iodine. The slap of waves underneath told him that it was a pier. Rico felt no pain now, but all of his will wasn't enough to get his legs under him.

The city overhead sounded like it was coming apart—screams and explosions were punctuated by small-arms fire, and already the air smelled of spoiled meat.

"Couldn't have worked better if we'd planned it that way," Father Free said.

He chuckled through a well-chewed Havana, then lifted Rico under the armpits and steered him towards the fishing boat that he rented out to tourists. Scholz followed, covering them with the Hornet.

"Love your toys," Rico said, nodding at the freshly painted boat.

"Worked hard for 'em," Father Free said. "Welcome to the *St. Elias.* I've got Wally on standby, in case we have to do a pickup on the kids."

Rico sat on the deck as Scholz slipped down the hatch.

"Who's Wally?" he asked.

"Wally's not a who, he's a what. Go ahead and get below."

Rico slipped his legs over the lip of the hatch, grasped the ladder weakly and tumbled in a heap onto the cabin deck. Father Free slid down the ladder behind him, and didn't miss a beat as he helped Rico to a chair beside the controls.

"Wally's a relic," Father Free said. "It's an old Coast Guard Sikorsky that I did some barter for a few years back. Runs like a dream—a loud dream. It's slow, but it'll make good backup if the kids get stuck. As Scholz pointed out, they're shooting down anything that goes up right now, and I don't want to lose this bird."

Susanna and Melissa had the screens up, and once again they tuned into the devastation that used to be Mexico City. Everyone was quiet now, as Father Free dogged the hatch. All ten people aboard had friends in Mexico City.

Colored overlays labeled "EMP Range" and "Biological Perimeter" clicked into place and far exceeded the blast site. Rico knew what it was before the calculations on the peel told him.

"Neutron device," he said. "Looks like a steamer trunk from Operation Trojan Horse. Deployed by rail to industrial centers or by ship to key ports. Kills people, leaves most of the goods intact. Solaris's idea."

"But does it kill viruses?" Spook asked.

Rico shook his head.

"Don't know. Chang would know. From what she told me, it could have already dispersed on the steam and smoke from the earthquake. . . . "

"There's probably a device here in La Libertad somewhere, right?" Father Free asked.

"Right," Scholz said. "In a shipping container, aboard the *Comet*."

"That derelict?" Spook laughed. "I wondered why anybody bothered to keep it afloat. So what's to keep The Man from setting off this one, too?"

"The Woman doesn't have to," Scholz said. "Solaris had the codes for every device in his region, and discretionary power to detonate. It's a hands-on action, though. A suicide mission. He can't do it by remote."

"Father," the redhead Melissa interrupted. "Wally, command line."

"Unscramble," Father Free said. "Speaker. Go, Wally."

"Targets secure," the voice said. Even the computer couldn't filter out the background noise of the old Sikorsky. "For your information, I had to launch. I'll set down as quick as I can. Big trouble out here."

Father Free rolled his eyes and spoke through teeth clenched tight to his unlit cigar.

"Go."

"Embassy's gone. I count six villages on fire, four more smoking and gone. A squad of Costa Brava regulars tried to grab my bird. Is there a war out here you didn't tell me about?"

"What villages?" Rico asked. He stood too quickly, and all the little mouths of the hundreds of wounds on his body screamed at him. He had to have confirmed what his gut already feared. "Where, exactly?"

"That string from the highway up to the Jaguars. Hold on, going up . . . yeah, hey, looks like a lot of smoke coming from your way, too. In town. Want me to check it out?"

Spook glanced at Rico, and Rico shook his head.

"Stand by targets. Watch out for bogies; they mean business."

"Roger," Wally said. "Targets moving your way, ETA ten minutes. Will stand by."

Father Free turned to the redhead, who had mounted her visor as well as her gloveware.

"Melissa?"

"On it, Father. Fire frequency shows more calls than units available in Zones Nine and Twelve. . . . "

"Mother of Mercy Hospital," Scholz said. "It's in Zone Twelve. . . . "

" . . . Where the airport highway enters town," Rico finished. "Can you give us a grid from the ViraVax site to La Libertad?"

"It's yours, Colonel," Melissa said.

Rico picked up a pointer and traced backwards from Mother of Mercy Hospital to ViraVax. The path included Valle Viejo, a dirt track that connected several Maya settlements and ended in jungle just outside the old ViraVax perimeter.

"You and Scholz don't look too well, Rico," Father Free said. "You're onto something. Want to fill me in?"

"The army was supposed to secure that area," Scholz said. "Nobody in, nobody out."

"Yeah, right," Rico muttered. "The lid was on. Orders were probably low priority—looter precautions, or some such shit that wouldn't get a whisper going."

Scholz stared at the peel as the data started fleshing in details and connecting the dots to the city. She spoke in a whisper so soft that Rico barely heard.

"Chang had some new projections," she said. "She said we might not need a vaccine. This thing moves so fast that it just might burn itself out right here."

In the stiff, momentary silence between them, Rico heard the hum of electric motors as the boat started to move.

"Mexico City doesn't matter," Rico told Father Free. "It's big-time infection here."

Father Free set his soggy cigar on his control panel,

sucked in a big breath and let it out very slowly while he
looked Rico in the eye.

"What are our odds?"

Melissa and Susanna had their visors up, fingers stilled,
and the rest of the crew seemed to be holding their collec-
tive breath.

"If the wind's been in our favor here, and we split now,
we might make it," Rico said.

He couldn't look anyone in the eye.

"*Might?*"

Rico nodded.

"Yeah," he said. "We were all exposed topside when
your customer went flambé. We thought yesterday that the
Gardeners just poisoned themselves off. This mess we're
into now must be phase two."

"Somebody's got to get on the air, warn people, get
them isolated," Scholz said.

Father Free surveyed the equipment aboard *St. Elias* and
his silent team of assistants, then made a decision.

"Here's what we'll do. The *Kamui* has excellent navigation electronics and a good transmitter. She's a blue-
water sailer. This thing's designed for day cruises and really
sucks the power. Wouldn't get us far on open water. You,
Scholz, me, Susanna and Melissa will take what we can
from here and start broadcasting from *Kamui*. There's
Wally for a short hop, maybe to one of the islands. If we
split up, we'll check in hourly and scramble via satlink on
command one. Wind is from the water; that gives us a
break. Let's get out to *Kamui now,* and from there to Maude
Island."

Maude Island had been a consulting project of Spook's
like ViraVax had belonged to Rico. It was a real island,
but hollowed out and fitted with warrens that sent explor-
atory fingers for kilometers under the Pacific. Rico knew
of its existence, but not its purpose. Father Free had quit
the Agency the day his portion of the Maude Island Project
was finished.

As they navigated the boat haven and nudged up to the
*Kamui,* Spook cracked the hatch. One by one, back in the
city, the frantic sirens fell silent as the wall of flame grew.

> *For now I will stretch out my hand,*
> *that I may smite thee and thy people*
> *with pestilence; and thou shalt be cut*
> *off from the earth.*
>
> —MOSES

# 41

EZRA HODGE WAS elated, but he didn't dare show it. Truly, the Lord's will was evident in the good fortune that fell his way. He monitored the White House orders to the offices of Pan-Pacific, and he made the right choice by heading straight for the airport. He had no idea how he was going to get the kids away from the Pan-Pacific boys, and the kids took care of that problem for him. He had no idea how to keep them from flying out of La Libertad, and then Flaming Sword, itself, came to his rescue. Now his only worry was how to eliminate Rico Toledo when they got to the harbor.

*The Lord will provide,* he reminded himself, and he was more confident of this today than ever before in his life.

"You get in the back," Harry told him, twitching the pistol. "I'll ride back there with you. Sonja can drive."

"Whatever you say," Hodge said. "Just so we make it to the harbor. I'm on your side, you know."

"You've had a helluva way of showing it," Harry said. "As far as I'm concerned, Sonja and I are on one side and the rest of the world is on the other. Hold that thought."

Hodge slid across the back seat and Harry got in beside him.

"Even your father?" he asked. "And Colonel Scholz?"

"Maybe," Harry said. "We'll see."

Sonja ran back from a quick inspection of the runway and jumped into the driver's seat.

"Can't do it," she said. "We'd have to use the road for takeoff, and nobody's going to let us through."

She toggled the doorlocks just as a group of wild-eyed men and women rushed the car. She spun the car around in a half-circle, tumbling them to the pavement, and fishtailed out the back gate onto the frontage road.

"Take Valle Viejo," Hodge told her. "The highway's jammed to a standstill."

"Take whatever road you want," Harry told her. "You can't believe this bastard."

"Harry," Hodge said, in his calmest voice, "I don't want to die out here any more than you do. Valle Viejo was clear ten minutes ago; the highway was not."

Ezra was relieved when Sonja took his advice. It was a step, a very small step, towards their trust. Soon, they would rely on him for everything; they might as well trust him. He noticed tears sliding down Harry's cheeks, and a disconcerting tremble in his gun hand.

"Are you all right, son?"

Harry's eyes snapped into a cruel gray duplicate of Rico Toledo, and the bore of the pistol stared Ezra down as Harry sneered, "What are you saying, Hodge? Did you have a little fling with my mother?"

Ezra felt his heart shift into triple-time. He had not expected this kind of aggression from the boy, but it was magnificent testimony to the handiwork of Dajaj Mishwe.

"No, Harry, I . . . I just . . . "

"Harry!" Sonja snapped. "Chill out. It's not his fault Marte died."

"Are you sure?" Harry said. "He works for the Agency, the Agency gave us ViraVax, and ViraVax gave us this . . . *this*!"

Harry waved his hand at a burning bus as Sonja swerved around it. Lumps of charred, steaming flesh littered the roadway, and Ezra felt the *thump-kathump* of something soft under the car. Sonja was an absolutely fearless driver; Ezra liked that about her.

"Marte came up with an answer," Harry said. He pointed to his head and patted the cube in his pocket. "It's here, and here. Now, we need to get it to someone who can grow the proper medium. Then they could be growing a counteragent within twenty-four hours. And we have to warn people not to drink that EdenSprings water."

Ezra shook his head.

"If you've got an idea of where to go," he said, "I'll be glad to get us there. But, as you can see, this bug is fast. Very fast. If anybody's alive at this lab you seek by the time we get there, what makes you think they'll let us in?"

"They don't have to," Harry insisted. "We can transmit the data and the warning about the water onto the web, and every lab in the world can get on it. That's what we're going to do."

"Hold on," Sonja said. "Roadblock."

It was a typical Costa Bravan Army roadblock, three burned-out civilian cars across the road with a squad of young, scared grunts on both sides. They held their rifles ready and their gazes swept the area, self-conscious in their vulnerability on the open road.

"Bust it," Harry said.

"Only in the movies, Harry," Ezra said. "You will be killed or the car will be destroyed. Either way, you help nobody. Put the gun away and let me handle this. I have clearance."

Sonja slowed nearly to a stop a hundred meters away from the roadblock.

"Ditches," she said. "I can't make it around, either. Shit!"

A sudden roar and a gust of wind pounded their car, and the army boys snapped rifles to shoulders. A pair of rockets streaked from somewhere overhead and blew the roadblock into a flaming fountain of junk. Then an old tin-can chopper dropped in front of their car and laid down a whirling storm of heavy red smoke while the grunts scrambled for the ditches.

"Go! Go! Go!" Harry hollered.

Sonja jammed her foot to the floor. A dozen rounds smacked into both sides of the car before they plunged into the smoke screen. They crashed through the twisted wreckage, bounced and skidded on the debris, and when they shot out of the other side of the smoke they were still on the road.

"Chill, girl!" Harry said, and slapped Sonja on the back with his free hand.

"Who was *that*?" Ezra whispered.

"A guardian angel," Sonja said. "Who cares? They got us through and we're almost there."

*She has her spiritual side,* Hodge thought, with growing satisfaction. *This is all as it should be.*

Two things worried him now. It was well past time for his antidote, and the drawbridge to the harbor was up. A kilometer or more of roadway was choked with cars stopped for the bridge, and several cars at the head of the line blazed furiously under thick, black smoke. The bridge-tender's shack was also ablaze.

"Do you have clearance for *that*, Hodge?" Harry asked.

Without waiting for a response, Harry picked up Hodge's Sidekick.

"Dad and Scholz," he demanded. "What channel?"

"Command one scramble," Ezra said, and he was surprised when Harry's fingers flurried the correct code.

There was no response.

"Transmitter's working," Harry mumbled. "They must have their hands full." He keyed "memo" and said, "We're stuck at the Valle Viejo bridge. We'll work our way north along the waterfront, look for a boat and retransmit every fifteen minutes."

"Sit tight, kid," a voice came back. The background was so full of engine noise and static that Harry could hardly understand him. "I've got two shadows on my tail. When I set down, you-all come a-jumpin'."

Ezra looked out the hole in their shattered rear window and saw the old Sikorsky racing the grasstops towards them.

"Let's go!" Harry shouted. "You, Hodge, this way!"

Harry kept the pistol trained on Ezra as he slid out Harry's side of the car. The chopper came in so low and fast that they heard the shriek of gravel against pontoons over the scream of the engine. Two Costa Brava choppers closed fast from a few kilometers back. Sonja dove headfirst into the loading door, then reached out a hand to Ezra. Harry only had one foot on the pontoon when the chopper surged skyward. He pinwheeled backwards and lost the pistol as he grabbed Ezra's waist. Sonja braced her feet against the doorframe and hauled them both aboard.

"This'll be quick," their pilot shouted. "I'll drop you at the harbor and lose those bogeys. Grab lifejackets; you're gonna get wet."

In less than a minute they hovered low over the end of the harbor pier where *Kamui* rocked in its slip.

"Can't get closer because of the masts," the pilot yelled. "You'll have to jump."

Ezra's heart dropped to his stomach.

"I can't swim," he shouted back.

"You'll be swimming one way or another," the pilot said. "Now, jump!"

A cannon burst stitched the water across their bow, and Ezra felt Harry's foot punch him between the shoulder blades. He tried to grab the pontoon, but slid off into the water, his lifejacket clutched in his fist. He held his breath as hard as he could and never lost sight of the surface. Sonja and Harry plunged through the sunlight nearly on top of him, and one of them pulled him towards the surface.

They broke through the debris-strewn chop together, and Ezra gasped down a quick three or four breaths. He clutched his lifejacket to his chest as somebody towed him with a hand under his chin.

The chopper must have been hit just as they jumped, because it lay smoking on its side halfway across the neighboring pier. The old chopper took several boats with it as flames blossomed from the cockpit and it sank into the harbor. There was no sign of the pilot, and the two pursuit choppers turned back towards the airport.

The three of them reached the pier after the longest minute of Ezra Hodge's life. Sonja and Harry clambered up the swim ladder, leaving Ezra to his white-knuckled grip on the bottom rung. He took several deep breaths, then climbed up after them on trembling legs. His abject fear turned suddenly to elation.

*We made it!*

Now, for everything to be perfect, he merely needed await the arrival of Rena Scholz, and they could be about the business of reclaiming the Garden of Eden for themselves, and for the Lord.

*With what measure you measure, it shall be measured to you.*

—JESUS

# 42

HARRY WOULDN'T HAVE recognized his father if Rico hadn't been with Colonel Scholz. The two colonels sat in the cockpit of the *Kamui*, looking like casual holiday boaters drinking their frosty lemonade, the whole city ablaze like a violent sunrise behind them. Both Scholz and Harry's father wore fire-blackened field pants and black T-shirts. Scholz's face was hollow-eyed, pale, and for the first time Harry thought she looked old. His father looked dead. *Kamui*'s clockwork diesel chugged in the waveslap, and rigging rattled over the *pop-pop* of small-arms fire.

Rena Scholz held her lemonade in one hand and a scorched palm-cam in the other.

"Hey, Harry," Rico rasped. "Good work, son. You too, Sonja."

Rico didn't attempt to rise to greet them, and Harry suspected that he couldn't.

"Thanks, Dad. So far, so good."

Sonja stood dripping on the pier in silence while she watched the city burn.

Rico's eyelids drooped, his hands trembled, but his mouth worked up a smile.

"Between us, Pan-Pacific's had a mighty bad day," Rico said. "Cast off the bow line and jump aboard. You remember how to sail this thing?"

Harry grunted, moved to the bow cleat and untied the line. He didn't ask about the fishing boat rafted to the rail of the *Kamui*. His father was only this casual when he had a trap ready to spring, and Harry expected that this time it was Hodge's neck that was on the line. He and Sonja had sailed aboard *Kamui* twice. Both times his father had secured the boat from the DEA so that he and Sonja's dad could take their families out. Both times Rico had failed to show up because he was drunk somewhere or chasing some skirt. But Harry, Sonja and Red Bartlett had enjoyed a few days sailing up- and down-coast.

"Come on, Sonja," Rena Scholz said. "Let me give you a hand up."

Sonja clasped the offered hand and climbed aboard, her wet tennis shoes slopping the deck.

A formation of Costa Brava's tank-killers screamed overhead, hugging the coastline south. Rico pointed them out for Hodge's benefit.

"Those boys have had enough," Rico said. "They're saving their own asses, heading for Costa Rica or Panamá. If they'd left a few minutes earlier, the Peace and Freedom boys might still have their chopper. What's the latest, Major?"

Hodge said nothing. He glanced around fearfully at the confusion of small boats that careened off each other and the pier in their frantic dash for the open water and safety. Overloaded barques pedaled a beeline for the channel.

Hodge avoided Rico's gaze and shifted from foot to foot on the wet pier. Harry saw Hodge eye the water, as though weighing the sure death by water against anything his dad might have to offer.

Harry coiled the bow line and tossed the loop to Rena Scholz. A burst of rifle fire ended in a grenade explosion at the head of the boardwalk. Two Harbor Patrol boats, loaded way beyond capacity with women, kids, luggage and chickens, screamed past their bow and snaked their way through slower traffic to the mouth of the harbor. None of those things distracted Harry from standing between Hodge and escape. Harry followed a silent, sullen Hodge over the rail.

The sailboat's diesel was smooth and nearly silent, but the rest of the world was noise. Several fireballs and concussions marked the destruction of the marina's fences behind them. Rico motioned Sonja to the topside controls.

"Scholz has the charts," Rico said. "Make for Maude Island when we clear the harbor. We've punched it into the navcom. Harry and I have some business with Major Hodge, here. Major? You don't seem very grateful that we just saved your slimy ass."

Major Hodge's gaze was fixed on two metal boxes that Rico held in his lap. Harry would bet big money that the metal boxes covered a pistol, too, the way his dad's hand lazed at the edge of them.

"I'm grateful," Hodge said, and tried a smile. He spread his hands slowly, water dripping from his clothing to the deck. "I'm very grateful. I'm just not quite sure how . . . "

"Yes," Rico said, " 'how?' is the great question of the hour, isn't it? Right after 'what?' " He tapped the top metal box with his index finger. "This, for example. What is it?"

Hodge glanced quickly towards Scholz, as though asking for help. She stood, impassive, behind Sonja at the wheel, fending off the fishing boat as they maneuvered away from the pier. Sonja held her head high, to see over the top of the cabin, and picked their way through the chaos of small-boat traffic. She pretended that she wasn't interested in Rico's game with Hodge, but Harry could tell that she was tuned in.

"It's insulin," Hodge said. He began to shiver as the wind from the fires whipped the wavetops and his wet clothes. "I'm a diabetic, and I need insulin."

Rico spoke in that calm, level voice that Harry knew always preceded a major explosion.

"If we had more time, I'd dick around with you," Rico

said. "But our circle of friends is narrowing fast, and you're insulting my intelligence. The least you could do is honor me with a good lie, one I might be proud to remember you by."

Rico held the top box over the rail, and asked again.

"What is it?"

"Allergy shots," Hodge said, speaking quickly. "They're in a series and I have to take one . . . "

When the metal tin hit the water, Harry heard a groan from Hodge's throat that was torn from the very bottom of his being. For a moment it looked to Harry as though Hodge would jump in after the box, but then the man remembered that he couldn't swim.

"Oh, no. Oh, no," was all Hodge could bring himself to say.

He grabbed a boathook and ran along the rail, trying to snag the silver box that now shone blue-green under the harbor surface. The blunt prong of his boathook just forced it under the surface that much faster. Then it was hit by a speedboat and sunk. Hodge dropped the boathook onto the deck, then turned a stricken face towards the others, hands outstretched as if expecting them to help him.

Rico picked up the remaining tin and held it over the rail, and Hodge dropped to his knees at Rico's feet, unmindful of the pistol in Rico's other hand.

"Please, no!" he begged. Hodge turned a desperate glance towards Scholz, who ignored him. "Please," he repeated, nodding towards Scholz, "don't drop it. She'll die. You don't want her to die."

"No," Rico said, "I don't want her to die. Does Scholz have diabetes? Allergies that she's not aware of?"

"You know what it is or you wouldn't be doing this to me," Hodge said. "Believe me, I was trying to save the children. . . . "

"A lot of interest in these kids, these days," Rico said. He kept his hand with the box over the rail. "Tell me about your newfound parental instincts. Tell me about your work with ViraVax."

"Mishwe owed me some favors," Hodge said. "He gave me two series of antidotes—one for me, one for . . . her."

Rena Scholz raised an eyebrow.

"How thoughtful of him," Scholz said. "And he didn't even know me."

Hodge turned to her in desperation.

"I got it for you. I talked him out of it. I didn't want you to . . . "

"To die like the rest of the world?" Rico interrupted. "How romantic, Hodge. You and Colonel Scholz, the new Adam and Eve of the Apocalypse. I'm touched. But why save the kids if they're just going to die later?"

"The GenoVax won't kill them," Hodge said. "They're immune. They're the real Adam and Eve."

Harry was stunned, hearing this from someone who wasn't merely speculating.

"So," Harry said, "Marte was right. She guessed as much when she went through the cloning data that Sonja's dad siphoned out of Mishwe's records." He clenched his fists and stood chest to chest with Hodge. "What else did you do to us?"

"That's all I know," Hodge said. His full, pale lips trembled.

Rico brought the case back into the boat and opened it. He selected one of the slapshots and squirted half of it overboard.

"No, no, no," Hodge cried. "Don't do that."

"The boy asked you a question, Major. If you answer it, I'll let you have one of these."

"There's a fail-safe," Hodge said. "That's all I know about."

Rico set the injector back into the case.

"That's better. What kind of fail-safe?"

"To make sure that they remain pure. He didn't want their genetic material wasted."

Harry felt himself dizzying with an unfamiliar but comfortable fury.

"What does that mean?"

Hodge stared at the puddle of water on the deck at his feet. He wouldn't look up.

"It means you can't have sex with anyone but each other," he said. "If you do, they'll die."

Harry screamed his rage, and his palms popped both of Hodge's ears.

"Marte!" he sobbed, then snap-kicked Hodge under the sternum. "Marte!"

Harry grabbed Hodge by both ears, then kneed Hodge's face and kicked his belly as he dropped to the deck.

"You bastard! You rotten sonofabitch!"

"Wait, Harry," Scholz said, with a hand on his arm. She moved quickly between them. "He'll get his punishment soon enough. He'll die like the rest of us." She glanced up at Rico and their gazes held for a moment, two. "Don't become what you hate, Harry, or it's all completely hopeless."

The sailboat lurched then as the fishing boat shoved itself into gear. Hull scraped hull as shouts came from below-decks, and a beautiful, terrified redhead reached up with a machete to chop their towline free. Sonja slipped the transmission into neutral as the *St. Elias* bounced back into their stern. It hung up in their rudder for a few seconds and spun them sideways, then pushed free.

The *St. Elias* wallowed away from them, already listing, and Harry saw thick black smoke and flashes of blue flame through the portholes. A small ski boat hit the *St. Elias* a glancing blow at the bow and the boat listed all the way over to its rail. Steam screamed from a jagged hole in the hull; then it started under in a boil of froth and foam. Father Free popped to the surface, holding a plastic bag out of the water.

"Spook!"

Rico tried to stand, and Hodge made a grab for his precious box. A runabout collided with *Kamui*'s bow and capsized a rowboat full of children. Hodge missed the grab and his case clattered to the deck, but Hodge's momentum carried him into Rico. The lurch of the collision tipped both men over the rail in a slow-motion ballet.

Harry was in the water before he knew it. Dozens of small boats swarmed overhead, blocking what little light penetrated the turbulent bay. Harry swam downward, kicking himself into a spiral as he groped around wildly for his father. He felt something solid hit his back. Harry reached around and made a blind grab, hoping for the best. He got his dad's hand with the pistol still in it.

Harry moved to get behind his dad's limp body, and that was when Hodge clutched him around the legs. Harry tried kicking free, but Hodge had him tight with both arms, dragging them down. Rico never moved, and his body was hot, too hot, with bubbles leaking out of his scalp, his shirt, his melted, empty eyes.

Harry yanked the pistol free and his father's finger stuck in the trigger guard. He pushed his father's corpse and its bloody froth away and felt the telltale mushiness of collapsing tissues against his palms.

Air leaked past Harry's lips as his lungs burned and Hodge dragged him further into the depths. Harry freed the trigger guard of his father's finger, pressed the Hornet against one of Hodge's arms, and fired. A dull *pat* and a burst of blood-stained bubbles rose past Harry, but Hodge held tight with his other hand. As the last of his breath whooshed out of him, Harry pressed the pistol to Hodge's head and fired again. He kicked and stroked upward, chasing his own leaking air. Harry hadn't broken the surface yet when he felt something snag the back of his shirt and yank him out of the filthy water.

Harry coughed and gagged as Rena Scholz hauled him alongside with the boathook. She dragged him by his belt over the rail, where he lay gasping beside a wet, gasping priest. Scholz hurried to the stern and began probing again with the hook.

"It's no use," Harry gasped. "Dad's dead."

"Dead?"

Sonja didn't hesitate. She slammed the *Kamui* into forward and jumped on the throttle without a word. She shoved her way through the small boats that jammed the narrow channel out of the harbor, her face set in a mask of anger and despair. Behind them, automatic weapons splintered a wallowing houseboat and stitched across their wake.

Scholz thrust a few more times off the stern with the hook, but her movements were slow, automatic, numb. She looked like a B-movie zombie, barely holding her balance. The ride was choppy with all the small boats around them, and Harry was afraid Scholz was going over the side. He crawled to the back of the cockpit and grabbed her arm.

"He's dead, Scholz," he said. "The Deathbug got him. And Hodge won't be coming up, either."

Scholz dropped the hook, and Harry caught it before it hit the water. He set it down on the deck and Scholz dropped heavily beside it. She stared back at the inferno that used to be La Libertad and said nothing. Harry picked up the metal case and handed it to her.

"Maybe this is what he said it is," he said.

She shook her head.

"Do you really believe that Mishwe would want to save a snake like Hodge?" she said. "It's probably just saline."

"You could take a little," he suggested. "Then we could get it analyzed, just in case."

"Yeah," Scholz said, her voice as hollow as her eyes, "we could do that."

Harry thought that she hadn't really heard him, and wouldn't really hear him for a while yet.

"What got Hodge?" Sonja asked.

They were just breaking out of the harbor and rounding the red channel marker, heading for the open sea. The Harbor Patrol was long gone, and a stream of small boats whined their way towards open ocean.

Harry tossed the little Hornet onto a cushion beside Sonja and ignored Father Free, who clutched a plastic bag to his chest and appeared to be praying to himself.

"I did," Harry said. "I'm going to put together Marte's

data for transmission. Can I get you something from the galley?''

"Coffee," Sonja said, not looking at him. She concentrated on staying away from the pack of boats fanning out from the harbor. "It's going to be a long night."

*So Joshua smote all the country of the hills, and of the south, and of the vale, and of the springs, and all their kings: he left none remaining, but utterly destroyed all that breathed, as the Lord God of Israel commanded.*

—JOSHUA

# 43

SONJA GOT THE *Kamui* twelve kilometers offshore before an uncontrollable shaking overcame her white-knuckled grip on the helm. Sonja, Harry, Rena Scholz and Father Free each had nursed their own grief in silence, busying themselves with the dozen small tasks of navigation and accommodation.

"I can hold a course," Rena told her. "Why don't you get some dry clothes and some sleep? There are things in the medical kit I could give you. . . . "

"No!" Sonja snapped. "I mean, no thanks, Rena. I don't want anybody giving me anything ever again."

She finished with a shrug.

"I understand," Scholz said. "Go ahead; I'll take it for a while. I need to be out here alone, anyway, I think."

Sonja stumbled through the hatchway and kicked off her wet shoes. Harry and Father Free were engrossed in the onboard Litespeed. She didn't feel like making small talk, so she hurried past them into the head. She stripped, toweled down, then zipped herself into a sleeping bag on a lower berth in spite of the heat and humidity. She couldn't seem to get warm, but once inside the bag she felt the shakes ease off.

Harry was consolidating Marte's data with Father Free's, adding whatever he could from memory. Father Free cabled up the palm-cam and dumped its memory to the Litespeed, too. They had worked without speaking, except to exchange tools, for two precious hours. It was Father Free who broke the silence.

"I don't think that tonight's holocaust came from the Sabbath Suicides," he said.

"Where else?" Harry asked. "Tonight it spread to Catholics, and they didn't all drink the EdenSprings water."

Father Free held up the plastic bag, with the items he'd rescued from the *St. Elias*. The data cubes were already dumped to the Litespeed, so the bag contained only the priest's personal kit: Breviary, stole, holy water and oil, a tin of communion wafers.

"For Easter Mass most of the churches used fresh hosts, just delivered on Friday. It's the only way I can think of to infect so many Catholics so quickly."

Harry stopped his editing chore and looked Father Free in the eye.

"You said an Easter Mass, too, didn't you?"

Father Free nodded solemnly and set the bag down.

"Yes," he said. "I had some old hosts from the cathedral that I preferred to use up rather than toss, so my mix was about fifty-fifty, old to new. My own kit, here, is old hosts. The one I took myself was old, because it was from a supply I left there last month."

"You'd better prepare a statement," Harry said. "We'll broadcast that with the rest. We're almost set, here."

Sonja lay in the starboard bunk beside the electronics and navigation equipment, and drifted in and out of sleep as Harry and Father Free worked their electronic magic.

"The trick," Harry said, more to himself than to Father Free or Sonja, "is to appear to be where we're not while we're sending. Or not to appear where we are."

"Do you really think they'll look for us now?" Sonja

asked. "Especially after you send whatever you're sending. There's no *reason* for them to come after us, is there?"

Harry frowned at his display, and Sonja saw the glimmering codes reflected off his gray eyes. He solved a problem with a grunt, then said, "As long as the U.S. government is intact, they'll come after us. Governments like things tidy, and we're the last loose end. Besides, as long as your grandfather's alive, they won't give up on you. You're the only living relative of the Vice-President of the United States."

She still couldn't get used to that thought, although her grandfather had been a senator or cabinet member as long as she could remember.

*It hasn't done us much good so far.*

"How could they find us aboard a sailboat?" Sonja asked.

"I found a locator beacon inside this Litespeed and tossed it onto another boat leaving the harbor," he answered. "That should throw off some of the dogs for a while. This boat's primary mission was entrapment of drug dealers, so I would assume it's black-wired from top to bottom. We could have half the intelligence agencies in the world listening in. I hope that we'll have them all listening in when we broadcast, but I don't want anybody tracking us down."

"If . . . if there's anybody left," Sonja said.

Past Harry, out the porthole, she saw the flare of another small boat burning in the dark. They had seen dozens of boats catch fire in the past couple of hours as the Deathbug relentlessly kept its gruesome appointments.

"There'll be people left, all right," Harry said. "Marte said that Mishwe made two mistakes—first, this is a multistage AVA, therefore fragile, so it can't last long outside the body; second, it works too fast. It kills people before they have a chance to get far."

"Harry, could you love me?" she asked.

He looked up in open-mouthed surprise, and Father Free cleared his throat.

"I'll go topside," he said. "See if Rena needs a hand."

"What was that again?" Harry asked.

"Do you think you could love me, after what we've been through? I mean, I've lost everybody I've loved. Everybody that I've lived with. I don't know if I can stand it happening again."

He closed his mouth and it slowly tilted into a smile.

"I've had a crush on you since we were six," he said. "Does that count?"

She was not too exhausted to blush.

"It's not the same."

"Then I'll have to confess, if I didn't know I loved you before, I knew it when you talked me up that elevator shaft at ViraVax. Maybe even before that, when they had us naked in that decontamination room and you were pacing around, looking . . ."

"Looking what?"

Sonja was up on one elbow now, watching him chew his lip and squirm.

"Looking sexy," he blurted. "I mean, even then, in all that trouble, I wanted to, you know . . . except we knew they were watching us all the time."

"That's different, too," she said. "That's combat bonding; I've read about it before. Foxhole buddies, that's what we are."

"I've never had a buddy that looked like *that*," he said.

Harry pressed a few keys, frowned at the display in front of him and shuffled his gloveware until the machine beeped at him.

"Chill," he said. He slipped out of his gloveware, rubbed his eyes, and when he returned his hands to the machine he spoke to the ceiling, not to Sonja.

"If those things aren't love, then why don't you tell me what is? Do you think love's only for people who don't die?"

Sonja took a deep breath, then asked the thing she was afraid would alienate him for good.

"Did you love Marte Chang?"

Harry didn't even take his hands out of the gloveware. He laid his forehead on the table in front of the Litespeed, and his body began to jerk with silent sobs. Sonja let him be. After a few moments he took a couple of deep breaths, but he didn't lift his head from the table.

"I . . . I didn't have the chance," he said, his voice almost too tight and squeaky for her to hear.

Another couple of deep breaths. Harry set the machine on standby and wiped his face with a napkin. He cleared his throat to get his voice under control.

"I really liked her, I know that," he said. "She was the smartest person I ever met. I kept having this dream. . . ."

Harry shook his head, still not looking at her. Sonja bit her lip, but kept quiet.

For the first time since she'd known him, Harry was absolutely still. She didn't realize until then how busy his body always was—not fidgeting, but busy. She wasn't even sure he was breathing until he spoke.

"What we did . . . it wasn't something that she should *die* for," he said. "But you heard Hodge. I killed her, as sure as if I'd put a gun to her head."

Sonja's shaking finally stopped. She sat up, gathered the sleeping bag around her and sat beside Harry. She took Harry's hand, squeezed it.

"You didn't kill her," she said. "ViraVax killed her. Hodge and Mishwe killed her. Your father and mine, keeping their secrets, they killed her. You helped her to feel something good one time before she died; you should be happy for that."

Harry's Litespeed beeped twice. He took another deep breath and let it out slowly.

"Okay," he said, "at least I'd better not blow my opportunity to make something out of all of her work. It's show time."

Then Sonja kissed him. She was as surprised about that as Harry was. They lingered at each other's lips until the machine double-beeped again, and Sonja pulled away.

"Okay, wizard," she whispered, "show your stuff."

The machine was set to Hodge's voice commands, so Harry slipped his hands back into the gloves and made the "go" motion. The telltale green light blinked off and on as the Litespeed uploaded to the satlinks.

"How did you fix it so they can't find us?"

"It's the same trick I showed your dad," Harry said. "The same one that Marte used to get information out of ViraVax. We're seeking and using channels that are already in use. We're doing this at random, using three hundred and sixty satellites, firing bursts of data into the worldwide system. Any traces will lead back to the original carriers, hundreds of them."

"If it's random, how do they make sense of what you're sending?"

Harry smiled, and this time it was his turn to take Sonja's hand.

"I wrote a find-and-collate program. It links all of the data fragments into the proper order and announces itself as a single file. Anyone looking at it would know it would take at least a half-hour to dump it into the system, so they'll be backtracking transactions that took at least a half-hour. But none of ours is taking more than a half-second, and it's riding on somebody else's, anyway."

"Where's it going?" Sonja asked. "I mean, besides just *out there*?"

"First, it's going out to twenty researchers that Marte recommended. Then to every newsgroup that I could get an address on. Then to all the boards on the web for anybody who wants it."

"Hey, crew," Rena Scholz called down, "did you save any of that coffee for me?"

Harry stood up and stretched.

"Coming, Skipper," he said. "We got busy here and forgot all about it."

By the time the coffee finished gurgling into its carafe, the palm-cam was transmitting the last of its tape into the void. Tired as they were, Sonja and Harry joined Scholz on deck for a sunrise toast to their success.

The weather had roughened considerably, and the spray bursting over the rails brought an uncharacteristic chill for these waters.

"Here's to success," Harry said, holding his cup out to the others.

They clinked cups, and each of them balanced on the rolling deck and sipped their hot coffee in the privacy of their thoughts, memories, sorrows, dreams.

"Another one," Rena said, pointing off the stern.

Then Sonja saw it, a blossom of flame thrown into the black throat of the oncoming wind.

*That one must be close,* she thought, *if we can see it through this weather.*

Father Free muttered a prayer to the wind.

When Sonja turned back to Rena, she saw the unguarded fear in the older woman's eyes. The glow from the gauges turned Rena's face a sickly green, and aged her far beyond her years.

"What is it, Rena?" Sonja asked. "Are you still afraid it'll get you, too?"

Rena sighed, and faked a smile.

"I thought I had enough luck for Rico and for me," she said. "He was a changed man, and he did the changing on his own. It was the real thing, and I let myself look forward to . . . well, I let myself look forward." She nodded towards the fireball, dying in the relentless mouth of the sea. "If I'm afraid of anything, it's that I'll burn up the boat and kill the two of you when I go."

Sonja couldn't think of anything to say, since the thought had occurred to her, too. And with his silence, Harry acknowledged his own thoughts on the matter. After a few moments, he was the one to speak.

"Let's get you and Father Free to Maude Island," Harry told Scholz. "You'll be safe there, and maybe you can get that kit analyzed, just in case it's the real thing."

"You don't sound like you're planning on staying at Maude Island," Rena said.

"This lab rat is through running mazes," Harry said.

"What I'd like to do, if Sonja's willing, is to sail off with her into the sunset, and find someplace where we can be invisible, take our chances on a real life."

"I can understand why you'd feel that way," Rena said. "How about you, Sonja?"

The chill she felt now had nothing to do with the weather. Sonja knew that in all of this dying, it was time to be born. They had few resources, and could very well starve at sea, but she agreed with Harry—she never wanted to be a specimen in a jar again. At least, not a live specimen.

"I love Harry," she said. "Where he goes, I go."

They tried on silence again for a while, and wore it well. Rena broke it with a sigh and a toss of her cold coffee overboard.

"Okay," she said, "if that's your plan, then I have a present for you. Call it a wedding present. Harry, if I give you some numbers, can you connect to them without giving away our position?"

"It might take me some time to access," he said, "and we might have to do some switching while you're on-line. Why?"

"If they're looking, they're after the sailing vessel *Kamui* carrying Harry Toledo and Sonja Bartlett. With a little fancy footwork and some help from you, I can get both of you protected identities with full documentation, and a new registration for the boat. That way, you can sell it when you get to a safe port. If there is a safe port."

"How about a pilot's license?" Sonja asked.

"We can do that," Rena said, "as well as transcripts, passports, the works. We can make you Australian, Canadian, Mexican. . . . "

"Chill," Harry said. "How about 'World Citizen'?"

Rena laughed.

"Well, Harry, we're trying not to call attention to you. How about American? Then you don't have to worry about your story or your accent."

"Simpler is better," Sonja agreed. "But we'll have to be older."

"Oh, God." Rena mocked a groan. "I've sunk to providing false ID for minors."

Rena threw an arm around Sonja's shoulders and gave her a hug.

"I'm really going to miss you two," she said. "Nobody else alive can possibly know what we've been through, and what you two accomplished for the rest of the world."

Harry cleared his throat.

"So, Scholz," he said. "Why don't you just stay with us?"

Rena Scholz shook her head slowly, and ran a hand through her buzz-cut hair.

"No," she said. "No. I can't do that, much as I'd like to. It would be desertion, you see, and I signed on to serve my country, not to leave it when it needs me most."

"But you might be immune," Sonja pointed out. "You've survived a lot of exposures. They'll turn *you* into a lab rat."

Rena laughed again.

"Yes, that's possible. But that's a service, too. And I agree with Marte Chang's assessment—by the time someone comes up with a vaccine or a cure, this thing will have run its ugly course. Someone's got to tell them how this all happened, so it won't happen again."

"Somebody's got to take the fall, you mean," Harry said. "They'll pin the whole thing on you; you're the highest-ranking survivor."

Rena shook her head.

"No, Harry, I have to go back. Even if it's to take the heat. I signed on for that, too, and I have to see this through. Your lives are just starting. Your father didn't turn tail and run when he had the chance, and neither will I."

Sonja saw Harry's spine stiffen, and his lips compress into a tight line.

"He accused me of that, once," Harry said. " 'Turning your yellow tail to run?' he asked me."

This time Scholz's arm went around Harry's shoulder.

"He told me about that," she said. "While he was getting patched up after the ViraVax flood, he told me a lot of things he had done to you and your mother that he was ashamed of, and that was one of them. He loved you, and respected you—both of you."

Sonja was glad that Harry hugged Rena back. It was obvious that Scholz had been in love with Rico Toledo for a long time. Now, in his exhaustion, Harry looked more like his father than ever.

*Harry must remind her of Rico*, Sonja thought. *I'll bet that's hard.*

"Will you stay in touch, Scholz?" Harry asked. "We have a lot of scramble skills between us, and almost a thousand satellites to shuffle through."

Scholz smiled, and kissed Harry's cheek.

"I think we could arrange something," she said. "You two . . . well, you're the only family I've got. I couldn't stand having you sail into the sunset without a trace."

Sonja felt a wave of happiness break over her tiresome despair. Yes, it was true; she was not dying, after all, but preparing to be born. She followed the others below and snugged the hatch behind her. Then she sat at the table and sipped another coffee as she waited to find out who it was that she was going to be for the rest of her life.

*The Way of the warrior is death. This means choosing death whenever there is a choice between life and death. It means nothing more than this.*

—YAMAMOTO TSUNENORI

# 44

FATHER FREE JUMPED into the surf next to Rena Scholz and pulled their inflatable raft onto the pebble beach of Maude Island. The two of them collapsed against a grassy dune and watched the sails of the *Kamui* disappear into the haze that was only now beginning to blend into the overcast. No one challenged them on approach or on the beach, and Father Free knew by this that everyone inside Maude Island was dead.

Rena caught her breath before he did, and only then did he realize the excellence of her physical shape.

"I'm glad you married them," Rena said. "At least we were able to give them *that*."

"Maybe they'll get lucky," he said. "But granddad's President Granddad now, and he seemed pretty determined to find them."

He smiled up at Rena, glad to be stranded with someone he liked and respected.

"Besides," he said. "They can always come back here."

"It's pretty quiet here for a high-security facility," she said. "What if they're all dead?"

Father Free chuckled.

"Then I guess we have the whole island to ourselves."

"You mean, *stay* here?"

"Why not?" he asked, and sat up. "I know the place; it's got everything we'd ever need. If there's a world left out there, they'll come and find us soon enough."

"What about the dead?"

"They'll probably stay dead," Father Free said, and laughed. "Harry had the right idea, after all."

"What's that?"

"He said something last night about Pandora's box. 'When Pandora opened the box, where was the safest place to hide?' "

"I give," Rena said. "Where?"

" 'Under the lid,' he said. 'Until they're all gone; then you can hide in the box.' "

Rena shaded her eyes and searched the area of sea where *Kamui* had been.

"So," she said, "they're going back."

"It's the life they know, with people they understand," Father Free said. "Grandpa President can look the wide world over, but I'm betting that they'll sail out their supplies and set up housekeeping back in Costa Brava. They have a coffee farm, a plane, new identities . . . I think they'll do just fine."

"And what about us?" Rena asked. "How will we do?"

"We'll find out soon enough," he said.

Father Free stood, brushed off his wet clothes and opened the plastic bag that he carried with him.

"What now?" Rena asked.

"Now it's time to say a Requiem for the dead," he said. "After that, it will be time to go on living."